The Bay of Glasstown. Watercolour by Charlotte Brontë
after John Martin

CHARLOTTE BRONTË

Five Novelettes

———

Passing Events
Julia
Mina Laury
Captain Henry Hastings
Caroline Vernon

———

TRANSCRIBED FROM THE ORIGINAL
MANUSCRIPTS AND EDITED BY
WINIFRED GÉRIN

LONDON
The Folio Press
1971

ISBN 0 85067 029 2

PRINTED IN GREAT BRITAIN

Printed and bound by W & J Mackay & Co Ltd, Chatham
Set in 'Monotype' Baskerville 11 point leaded 1 point
Illustrations printed by Jarrold & Sons Ltd, Norwich

CONTENTS

ILLUSTRATIONS

GENERAL INTRODUCTION

Charlotte Brontë wrote the following novelettes between the years 1836 and 1839, from the time when she had just turned twenty until her twenty-third year. They cannot, therefore, be technically reckoned as belonging to her juvenilia, but their emergence from, and continued commitment with, the subjects of her childhood writings, connect them indissolubly with her earliest work. At the same time as they foreshadow the themes and characters of her mature novels, they show the author of *Jane Eyre* and *Villette* in the process of becoming the Currer Bell who took the town by storm overnight with her first published work. Their interest, therefore, and value to students of literature, is unique as affording an insight into the processes of artistic creation through which an author's first shapeless idea passes before assuming a definitive form.

Origins
The earliest preserved writings of Charlotte Brontë date from March 1829, a month before her thirteenth birthday, when, in a *History of the Year*, she set down in journal fashion the current circumstances of family life and the origins of their "Plays", as the Brontë children called their make-believe dramas. These, as might be expected on the part of precocious children for whom books were the principal enjoyment of life, were derived from such widely divergent sources of reading as the Tory Press, *Blackwood's Magazine* and their favourite childish books—*Aesop's Fables* (in the translation of Samuel Croxall of 1825), *The Arabian Nights Entertainments* (from the French text of Galland of 1787) and Sir Charles Morell's *Tales of the Genii*, published in 1764 and an equal source of inspiration to young Dickens and Thackeray of whom, as yet, the young Brontës knew nothing. The result was a medley of Eastern Tales, Parliamentary Reports and, above all, of hero-worship for the famous men of the immediate historic past, Wellington and Bonaparte in particular.

From the Duke's Peninsular campaigns, with which the children were familiarised through the memoirs and eyewitness accounts appearing in *Blackwood's* for the 1820s, they adopted the place-names and the titles of their fictional characters, noticeably Spanish in trend. Thus the title of Marquis of Douro, which Wellington earned for his victorious campaign along the course of that river in North-West Spain, became permanently associated with Charlotte's hero in the "Plays", while the further title of Zamorna was derived from the province and town of Zamora on the Douro. Equally, Branwell, whose sympathies went to Wellington's enemies, the French, identified himself with Marshal Soult and the members of the French General Staff whose names appeared as contributors to his *Branwell's Blackwood's Magazine* and its sequel, *The Young Men's Magazine*, a home-production imitating in all parts the Edinburgh original.

"Our Plays were established", wrote the twelve-year-old Charlotte in an attempt to bring order out of the chaos of their prolixity, "*Young Men* in 1826; *Our Fellows* July 1827; *Islanders* December 1827. These are our three great plays, they are not kept secret. Emily's and my bed-plays were established the 1st December 1827; the others March 1828—Bed-Plays mean secret plays—they are very nice ones—all our plays are very strange ones—*The Young Men's Play* took its rise from some wooden soldiers that Branwell had; *Our Fellows* from Aesop's Fables, and the *Islanders* from several events which happened . . ."

It is clear that *all* events, the fabulous and the founded, were grist to these children's imaginations, and had their part in creating the composite universe which they erected within the confined walls of their home. Some influences were more marked than others, like their interest in the *Travels of Mungo Park* and his explorations into the source of the Niger, and Major Denham's successive expeditions from 1822 to 1825 into the North and Centre of the African Continent, of which the young Brontës read accounts in *Blackwood's* and which lent a solid topographical background to their conceptions of *The Arabian Nights*.

From this emphasis on Africa, it follows that the earliest enemy figuring in their games were the Ashantee tribesmen, and especially the hereditary prince, Quashia Quamina, who opposed the landings of *The Twelves* (as the wooden soldiers became known) in their reputed invasion of the Gulf of Guinea. As readers of *Caroline Vernon* will find, Quashia Quamina continued to figure (albeit briefly) even as late as 1839.

The advent of the box of twelve wooden soldiers at the parsonage (a gift of Mr Brontë's to Branwell on his ninth birthday) was momentous in its consequences for the children. Identifying themselves with the distinct individuals which each represented (they were not uniform either in size or costume) the children used them as performing puppets on whom they bestowed eponymous names to play their own parts in the game of Genii versus Ashantees.

Thus Branwell, whose admiration for Napoleon had been fired by Scott's sympathetic *Life* of the Emperor, identified his chosen soldiers with Bonaparte; and Charlotte, inheriting her father's hero-worship for "The Great Duke", snatched up a soldier on first receiving them—"the prettiest of the whole, and the tallest, and the most perfect in every part"—and tells us that she cried "This shall be the Duke of Wellington! This shall be the Duke!"

From the day of her thirteenth birthday onwards, she was writing without intermission on the subjects of her most ardent loyalties, English politics and the Duke. In a MS of that year, *Anecdotes of the Duke of Wellington,* she was already chronicling his deeds and modifying the portrait of Sir Arthur Wellesley as presented by Scott* to fit in with the fabulous elements with which the *Tales of the Genii* had familiarised her. "The character of the Duke of Wellington is one of the most wonderful that ever any man had. it is noble dignified & vigorous in the extreme; He appeared to possess the gift of preciance [*sic*] the past and the future are all alike before him. His vision is uncommonly acute and his finely formed frame is so knit & moulded as to be equal to the greatest hardships of the most terrible campaign; it is light active muscular & symmetrical. His mind approaches as nearly to the perfection of greatness & wisdom as human faliability [*sic*] will allow . . ."†

In Wellington, Charlotte found the prototype of her Ideal Hero. Branwell, who did not blush to espouse the cause of Wellington's enemies, and identified himself with Marshal Soult, Lucien Bonaparte, Marmont and even Chateaubriand in turn, adopted an altogether more equivocal attitude in his conception of a hero. Soult was soon degraded from the rank of Marshal of the Empire to that of an adventurer, and appeared again in the role of Alexander Rogue, from whose shady fortunes sprang the personality of Alexander Percy, Earl of Northangerland, who figures so largely in Charlotte's novelettes.‡

The main feature of the young Brontës' "Plays" was their shared character. They all four contributed to the plots, even if the younger Emily and Anne did not contribute to the *written* saga, and they all directed the adventures of their titular heroes— Wellington, Bonaparte and, in the case of Emily and Anne, the arctic explorers Parry and Ross, whose names became rooted in the action and topography of the tales long after their sponsors had

---

* See *Life of Napoleon*, Vol. II, Chap. 45   † 30 September 1829
‡ Northangerland is an obvious adaptation from Northumberland, and the Percys of Alnwick, dear to the Brontë children, sprang from the pages of Percy's *Reliques*

seceded from collaboration with their elders. Thus in Branwell's plan of the country of their "Plays"*, copied minutely from the Map of the Gulf of Guinea published in *Blackwood's* for June 1826, there appear the four provinces controlled by the eponymous heroes—Wellingtonsland (the former Senegambia), Parry's Land, Ross Land and Sneacky's Land (after the invidious title finally given to Branwell's French, and hence untrustworthy hero).

The solid topographical background to the "Plays" was not their least original feature: the action was played out against such permanent recognisable localities as the Mountains of the Moon, the rivers Calabar and Etrei, Ardrah, the capital of the Ashantee country, and the Plain of Dahomey—all situated on the Gulf of Guinea—all of which persisted into the later novelettes, as readers of the following selection will find. The Marquis of Ardrah who figures conspicuously there was Arthur Parry, son of the explorer William Edward Parry, Emily's hero and the King of Parry's Land, whose capital was Edwardstown to the north of the territory.

The Brontë Juvenilia

Such were the elements from which was drawn the complex of plots and characters on whose invention the children spent the leisure hours of their growing years. In their childish "Plays", as in their mature novels, the Brontës placed great importance on landscape, on the setting to their dramatic scenes, visualising them in the concrete terms not only of the homes where they lived but of the regions, whether mountainous or flat, and of the climate that influenced their temperaments. Emphasis is laid on the fact that both Miss Laury and her lover Zamorna were natives of the moist West—in other words, Ireland—born with ardent temperaments. Zamorna, indeed, calls her his "Beautiful Western".

Where no details were left vague, the very architecture of their tales had a distinct character drawn from the pictures of John Martin, prints of which hung on the walls of their home, and whose vast Assyrian complexes of battlemented buildings, reflected in the waters of Babylon, gave the name and the style to their great Glasstown Confederacy, as they came to call their imaginary country. This country was created in three stages, all of which find their echoes in the novelettes: there was first the Kingdom of the Twelves, when the dramatis personae were confided to the wooden soldiers; this was followed by the great Glasstown Confederacy whose boundaries followed Branwell's map of the Gulf of Guinea; finally, there was the Kingdom of Angria, into which all the terri-

* Reproduced as the endpaper to this volume

tories were absorbed while maintaining separate provincial status
and local governments. This greatly enlarged conception of their
fabulous country was the work of Branwell, begun at a time when
Charlotte was away at boarding-school. Branwell excelled in the
machinery of government, in defence, finance and population
returns. He worked out the differences in mileage separating the
capitals (Verdopolis, Freetown, Edwardstown and the federal
capital, Adrianopolis) of the original four—later seven—provinces,
with their respective produce and trade figures, military strength
etc. No aspect of mercantile or political life was overlooked by
Branwell in his description of the Confederation in his huge output
for the years 1830–7.

Where descriptions of natural and artistic beauty were needed
to amplify Branwell's monotonous cataloguing (he was studying
Homer with his father at the time and was much impressed by
the Catalogue of Greek ships), Charlotte exercised her imaginative
faculty with ever-increasing powers. These extracts from her early
descriptions of the Glasstown cities contain already in embryo the
romantic quality of her mature writings, and match the barbaric
splendours of Martin's presentation of Nineveh and Babylon. The
first was recognisably inspired by Martin's *Fall of Babylon*, cedars
and all. Of Douro's palace she wrote that it was "situated on a
lofty hill which on one side fell sheer down to the sea in a perpen-
dicular precipice 250 ft high. Huge oaks and cedars grew on its
brink, some of them so lofty that their topmost boughs swept the
palace dome. Lawn and garden with grove of palm and myrtle
covered the rest of the hill . . ."*

With the shifting of the capital city from Verdopolis to Adrianopolis, Charlotte took a last nostalgic look at the ancient city,
apostrophising it as the "Queen of the Earth, who looks down at
her majestic face mirrored in the noble Niger, and sees the far
reflection of her valley and turrets caught by the flashing Guadima
& flung with beauty unimaginable on the glass that her harbour
gives her. to hear them prefer the marble toy-shop of Adrianopolis,
the mushroom of the Calabar, to a Babylon so steadfastly founded,
an oak whose roots have struck so deep as the city on the Guinea-
Coast, is most hateful, most maddening to any man cursed with a
tithe less folly than themselves . . ."†

Adrianopolis, "the mushroom of the Calabar", was as much
inspired by Martin's grandiose conceptions of the fallen eastern
empires as had been Verdopolis. Describing its features, Charlotte
wrote "A row of marble pillars pale and gleaming as ice, receded

* *The Foundling*, May–June 1833   † *My Angria & the Angrians*, 1834

in their grand perspective before me. Their eternal basement, their Giant shafts, their gorgeous capitals, the long long high-uplifted cornices that ran above them, were all of the purest, the most Grecian moulding. All breathed of Ionia in her loftiest time— Beyond the Palace, the Calabar was rolling all its broad smooth billows. I heard them kiss the marble walls as they swept on . . .''*

To readers of the following novelettes, the Calabar at Adriano-polis will become a familiar landmark on the Angrian scene. Long familiarity with these topographical features lends to Charlotte's tales a verisimilitude which their plots alone could not have done. The modern reader feels himself on solid ground with each return to these sites and is fully able to suspend disbelief when, for instance, Charles Townsend takes the Angrian stage-coach from Adrianopolis to Zamorna town at the beginning of *Captain Hastings*, where the passengers are put down at the Spinning-Jenny Inn.

The range and completeness of the young Brontës' invention, which extended to the climate of the different provinces and the characteristics of their inhabitants, was only one of the many devices that made them so compelling. Against this haunting topo-graphical background, Charlotte could construct the complex scenario of her romantic tales. Much as she responded to natural and artistic beauty of all kinds, it was the human element that fired her imagination most keenly. It was to allow herself greater liberty of invention, no doubt, that she replaced the central figure of the "Great Duke" with his two sons, Arthur and Charles Wellesley, the former of whom became her type hero and the latter her mouthpiece, prototype and pseudonym, in whose name she signed her stories from 1830 onwards, modifying it to the initials "C.T."—for Charles Townshend—in a gesture of final emancipation.

Arthur Adrian Augustus Wellesley, on whom descended his father's title of Marquis of Douro, became her darling, upon whose portrait she lavished pages of lush description. The character, which suffered many modifications and much moral deterioration as time passed, was initially that of an innocent, effeminate youth bent on pleasing his parents, as in *Tales of the Islanders* (1829). In 1834 "He seemed to be in the full bloom of youth; his figure was toweringly, overbearingly lofty, moulded in statue-like perfection, and invested with something which I cannot describe—something superb, impetuous, resistless. His hair was intensely black, curled luxuriantly, but the forehead underneath . . . looked white & smooth as ivory. His eye-brows were black—broad, but his long

* *My Angria & the Angrians*

eye-lashes & large clear eyes were deep sepia brown . . . The upper lip was very short—Grecian—& had a haughty curl . . . At the first glance I discerned him to be a military man . . ."*

In a slightly later sketch, patently inspired by Finden's engravings of Byron's poems, Douro is described as "A youth of lofty stature and remarkable graceful demeanour, attired in a rich purple vest & mantle, with close fitting pantaloons of white woven silk, displaying to advantage the magnificent proportions of his form. A richly adorned belt was girt tightly round his waist from which depended a scimitar whose golden hilt, and scabbard . . . glittered with gems of inestimable value. His steel-barred cap, crested with tall, snowy plumes, lay beside him, its absence revealing . . . the rich curls of dark glossy hair clustering round a countenance distinguished by the noble beauty of its features, but still more by the radiant fire of genius and intelligence visible . . . in his large, dark, and lustrous eyes . . ." As readers of the novelettes will find, such a description remained typical of the Duke of Zamorna into whom Douro evolved except for the addition of his Byronic wickedness.

It has to be remembered that the impact of Byron's poetry was equal to that of the Napoleonic wars as a source of inspiration in developing the young Brontës' creative bent; Charlotte was acquainted with Byron's poetry by her tenth year and quoted from *Manfred* and *Cain* with glib familiarity in *The Islanders* (1829). In due course, it was inevitable that she would endow her hero with the demonic attributes proper to the Byronic male.

While her strong love of adventure, stimulated by the nocturnal promptings of her collaboratrix Emily, fired her to write such purely fabulous stories as *The Twelve Adventurers, The Search after Happiness, The Islanders, The Spell, The Fairy Gift*, etc., an irresistible urge towards romance soon took control of her imagination and by her fourteenth year the love element was introduced into her tales. From then on, it became the dominant subject of all her writings, childish and mature, and earned Currer Bell the reproof of Harriet Martineau who considered that she saw all things too much through "the one medium of the passion of love".

With the advent of Zamorna, a purely fictional character based on Douro and still supposedly a Wellesley, Charlotte felt herself free to portray a thorough-paced libertine in the Byronic style. In Branwell's history of the Angrian wars, Zamorna triumphed over the Ashantees and claimed in guerdon of his victories a crown— that of Angria—which would place him above the provincial

* *My Angria & the Angrians*

rulers of the Glasstown Confederacy, and he was granted his heart's desire. With Percy as his first Prime Minister, with whom he allied himself by marrying his daughter, his reign started auspiciously enough. The treachery of Percy, who raised a faction in the field against him, provoked the civil wars whose aftermath appears in the novelettes, and left a permanent scar on Zamorna's mind. Here he is, seen in a sketch of 1834, *A Peep into a Picture-Book*, with his Byronic attributes upon him and a new satanic power investing him. "Fire! Light! What have we here? Zamorna's self, blazing in the frontispiece like the sun on his own standard. De Lisle has given him to us in full regimentals—plumed, epauletted, and sabred . . . he stands as if a thunderbolt could neither blast the light of his eyes nor dash the effrontery of his brow. Keen, glorious being! tempered & bright & sharp & rapid as the scimitar at his side . . . O Zamorna! What eyes those are glancing under the deep shadow of that raven crest! They bode no good. Man nor woman could ever gather more than a troubled fitful happiness from their kindest light. Satan gave them their glory to deepen the midnight gloom that always follows where their lustre has fallen most lovingly . . . All here is passion & fire unquenchable. Impetuous sin, stormy pride, diving and soaring enthusiasm, war and poetry, are kindling their fires in all his veins, and his wild blood boils from his heart & back again like a torrent of new-sprung lava. Young duke? Young demon! . . ."

In his innocent pre-Byronic days, Zamorna fell in love with a fifteen-year-old girl, Marion Hume, whose character and frail beauty, as well as her name, are an early sketch for Paulina Home in *Villette*. Hers is the first of the long line of female portraits to come from Charlotte Brontë's pen. She is seen first as a "beautiful girl in a white dress and green sash without any ornament on her head except a profusion of chestnut curls which, clustering in the most luxurious ringlets, obliged her every now and then to raise her small hand in order to put them back from her snowy forehead and laughing blue eyes . . ."*

Immediately after her marriage to Douro, she is seen at the theatre. "Her cheeks were tinted with a rich, soft crimson . . . the clear light of her brilliant hazel eye & the soft waving of her auburn ringlets . . . The only ornaments she wore were a long chain . . . which hung lower than her waist, together with a small crescent of pearls glittering on her forehead (which is always worn by the noble matrons of Verdopolis) betokened she had entered the path of wedded life . . ."†

* *The Tragedy and the Essay*, November 1833   † *The Bridal*, 1832

A drawing of Charlotte's, a copy of Finden's engraving of the Countess of Jersey (see illustration facing p. 112) which figured in the illustrated edition of Byron's works of 1834, shows precisely the ornaments described here, and affords the clue to the pictorial origin of Charlotte's heroines. They were all too obviously taken from the engravings of Society Beauties reproduced in the fashionable Annuals and other illustrated periodicals of the day of which Charlotte saw a good proportion. She must regularly have seen *Forget-Me-Not, Friendship's Offering*, Heath's *Book of Beauty* and *The Keepsake* from which she copied several prints and whose vogue reached its apogee in the 1830's. From such sources came her undoubted models for the Duchess of Zamorna, for Zenobia Ellrington, Julia Wellesley and other heroines who figure in these novelettes. The pictorial origin of her heroines can be traced furthermore in the details of dress, which must otherwise have been unknown to her in the quiet provincial circles where she lived, and in the very attitudes in which she presents them to the reader. Here is an early sketch of Julia Wellesley: "She was dressed in a violet silk mantle and hat with a long white veil which concealed her face . . ." At a ball, Julia is further described as dressed in "a rich dark satin robe ornamented with a profusion of jewels. A diamond aigrette glittered in her hair, surmounted by a stately drooping plume of white ostrich feather . . ."* (See illustration facing p. 97) On yet another occasion "Her ivory fan and her as ivory arm were raised with an arch graceful gesture, and the scarlet plumes nodded proudly on her head as she bent it coquettishly to one side . . ."† Zenobia Ellrington, one of Zamorna's early flames who consoled herself for his infidelity by marrying Percy, was introduced to the reader thus: "What eyes! What raven hair! What an imposing contour of form and countenance. She is perfectly grand in her velvet robes, dark plume and crown-like turban . . ."‡

Starting from the pictured image of a woman, Charlotte Brontë's heroines soon evolved personalities of their own, from which grew the complexities of the plot spreading about the central figure of Zamorna, and the analysis of human relationships in which already the young author excelled. The main dramatic theme on which the literature of Angria was based was the rivalry between Zamorna and Percy—the prince of the blood and the unscrupulous demagogue—and the infidelities of Zamorna, which further envenomed the relationship between the two men since Percy's daughter, Mary, was Zamorna's second wife. It was

* *The Foundling*, May–June 1833   † *My Angria & the Angrians*
‡ *A Peep into a Picture-Book*

natural that, in the division of labour which such a scenario entailed, Branwell should assume the responsibility for the political and military incidents, and Charlotte for the royal amours. From her first attempts at portraying the devastations of love, she showed herself an adept at the theme. She early accepted that a woman could die of sorrow, and demonstrated it in Marion Hume who pined away under the loss of Zamorna's love.

Branwell occasionally took a hand at advancing the plot when Charlotte was away and on one occasion wrung her heart by killing off the Duchess of Zamorna. In her dismay, Charlotte confided her feelings to the spasmodic journal she kept at the school. "About a week since I had a letter from Branwell containing a most exquisitely characteristic epistle from Northangerland [Percy] to his daughter . . . I lived on its contents for days. in every pause of employment it came chiming in like some sweet bar of music, bringing with it agreeable thoughts such as I had for many weeks been a stranger to . . . I wonder if Branwell has really killed the Duchess? Is she dead, is she buried, is she alone in the cold earth on this dreary night with the ponderous gold coffin plate on her breast under the black pavement of a church in a vault closed up with lime and mortar. Nobody near where she lies . . . now quite forsaken . . . A set of wretched thoughts are rising in my mind, I hope she's alive still, partly because I can't abide to think how hopelessly & cheerlessly she must have died, and partly because her removal if it has taken place, must have been to Northangerland the quenching of the last spark that averted utter darkness . . ."*

The obsessional nature of the young Brontës' make-believe world, apparent in this passage, where the reality of the imagined event is never questioned, was the chief characteristic of their writing. At this stage, Charlotte could not, without much agony of mind, separate the ideal world of her fabrication from the dreary reality of her life as governess in a girls' school, though she came to do so later. (It was Branwell's tragedy that he never succeeded in coming to terms with reality.) There was, as Charlotte's school journals reveal, a trance-like quality in her method of writing which excluded all possibility of self-criticism and almost, one is tempted to think, suspended consciousness. She wrote with her eyes shut, as she confided to her journals and as the irregular lines of her manuscripts attest, and did this intentionally the better to sharpen the inner vision and to shut out her bodily surroundings. In the same year that she wrote *Passing Events*, in August 1836,

* *Roe Head Journal*, 1836

having returned to school after the holidays, she noted in her journal for 11 August: "All this day I have been in a dream half miserable and half ecstatic—miserable because I could not follow it out uninterruptedly, and ecstatic because it shewed almost in the vivid light of reality the ongoings of the infernal world . . . The parsing lesson was completed, a dead silence had succeeded it in the school-room and I sat sinking from irritation and weariness into a kind of lethargy. The thought came over me am I to spend all the best part of my life in this wretched bondage . . . After tea we took a long weary walk. I came back exhausted to the last degree . . . The Ladies [pupils] went into the school-room to do their exercises & I crept up to the bed-room to be alone for the first time that day. Delicious was the sensation I experienced as I laid down on the spare bed & resigned myself to the luxury of twilight & solitude. The stream of thought, checked all day, came flowing free & calm along its channel. My ideas were too shattered to form any defined picture as they would have done in such circumstances at home . . . the toil of the day, succeeded by this moment of divine leisure had acted on me like opium & was coiling about me a disturbed but fascinating spell such as I never felt before. What I imagined grew morbidly vivid. I remember I quite seemed to see with my bodily eyes a lady standing in the hall of a gentleman's house as if waiting for some one. It was dusk & there was the dim outline of antlers with a hat & a rough great-coat upon them. She had a flat candle-stick in her hand & seemed coming from the kitchen or some such place . . . As she waited I most distinctly heard the front-door open and saw the soft moon-light disclosed upon a lawn outside, and beyond the lawn at a distance I saw a town with lights twinkling through the glooming . . . No more. I have not time to work out the vision. At last I became aware of a heavy weight laid across me—I knew I was wide awake & that it was dark & that moreover the Ladies were now come into the room to get their curl-papers . . . I heard them talking about me—I wanted to speak, to rise, it was impossible . . . I must get up I thought, and did so with a start . . ."*

Such a passage, rare in the annals of literature for its perception of the actual creative processes at work, explains in great measure both the weakness and strength of the young Charlotte's writings. She was like a medium through whom a spirit worked without control, and who could at the same time clearly register the sights and sounds, though not the significance, of what she saw. While she was, as she herself revealed, under the effect of a "spell"

* *Roe Head Journals*

comparable to opium, her critical faculties were dormant, and she could not be said, in any artistic sense, to be in control of the workings of her imagination.

She was already twenty and in many ways, despite her mental brilliance, retarded for her age. Shut in upon herself by her detestation of her employment as teacher, frustrated in every artistic impulse, separated from those she loved, she suffered all the agonies of a shy nature unable to liberate itself except by recourse to a drug-like dream which had little to do with either life or art.

The Novelettes

It was no easy task to shake off the dream and win her artistic independence, yet she was too much of an artist not to attempt it. Like all growing creatures, she took one step forward for every two she slipped back, but the advance was undeniable and the gain assured. The interest and importance of the novelettes is precisely in this progression because, from *Passing Events* to *Caroline Vernon*, it marks the transition from writing as an addiction to creative writing impelled by an awakened critical faculty. From being incapable of escaping from the "spell" that "coiled" about her in her frustrated days in school, she could get outside her visions and judge her characters objectively, as she did Elizabeth Hastings and Caroline Vernon, with wisdom and sympathy. They are no longer Society Beauties whose attraction lay in their elaborate dress, but sentient individuals responsible for their actions.

How difficult it was for Charlotte to shake off the dream, even after the emancipation of years, can be seen in her confession written to Branwell from Brussels, when she was alone in the Pensionnat during the Long Vacation and when the old loneliness in isolation and the old passionate dissatisfaction with her lot provoked the old response and drove her, like a drug-addict, back to the old recourse. "It is a curious metaphysical fact", she wrote on 1 May 1843, "that always in the evening when I am in the great dormitory alone, having no other company than a number of beds with white curtains, I always recur as fanatically as ever to the old ideas, the old faces, and the old scenes in the world below . . ."

Nine years had passed since the *Roe Head Journal* quoted above was written, yet the same expressions linger: the "infernal world" of those days and the "world below" of Brussels meant only one thing to the former collaborators, Branwell and Charlotte, it meant Angria, Zamorna and Percy—"all that mighty fantasm that we have conjured from nothing", as Charlotte called it.

The wonder is that being still assailable by the old magic formulas, Charlotte resisted their appeal to the extent of apparently writing nothing in the years immediately following *Captain Hastings* and *Caroline Vernon*. From 1840 to 1844, when she returned from Brussels, there are no preserved manuscripts to attest to any literary activity, but even though she was much preoccupied with a project for opening a school of her own at the parsonage and other practical plans, this is not to say, of course, that she wrote nothing, simply that if she did, she did not keep it. The gesture is significant and eloquent of a new-born attitude to her writing: it shows that she regarded it no longer as an escape from reality, dependent on no rational laws of cause and effect, but as the record of experience personal to herself of whose truth she had become the guardian. Immersed in literature as she had been all her life, reading nothing but standard authors, her sense of the writer's obligations to society were exalted, and once the canon of perfection was applied to her own work, with the growth of an artistic conscience, it was inevitable that "divine discontent" should set in and decree the destruction of all but the very best.

Two documents remain of this time to show her changing attitude towards these subjects: one is a letter she wrote to Hartley Coleridge some time in the summer of 1840, and the other is her so-called *Farewell to Angria* in which she took leave of her former "friends". She had already, in 1837, applied to the Poet Laureate, Southey, for an opinion on her work, and had received a very discouraging reply. In 1840, while Branwell was tutor to a family in Broughton-in-Furness, he approached Hartley Coleridge and was invited to visit him at Ambleside. Unlike Southey, Coleridge showed Branwell much kindness and thought well of his latest work, a translation of the first book of Horace's *Odes*. Emboldened by Branwell's success no doubt, Charlotte sent Coleridge a couple of her novelettes (the word is her own) and received a cautious though kind reply in return. The tenor of his letter can be judged from her response. Signing herself "C.T." ("Charles Townshend") her usual pseudonym at the time—and so preserving the secret of her sex—she wrote in a very bantering vein which did not, however, hide her chagrin at his poor opinion of her work.

"I am very much obliged to you for your kind and candid letter", she wrote, "and on the whole I wonder you took the trouble to read and notice the demi-semi novelette of an anonymous scribe who had not the manners to tell you whether he was a man or woman or whether his common-place 'C.T.' meant Charles Tims or Charlotte Tomkins . . ." The most revealing passage in her letter was that which concerned her Angrian creation. "It is very edifying and profitable to create a world out of one's brain and people it with inhabitants who are so like many Melchisedecs—without father, without mother, without descent, having neither beginning of days nor end of life. By conversing daily with such beings and accustoming your eyes to their glaring attire and fantastic features—you acquire a tone of mind admirably calculated to enable you to cut a respectable figure in practical life—If you have ever been accustomed to such society Sir you will be aware how distinctly & vividly their forms & features fix themselves—on the retina of that 'inward eye' which is said to be 'the bliss of solitude' . . ."

The impracticability of the kind of writing in which she had indulged up till then had, at last, struck Charlotte and decided her to make a radical change. However Coleridge worded his advice, it could only have urged a more disciplined approach to her work. In the undated document, generally attributed to this time and known as her *Farewell to Angria*, she took this advice to heart and made a formal renunciation of the subjects and style of her youthful writings. "I have now written a great many books", she said, "and for a long time have dwelt on the same characters and scenes & subjects . . . but we must change, for the eye is tired of the picture so oft recurring & now so familiar. Yet do not urge me too fast, reader, it is no easy thing to dismiss from my imagination the images which have filled it so long; they were my friends and my intimate acquaintances . . . When I depart from these I feel almost as if I stood on the threshold of a home and were bidding farewell to its inmates . . ."

In a felicitous phrase that conjures up the long procession of figures that had animated her pages, from the Genii of the Arabian tales to her latest inventions—evoked here in valediction—she gave evidence of a new artistic awareness of the right paths for her to pursue. The future author of *Jane Eyre*, *The Professor* and *Villette* stands revealed in a declaration of literary faith. "I long to quit for awhile the burning clime where we have sojourned too long—its skies flame—the glow of sunset is always upon it—the mind would cease from excitement and turn now to a cooler region where the dawn breaks grey and sober, and the coming day for a time at least is subdued by clouds . . ."

True to the resolution taken then, Charlotte applied the new criteria to her writings with such severity that none remain for the period immediately following her return from Brussels. In the Preface to *The Professor* (written between the autumn of 1845 and

June 1846) she told how ruthless she had been. Making no claim to its being apprentice work, she wrote: "A first attempt it certainly was not, as the pen which wrote it had been previously worn a good deal in a practice of some years. I had not indeed published anything before I commenced *The Professor*, but in many a crude effort, destroyed as soon as composed, I had got over any such taste as I might once have had for ornamental and redundant composition, and come to prefer what was plain and homely . . "

Without the evidence of Charlotte Brontë's novelettes, it would be hard to believe that her tastes had ever been for what was *not* "plain and homely", so completely did she come to identify herself with the strictly sober and concrete style of the novels that made her famous. Without knowledge of the Angrian literature that went before and of its protagonists, her deliberate choice of hero, as set forth in the Preface to *The Professor*, would have nothing so remarkable in it—except in so far as it was remarkable for a woman of her time to make such a choice at all. "I said to myself that my hero should work his way through life as I had seen real living men work theirs—that he should never get a shilling he had not earned—that no sudden turns of fortune should lift him in a moment to wealth and high station; that whatever small competency he might gain, should be won by the sweat of his brow; that, before he could find so much as an arbour to sit down in, he should master at least half the ascent of the 'Hill of Difficulty'; that he should not even marry a beautiful girl or a lady of rank. As Adam's son he should share Adam's doom, and drain throughout life a mixed and moderate cup of enjoyment . . ."

It is a far cry, indeed, from Zamorna to such a conception of the Ideal Hero, but in the interval Charlotte had learnt something of real life, she had travelled and worked abroad and come under the influence of a compelling personality, her Brussels teacher, Constantin Heger, whose philosophy of work and moral rectitude were very far indeed from the Byronic model of a man. His image it was which patently inspired the new concept of a hero introduced into *The Professor*—and still more into *Villette*.

Even so, the ghost of Zamorna haunts the pages of Currer Bell. Without Zamorna, Rochester would never have had those French mistresses and that illegitimate child, nor have boasted of them to that child's governess! And after the disclosure of his unhappy secret, Rochester would never have proposed to a girl of Jane's rectitude to live as his mistress. Once explained, how much more understandable Rochester—and even Paul Emanuel—appear through a knowledge of Zamorna. Though invisible, like the dark side of the moon, we know he is there, present even in the master-pieces.

While the distinguishing traits of the men and women in the novels of Currer Bell are Mind and Conscience—and these are conspicuously absent in the novelettes—one characteristic trait is common to all: a passionate nature that makes them all akin. Mina Laury, the "servante maitresse" of Zamorna's clandestine establishment, is already the prototype of Frances Henri and Jane Eyre. However much Charlotte Brontë conquered her tastes for extravagance and titles in the later novels, a study of the early writings shows us that, fundamentally, all her work was one. The subject of her finest penetration, first and last, was the power of love: whether its assaults were met with conscience, as by Jane Eyre and Elizabeth Hastings, or with abandon, as by Caroline Vernon and Zoraide Reuter, it is all-pervading throughout her work.

The interest of the novelettes as an introduction to the later works is, therefore, considerable. For all their immaturity—and it is conspicuous—especially in the treatment of servants and the use of titles (Dukes and Earls are equally addressed as "Mr Wellesley" and "Mr Percy", and the Queen of Angria as "Miss Percy") their humanity, faulty as it is, is not in doubt. It is the humanity of a primitive society—predatory, vainglorious, rapacious, spiteful—a nursery society, but throbbingly alive.

A comparison between the early and later works shows us, moreover, that though experience of life replaced the drug-like dream and dictated the style and substance of the published writings, there is no split apparent in the workings of the author's mind. Experience and the growth of the artist's powers only deepened and confirmed what was already there, the bent and aspirations of a nature equally compounded of intelligence and imagination. What happens in the novelettes to make them so remarkable is but the effect of precocity in a child, which permits it to see, as in a glass darkly, the human condition revealed in a game of puppets.

The Text

The text of the novelettes, only one of which is titled, and not all of which are signed or dated, is drawn from five separate manu-scripts now in the United States and written in Charlotte Brontë's habitual microscopic script that aimed at an imitation of type. The impression made by a page of any one of these manuscripts is that it was written at a feverish speed which nothing was allowed to impede, even to the detriment of sense. Paragraphing is minimal, capitalisation is eccentric and haphazard (not even new sentences necessarily call for the use of a capital), spelling aberrations are frequent, and punctuation (where it exists) consists very largely of dashes. All this, however, is so revealing of the author's creative process that every effort has been made to ensure that the present text faithfully reproduces what Charlotte Brontë wrote. At the same time, without some additional punctuations at least, it was felt that the reading of the novelettes might well become more laborious than enjoyable. That Charlotte herself was fully aware of her failings in this respect is clearly shown in what she wrote to her publishers at the time when *Jane Eyre* was going through the press: "I have to thank you for punctuating the sheets . . . as I found the task very puzzling. I consider your mode of punctuation a great deal more correct & rational than my own." Where, in this edition, punctuation has been added, it has been set in semi-bold type so that it can easily be distinguished from Charlotte's own. On rare occasions, where some interpolated mark of punctuation is totally uncalled for (as with a second opening quotation mark in the middle of a speech) it has been deleted without comment, as have terminal dashes at the end of lines which serve no other function. Spelling mistakes have been left as written without attention being drawn to them by a continual use of "[*sic*]".

PEOPLE AND PLACES
IN THE ANGRIAN CHRONICLES

ADRIANOPOLIS. The capital city of the Kingdom of Angria on the Calabar river. Named after the Duke of Zamorna, it is 150 miles from the old capital, Verdopolis.

ALNWICK. The family home of the Percys, after the historical home of the Percys of Northumberland.

ANGRIA, Kingdom of. Created from the African territories conquered by Zamorna and given him in recompense for his victories.

ANGRIA HOUSE. Zamorna's town house at Adrianopolis.

ARDRAH, Arthur Parry, Marquis of. Only son of William Edward, King of Parrysland; leader of the Reform Party and, as Percy's ally in his rebellion against Zamorna, was routed by the loyal Angrians under Warner.

ARUNDEL. One of the provinces of Angria.

ARUNDEL, Frederick, Earl of. Lord Lieutenant of the Province of Arundel, "the gallant, courteous chevalier", Grand Chamberlain to the Angrian Court and godfather to Zamorna's elder twin son, Victor Frederick.

DANCE or DANCI, Louisa. Formerly an opera-singer and ballet-dancer, and previously married to Zamorna's uncle, the Marquis of Wellesley. She later married Mr Vernon but, during his successful rebellion against Zamorna, became Northangerland's mistress and the mother of Caroline Vernon. On Zamorna's victorious return, he placed her under house-arrest.

DOURO, Marquis of. See Zamorna.

ELLRINGTON HOUSE. The Northangerlands' town house at Verdopolis.

ELLRINGTON, Surena. A relation of Zenobia's, probably a brother.

ELLRINGTON, Zenobia. Formerly in love with Douro and jealous of his passion for Marion Hume, she later married his rival, Alexander Percy, and, as Countess of Northangerland, held high state at the Angrian Court. She was variously described as "the prima donna of the Angrian court, the most learned woman of the age, the modern Cleopatra, the Verdopolitan de Staël . . ."

ENARA, General Henri Fernando di. Known as "The Tiger" or "The Colonel of the Bloodhounds", and Lord Lieutenant of the Province of Etrei.

FIDENA, John, Duke of. Leader of the Constitutional Party.

FIDENA. Capital city of the former Kingdom of Sneachiesland.

FITZ-ARTHUR, Ernest Edward Gordon Wellesley, Baron Gordon. Zamorna's son. In earlier accounts he was described as the child of Marion Hume and, on her early death, was confided to the keeping of Mina Laury. In another, later tale, he was described as the illegitimate son of Lady Helen Victorine, and was again confided to Mina Laury who, in both versions, fought for his life during the civil wars, and in whose arms he was murdered by Zamorna's enemies.

GIRNINGTON HALL. The home of the Thorntons.

GORDON, Baroness. Usually referred to as the Marchioness of Wellington, the mother of Zamorna and Charles Townshend.

GORDON, Baron. See Fitz-Arthur, Ernest.

GUADIMA. The river on whose banks was built the old capital of the Glasstown Confederacy, Verdopolis.

HARTFORD, Lord Edward. A General in the Angrian army and the commanding officer of Captain Henry Hastings, towards whom he had a special animosity.

HASTINGS, Elizabeth. The sister of Henry Hastings and lady-companion to Jane Moore.

HASTINGS, Henry. A creation of Branwell's and a self-projection of his own character. A poet and the chronicler of Angrian history, he rose to be a Captain in the 19th Regiment of Foot.

HUME, Marian. Zamorna's first wife whom he repudiated for Mary Percy.

JORDAN, Earl of. Lord Lieutenant of the Province of Douro.

JULIA. See Wellesley.

LAURY, Mina. Zamorna's mistress. Faithful to him in all circumstances, she guarded his son Ernest Fitz-Arthur and tried to save him from Zamorna's enemies. She followed Zamorna into exile and prepared his restoration with the loyal forces under Warner.

LOFTY, Lord Macara. Leader of the Republican Party. Together with Montmorenci, he fell from power when Northangerland was defeated. Described as addicted to opium, he was a creation of Branwell's.

MACARA. See Lofty.

MacTERROGLEN. General in command of the insurgent forces and a temporary victor during the civil war.

MARY HENRIETTA. See Percy.

MOORE, Jane. A Society beauty who figured in early Brontë narratives and was known as "The Rose of Zamorna" for her loveliness.

MONTMORENCY or MONTMORENCI, Hector de. One of the frenchified characters inspired by Charlotte's reading of contemporary French novels, he also figured in some of Branwell's tales. One of Zamorna's enemies, in league with Northangerland and Ardrah.

NORTHANGERLAND, Countess of. See Ellrington, Zenobia.

NORTHANGERLAND, Earl of. See Percy, Alexander.

PERCY, Alexander. Originally known as "Rogue" and a key figure in Branwell's early narratives. He represented the opposition-figure to Charlotte's Wellingtonian hero, the Marquis of Douro, later Zamorna. Percy was leader of the Democratic Party and early raised the standard of revolt against the four kings of Glasstown, even before Zamorna was made King of Angria. In temporary alliance with Zamorna, he allowed the marriage of his daughter Mary with the new king, but soon betrayed him again. Successful for a time, he was finally defeated but, because of their family ties, was shown leniency by Zamorna and was allowed to live on his estates at Alnwick and to retain his title of Earl of Northangerland.

PERCY, Edward. Half-brother to the Duchess of Zamorna, and like his brother William, rejected by his father, Northangerland. Ruthless and capable, he started from nothing, but rapidly made a fortune as a mill-owner.

PERCY, Mary Henrietta. Northangerland's daughter and Zamorna's second wife. A victim of her husband's infidelities, she yet remained deeply devoted to him and never abandoned hope of reconciling her husband and her father.

PERCY, Sir William. Brother of Edward Percy but, unlike him, a weak and romantic figure. The animosity between the brothers foreshadows the situation in *The Professor* between the brothers Edward and William Crimsworth.

QUASHIA. Son of the Ashantee Chief Quamina who was killed at the Battle of Coomassie, Quashia was adopted by Wellington but later rebelled against his benefactor.

RICHTON, John, Baron Flower. A creation of Branwell's and Minister of War in the Angrian government, he was an incorruptible politician and a deeply religious man.

ROGUE, Alexander. See Percy.

ROSIER, Eugène. Zamorna's French valet.

SHAVER or SHERER, James. Northangerland's valet.

THORNTON, Julia. See Wellesley, Julia.

THORNTON, General Sir Wilson. A rough-spoken hearty York-shireman, the first sketch for Hiram Yorke in *The Professor*. After her divorce from Edward Sydney, he married Julia Wellesley and was Lord Lieutenant of the Province of Calabar.

TOWNSHEND or TOWNSEND, Charles. An amplification of Lord Charles Florian Wellesley and, therefore, the supposed son of Wellington and brother to Zamorna. The narrator in some of Charlotte Brontë's tales and a mischievous, prying, quarrelsome character, he was a caricature of Branwell.

VERDOPOLIS. The old capital of the Glasstown Confederacy on the Guadima river, a confluent of the Niger. Abandoned as the seat of government when a new capital was created in Adrianopolis.

VERNON, Caroline. Northangerland's illegitimate daughter by Louisa Dance, her appearance as a child in *Julia* pre-figures the creation of Pauline in *Villette*.

VERNON, Louisa. See Dance.

WARNER, Warner Howard. Succeeded the defeated Northanger-land as Zamorna's Prime Minister. One of Zamorna's most faithful adherents, he frequently acts as his conscience and, because he always advocates what is right, is often repulsed.

WELLESLEY HOUSE. Zamorna's town house at Verdopolis.

WELLESLEY, Julia. Zamorna's cousin. First married to Edward Sydney, she later married General Thornton. When the newly-created Angrian Court moved from Verdopolis, Julia was left behind. (See *My Angria and the Angrians*.)

ZAMORNA, Arthur Augustus Adrian, Duke of, and King of Angria. Formerly Marquis of Douro, Zamorna was supposedly Wellington's son (whose real title it was) and his career was based on that of the Duke, though his immoral character was founded on that of Byron. He figures throughout Charlotte's juvenilia as the predominant character.

ZAMORNA, Duchess of. See Percy, Mary Henrietta.

ZAMORNA, Province of. Probably named after the Spanish town Zamora on the Douro.

ZENOBIA. See Ellrington.

The previous narratives in which these characters appear are:
Branwell Brontë: *Letters from an Englishman* (1830–2), *History of the Young Men* (1831), *The Pirate* (1833), *The Wool is Rising, or the*

Angrian Adventurer (1834), *The Massacre of Dongola* by Henry Hastings (1835), *The History of Angria in Ten Parts* purporting to be written by Henry Hastings (1835–7) and *The Life of Warner Howard Warner* (1838).

Charlotte Brontë: *Characters of the Celebrated Men of the Present Day* (1829), *Albion and Marina* (1830), *The Bridal* (1832), *The Foundling* (1833), *Politics in Verdopolis* (1833), *The Tragedy and the Essay* (1833), *Arthuriana* (1833), *A Peep into a Picture-Book* (1834), *My Angria and the Angrians* (1834), *The Spell and Other Tales* (1834), *The Scrap Book* (1835), *Zamorna's Exile—Zamorna's Return* (1837) and *The Duke of Zamorna* (1838).

PASSING EVENTS

INTRODUCTION

Charlotte Brontë began this manuscript on her twentieth birthday, Thursday 21 April 1836, and finished it eight days later. She was engaged as teacher at the time at the Miss Woolers' school, Roe Head, Mirfield Moor, where she remained from August 1835 to June 1838, but she wrote at home during her Easter holidays.

*The series of episodes which the MS contains stands midway between her juvenilia (dating from 1829) and the maturer fragments written in her early twenties. It is of special interest, therefore, in marking the transition period during which she emerged from the direct collaboration with her brother Branwell (his influence is still apparent in certain features of this MS) to independent authorship. While still assuming the masculine—and Branwellian—characteristics and nom-de-plume of 'Charles Townshend' or 'Townsend', she is seen moving here towards the more feminine and analytical view-point of the maturer compositions which follow—*Mina Laury, Captain Hastings *and* Caroline Vernon.

The MS is divided into seven loosely-connected episodes, the first of which, comprising six pages of script, is most revealing of the author's processes of creation. She writes for the pleasure of writing but without a theme, waiting for inspiration to dictate one. After filling three pages with desultory reportage, she ejaculates: "Reader, as yet I have written nothing, I would fain fall into some regular strain of composition, but I cannot, my mind is like a prism full of colours, but not of forms . . ."

The nature of Charlotte Brontë's imagination is here clearly revealed: it was a visual imagination dependent on images—not on ideas—to stir it to life. She recognised this herself: groping for a subject, she noted: "A panorama is round me whose scenes shift before I can fix their features—first a Saloon in Ellrington Hall . . ." The meaning of what she sees is, moreover, not always immediately apparent to her, as she says: ". . . my mind feels a vague impression that some incident is transpiring though I know not its nature . . ." Her descriptions are therefore visual before becoming an intellectual fact; they partake of the nature of dreams rather than of observed reality. This is an important—and characteristic—aspect of her early compositions.

The appearance of her manuscripts, furthermore, where the lines are frequently broken and overflow into each other, confirms her method of writing with her eyes closed, which she did to preserve the inward vision from interference from without. A passage from one of her journals kept at Roe Head during this summer of 1836 is illustrative of this. She is supervising a class-room of girls at their home-work and has been carried away by her mental visions while painfully conscious of their presence: ". . . encompassed by bulls (query calves of Bashan) all wondering why I write with my eyes shut—staring, gaping long their astonishment . . . stupidity the atmosphere, school-books the employment, asses the society. What in all this is there to remind me of the divine, silent, unseen land of thought, dim now and indefinite as the dream of a dream, the shadow of a shade . . ."

Two paramount influences of her girlhood, her brother Branwell and the poetry of Byron, are still dominant in these episodes. The characters and careers of Lord Richton, of Warner Howard Warner, of Captain Henry Hastings and, essentially, of Alexander Percy, Earl of Northangerland, are Branwell's creations taken over from his earlier MSS. The demoniac centre-figure of all Charlotte Brontë's youthful writings, the Duke of Zamorna, owes far more to the Byronic conception of the tragic hero, than to the historic Duke of Wellington with whose physical traits, titles and campaigns Charlotte endowed his figure. In the last episode of Passing Events *he is presented even as suffering from Byron's epileptic instability.*

Passing Events was written at a time of acute religious crisis in Charlotte Brontë's own development, and is singular among all her juvenile writings for its references to religious themes—conspicuous by their absence elsewhere. In the sixth episode, where Zamorna persists in repudiating his wife, his virtuous Home Secretary, Warner, tells him that despite his splendid endowments he has "no place amongst the elect of God. Long before the foundations of the world were laid you were numbered with the ever-lastingly condemned . . ." This was the Calvinist tenet which caused Charlotte such acute mental suffering at the time, and against which she eventually rebelled. In the letters of that summer to her former school friend Ellen Nussey, she wrote: "Don't deceive yourself that I have a scrap of real goodness about me . . . If you knew my thoughts; the dreams that absorb me; and the fiery imagination that at times eats me up . . . you would pity and I dare say despise me . . . If the Doctrine of Calvin be true I am already an outcast . . ." Such parallels between the fictional and the personal writings of Charlotte Brontë's twentieth year are symptomatic of the final stages of her development towards authorship, when her work began to assume an artistic entity distinct from her life.

The manuscript of Passing Events *is currently in the possession of the Pierpont Morgan Library of New York, by whose kind permission it is printed here. Only the second episode (pp 42 to 48) has been previously published, by Shorter and Hatfield in their edition of* The Twelve Adventurers, *Hodder, 1925.*

PASSING EVENTS

Every man to his trade, the blacksmith to his anvil, the tailor to his needle. Let Richton take his seat at the council board of war or peace, let him paint to the life, the members gathering round that table of heavy & dark honduras whose large circle groans under the piled documents of state, let him describe the mood of ire or thought or pride or scorn, that contracts the brow of each haughty councillor—let him detail with graphic skill the imperious bearing contrasted with the civil garb of one, & the martial dress & grave deliberate aspect of another. let him with magic power show the whole room haply adorned with mirrors where are seen the reflected figures bending over the table, now in deep consultation, now in fierce dispute. let him write so well that each separate voice shall speak out of the page in changeful tone, the word passing from mouth to mouth, the flexible lip & the rapid tongue of Edward Percy succeeding in raised bass the energetic silver dictum of Howard Warner. Let him show us even those details that give truest life to the picture, the pocket-handkerchief drawn out with a flourish, as altercation kindles, the snuff-box hurriedly produced & replaced, the gold repeater glanced at while the pre-occupied aspect of the speaker's eye testifies that he has derived no information from its enamelled plate. Castlereagh's involuntary adjustment of chain or stock, his unconscious use and recurrence to the habits of the coxcomb when his whole soul is truly absorbed in the duties of a statesman. Arundel's hand run through his fair locks arranging them as he does at the toilette when meantime he enforces with fluent power & reckless self-abandonment, some favourite measure of his party. Thornton warms to the discussion of serious danger, forgetting his beloved Doric & launching into the very voice & accent, deep, pure except a momentary whistle of the North wind, of his abhorred, & abhorring brother. Let Richton do this & astonish us & let Hastings familiarise us with the terms & tactics of war, let him stir us up with the sweet & warlike national airs of Angria, let him lead us along her many & splendid streams, not through green pastures or by still waters, but through the haunts of herons & curlews & water-ousels & lamenting bitterns, fringed with sedges & canes & long-jointed dog-grass. let him reveal to us the Calabar or the Etrei (the wild eerie Etrei a battle-stream, whose pitchy billows evermore carry a vein of negro blood to the ocean) by moonlight, the first & royal river washing the white-walls of the capital, the devoted young & beautiful capital of the east, & rolling its broad & profound torrent, as if jealous of the very light of heaven cast on its white foam and on its magnificent sheet of bounding flashing water.

The last, Ah! the last is all black with the shade of its brakes & morasses, when in the storm or in the calm summer midnight we bivouac with Hastings beside it, we strive in vain to sleep, thoughts of the concealed man Alligator of the African hid in the giant-rushes will not let us. Let Hastings speak of Gazemba, shew the armed houshold and bandit vassallage of Enara, the rendezvous of regiments, the head quarters of General officers. polished, brave, intriguing, ambitious, scoundrelly, sagacious men. General Lord Hartford, smoothed by travel & knowledge of the world, a frank cultivated gentleman, an impetuous daring skilful soldier, a dark aspiring Aristocrat, of liberal & bland though lofty bearing towards the world at large, yet arrogant & insolent to the last degree in asserting the claims of Angria, a thought dissolute as his underlip & marked face shew, yet a man of honour & of his word. feudal in his ideas of birth & caste, firm & soldierly in his allegiance to the King, generous when obeyed, oppressive when opposed, kind to submitting inferiors, jealous of equals, acknowledging no superior except in the single area of rank when he yields with a good-grace & ungrudgingly—handsome but for a distorting scar on his fore-head, of cheerful & noble demeanour—a sort of Angrian Great-heart in the field & in the council. One who wherever he went would be of consequence & high consideration. Let Hastings shew us Hartford & such as Hartford for Angria has not a few like him, let him unveil to us the Chambers where they walk & converse together, the courts whose flags ring to the tread of the iron shod boot, as alone or in leashes those men walk, the Nobles & Esquires of the East, all born of Earth's first blood & expressing their strong thoughts in language as strong & in the sonorous tones bestowed by Health & energy. It may be the eve of battle, the sun perhaps is setting calm & glorious, the possible Death of war near at hand, the solemnity of the evening sky has hushed the riotous mirth of some amongst those gallant Gentlemen, they lean on the coping of the fortalice & listen silently while the bands of their regiments play along the Etrei. yes Hastings, we hear that wild music in thy page most distinctly. National melodies that neither private nor officer would exchange for the fine opera of Italy. Each of the seven provinces had its air, mostly triumphant but now & then inspired with a thrilling wildness that might touch the nerves of a

nation!—"Sound the loud trumpet o'er Afric's dark sea!"* Sublime!
—but stop, my recollections of Hastings have led me too far astray.
let the Earl & the Major say I dilate on these things, let them rush
upon that noble quarry, they are eagles, let them travel that broad
road, they are mounted on chargers of the Ukraine. for me I am
but a crow, so I must be well content in the rookeries that shade
Africa's ancestral Halls. I have but my own shanks to go on, therefore I can travel no farther than the groaning park-gates of the
magnates. While Thornton far off, wrapped in his furred roquel-
aure sits by the bivouac fire & as he discusses the viands his
canteens supply & hears the sounds of the encamping army, the
wail of the wind & the hissing of the rain as it falls on that un-
quenched flame before him. thinking meantime of his young gude-
wife, his bonnie Julia, & wishing that her warm & soft white hand
were now resting in the grasp of his own vigorous fingers & that her
dark bewitching eyes were laughingly eluding his hawk-like
glance. While he, I say, muses thus, I stand by Julia in her chamber,
I watch her as she sits alone on a low stool before her glowing
hearth, her etherial spirits ebbing low & her lovely head declined
upon an arm of marble, the hearth-light suffuses her with its glow,
her raven curls are dishevelled upon her knee where the forehead
rests upon the clasped hands & her robes of bright silk are spread
over the purple & green & crimson dyes of the carpet. She too
wishes that Thornton, her falcon-eyed & bold & frank Thornton
were there. could he be restored to her at that moment she would
even let him repose his head if it ached on the lace pelerine that
shades her neck & shoulder & veils the lustrous silk of her sleeves.
She might touch his brow, hard-looking & daring as she remembers
it to be, with her coral lips. but then she would torment & tantalize
him to the farthest limits of endurance too. But Julia's lightsome
& proud heart beats in the breast of a true Wellesley. She cannot
droop long. This momentary dejection is succeeded by an elastic
spring. Starting from the foot stool, she is in a moment seated at
that splendid instrument in the recess, her fingers wake like
lightning the satisfying & rich melody of its tones, and the voice,
not of a Seraph but of a beautiful woman with clear, silvery utterance, steals through the tumultuous sweetness, like a moonbeam
through bright but confused clouds.

I've a free hand & a merry heart
I dwell in gay Madrid,

* Verses by Branwell Brontë, written June–September 1834. The allusion, here, to
Hastings is an indication of the closed circle of Charlotte Brontë's juvenile readers

My hair is like a night-cloud when
   Its veil the moon has hid.
My blood is not the high Castile,
   The Moor has breathed his flame
Through every blushing artery
   That leads the crimson stream.
And yet I am of noble birth,
   My father's long ago
Where mighty lords [*illegible*] Granada
   Quailed to the Christian foe.
But what care I for noble birth,
   I'm young & gay & free,
I've jet-black eyes & coal-black locks
   & brow of ivorie.
I've a quick hand & a sweet guitar
   And a light foot for the dance,
And many a mystic reel I know
   And many a blithe romance.
When I see the clear blue skies of Spain
   And feel her glad warm sun,
I've nought to jar the harmony
   They breathe my soul upon.
I'm happy when the early light
   Looks through my casement panes,
I'm happy when the sun's farewell
   Their hew with amber stains,
I'm happy when the moon uplights
   The green vine's leafy veil
And smiles as I lie wakefully
   To meet her lustre pale.
And Oh! when far beneath my bower
   A wild sweet air is played,
My soul leaps up to bless the hour
   Of star & Serenade.

This is a song that suits Julia and she sings it in a style that even relaxes the critical severity of her awful & fastidious cousin.* He thinks her a pretty woman, one of the prettiest in Africa, & I've seen him regard her with a very indulgent & gratified smile when she has been singing this little ballad. Reader, as yet I have written nothing, I would fain fall into some regular strain of composition, but I cannot, my mind is like a prism full of colours but not of

* Zamorna

forms. A thousand tints are there, brilliant & varied, & if they would resolve into the shade of some flower or bird or gem, I could picture before you. I feel I could. A Panorama is round me whose scenes shift before I can at all fix their features. first a saloon in Ellrington-Hall with wide sash-windows through which flashes a gleam of the sea thundering in sunshine. the Countess* by one open casement, seated & leaning thoughtfully back in an arm-chair, the breeze from a garden playing over her face & fluttering her sable plume & tresses. an open letter lies on the carpet at her feet which has dropped unconsciously from her relaxed hand. Over this scene of daylight rolls a gloomy mass, which the eye cannot at first comprehend. by and bye it is discovered to be a court in Waterloo Palace. a pile of grey shade silvered with moonbeams. it is silent, I hear nothing. It is lonely, I see nothing but the walls & arches, the statues of stone & flags of solid granite. an aimless picture, yet now & then, a light waving object like a lady's veil, glints uncertainly through that dark row of pillars. a scarcely audible step flits along the hidden recesses & my mind feels a vague impression that some incident is transpiring though I know not of what nature. the court & moonlight are gone. it is high noon & I am conversing with Greenwood Peascod in his own apartment at Wellesley-House, a round table covered with newspapers, a cold chicken & a pleasant bottle of French wine are between us. Her Grace's gentleman regales me with a thousand anecdotes of court-scandal, boasts of his own importance & points out the paragraphs he has furnished to the papers. a bell rings, Greenwood knows his summons, he & his parlour both vanish. Go to. the first scene on my list is Ellrington Hall. let us dash at once into it.

It was night, the clocks had all chimed twelve, the saloons were fireless, & lampless, no company had enlivened them that night or for many preceding ones. Zenobia, as she glided past their portals, thought how lonely their silence & darkness was. with a less inceding† & slower tread than was customary to her, she ascended a private stair-case & sought her chamber with the intention of retiring to rest. for she was weary of sitting up alone & struggling against thoughts that tamed her pride & lowered her soaring spirits. She had been by herself all day, solitude is not the nurse of haughtiness, & the very imperial expression she usually wears had faded gradually from her face, her hair was uncurled a little & drooping on her neck. She wore no plume & no gem, chain or crosslet. A fine woman she looked with a solemn but not sad aspect in her eyes as she opened the door & crossed the threshold

* Zenobia   † One of Charlotte Brontë's favourite adjectives

of her dressing-room. Why does she stop? what means that look of astonishment changing quickly into one of a different & inscrutable meaning. that parting of the beautiful lips & that sudden erection of the splendid bust? Her sanctum is as it should be—the wax tapers are lighted, the fire burns red & clear, there is the mirror on the polished toilette, there are the dressing-cases open. Velvet draperies shroud the windows like palls, a light perfume, a silence fill the chamber. But it is not empty of more substantial tenants, a tall shadow quivers on the walls & ceiling. look yonder! that is a human being! a man! a gentleman! Yes! one in a black dress with a white forehead & fine nose leans against that cabinet with folded arms & eyes directed straight, daringly & unblinkingly towards the awful Countess! The first petrifying effect of this apparition over, Zenobia closed the door, then she moved to the fire, & mutely gazed on the ascending flame. in a moment she turned & glanced again on the intruder as if to be certain he was still there—he was indeed but he had changed his place & stood close beside her—The word Percy burst from her lips & flashed from her eyes, into which, black & spirited as they were, at the same time gushed a lustre that told some warm almost resistless feelings were impelling her to forgiveness, a cordial welcome, forgiveness without a hearing & welcome before it was asked. The Earl* coughed & looked at her & then said, "Why my dear Zenobia this excitement makes you look very interesting, almost as much so as—" he paused & then said—while his lip curled & a low laugh escaped him "as Louisa Vernon". The trembling light in Zenobia's eyes ran over—but Oh! how it was dashed away! & how she snatched her hand from the aristocratic fingers that were enclosing them in their grasp. "My Lord I am a Western!† and the Heiress of Henry Ellrington of Ennerdale & the Grand-daughter of Don John Louisiada. I will not be insulted—by my life" continued the Countess using unconsciously her husband's oath. "I would have forgiven you & loved you again at that moment because you looked pale & weary—but I'll not now—you did ill to speak of Louisa Vernon—I thought you were tired of your false rest & come back to lean upon your true one in adversity." "I am, my Countess" said the Earl, gazing at her as she agitatedly paced the room. "And a most placid rest I've found, you look all repose, Zenobia." "He is possessed!" exclaimed his wife, "he is sick at heart I see & satiated & utterly without hope, & yet there's a light

* Alexander Percy, Earl of Northangerland, her husband
† i.e. a native of the western provinces within the original Verdopolitan Confederation, founded before the conquest of the Angrian provinces

foam on his desperation that churns up the more wantonly & fantastically, the more madly the torrent rushes." "An Evangelical truth!" ejaculated Percy. "Verily your ladyship speaks right. Satiated I was with the semi Gallic, semi Italian & wholly Paradisaical graces of my delightful Louisa ——— with her elegance & her caresses & her lusciously sweet voice & her fastidious boudoir with its too perfect taste & luxury & her animated intelligent daughter* (mine too by the bye), ennuyé utterly by her grasping monopoly of my precious self & her tiresome jealousy of my favours—frightened (you know I've weak nerves) at her violence & her propensity to scenes—I began to long for the dying scene as a relief, but as it never comes I took myself off, & in a very queer mood of mind not at all myself, forgetting my partiality to close carriages, hotels bespoken beforehand &c., I wandered here I scarcely know how, actually without the company of James Sherer.† & when I'm at last arrive[d], after an absence as they say in newspapers of nearly three months, my wife's first greeting is couched in a genealogical account of herself & her family." there was sorrow & even concealed alarm in the expression of Zenobia's countenance as in a tone of strange levity Northangerland ran on thus. He divined what her thoughts were & continued "I say, my Castillian Countess, are you quite sure that you are the Daughter of Henry, lord Ellrington? I've heard of the Donna Ranline in my young days. She was a court beauty her contemporaries say, such a one as is never seen now, and that Scoundrel of Grassmere, that Macarthy, for a long time did homage at her shrine. you may be his daughter & in that case you're a sort of left-handed aunt of Zamorna's." Zenobia, with a coolness unusual in her, stood at her mirror quietly arranging her hair for the night. she did not speak, the Earl went on. "talking of those times reminds me of one Alexander Percy that I used to know. It's long since & I remember very little about him, except that his brains were less irretrievably cracked than those of the present most mighty Earl of Northangerland. Zenobia! what did that glance mean! it meant that you thought me mad. you are frightened at hearing my jaunty desperation. Zenobia" the earl drew near & laid his hand on her shoulder & looked at her with a kind of heart-broken expression. "Zenobia! I don't pretend to say I've lost my senses, or that I'm much wronged or in phrenzied despair—to speak truth, I'm only horribly dissatisfied—but—but my lady, that's the worst of all miseries. I've striven hard to get a moment's rest & content & I cannot. Louisa sickens me & I hate France & I abhor Africa. Eden Cottage, the

* Caroline Vernon   † His valet

villa at St Cloud, Alnwick & Ellrington house are equally loathsome to me." "Then" said the Countess turning quickly "lash
your broken helmless bark wholly to myself my lord, I've enough
firmness & fidelity to be a most steadfast anchor, trust me."
Northangerland looked in earnest for a moment, then he laughed
& swerved adrift again. "That is to say in other words" he
answered "Tie yourself to my apron-string. I might have yielded,
but another thought has just struck me—there's one quarter I've
left untried, a project that entered my head, shabby, despicable &
contemptible in its nature & therefore the more in harmony with
the whole state of my feelings. Good night Zenobia—" the Countess
said nothing, she could not speak, but a destructive crack & the
splendid fragments of a shivered mirror told what she felt.

*

The Cross of Rivaulx!* Is that a name familiar to my readers? I
rather think not. Listen then, it is a green delightful & quiet place
half way between Angria & the foot of the Sydenham Hills, under
the frown of Hawkscliffe on the edge of its royal forest. You see a
fair house whose sash windows are set in ivy grown thick & kept in
trim order, over the front door there is a little modern porch of
trellis-work, *all* the summer covered with a succession of verdant
leaves & pink rose-globes, buds & full-blown blossoms. Within this,
in fine weather, the door is constantly open & reveals a noble
passage, almost a Hall, terminating in a staircase of low white
steps, traced up the middle by a brilliant carpet. there are no
decided grounds laid out about the Cross of Rivaulx, but a lawn-
like greenness surrounds it & the last remnants of Hawkscliffe
shade it in the form of many wild rose trees & a few lofty elms. You
look in vain for anything like a wall or gate to shut it in—the only
landmark consists in an old Obelisk with moss & wild flowers at its
base and an half obliterated crucifix sculptured on its side. Well,
this is no very presuming place, but on a June evening not seldom
have I seen a figure whom every eye in Angria might recognise
stride out of the Domestic gloom of that little hall & stand in
pleasant leisure under the porch whose flowers & leaves were
disturbed by the contact of his curls. Though in a sequestered spot,
the cross of Rivaulx is not one of Zamorna's secret houses, he'll
let any-body come there that chuses. It is but a lodge to the
mighty towers of Hawkscliffe, which being five miles distant,
buried in the chase, are of less convenient access. The day is

* The subject of a drawing by Charlotte Brontë

breathless, quite still & warm. the sun, far declined for afternoon, is just melting into evening, sheds a deep amber light. a cheerful air surrounds the mansion whose windows are up, its door as usual hospitably apart, & the broad passage reverberates with a lively conversational hum from the rooms which open into it. the day is of that perfectly mild sunny kind that by an irrisistible influence draws people out into the balmy air, & see, there are two gentlemen lounging easily in the porch, sipping coffee from the cups they have brought from the drawing-room & a third has stretched himself on the soft moss in the shadow of the obelisk. but for these figures, the landscape would be one of exquisite repose. They break the enchantment of sun, sky, pleasant home & waveless trees. their dress is military, they are officers from Angria, from the head-quarters of Zamorna's grand-army. Two at least are of this description, the other reclining on the grass, a slight figure in black, wears a civil dress. that is Mr Warner the home Secretary & another person was standing by him whom I should not have omitted to describe. It was a fine girl dressed in rich black satin, with ornaments like those of a bandit's wife in which a whole fortune seemed to have been expended, but no wonder, for they had doubtless been the gift of a King. In her ears hung two long clear drops, red as fire & suffused with a purple tint, that showed them to be the true oriental ruby. bright delicate tints of gold circled her neck again & again, & a cross of gems lay on her breast, the centre stone of which was a locket enclosing a ringlet of dark-brown hair—with that little soft curl she would not have parted for a kingdom, it had been severed from the head of the Lord's anointed. Warner's eyes were fixed with interest on Miss Laury as she stood over him, a model of beautiful vigour & glowing health. a kind of military erectness in her form, so elegantly built, & in the manner in which her neck sprung from her exquisite bust & was placed with graceful uprightness on her falling shoulders. her waist too, falling in behind, & her fine slender foot supporting her in a regulated position, plainly indicated familiarity from her childhood with the sergeant's drill. All the afternoon she had been entertaining her exalted guests, the two in the porch were no other than Lord Hartford & Enara, & conversing with them, frankly & cheerfully but with a total absence of levity, & a dash of seriousness, an habitual intentness of purpose that had more than once attracted to her the admiring glance of the Home Secretary—these & Lord Arundel were the only friends she had in the world. female acquaintance she never sought, nor if she had sought would she have found them. And so sagacious, clever & earnest was she in all she said & did that the haughty Aristocrats did not hesitate to communicate with her often on matters of first rate importance.

Mr Warner was now talking to her about herself. "My dear Madam" he was saying in his usual imperious & still dulcet tone, "It is unreasonable that you should remain thus exposed to danger. I am your friend, yes madam your *true* friend, why do you not hear me & attend to my representations of the case. Angria is an unsafe place for you. you ought to leave it." the lady shook her head. "Never till my master compels me, his land is my land." "But— But Miss Laury you know that our Army have no warrant from the Almighty of conquest. this invasion may be successful at least for a time & then what becomes of you? when the Duke's nation is wrestling with destruction, his glory sunk in deep waters & himself striving desperately to recover it, can he waste a thought or a moment on one woman? You will be at the tender mercies of Quashia* & of the Sheik Medina, I mean of that detestable renegade Lord before you are aware." Miss [Laury] smiled. "I am resolved" said she. "My master himself shall not force me to leave him. You know I am hardened Warner, shame & reproach have no effect on me, I do not care for being called a camp-follower. In peace & pleasure all the ladies of Africa would be at the Duke's beck, in war & suffering he shall not lack one poor peasant-girl. Why Sir, I've nothing else to exist for, I've no other interest in life. Just to stand by his Grace, watch him & anticipate his wishes or when I cannot do that, to execute them like lightning when they are signified. To wait on him when he is sick or wounded, to hear his groans & bear his heart-rending animal patience in enduring pain. To breathe if I can my own inexhaustible health & energy into him & Oh, if it were practicable, to take his fever & agony. to guard his interests, to take on my shoulders power from him that galls me with its weight. To fill a gap in his mighty train of service which nobody else would dare to step into. To do all that Sir, is to fulfil the destiny I was born to. I know I am of no repute amongst society at large because I have devoted myself so wholly to one man. And I know that he even seldom troubles himself to think of what I do, & has never & can never appreciate the unusual feelings of subservience, the total self-sacrifice I offer at his shrine. but then he gives me my reward & that an abundant one. Mr Warner, when I was at Fort Adrian & had all the yoke of Governing the Garrison & military houshold, I used to rejoice in my

* Quashia, son of Quamina, King of the Ashantees, adopted by Wellington after the African's defeat. See *The Green Dwarf* (1833) and *The African Queen's Lament* (1833)

responsibility & to feel firmer the heavier weight was assigned me
to support, & when my master came over as he often did to take
one of his general surveys, or on a hunting expedition with some
of his state officers, I had such delight in ordering the banquets &
entertainments & in seeing the fires kindled up & the chandeliers
lighted in those dark hall[s]—knowing for whom the feast was
made ready, & it gave me a feeling of extasy to hear my young
master's voice, as he spoke to you or Arundel or to that stately
Hartford, & to see him moving about secure & powerful in his own
stronghold, to know what true hearts he had about him, assured as
I was that his Generals & his ministers were men of steel & that his
vassals under my rule were trusty as the very ramparts they garrisoned. & besides Sir, his greeting to me & the condescending
touch of his hand were enough to make a queen proud (let alone a
Sergeant's Daughter). that is an Irishism, Warner. Then, for
instance, last summer evening that he came here, the sun &
flowers & quietness brightened his noble features with such happiness. I could tell his heart was at rest for as he lay in the shade were
you are now, I heard him hum the airs he long, long ago played on
his guitar at Mornington.* I was rewarded then to feel that the
house I kept was pleasant enough to make him forget Angria and
recur to home. You must excuse me Mr Warner, but the West, the
sweet West, is both his home & mine." Mina paused & looked
solemnly at the sun, now softened in its shine & hanging exceedingly low. In a moment her eyes fell again on Warner—they seemed
to have absorbed radiance from what they had gazed on, light like
an arrow point glanced in them as she said "this is my time to
follow Zamorna. I'll not be robbed of those hours of blissful danger
when I may be continually with him. My kind noble master never
likes to see my tears & I will weep before him day & night until he
grants what I wish. I am not afraid of danger, I have strong nerves,
I don't wish to fight like an Amazon a fatigue I never felt, I will
die or be with him." "What has fired your eyes so suddenly Miss
Laury?" asked Lord Hartford, now advancing with Enara from
their canopy of roses. "The Duke, the duke" muttered Henri
Fernando.† "You won't leave him I'll be sworn." "I can't General"
said Mina. "No" answered the Italian "& nobody shall force you.
you shall have your own way, madam, whether it be right or wrong.
I hate to contradict such as you in their will." "Thank you General,
you are always so kind to me." & Mina hurridly put her little hand

* Mornington was one of the titles of the Wellesley family, and is used here as
the name for their home
† Enara

into the gloved grasp of Enara. "Kind madam!" said he, pressing it warmly "I'm so kind that I would hang the man unshriven who should use your name with other than the respect due to a queen." The dark hard-browed Hartford smiled at his enthusiasm. "Is that homage paid to Miss Laury's goodness or to her beauty?" asked he. "To neither my lord" answered Enara briefly "but to her worth, her sterling worth." "Hartford, you are not going to despise me? was that a sneer?" murmured Mina aside. "No, No, Miss Laury" replied the noble General seriously. "I know what you are, I am aware of your value. do you doubt Edward Hartford's honourable friendship? it is yours on terms such as it was never given to a beautiful woman before." Before Miss Laury could answer, a voice from within the mansion spoke her name. "It is my lord!" she exclaimed & sped like a roe over the sward, through the porch, along the passage, to a summer parlour, whose walls were painted fine pale red, its mouldings burnished gilding & its window-curtains artistical draperies of dark-blue silk, covered with gold waves & flowers. Here Zamorna sat alone, he had been writing one or two letters, folded, sealed & inscribed with western directions lay on the table beside him, his gloves & cambric handkerchief with a coronet wrought upon it in black-hair appeared on his desk, he had not uncovered since entering the house three hours since, & either the weight of his Dragoon Helmet or the gloom of its impending plumes or else some inward feeling, had clouded his face with a strange darkness. Mina closed the door & softly drew near, without speaking or asking leave, she began to busy herself in unclasping the heavy helmet, the Duke smiled faintly as her little fingers played about his chin & luxuriant whiskers & then, the load of brass & sable plumage being removed, as they arranged the compressed masses of glossy brown ringlets, & touched with soft cool contact his feverish brow. Absorbed in this grateful task she hardly felt that his Majesty's arm had encircled her waist, & yet she did feel it too and would have thought herself presumptuous to shrink from his endearment. She took it as a slave ought to take the caress of a Sultan, & obeying the gentle effort of his hand, slowly sunk on to the sofa by her master's side. "My little physician" said he, meeting her adoring but anxious upward gaze, with the full light of his countenance. "You look at me as if you thought I was not well—feel my pulse." She folded the proferred hand, white supple & soft with youth & delicate nurture, in both her own, & whether Zamorna's pulse beat rapidly or not, hiss handmaid's did as she felt the slender grasping fingers of a Monarch laid quietly in hers. He did not wait for the report, but took his hand away again & laying it on her raven curls said "So Mina, you won't leave me though I never did you any good in the world. Warner says you are resolved to continue in the scene of war." "To continue by your side, lord Augustus, I mean my lord Duke." "But what shall I do with you Mina? where shall I put you? my little girl, what will the army say when they hear of your presence? you have read history, recollect that it was Darius who carried his concubines to the field not Alexander. The world will say Zamorna has provided himself with a pretty mistress. he attends to his own pleasures & cares not how his men suffer." Poor Mina writhed at these words as if the iron had entered into her soul. a vivid burning blush crimsoned her cheek, & tears of shame & bitter self-reproach gushed at once into her bright black eyes. Zamorna was touched acutely—"Nay my little girl" said he, redoubling his haughty caresses & speaking in his most soothing tone "never weep about it, it grieves me to hurt your feelings, but you desire an impossibility & I must use strong language to convince you that I cannot grant it—" "Oh! don't refuse me again" sobbed Miss Laury. "I'll bear all infamy & contempt to be allowed to follow you, my lord. My lord, I've served you for many years most faithfully & I seldom ask a favour of you, don't reject almost the first request of the kind I ever made." The Duke shook his head, & the meeting of his exquisite lips, too placid for the term compression, told he was not to be moved. "If you should receive a wound, if you should fall sick" continued Mina "what can surgeons & physicians do for you? they cannot watch you & wait on you & worship you like me, & you do not seem well now the bloom is so faded on your complexion & the flesh is wasted round your eyes. My lord smile & do not look so calmly resolved—let me go!" Zamorna withdrew his arm from her waist. "I must be displeased before you cease to importune me" said he. "Mina, look at that letter, read the direction," pointing to one he had been writing—she obeyed, it was addressed to "Her Royal Highness Mary Henrietta, Duchess of Zamorna, Queen of Angria, Duchess of Alterwood, Marchioness of Douro &c." "Must I pay no attention to the feelings of that lady?" pursued the Duke, whom the Duties of war & the conflict of some internal emotions seemed to render rather peculiarly stern. "her public claims must be respected whether I love her or not." Miss Laury shrunk into herself, not another word did she venture to breathe, an unconscious wish of wild intensity filled her that she were dead & buried & insensible to the shame that overwhelmed her. She saw Zamorna's finger with the ring on it still pointing to that awful name, a name that raised no impulses of hatred, for too high & blessed the exalted

Lady seemed for that, but only bitter humiliation & self-abasement. She stole from her master's side feeling that she had no more right to sit there than a fawn has to share the den of a royal lion, & murmuring that she was very sorry for her folly was about to glide in dismay & despair from the room. But the Duke, rising up, arrested her and, bending his lofty stature over as she crouched before him, folded her again in his arms. his countenance relaxed not a moment from its sternness, nor did the gloom leave his magnificent but worn features as he said "I will make no apologies for what I have said because I know Mina that, as I hold you now, you feel fully recompensed for my transient severity. before I depart I will speak to you one word of comfort which you may remember when I am far away, & perhaps dead. My dear Girl! I know & appreciate all you have done, all you have resigned & all you have endured for my sake, I repay you for it with one coin, with what alone will be to you of greater worth than worlds without it. I give you such true & fond love as a master may give to the fairest & lordliest vassal that ever was bound to him in feudal allegiance. You may never feel the touch of Zamorna's lips again, there Mina" & fervently, almost fiercely he pressed them to her forehead. "Go to your chamber, to-morrow you must leave for the West." "Obedient till Death" was Miss Laury's answer as she closed the door & disappeared.* Four horses were now brought out on to the lawn. Hartford, Warner & Enara were already mounted, the Duke clasped on his helmet, assumed his gloves & proceeded to the front-door, & was just crossing the threshold when a soft voice called to him to stop, an elegant female figure clad in azure gauze was running down the stair-case. "The D——l!" exclaimed Zamorna when he saw her. "this is lax, ward, how dared you leave your room —" It was chilling to hear his voice assume that tone to the fine pleasing woman of about seven & twenty who now stood at his elbow. She pressed close to him & looked up in his face with an affected expression of appealing languor. "I am so weary of my chamber" said she "& it is such a sweet evening—do give me leave to take a stroll along the Arno just as far as your own birch." "Take it & be d——d" said Zamorna, fastidiously receding from her approach & his dark eyes looking most freezingly haughty from the shade of his curls & casque. a kind of momentary convulsion flitted over the lady's features, yet she seemed to notice neither his coldness nor his

* Hatfield's extract, published in *The Twelve Adventurers*, ends here. Because of its main protagonist, this section of manuscript is sometimes referred to as *Mina Laury I*, and the main novelette that followed later is consequently known as *Mina Laury II*

curse—"Oh! how infinitely I am obliged to you my dear Arthur" said she—"but how are you this evening? you do not look well" & assuming an air of interest she again drew near & looked into his face. "Have done with your canting hypocrisy" returned he, colouring deeply with annoyance & disgust & making a stride from her on to the lawn. She followed & taking his hand hung tenderly upon it. "Do bid me good-bye my lord before you go"— "Begone" was his peremptory mandate. "I will" she answered patiently "but just speak one kind word to me ere we part." Zamorna shewed his teeth & scowled most threateningly—he pushed her slightly from him, she still retained his hand however & bending her head over it seemed to press her lips to it. She let it drop, he had neither started nor spoken, but the blood was trickling rapidly from it & there was a deep incision made by the teeth of the she-tigress. "Louisa Dance, you may still have your walk" said Zamorna, coolly binding it with his pocket-handker-chief—"but mind a footman goes with you." he touched the mane of the noble horse that stood proudly pawing the green-sward, vaulted into the saddle and touched its flank with his armed heel & away cantered himself & his gallant staff.

Louisa Dance did go that evening to take a walk along the banks of the Arno but she never came back. The moon had risen when she reached the splendid weeping birch called Zamorna's tree. She sat down & fixed her eyes on the high road through Hawkscliffe forest which might be seen from thence. erelong there came an open carriage bright green & with a coat of arms emblazoned on its pannels, the horses that drew it were four grey Arabians and their harness & caparisons were most sumptuous. It suddenly drew up, Louisa waved her handkerchief & a tall slender gentleman in a cloak dismounted from it. Before the attendant footman was aware, he had reached Louisa & tucked her under his arm while he himself was stunned by a blow from behind. I know no more but she has not since been heard of.

April 21st —36   C. Brontë

*

What a queer disjointed world this is. No man can for a moment say how things will turn. All the body politic of Africa seems delirious with raging fever, the members war against each other, Parties are confounded, mutual wrath increases. it was not enough that the embodied forces of Ardrah, of the French & of the

Aborigines, should assume the front of deadly conquest against arrogant Angria. that the Northerns & the Westerns should threateningly possess themselves of the ground Debatable. But Northangerland must also begin to awaken motion against its undefined masses of followers. A fluctuating uncertain movement, which way tending none can yet say, the result of a wild impulse which they have seen in their leader. Signs he has given distinctly intimating that his rest is at an end, but mysteriously veiling the aims of the approaching turmoil. It is not for nothing he has dismissed Northangerland & recurred to Rogue,* his late disreputable & eccentric proceedings are not a disease in themselves but merely the symptoms of some grand latent malady. You see only the gyrations of the sling now round the head of David, preparatory to that final launch which shall fix the stone deep in Goliath's forehead. The Tiger is crouched, he looks round, in what direction is he going to spring? Many, Many ask themselves this question besides me and some whose hearts throb agonizedly for an answer. Occasionally in the course of ones life, one does see & hear things that make one doubt whether ones head or one's heels are uppermost. It is now said all over Verdopolis that Northangerland is somewhere in the City, living incognito with the lady whom his knight-errantry rescued from a prison. Northangerland, who erstwhile scintillated between Ellrington Hall & Wellesley-House, & would not for a Dukedom have stooped his head to enter a lowlier portal, Northangerland the husband of a woman who in her thirtieth year has waxed so imperially stout & high that she will not even leave her own saloons for the benefit of fresh air. Ochone! this world's but a vertigo & the best of us is but dust & ashes! A thousand rumours are afloat: some say the earl has yielded himself to the fraternal embrace of Ardrah, others that he has sought respose on the sympathising bosom of Montmorency. Others that himself & Richard Magne, aided by the people, are about to defy all Africa and once more give to the winds the blood red flag of Revolution. A fourth party affirm that he has oppened a correspondence with Quashia & that the above-mentioned & respectable individual stipulates, that in case their mutual manoeuvres should be crowned with success, his share of the spoil should consist in the Kingdom of Angria & the hand of the Duchess of Zamorna. My readers are,† I have no doubt, aware that on a Sunday evening I generally make

* Alexander Percy's name before he rose in the social scale to become Zamorna's Prime Minister and Earl of Northangerland. He dates from the earliest Brontë tales
† No break exists in the MS between the preceding narrative and the fresh

a point of attending the ministry of Mr Bromley, at the Wesleyan Chapel, Slugg Street.* Accordingly, last Lord's day after tea, Mr Surena Ellrington and myself accompanied by Lord Macara Lofty, who had called on us in the course of the afternoon, & whom in spite of his Voltaire sneers & insinuations we had easily persuaded to go with us, proceeded arm in arm to our accustomed place of worship. Being arrived & having taken possession of our usual pew in the gallery, each man, after a private hiding of his face in his hands & a few internal groans, sat quietly down. a devout set we must have looked, seated in that long front pew, which I forgot to say was also occupied by Mr Timothy Steaton. Surena, who was suffering from a cold in a great coat & a large spotted blue & white shawl envelloping his neck & chin, from which emerged the most insignificant physiognomy mind can conceive, crowned by a peak of hair surmounting the low mean forehead & hungry eyes. Macara, whose delicate health likewise required care, in a cloak with a high stiff collar & black silk kerchief genteely adjusted over his black stock, forming an exquisite contrast to the ghastly rakish white of his physiognomy, in which all the lines of profligacy had been ploughed by courses of secret but delirious debauchery. Tim in his Sunday's suit of brown & drab with a coloured neck-cloth, grey worsted gloves, & greasy hair of a dark mouse colour combed straight over a brow invested with no expression but that of low scowling depravity. Myself in a jauntily cut costume consisting of dark-green frock-coat, pale buff vest & nankeen pantaloons, my locks singularly light in their hue brushed smartly on one side, my dandy primrose gloves laid across over my hymn book on which rested my truly patrician hand decorated with a ring on the little finger, the habitual smirk of my face subdued to gravity & a preternatural groan every three minutes emitted from the bottom of my lungs. Mr Bromley's short broad Athletic figure having entered the pulpit & having delivered [? the hymn] with suitable power & pathos, all the congregation joined in singing it in strains of such melody as was fitted only for the ears of seraphs.

* In a parallel satire upon Methodist services, Branwell gave the name Slugg— The Rev. Simon Slugg—to the preacher in his *And the Weary are at Rest* (1845), and Bromley also figures as a Methodist Class-Leader in Branwell's narratives

---

subject introduced here, but this is typical of Charlotte Brontë's precipitate manner of composition. The first person is now introduced for the first time, the speaker being, as usual, Charles Townshend, a Wellesley and Zamorna's brother

While the last stave was being thundered forth, I noticed that a lady came gliding up the gallery stairs, & as she stood still & seemed in doubt were to go, lord Macara, who sat at the end of our pew, opened the door & signed to her approach. she advanced without hesitation, bowing graciously to Lofty as she seated herself at his side. the sun being now set & the red glow it had left behind being greatly obscured by the oil paper windows of the chapel through which it had to make its way, I could discern only the outline of the lady's form which was graceful & prepossessing enough. Amidst the increasing gloom the hymn ceased & Bromley knelt down to pray. As Macara & his companion inclined forwards, I saw the former insinuate one of his sinister & revolting squints under her bonnet & by the sudden biting of his under-lip I judged he had made a discovery. I would have asked him what it was but Bromley burst upon us in thunder. "O Lord! A more infernal pack of defiled, depraved, bemired, besotted, bloody brutal wretches never knelt to worship in thy presence!" Loud, deep, genuine & heart-felt rung the responding Amen as Bromley paused to breathe after this first clause of his vesper. he went on "Filthy rags are we, potsherds were with the leper has scraped himself, bowls of the putrid blood of the sacrifices, sweepings of the court of thy temple, Straws of the dunghill, refuse of the kennel, Thieves, murderers, slanderers, false-swearers." "Amen, Amen!" groaned every hearer from his innermost soul. "Cheats, Usurers" added I, looking at my right-hand neighbours Tim & Surena. "Furniture & fuel for the D——l" subjoined a strange voice from the body of the chapel. I started & looked over the gallery, but impenetrable obscurity covered the scene beneath. Mr Bromley proceeded "were we to show all that we have done, all that we have thought during the half-hour we have been beneath this roof, the sun would turn black at the abomination! O shed thy grace upon us like a water-spout, wash us, scour us with sand & soap, heave us neck & heels into Nebuchadnezzar's furnace, bound in our coats & hosen, our garments, our shoes & our hat, our bed & bedding, our sheets, blankets, bolster-drawers & pillow-slips. In with our fish-kettles, warming-pans, our gridirons & our porridge-pot, our tureen & our soup-ladle, let nothing escape for the plague of our iniquity is upon all—O! may we burn through & through, may we be as cinders & ashes upon the alter. let us not come out like Shadrach, Meshech & Abednego without a hair of our head being singed or without the smell of fire having passed over our raiment. No lord! do thy work thoroughly, when the fire is raked let there be plenty of coke!!" A sharp & simultaneous shout of "Amen!" again signified the flock's acquiescence in their Pastor's pleading. the voice which had spoken before again contributed its appendix. "And speedily O lord shew forth thy mercy & thy power upon our brother Bromley, let him be as a heap of ashes & of slates when the range is sealed." This voice was different indeed from the rough bass of Bromley, calm & penetrating, rather loud & intensely distinct, with a pure accent & an appalling twang. After an hour of morbid sufferance, the prayer wound up, the Door-keeper burning two mould candles (bought I have no doubt out of *our* shop) was now seen posting out of the vestry. these being elevated in brass sconces, one on each side of the pulpit, dissipated the midnight darkness which had involved the chapel, & shed a light which, though dim, was sufficiently clear to reveal to me the person of the lady occupying the further end of our pew. She wore a silk gown & was envelloped in a large & handsome shawl, it was evident a recognition had taken place between her & Macara, for her hand was lying in his & they were talking in very low whispers. Her head being thus turned towards me, I had a full view of her countenance. In the regular pleasing features, the languid blue eyes, the wan complexion & light reddish hair which I saw suffused with sheepish coquetry & superficial meekness, it was no difficult matter to recognise my aunt, the ci-devant Marchioness of Wellesley*—Not chusing however to acknowledge her at that moment, & secure from remark in the thorough alteration that had taken place in my own person since she last saw me, I did not speak, but again turned my attention to the pulpit. Lo! the scene was changed or at least the actor, two men now filled the little pulpit, and seemed as if they would split its sides. One, the square lateral image of Mr Bromley, was seated; the other, stood full in front, was an exceedingly tall man & as slender as he was elevated, with a peculiar face, thin & wasted, having features most finely & exactly cut, a shock of dark hair encroaching on his forehead, & eyes that wandered with an excited or disturbed glance over the congregation. his dress was plain & genteel but the emaciation its close adjustment revealed about the waist & loins was frightful. He took his text without opening the bible: "I came not to save but to destroy". And as he uttered it, I knew his voice to be the same I had heard from the body of the chapel. A sermon followed, wandering & wild & terrible, now it was all curse & denunciation, then it diverged into a strange political harangue, and again the speaker assumed an insane & preposterous tone of scoffing at what himself had said. he seemed to reserve his strength to the conclusion & then he poured it out in a powerful exhortation

* Louisa Dance

to a religious revival. He descended from the pulpit amidst groans & cries & ejaculations. Mr Bromley had introduced him as our Dear Brother Ashworth, but ere ten minutes of the sermon had elapsed there was scarcely one in the Chapel who did not know Alexander Percy! As our party, having reached the chapel door, were just beginning to feel the stream of fresh air & to catch a glimpse of the cool bright heavens & glittering starlight, a gentleman in a travelling cap pushed through the crowd round us. He laid his hand on Miss Dance's shoulder who had put herself under the escort of Macara Lofty. "Mrs Ashworth" said he, "a prayer-meeting will take place in the vestry, you must wait till it is over." That was Northangerland, the exclusive, the etherial, standing to be elbowed by the crowd of a suburb schism-shop! Macara & Tim & Surena & myself had some queer talk that night over a mutton-chop & a glass of gin & water.

*

While listening to the talk of coffee-houses, hearing the gossip of news-rooms, & reading the speculations of public-prints, amusing ourselves in short with the chit-chat & scandal rife in a great city respecting the characters, ongoings & probable destinies of eminent men, we never reflect that the relatives, the wives & daughters of those men, buried out of our sight amidst the seraglio existence of palaces, hear the same reports that we hear & feel as storms what we consider but slight clouds, & as arrow-heads what seem to us only snow-flakes. We view their domes from a distance like shrines, we pass under them, nothing of life appears from their veiled windows & the imagination will not stretch to the reality of human-beings dwelling within, subject to all the passions & distresses & hopes & fears of mortality. Now in this sweet April evening, look at Wellesley-House! The morning was showery, but the clouds are all dispersed now & the sun in its decline sheds so rich & mild a light that the white mansion seems absolutely to slumber in gold. go close up to it, ascend the steps & stand under the vestibule. Not a voice is heard from within, the square lies silent & solitary, the vast murmur of Verdopolis rises all round, & beyond that of the sea. but these far-off sounds add only to the calm pervading this immediate neighbourhood. Do you think of sorrow & of turmoil now, of hearts which throb to hear the Acclaim of the great world, to read the columns of the daily newspapers, to receive the tidings of the morning & evening Post? you do not, "mais allons, nous verrons davantage". "The duchess will take tea in the West drawing-room to day Greenwood." "Yes Madam, Williams has carried the equipage there." "there is a card, Madam, for my lady." "a card! Hah! this is right; bring that writing-case Greenwood." Mr Peascodd obeyed, and the lady who spoke, sat down at a table & taking a sheet of satin note-paper began to write. She & the gentleman in waiting were the only figures in a large hall, the only figures I mean that had life, for silent forms in marble stood in many a niche, some reposing pallid & cold in the shade, others kindling almost to animation, as the glowing sunbeams streamed on them through the windows. One level ray rested also on the lady above alluded to, it suffused with warm light a tall well-modelled woman of five & twenty with very black hair curling down on her neck, a sallow complexion, long face, Italian features, expressive & solemn dark eyes & a carriage of aristocratic dignity. She was attired in black silk, having robings of some rich fur down the front & large hanging sleeves of white lawn, a full boa of the same fur loosely encircled her stately neck, round which also were clasped a collar of pearls & silver. having finished her billet she called for a taper, sealed it & delivered it into the hand of Greenwood, saying "let it be transmitted immediately". She then rose & glided on to the West drawing-room. Now the West drawing-room is a very pleasant apartment, with windows that open onto a terrace of flowers & greensward checquered whether by sunlight or moonlight with the trembling shadows of some slim young aspens.

Away from these windows, out of sight of the sun-shine & out of hearing of the whispering aspen leaves, the Queen of Angria was sitting close by a large bright fire. her sofa was covered with many beautiful little volumes, bound in white & crimson & green & purple Russia. Some were open, displaying exquisite engravings on silver paper & fair type on a surface almost like ivory. One had dropped from her hand & lay at the footstool at her feet & she was leaning back with her eyes closed & her thoughts wandering in day-dreams either of bliss or mourning. The opening of the door and the approach of Miss Clifton did not rouse her. "This will never do" said that lady in an undertone, looking anxiously at her royal mistress's relaxed form supported by sofa cushions, & at her features whose expression or rather whose want of expression intimated that her mind had slid into a voluntary syncope of exertion. She shook her gently. The Duchess unclosed her eyes & said with a faint smile "I was not asleep". "But you were unconscious my lady" answered Miss Clifton. "Nearly so, but Amelia what time is it? are the mails come in? are my letters arrived?" "No, my lady, it is not yet seven o'clock—but your Grace will take tea now" and Miss Clifton proceeded to busy herself with the silver equipage glittering on the table. The Duchess dropped her head on her hand. "Is the sun shining hot this evening?" said she. "I feel very languid & inert." Alas, it was not the mild sun of April glistening even now on the lingering rain drops of the morning which caused that sickly languor & so Miss Clifton thought, but she held her peace. "I wish the mail would come in" continued the Duchess. "how long is it since I've had a letter now Amelia?" "Three weeks my lady." "If none comes this evening what shall I do Amelia? I shall never get time on till to-morrow. Oh, I do dread those long weary sleepless nights I've had lately, tossing through many hours on a wide lonely bed, with the lamps decaying round me. Now I think I could sleep if I only had a kind letter for a talis-man to press to my heart all night long. Amelia, I'd give any-thing to get from the east* this evening a square of white paper directed in that light rapid hand. but no—the rumours we have heard in Verdopolis have spread to Angria by this time, it is that my father† has seen Ardrah & in that case I may go to Alnwick‡ & hope no more—would he but write two lines to me signed with his name." "My lady" said Miss Clifton as she placed a little silver vessel of tea & a plate of biscuit before her mistress "you will hear from the East this evening & that before many minutes elapse. Mr Warner is in Verdopolis & will wait upon you immediately." It was pleasant to see how a sudden beam of joy shot into the settled sadness of Queen Mary's face. "I am thankful to heaven for it" exclaimed she "even if he brings bad news it will be a relief from suspense, & if good news, this heart-sickness will be removed for a moment." as she spoke, a foot was heard in the antechamber, there was a light tap at the door & Mr Warner entered closely muffled, as it was absolutely necessary that he should avoid remark, for the sacrifice of his liberty would have been the result of recognition. With something of chivalric devotedness in his manner he sunk on one knee before the Duchess, & respectfully touched with his lips the hand she offered him. A gleam of eager anxiety darted into his eyes as he rose, looked at her & saw the pining & joyless shadow which had settled on her divine features, her blanched delicacy of com-plexion & fragile attenuation of [?form].

"Your Grace is wasting away" said he abruptly, the first greet-ing being past. "You are going into a decline, you have imagined things to be worse than they really are, you have frightened your-self with fantastic surmises." "I wish I could think so" said the

* The seat of government, Adrianopolis   † Northangerland
‡ In other words, into exile

Duchess. "I wish I could believe that my apprehensions have been all fanciful, that I have distressed myself with nervous terrors, prove it to me. I will hold myself your debtor for life." Mr Warner made no direct answer. he walked twice or thrice across the room, then sitting down began instantly to enter upon the business that had brought him there. It was to examine & re-arrange some state-papers which had been placed in the Duchess's custody when she was Regent during the last Etreian campaign. having received the documents & acquired the necessary information, he sat for a moment silent. The Duchess was standing near the window, gazing on the alternation of silver & green, golden-sunlight visible in the play of the aspen leaves, but not thinking what her eyes rested upon. She was pondering how to bring forward subjects which lay bitterly at her heart. Warner had given her no letter yet, no verbal message, he had not so much as mentioned the name that ever rung in her ears. While she waited in racking impatience, Mr Warner broke the silence. "My Lady" said he speaking soft & low "may I presume to ask if you know anything of the proceedings of the Earl your father? if you have seen him since he arrived at Verdopolis?" "I have not. neither have I heard from him, the rumours of the press are all I have to depend on for information respecting him, & the press always belied him. but, Mr Warner, what have you heard in Angria regarding his movements?" "That he has opened two lines of communication, one with Ardrah & one with Montmorency" returned the secretary concisely. "And what effect has that intelligence produced?" "It has revolted the minds of the army & nation most utterly. the Angrians feel themselves to be men of strong passions, my lady. when they hear that their prime minister is in alliance with their deadly foes—" Mary Henrietta turned from the window. "Mr Warner" said she, suppressing her voice almost to a whisper "you know I have interest in this question, answer me without reserve, what does my lord, what does the Duke of Zamorna say to all those evil tidings?" Warner knitted his brows. "I would have avoided this subject" returned he "But since your Majesty commands me, I must speak. The Duke says nothing!" "But what does he think?" pursued Mary eagerly, following up the path into which she had struck. "how does he look? you can read his countenance surely at least. I could." "his countenance is paler than when your Grace last saw him & it expresses thought & mental disquietude." "And — and" continued the Duchess, throwing off restraint & writhing with impatience as she spoke "Have you no letter for me, Mr Warner? do you bring me no message, no word of his welfare & no inquiry after mine?" "My lady, I have not so much as a syllable for you, not so much as a scrap of paper." "Then his children" said she, her excitement still increasing "he must have mentioned their names, Frederick & Julius, he must have spoken of his sons! they are his own flesh & blood, and my little Arthur who was only two months old when he went, he must have wished to know whether he still promised to be as exact a copy as ever." "My lady, he did mention his children, he said if you see the boys tell me how they are, & he looked as if he would have said something more, but when I stopped to receive further directions he dismissed me hastily. do not doubt however that he was thinking of yourself."

"And he would not mention my name!" said the Duchess. "I am nothing to him. I am utterly compr[om]ised by my father's actions. Oh, I used to be so sinfully proud of such a father & I am so still, but my pride is eating away my happiness like rust. Mr Warner, you don't know what I feel just now, a restlessness, a trembling all over which I cannot endure. To let the Duke of Zamorna lose his impressions of me & familliarize himself with dark looks, and grow like rock in his resolutions to make me the atonement for his premier's awful wanderings! And I cannot try one effort to soften him, separated by one hundred & twenty miles. He would think of me more as a woman I am sure & less as a bodiless link between himself & my terrible father if I were near at hand. Warner, this irritation throughout all my nerves is unbearable. I am not accustomed to disappointment & delay in what I wish—when do you return to Angria?" "Tomorrow my lady, before day-light if possible." "and you travel incognito of course?" "I do." "Make room in your carriage then for me—I must go with you. not a word I implore you, Mr Warner, of expostulation. I should have died before morning if I had not hit upon this expedient." Mr Warner heard her in silence & saw it was utterly vain to oppose her, but in his heart he hated the adventure. he saw rashness & peril, besides he had calculated the result of the Duke's determination over & over again. He had weighed advantages against disadvantages, profit against loss, the separation from the father against the happiness of the Daughter, & in his serene & ambitious eye, the latter scale seemed far to kick the beam. He bowed to the Duchess, said she should be obeyed, & left the room.

Morning was just awakening, but the hush of the darkest hour of night pervaded all the Palace. One room in the centre of the West wing nestled in especial shade & silence, & a slumberous gloom increased by the dark & rich dyes of its hangings & carpet filled the air. Dawning, dim & doubtful, stole through the windows, but it scarcely as yet paled the light of an alabaster lamp suspended from the ceiling. this light shone full on two fair white beds placed side by side. Small in size & exquisitely classical in design, the snowy curtains being looped up with white silk cords, there appeared buried in down & spotless cambric three sleeping infants. their heads were unprotected by coverings & the dark curls of one little rosy model & the golden ringlets of the two fair elder children, gleamed richly in the lamplight as they rested on their small serene brows. all had eyelids of beautiful form & polished long romantic eye-lashes pencilled like dark fringes round the lid. they lay in happy slumber, symbols of tranquillity. Day kindled & the light waxed dim, the changing light roused the youngest sleeper. it woke, & according to the custom of childhood, for it was a living baby & not a mere waxen image, it began a piping lament to find itself alone. Presently the others unclosed their superb eyes as dark as midnight. one of them rose & peeped with uncanny keenness over the side of his own crib into that of his little brother. it pushed its tiny hand upon the other's mouth, & creeping quickly to its nest, proceeded to enforce silence by manual discipline, intermixed however with kisses & such expressions as "little Arthur!" little [*half a line illegible*? its own cub conscience]. Happy was it for the peace of the Royal nursery that at this moment there softly entered one to intercede. It was a lady dressed in a pelisse of grey silk with silver clasps down the middle, a small straw cottage bonnet placed far back on her head & shewing light auburn curls clustered over a brow of perfect parian, a large veil of gauze thrown over this & a muff of ermine in her hand. She was an elegant creature, a perfect lady. Not a queen or a duchess, not a conservatory plant nor a wild rose, but a graceful garden Narcissus. She glided to the twin beds, & bending over, looked at her children, for they were hers. in the sweetest tone she chid the diminutive tyrant & took the small sleeper warm & cosy in its muslin night chemisette to her bosom. it smiled & was still the moment its cheek was pressed to that sweet rest. then reproachfully yet indulgently she looked at the other two & a ray of pride kindled her glance as she saw the life & brilliancy of their aspects, & viewed their quick & healthy movements as they clung about her & pushed their curled heads into her bosom to share the pillow pressed by Arthur. It was a group worthy to be seen & one that Mary felt even her Husband's haughty soul would have been gratified to witness. She was white as marble when she came into the room, but her cheek glowed animatedly as she caressed the King's children & remembered that they were the King's. "Good-bye Romella, good-bye Hawkscliffe" said she, proud to give her first-born their titles & clasping the twin heirs to a military throne at once in her arms, & "Good-bye Arthur Welles-ley" she continued, dropping her tenderest kisses on the child that had most of her own pale refinement & most of its father's luxurious & rosy beauty. "Papa shall hear of you to night if mamma is well enough received herself, to dare to plead for others. I may draw a little on his kindness since I am the mother of two such noble boys." she laid them all in their nests, gently spread the covering over them &, committing them to the care of their nurses who had now entered the room, she departed. In an hour's time the disguised Queen & the outlawed secretary of Angria had left Verdopolis & safe in their own rebellious but beautiful country were rolling eastward with all the speed six gallant bays could muster. the Queen's oppressed spirits rose as she felt the excitement of rapid motion, saw the lovely province of Arundel unfolding round her & beheld the glorious, glorious Sun which, just risen, seemed advancing to meet them. "May my lord shine on me as his symbol does now" thought she. "What am I? I am not an atom in the scale of existence, I am the only daughter of Percy, who now troubles Verdopolis, & beneath his foundations opens flood-gates which perhaps none may close. I am the wife of that military adventurer, that prince of my native West who now heads this young country in its desperate resistance to old allied nations. I have a great stake in the Royal game now playing. If Northangerland & Zamorna make me the link between them, must not I who have a separate existence, urge my separate claims, and still try to work for myself an even path in this vale of tears through which we are all travel-ling? Must I not be my own intercessor before Zamorna? Who else will step into the gap between the living and the Dead?" none. "Nil desperandum."

*

Night closed on the holy city of Angria!* the ecclesiastical city! now alas the depot of war. Former[ly] that ancient town rested quietly among the moors under the shade of the minster, now it seemed but one great barracks. The evening drum, the twilight bugle, sounded from the band of many a regiment. Soldiers & plumed officers were parading the streets where staid civillians formerly walked. the peal of the minster-bells was drownded in the deep boom of the sunset gun—and the blue Guadima! the verdant Ings† declining to its waters! they should have been asleep in the

* Adrianopolis   † A north country term for fields

parting glow of day. look! hundreds of cavalry men are washing &
watering their horses in that clear river, some are caracoling their
chargers along its banks & some are swimming them down the tide,
while laughter & shouts & snatches of songs, pass merrily from
group to group. It was the 23 of April, I shall remember it, for
standing on Richmond Bridge I saw the scene above described.
The heavens were gathering their sombre blue, in the quarter
where the full & newly-risen moon hung over the Warner hills,
that blue was softened by a suffusion of mellow gold, the Zenith
was dark & little stars were kindling out of its gloom. "Is any one
man amongst the scores that surround me thinking about that
sky?" said I, speaking unconsciously aloud—"No, why the d——l
should they, Mr Townshend?" answered a voice close at my elbow.
I looked—a young officer in scarlet & white, stood carelessly leaning against the parapet—as my glance encountered his light &
rather reckless eye, he laughed & said "You know William Percy I
dare say, so there's no need of introduction—You seem to think
there is something very charming in that sky, Mr Townshend. I've
seen far finer when I was a gipsy in the West. You know I had
opportunities star-gazing then—for the d——l a roof I had to roost
under in the night there, and as an old ditty of Cacillia goes

> Lanes were sweet at summer midnight
> Flower & moss were cool with dew
> There was neither blast nor breezes to chill me
> Silent shade of solemn hue
> Stole o'er skies intensely blue.
> I looked & thought the stars were piercing
> That gazed on me like eyes of light
> So still & fixed they seemed to watch me
> Ranked in myriads high & bright
> Kindling, burning through the night.
> If the hazel waved above me
> Or the wild-rose stretched its spray
> O'er the green & dewy coppice
> I have shuddered where I lay
> At thoughts which never came by day.

Hum! that's not true. I believe I was too stupid in those days to be
afraid of anything." "Are you of a poetical temperament Major
Percy?" asked I. "You be d——d" was the civil answer. "No, the
only poetical propensity I have is to prefer the smell of the earth to
that of a cotton-mill, wherein I diametrically differ from that

grubbing ear-wig* at Edwardston. I say, Mr Townshend, whose cab
is this coming? I'll be sworn the worm in that shell thinks itself a
man of importance, he drives at such a rate." A close carriage
dashed past us as he spoke. It stopped at the toll-bar to pay.
change was wanting & during the five minutes delay that intervened there came gallopping down from the city along Howard
Road, eight splendid steeds each attended by a groom in scarlet,
their pampered & glossy flanks covered with ample embroidered
horse-cloths to keep them from the cold night-air. The shores & the
stream resounded with their neighing & prancing & pawing when
they were reined up on the other side. More magnificent animals
never neighed by the tents of an Arab warrior. They looked like
spirit steeds as they stood bending their necks clothed in thunder to
drink the moonlight waves, & surrounded by the dark flitting forms
of their attendants. "Those are the Duke's horses" said a voice
within the carriage—the flutter of a gauze veil caught my eye as a
lady bent from the window for a moment, her form vanished
instantly & the barouche drove on. The gas-light at the toll-bar
had shot a strong clear beam on her features. Their divine beauty
thrilled my heart, I felt as an Italian might feel on suddenly
recognising a head of the Vatican Aphrodite in a foreign land.
"That is a lovely creature" said I, turning to William Percy.
"Yond's the secretary Warner's carriage" he answered—"though
it does not bear his arms. It comes from Verdopolis & by my life
that face was a bit like my own.† I should not be surprised if my
august brother-in-law get's a start to night, but Mr Townshend just
keep a quiet tongue in your head—it will do no good talking of the
thing—I guessed this up-shot when Warner was sent to Verdopolis. Now there's a sort of convenience in having little connection
with my illustrious sister, I'm not obliged to distress myself about
her welfare. but good-night, Mr Townshend, those Tom-fools of our
mess-table are coming this way & I'm not anxious for their
company—"

We parted on the Bridge & each went his separate way. As I
strolled in the pleasant soft air, the clear darkness of heaven, the
sight of its moon & stars in the Guadima, & the sound of warlike
tunes still swelling from the streets of Angria filled my mind I know
not how with delicious yet vague associations of the West &
snatches of old long forgotten songs came gushing back, songs that I
used to read from my mother's cahier of romances. Songs that I

* His brother Edward Percy. Here is the origin of the brother theme exploited
by Charlotte Brontë throughout her juvenilia and into *The Professor*
† The Percys were brothers to the Duchess of Zamorna

knew lord Douro had sung to the Baronness of Gordon far off in
hallowed Glen-Avon.

> The chapelle stood & watched the way,
>   Its cross still mouldered there,
>   But neither priest not penitent
>   Now bowed the knee in prayer.
>
> The lamps around our Lady's shrine
>   Were dimmed, were quenched for aye,
> but still upon her brow divine
>   The moon-beams slumbering lay.
>
> That night Maria thought her fair
>   And pure & meet to be
> The offer of a fervid prayer,
>   O! God in heaven to thee!
>
> And for her fierce & faithless love
>   Maria wildly prayed,
> St Mary did'st thou smile above
>   Thine altar's solemn shade?
>
> As rose amid the eerie hush,
>   All through the lone chapelle
> Petitions breathed in agony
>   For one beloved too well.
>
> Maria, die before that shrine,
>   Thy lord will love thee then,
> When thou art gone in bitterness
>   He'll wish thee back again!
>
> Amid a life of woes & tears
>   O brightest! cease to stay,
> Hark the wailing wind in the rifted arch
>   Says "lady pass away".
>
> The Lake the chapel looks upon
>   Is calm & still & deep,
> Maria thinks how pleasantly
>   She there might sink to sleep.

The Chapelle & the holy [? Cross]
  Gaze calmly from the brae
On another shrine & crucifix
  As fair & clear as they.

It chanced upon that summer night
  Dark Henry home did ride,
For ancient fondness fitfully
  Came o'er him for his bride.

Dark Henry sought his lady's bower,
  But his lady's bower was lone,
It was mirk midnight at that shadowy hour,
  O! where could she be gone?

Dark Henry hies to St Mary's lake,
  He hied to Madonna's shrine,
Not a whispered word does the silence break
  That reigns where those wall-flowers twine.

A ripple curls on the placid mere,
  Though there is no wind to sigh,
And a single foam-bell bubbles clear
  Where the leaves of that lily lie,

For Far under that fairy sea
Slumbers Maria placidly!

*

Angria-House is a large simple stone-building perfectly unadorned
in its architecture, but having a handsome door-way & a noble
flight of steps in front. It is, my readers know, the residence of
Warner Howard Warner Esqr & at this time the head-quarters of
the King. On the night in question many staff officers & field-
Marshalls of the Angrian army were gathered in the great dining-
room of this mansion. The guests were principally grouped about
the large fires that glowed at each end. at either side of one mantle-
piece stood two arm-chairs, wherein appeared the stately forms of
General lord Hartford & Field-marshall the earl of Arundel,
leaning easily back with their lengthy limbs crossed & their heads of
black & flaxen hair supported on hands sheathed in white gauntlet
gloves. General Thornton & Viscount Castlereagh stood on the rug

between & the whole four were absorbed in an animated strain of conversation. "I like this deepening of the plot" lord Hartford was saying. "A sudden dissolution, might be followed by a sudden reunion—But this gradual aggravation, the slow heaping up of injuries on each side, will terminate in some lasting catastrophe, depend on it." "Aye" said Thornton "I, I, no, nobbut an outbreak of passion fra' the Duke, he'd repent on't but he like gets blacker & blacker every day, na' at dinner this afternoon, he niver smiled nor spak a word except to say something to Enara abaat picquets." "And he took no wine either" added Castlereagh "I was quite scandalised at him for my part when he rose from table without even sipping his usual glass of champagne." "But" continued Arundel "He looks at us all with a very peculiar expression sometimes, now yesterday when he was reviewing the troops with his whole staff about him, there was something in his face which seemed to say "these are men worth their ears & who can hold their own & fight for their honour & their country right gallantly. are they not better to me than ten Traitors? a throne may be shaken that does not rest on their shoulders for support"." "It will be found that we are men whom it is dangerous to insult grossly & brutishly" returned Hartford. "there was a speech made once in that Parliament-House at Adrianopolis by a bad man* coming back from exile, which furiously & insanely assaulted men of high birth, of hereditary pride of feudal ideals respecting aristocracy, of constitutional vigour & hardihood, Men that had never before received an insult without wiping it out instantly in the blood of the offender, & this atrocious speech was uttered under circumstances which entirely prohibited revenge. Blood which boiled, hearts which panted & thirsted for vengeance as theirs did on that memorable night, can never either be cooled or satisfied till the blast of the last Trumpet shall summon all flesh to a final settlement of accounts." "God knows I have a heavy book to lay open" exclaimed Arundel "but there's the millenium, the thousand years of peace! Ochone ari! as we say in the West, & that horrible battle of Armageddon to intervene before the Judgement-Day. and though such free Bachelors as you, Hartford, may not understand me, I can tell you I've a lady-love at Mournly Cres in my own Savannah's South awa, whose black eyes I have more than once seen filled with tears when she read & heard the blackguard abuse vomited forth by that Demon on her Chevalier—I should like to get payment for those tears before the day comes when I may prefer my claims before the throne of the Ancient of Days." "Harriet

* Northangerland

never cried about me" said Castlereagh "but the fellow's a traitor-
ous overbearing rascal with neither the feelings nor ideas of a man
of honour, & it would do both my heart & my eyes good to see him
hanged as high as Haman—" "And mine too!" added Thornton.
"And if Edward Percy would let me kick away the scaffold fro
under him he sud knot the rope ower his jugular." "What is this
revelation of a most unchristian spirit that I hear" said a most
dulcet voice in the back-ground. "Gentlemen, did you ever read the
bible or repeat the Lord's prayer in your lives? this blood-thirsty
conversation will do much more harm to yourselves than to the
sinful & miserable man against whom it is directed. The Arbiter of
Heaven punishes Northangerland's vices by his own mind. The
blighted Traitor's thoughts are the continual scourge of his
actions. It would become you, instead of anticipating revenge with
the same kind of animal joy that your dogs feel when they are
upon the traces of a deer: to take warning in silence from the
unhappy criminal." It was Warner who spoke. he had entered the
room in his travelling-dress, pale & evidently fatigued but with his
indomitable soul flashing out from his unquenchable eyes. The
military Gentlemen warmly congratulated him on his safe return
from his perilous expedition to Verdopolis—as Castlereagh shook
hands with him, he said "Would you let the earl go then, Warner, if
you were to catch him?" "No, I would remove him from the world
as speedily as might be, but decently and with all the privileges of
religion at his command—" "Have you seen the Duke since your
return?" asked Hartford. "I have not & I wish to see him now &
thought perhaps he might be here." "Oh! no, he has never stirred
from his own apartment this evening." "Hah!" replied Warner.
"Gloomy, that is right. I wished that mood to continue." so saying
he departed to seek his master.

Warner paused a moment before he entered the apartment where
he knew Zamorna to be. all was silent. he tapped. a very, very
light step was heard from within, the door was opened by a slim
fairy figure of about three feet high with a graceful head of brown
curls. In a voice of childish treble but with singular sweetness &
purity of accent, the little Porter animatedly welcomed Mr Warner.
"Come in" said he "I'm so glad you've escaped from that kidnap-
ping Ardrah, but tread softly for Papa is asleep." The room was a
library, shelves & volumes formed the walls & the few other
articles of furniture that appeared were simple & in fine taste.
There was a sofa near the fire & on that sofa, lay the long, long
figure of Zamorna with arms folded on his bosom & eyes closed.
The aspect of the sleeping monarch fixed his minister in attention

for a while. There lay a symmetrical, compact & imposing form, limbs all splendidly developed, head chiselled & moulded to imaginative beauty, dark profuse hair, finely relieving the brilliant tint of a complexion that whatever it might be sometimes was glowing enough this evening. But notwithstanding all this outside shew of rich vigorous health, Warner felt with startling force at the moment a conviction he had long entertained, that in the timber of this stately tree there was a flaw which would eat ere the lapse of many years to its heart. turning his excited glance on Ernest he said abruptly "wake your father, my lord Gordon."* The boy climbed onto the sofa & creeping to his father's breast, roused him by whispering softly in his ear. The Duke's eyes unclosed, he removed Ernest with a kiss & a slight expression of pain from him as if he could not bear the child's light weight on his chest. his glance encountered Warner's. It brightened. "I knew you were come, Howard" said he "for I heard your voice below a quarter of an hour since. Well, have you procured the documents?" "Yes, & I have delivered them to your Grace's private secretary." "They were at Wellesley house of course?" "Yes, in the Duchess's own keeping. she said you wished them to be preserved with care." "Her Grace" continued Warner after a brief pause "asked very anxiously after you." The stern field-marshal look came over the Duke as he lay Giant-like on his couch, & the momentary mildness melted away— "I need not ask you how Mary Wellesley looks" said he in his deep undertone. "Because I know better than you can tell me. She looks like one condemned to wish intensely for something she can never get, that is white & worn as the beau-ideal of a beauty in a shroud. I say, Howard, did she not ask you for a letter?" "She did, she almost entreated me for one." "And you had not one to give her" answered his Sovereign, while with a low bitter laugh he turned on his couch & was silent. Warner paced the room with a troubled step. "My Lord, are you doing right?" exclaimed he pausing suddenly—"the matter lies between God & your conscience. I know that the kingdom must be saved at any hazard of individual peace or even life. I advocate expediency, my lord, in the Government of a State, I allow of equivocal measures to procure a just end. I sanction the shedding of blood & the cutting up of domestic happiness by the roots to stab a traitor to the heart. But nevertheless I am a man Sire, & after what I have seen during the last day or two, I ask your Majesty with solemn earnestness, "Is there no way by which the heart of Northangerland may be reached

* Ernest, Lord Gordon, Zamorna's eldest son by an early marriage. See Charlotte Brontë's MS tale *The Spell* (1834)

except through the breast of my Queen?" "Warner!" answered
Zamorna, still not stirring from his recumbent position "But two
living creatures in the world know the nature of the relations that
have existed between Alexander Percy & myself. from the very
beginning, in my inmost soul, while I resisted his devious & eccentric
course, I swore that if he broke those bonds & so turned to vanity
& scattered in the air sacrifices that I had made, & words that I
had spoken, if he made as dust & nothingness causes for which I
have endured jealousies & burning strife, emulations amongst
those I loved. If he froze feelings that in me are like living fire, I
would have revenge. In all but one quarter he is fortified &
garrisoned, he can bid me defiance, but one quarter lies open to
my javelin, & dipped in venom I will launch it quivering into his
very spirit—So help me Hell!" "Hell will help you" returned
Warner quite coolly. "And I fear my lord, God will veil his face
from you for-ever—remember, men may so tempt the Holy Spirit
that it will finally leave us. I do not expostulate, I know you are
decided. but I fear a man reprobate & d——d in this life is my
Sovereign—I fear I serve [*illegible*] incarnate!"

A sad smile, a sort of mournful reminiscence of what Zamorna is
in his hours of sociability, softened the monarch's eyes. he held out
his hand to his Secretary, saying "touch me Howard, I am kindly
flesh & blood yet". Mr Warner wrung that hand until the rings
nearly entered the slender finger, & holding it fast clasped in both
his own said with earnest emphasis "O Sire, what am I to you?
I am neither of your name nor your kindred, neither are you of
mine. you are above me in rank & it is human nature to hate our
superiors. I do *not* hate you. I have an interest in you, a deep
interest. I who am a man under authority having soldiers under
me & I say unto this man go & he goeth & to another come & he
cometh. I have condescended to grow attached to a stranger who
has come from a distant country & over my hereditary hills has
stretched a sway paramount to my own, & incessantly I am
haunted by the certain knowledge that this man who has his
reward on earth in superior gifts & more splendid endowments
than other men, that he has no place amongst the elect of God.
Long before the foundations of the world were laid you were
numbered with the everlastingly condemned,* all your thoughts
& your words, the whole bent of your mind, prove it. When you
die Sire, & you are not formed for a long life, I shall bid you an

---

* The Calvinist doctrine with which Charlotte Brontë was much concerned at
the time. See her letter of 1836: 'If the Doctrine of Calvin be true, I am already
an outcast . . .'

eternal farewell—your pulse once at rest, we may never meet again! There is a lady in the next room wishes to see you" continued Warner, hastily changing his tone & manner. "The wife, I think she says, of an officer in the Angrian Army. she seems exceedingly anxious to have an audience. may I admit her here?" "As you like" replied the Duke, scarcely seeming conscious of what he said.

In about ten minutes after Warner's departure, the lady in question entered the room by an inner door. Zamorna was now risen from his couch & stood in full stature before the fire. he turned to her at first carelessly, but his keen eye was quickly lit up with interest when he saw the elegant figure whose slight youthful proportions & graceful carriage agreeing with her dress, the simple pelisse, the pretty cottage bonnet & the costly ermine muff produced an effect of such lady-like harmony—While dropping a profound obeisance she contrived so to arrange her large veil as to hide her face. as she did this her hand trembled—then she paused & leaned against a book-case near the door. Zamorna now saw that she shook from head to foot. Speaking in his tone of most soothing melody—he told her to draw near & placed a chair for her close by the hearth. She made an effort to obey but it was evident she would have dropped if she had quitted her support. his Grace smiled, a little surprised at her extreme agitation. "I hope Madam" said he "my presence is not the cause of your alarm", & advancing, he kindly gave her his hand & led her to a seat. As she grew a little calmer he addressed her again in tones of the softest encouragement. "I think Mr Warner said you are the wife of an officer in my army, what is his name?" "Archer" replied the lady, dropping one silver word for the first time. "And have you any request to make concerning your husband? Speak out freely madam, if it be reasonable I will grant it." She made some answer but in a tone too low to be audible. "Be so kind as to remove your veil madam" said the Duke. "It prevents me from hearing what you say distinctly." She hesitated a moment, then as if she hat formed some sudden resolution, she loosened the satin knot that confined her bonnet & taking off both it & her veil let them drop on the carpet, his majesty now caught a glimpse of a beautiful blushing face, but in a moment clusters of curls fell over it & it was likewise concealed by two delicate little white hands with many rings sparkling on the taper fingers. The Sovereign of the East was non plussed; he had an acute eye for most of these matters, but he did not quite understand the growing trembling embarassment of his lovely suppliant. He repeated the question he had before put

to the lady respecting the nature of her petition. "Sire" said she at
length "I want your Majesty's gracious permission to see my dear,
dear husband once more in this world before he leaves me for
ever." She looked up, parted from her fair forehead her auburn
curls, & raised her wild brown eyes, tearful & earnest & imploring,
to a face that grew crimson under their glance. The King's heart
beat & throbbed till its motion could be seen in the heaving of a
splendid chest, he seemed fixed in his attitude standing before the
lady slightly bent over her, an inexpressible sparkle commencing &
spreading to a flash in his eyes—the current of his life-blood rising
to his cheek & his forehead dark with solemn awful desperate
thought. Mary clasped her hands & waited. She did not know
whether love or indignation would prevail. She saw that both
feelings were at work. her suspense was at an end, the thunder-
cloud broke asunder in a burst of electric-passion!—He turned
from his Duchess & flung open the Door—a voice rung along the
Halls of Angria-House summoning Warner—a voice having the
spirit of a trumpet, the depth of a drum in its tone—, before it
could possibly be answered the invocation was repeated, with the
impatient haughty terrible accent of a Despot driven to desperation. "WARNER!" The Secretary was now in the dining-room
with the staff, all heard the voice & were witness to the stricken
look of Warner & the exclamation of "My God what has come
across him!" which accompanied it. He went in a minute, he
found himself in the library, he shut & bolted the double door
mechanically. The Duke fronted him, animated not with Prome-
thean fire but with real lightened*—"How dared you do what you
have done?" said he at once. "How dared you bring my wife here
when you know I'd rather have an evil-spirit given to my arms this
night? you must have been conscious, Sir, that I had wrought up
my resolution with toil & trouble, that I had decided to let her die
if her father cut loose & deceived [me] with agony, & what
possessed you to ruin it all & set me the whole tormenting task over
again? You know this mental anguish shortens what you said here
an hour since, & what I knew before to be my very brief allotment
of life on earth. You know [in] what accursed way I take after my
Mother, & you know how I loved Percy & what it is costing me to
send him to the D——l!! Look at his Daughter. I'm to stand her
devotion & beauty, am I? but I will, though you've swept away all
perception of the reasons why I should, I'll go on the tack of blind
obstinacy now. leave me Warner, I feel as if I could shoot you. five
minutes since, I was persuaded it was the putting back of the stone

* Presumably, intended to read 'lightning'

Sysiphus had got to the top of the hill, & his sinews being all cracked he felt as if he could never get it up again. I'm a little cooler now, leave me!" Warner, whose Angelic philosophy had been little shaken by this appaling hurricane, would have stopped to give his Grace a brief homily on the wickedness of indulging in violent passions—but a glance of entreaty from the Duchess prevailed on him to withdraw in silence.

It was with a sensation of pleasurable terror that Mary found herself again alone with the Duke, he had not yet spoken one harsh word to her, he had even said what thrilled her with delight. Still it was awful to be Zamorna's sole companion in this hour of his ire. & how much better than to be one hundred & twenty miles away from him. She was soon near enough. The Duke, gazing at her pale & sweet loveliness till he felt there was nothing in the world he loved half so well, & conscious that her delicate attenuation was for his sake, appreciating too the idolatry that had brought her through such perils to see him at all hazards, threw himself impetuously beside her & soon made her tremble as much with the ardour of his caresses as she had done with the dread of his wrath. "I'll seize the few hours of happiness you have thrown in my way, Mary" said he, as she clung to him & called him her adored glorious Adrian, "but these kisses & tears of thine & this intoxicating beauty shall not change my resolution—I *will* rend you my lovely rose entirely from me, I'll plant you in your father's garden again, I must do it, he compels me." "I don't care" said the Duchess, swallowing the delicious draught of the moment & turning from the dark future to the glorious present shrined in Zamorna. "I feel now as I did for one instant when we parted on that winter's morning—& I am far happier now, for you were to leave me before the sun was up & to-night I may stay with you for many hours— but if you *do* divorce me Zamorna, will you never, never take me back to you? must I die inevitably before I am twenty?" the Duke looked at her in silence, he could not cut of hope—"The event has not taken place yet, Mary, & their lingers a possibility that it may be averted. but, love, should I take the crown off that sweet brow, the crown I placed over those silken curls on the day of our coronation—Should you be transplanted to Alnwick, do not live hopeless in the old mansion. You may on some moonlight night hear Adrian's whistle under your window when you least expect it, then step out on to the Parapet & I'll lift you in my arms from thence to the terrace—& from that time for ever, Mary, though Angria shall have no Queen—a Percy shall have no daughter. Yet Zamorna shall not be a widower though the world may call him so—" "Adrian" said the Duchess "how different you are, how very different when I get close to you. you never seemed stern yet when I was near enough to touch you & look into your eyes, but at a distance you appear quite unapproachable. I wish, I wish my father was as near to you now as I am or at least almost as near, not quite. because I am your creeping plant, I twine about you like Ivy. & he is a tree to grow side by side with you. if he were in this room I should be satisfied. Matters would assume a different aspect then." What answer Zamorna made I know not, but he [?brought down the] curtain. I don't know when the Duchess returned to Wellesley house, but she is there now. Good-bye Reader.

April 29th 1836

*

It is all up! I never thought to have seen this! What, the Invincible! where's the use of a nick-name. Let no man henceforth be proud of a good leg, it will not supply the place of brains. After all there is a shade of difference more important than plurality between understandings & understanding. Men are beginning to despise this hasty sun which sets before nine o'clock in the morning. they ask was it but an overgrown farthing-candle? & that blade of Damoscene steel on which they leant with such confidence, lo! it has crashed under them & they demand was it Harlequin's sword of lath? Gentlemen & ladies walk in, here's the modern Alexander cotched & chained, to be seen at the low price of six-pence for grown-up people & three-pence halpenny for children & nurse-maids. There, that's the Eastern Bonaparte, the Juvenile Cesar, the Hannibal, the Scipio Africanus, the Pyrrhus, the Pompey, le Charles douze, le Grand Frederic of the Levant. him you observe in the shabby genteel black coat with the pepper & salt trowsers like a broken-down military chaplain. he's got a pipe in one hand & an old Gazette in the other & the liquor in that glass at his elbow is Gin. Come forward Ladies & Gentlemen—the young people need not be afraid, he'll do them no harm. Now Sir, be so good as stir your stumps, stand up & tell the swells how like little wanton boys that swim on bladders this many summers in a sea of glory, you've floated on till your high-blown pride at length broke under you.* "there, speak out, his voice, gentlemen, is not what it used to be. Gin & bad-habits have cracked it. So, Sir, sing a little clearer, that'll never do, that's a mere asmathic wheeze d'ye hear me, ball out smart or I'll—" here a floorer concluded the

* From Cardinal Wolsey's speech in Shakespeare's *Henry VIII*, Act 3, Scene 2

FACSIMILE OF CHARLOTTE BRONTË'S MANUSCRIPT

scene. Ain't that pretty, Reader? What a nice thing that we have the Gilded Globe on the top of St Michael's dissevered from the cross & cupola by a thunder-storm to kick about as a foot-ball. the following is a paragraph from the Warning Binnacle. "We really doubt whether much of the blame resulting from the late bloody proceedings in the East is to be laid on the head of the nominal leader of the Rebels. We learn from the most authentic sources that his Grace has in verity been for the last month non compos mentus, absolutely unfit to originate the slightest order, that his acknowledged tendency to insanity having first declared itself in the most ridiculous & even disgusting forms, has finally merged into idiocy. The Duke's military counsellors have had hard work of it first to conceal & then to supply their master's loathsome deficiencies." What succeeds is from the [?Lobe]. "We in our times have seen a representation of Alexander the Great performed as Shakespeare's brutal & ignorant Athenian Clown's performed their parts in the Midsummer night's dream, the beastly blending with the comic checks our laughter but still we might have indulged in a little exercise of the cachinnatory organs, had not the spectacle of devastation so widely spread, of blood so ruthlessly poured out, the Gates of war not only flung open but also chained back by hands that should themselves have been fettered to the oars of the Galley, had not these things, we say, brought the blood hot to our hearts & changed mirth into ebullient indignation." The Freeport Hermes shall furnish our last extract. "Should the defeated Rebel's fate be referred to the Marquis of Ardrah's decision, we trust that noble individual will not allow just wrath against the convicted incendiary to overcome magnanimous clemency towards the wretched incapable. We believe in our hearts the ci-devant King of Angria is scarcely responsible for his own actions. With a disposition naturally mean & vindictive, a temper whose impotent violence & weather-cock caprice have averted from him the affections of his nearest relatives, & a foolish exaggerated vanity which it humiliates us to think of & which leads to actions of Nero-like brutality, ferocity, absurdity & filth, with all these his Grace Arthur, Augustus, Adrian unites a fatuity, an imbecillity, an obtuse Dutch stupidity, a gross, grovelling vacuity, a sensual swinish insensibility—which at once deprives him of the power of devising evil without suggestion & flings him prostrate at the feet of men of keener wits & nearly as depraved inclinations. The first part of his character would, we know, suggest to the pure & lofty mind of our Premier, immediate Death, the latter part will, we trust, appeal to his humane & philanthropic heart to spare a being so degraded by Nature & shielding him for life from the scorn of the world in some asylum where his support may be of the least expense to the nation, grant him space & opportunity for that repentance which he so greatly needs. Above all things" proceeds Mr Haines "We deprecate the idea of merely depriving the Traitor of his property & then allowing him to go at large. Will not the dog return instantly to his vomit & the sow to her wallowing in the mire." Some of our fellow-journalists have insinuated that the law will not bear out the ministry in a severer course. Ought such an obstacle to be a moment allowed to block the way as our contemporary the Inquirer suggests. if existing laws won't do, blot them out & make new ones. nay, in a case so urgent as the present, we should think that Administration blameable which should pause for the manufacture of fresh statutes. let the Premier exert his father's prerogative. the People will support his conduct, the people & their Representatives of the lower House, though the Asinine Peers should ever so fiercely bray against it." I said this should be my last extract, but I have just one more to make. it is from an Angrian Print, the Zamorna Telegraph. "What we predicted in our last is even now taking place. The forces on both sides are disposed:

"MacTerreglen has taken up the ground between Edwardston & Verdopolis, & our own troops occupy the range of country from Northangerland Hall to Stuartville. the sword is drawn, the arm uplifted, in the space that will intervene before the impending blow falls. Let Zamorna listen to the voice of his shuddering country, we will faithfully speak what she breathes in the hour of suspense, her head on the block & the executioner's axe hanging over it. "Sovereign! I was fair, flourishing, the happy Province of a mighty mother state. You saw me & I kindled your ambition—though the apparent heir to another throne, you would not wait till Death should take the Diadem from your father's brows, your father an old man who had nearly numbered all the years of mortality. you would not wait till his decease should make you a King, but you sprung at the Empire I offered. You built a capital, you raised Towns, you encouraged commerce, you modelled an army, you made me splendid without. I was gilded by your hands from the crown of my head to the sole of my foot. To attain this magnificence I was laden with debt. Young aspiring adventure[r]s vested in me the fruits of their industry. I became the repository of their hopes & fears, their high anticipations, the result of their heavy toil by day & night. In this state I stood, inspiring Sunshine on me & reviving Gales blowing round me. Now Zamorna, you should have been my mantle & my shield, a helmet for my head & a buckler for my bosom, you should have been my protector, my warder, my counsellor, have you been this? Where is my capital, besieged, stormed, taken, a broken wall a dwelling for negroes. where are my towns? ruined. my fields? barren. my commerce? annihilated. Where are the men who supported me? where are their hopes, anticipations, the hard-earned reward of their labours, all shattered, overthrown, involved in the general wreck of the Kingdom? lastly, where is my army—I see it there, it stands dispirited, enfeebled, wasted by disease & defeat. still rallying round your banner, still devoted to your cause, still obedient without murmur or mutiny to him for whose sake their homes—& what has a man dearer than his home—are so lifeless & desolate as the fanes of the Indians in Peru. Still willing to preserve even life as their last sacrifice in his service, their last stake in the bloody game playing on his account, waiting patiently, valiantly, to hear the word from your lips which shall send them to destruction or a gory victory. Pause a moment Zamorna—should that first event rush on them without hope of the last, should the reprieve delay & the axe descend, how will you feel as my blood streams over the scaffold? for my part I, yes I your martyred Angria, will curse you with my dying breath. I will curse you for your rashness, your cruelty, your selfishness, your incapability, for the mean atrocity of hazarding a nation & the welfare of a nation, to satisfy the puerile ambition of a silly & inconsiderate boy who wished to play at Alexander!—I will despise you & hate you & so will my children & their children to the third & fourth generation. You thought to be called the founder of a dynasty that should rule half the world. If to-morrow fate should prove adverse, you will be called the impious fool who aimed at Heaven, slipped & fell into Hell!"

It was after reading this & a hundred other long dark paragraphs similar to this, that I took a stroll last Friday evening up the valley, leaving Verdopolis gloomy & shrouded in sullen calm behind me. though the evening was very wild & wet, scores of Pedestrians & equestrians crowded the road. I just strolled on, following where the horsemen & foot-passengers led, & in about an hour found myself at the entrance of the Ashburnham estate. The people there I observed all unceremoniously turned in at the open park-gates & I was not surprised at this for numberless placards posted in the City had told me long before that on the 24th instant a Grand Auction was to take place by order of the Government of the Goods & chattels of Douro Villa, being the confiscated property of

A.A.A. Wellesley prescribed outlaw & arch traitor. I shall long remember the scene that met my eyes as after crossing the park by a short cut I reached the flowery knoll of velvet sward on which the Villa stands. The house had been gutted, the furniture, the statuary from the Halls & the plants from the conservatory, were piled in strange splendid confusion on the lawn. Throngs of people, in cloaks & great coats defending themselves from the incessant rain as well as they could by means of umbrellas, crowded thickly round. the finely-grown orange-trees & dense cypresses afforded shelter to some and others had taken refuge in the empty saloons & Atria of the interior. The Auctioneer, as I came up, was disposing of his last lot of plants, a splendid tree stood before him, bending in an arch from the deep china tub in which it grew, covered with large blue white balls as pure as snow. "Here" said he "is the magnificent Daitura Arbora, procured by the Lord Douro for his late mar-chioness at a costly price from India. who bids? I must have a regal sum for this, behold how the flowers, white as lady's note-paper, contrast with the broad emerald leaf. here is an article that will shine like the sultan of shrubs in any Gentleman's green-house, or in case of company may be introduced with advantage into the dining-room & placed as a grand natural èpergne in the centre of the table. ladies & Gentlemen what will you bid?" "Sixteen shillings!" said a fat man in gaiters speaking from the depths of a cravat, whose points nearly met above his eyes. "Seventeen & six-pence" counter-screamed an elderly woman in widow's weeds. "eighteen shillings!" responded the fat man. "a sovereign" shouted one whom I instantly recognised as Mr Ellrington's young gentle-man, alias apprentice. "One pound ten" said the voice from the cravat, who I afterwards found was a fancier of Green-house plants. "two pounds" ejaculated the widow, panting. "two pounds five" answered the apprentice with a laugh. "three pounds!" roared the fat man looking fierce—there was a pause. "going, going" said the auctioneer, vibrating his hammer. another pause. "Going, Going" continued Mr Hobbins. "what, will no gentleman bid more than three pounds for the Indian Daibura Arbora, the unparalled fine shrub brought from Delhi, the superb bridal present which lord Douro made to his lady?" no answer. what did all those respectable cloaked & hatted people care for Marian's* flowers—"Going, going, going—Gone—it's yours Mr Prettyman." the hammer fell & Mr Prettyman bore away his prize. "She did used to like that plant" said a quick feminine voice close by me, "A ball of it lay on her pillow when she was dying & its leaves were scattered in her

* Marian Hume, Zamorna's first wife

coffin." I turned to the person who had spoken, a handsome young woman with two or three children about her. I knew Mrs Sherwood. I addressed her but she did not answer me, all her faculties were wound up in the interest of the scene before her. I cannot describe the expression of her face as she watched keenly & jealously the despoiling of the house to which she & her husband were such devoted vassals. her eyes glittered sometimes as if they would over-flow, but still she restrained her feelings & bit her lip & knit her brave forehead. rocking the baby in her arms & saying earnestly to a fine boy at her knee "Arthur, remember this, never forget the sale at the Villa. you can recollect the Gentleman who used to come on Sunday evenings to our Lodge & hear you say hymns & read to him from the Bible, they are robbing his house & hunting him to death, as your father's dogs hunt the stags." "Who, mother?" asked the boy. "the Scotch, bairn, the Scotch, hate the Scotch, Arthur, as long as you live." The day's business now drew to a close. But one lot remained to be disposed of, it was a picture, as I could see by the gilded frame glittering through its canvass wrapper. Mr Hobbins uncovered it, an open space was now cleared round him. the various lots had been removed by their separate purchasers. the crowd stood without the temporary palisading round his table. He placed the large painting against a weeping cypress whose draperies fell over it like a pall. He stepped back, leaned his head on one side & looked in silence, so did I, so did all present. Well Zamorna, the lips of your very shadow seemed to murmur Ichabod! at that moment. The Painting was Lord Douro's portrait taken nearly five years since, at the age of nineteen. I remembered when De-Lisle* sketched it, the scene, the place, all the attendant circumstances. It was at Mornington on the evening of the longest summer's day. My Mother, then not far from her death, had that sweet warm afternoon been brought down into the drawing-room & lay on the sofa in a dress of white crape—her fallen wasted cheek suffused with the fever of her disease & the delicate glow of the crimson cushions she reclined on. The Duchess had called her son to sit by her & she was looking at him & perusing his features, where her own once divine beauty was so wondrously mingled with the Wellington severe Roman graces. She was thinking of her own early life at Grassmere before she ever dreamt of becoming the mother of that stately boy, when she was his father's young & recluse ward. Also she was thinking of the hour now rapidly draw-ing near which she had seen far off so long a time, the hour that was to separate her suddenly, perhaps eternally, from the being

* De-Lisle figures as the fashionable portrait painter in all the Brontë juvenilia

she had doated on from infancy to manhood. Often had Augustus
wrung her heart with his crimes & follies. for many years she had
stood a weeping intercessor between himself & his stern Father, but
all her sufferings for him melted from her fading vision & dying
memory. deep fondness only remained, shining in her mild earnest
eyes that watched him as if he was the last object they wished to see
on earth. I remember she made a feeble effort to change her position
as she lay on the couch, but was now grown too feeble to move her
limbs. Douro took her in his arms, he could lift her easily, tall as
she was, for consumption had worn her to shadowy attenuation, &
turned his mother's face to the setting-sun. the tears slid one after
another from her long raven eye-lashes as she received this attention from her darling. "Well, but what has all this to do with
the picture—nothing reader, only the atmosphere that always
hung over the dying Duchess lingers about this portrait of her
son.

I looked at the young face, the melancholy & dark eye, the long
curls silken & luxurious, I gazed on the fine features so pure so
unsensual, on the brow full of pride but banishing by its even
white expanse, by its deep shadow of thought, every dream of
mental deficiency—on the fresh youthful lips whose bright dyes &
refined compression seemed as if they never for one moment could
be tainted or relaxed by grossness. Whilst I looked, I thought on
what I had read but hours since, & who could reconcile the mighty
contrasts? The figure verily seemed to rise into life, it was represented leaning on a stone balcony beneath the library window—
It mingled the air of the deep-learned student with something
more, a wakening, a fiery dawn of the passions such as did, I well
remember, burn at that time in every glance of the original. & the
profound touching sorrow of his beautiful eyes, not flashing for the
lids were drooped, but beaming with full clear darkness On the
profanation of his shrine—that expression did not make me pity
him or love him, but it made me look long at his picture. The rain
now descended in drenching torrents & a gusty wind drove it
aslant, beating against the tender foreign shrubs on the lawn &
destroying the delicate bloom of the Orange-trees. Through the
empty Villa it moaned in tones of the wildest sadness, no other
voice, however, but that of the wind lamented its disarray—Mr
Hobbins commenced his slang—"Now Gentlemen & Ladies, here
is a very valuable picture from the universally celebrated pencil of
John Martin Dundee,* a portrait as you will perceive of the former

* Dundee, like De-Lisle, figures in the earliest Brontë MSS. His christian names
sufficiently indicate his origin in the Brontës' favourite painter, John Martin.

owner of this highly eligible residence." (His speech was here interrupted by a deep groan) "Aye, Aye" he continued "The subject his undoubtedly bad, the tenth transmission of a foolish face. Nevertheless the execution is fine, & an ass naturally painted is considered by connoisseurs a triumph of the Art. What then will you bid Gentlemen for this highly valuable & superbly finished delineation of the Greatest Donkey of this or any other age?" No answer followed but laughter & groans, not a bid was made. "That last lot of yours is no go, Mr Hobbins" shouted one. "Turn it over as a present to the bloody Dolt himself, he'll like it next best to looking-glass" suggested another—"Aye, as flattered likeness always pleases ninnies" added a third, "by the by if that was ever a good resemblance, he's grown grossly coarse since." I felt a kind of thrill pass through me, as I heard those words & they looked at the still melancholy picture, so very unlike the portrait of a brutal sumph, with the cypress streamers waving round it, & the gloom of that tempestuous evening stealing every moment darker over it. The contrast of past & present times stood bright as the sun & black as midnight before me. Could the Duchess of Wellington have foreseen this hour, how miserably she would have died! but she thought her son a God whom all Africa & the world must worship. This picture could not be disposed of that night, but I afterwards learnt it was bought by a publican, who had a fool's cap painted on the head, a pot of porter in one hand & a pipe in the other, & as a good joke hung it over his door by way of sign.

There is something very congenial to my feelings in the present state of Verdopolis. the expectations of some mighty new event, we know not what, of some vast change we are ignorant of what nature, The relishing excitement diffused through all the sections of social life. The Gloomy sort of holiday which all ranks of the people scorn to be keeping, as if they were determined not to work till they knew whether their labour would profit them. All this to a single Gentleman like me is pleasant, I have no wife, no family to potter me, no stake in commerce, no landed possession, no property in the Funds to bother myself about, I laugh at the anxiety written on the brows of monied men who in the grand suspense know not whether tomorrow may not behold them bankrupts. What goods I have are portable, two or three suits of clothes, a few shirts, half a dozen dickies, half a dozen cambric handkerchiefs, a cake or two of windsor soap, a bottle of Macassar oil, a brush & comb & some

Charlotte Brontë obviously forgot that she had already attributed the picture to De-Lisle other material of the toilet. the few sovereigns I have in ready money may be easily secreted about my person &, in case of the worst, what is there to which I cannot turn my hand for a livelihood? Not an atom of pride do I possess to check me! I'd as soon be a shoe-black in a merry jovial servants hall as heir-apparent to Wellingtonsland. I'm burdened neither by domestic ties, religious scruples nor political predelictions. I never could understand what home-pleasures & family affections meant. the seat of which I am a member is sunk so low that nothing can degrade it further. My political lungs would have the freest play in such a current of air as a hurricane revolution might create. Rogue* will never prescribe me, & if he does, where are the policemen, the bailiffs, the bloodhounds that could catch me? the jail that can hold me? the halter that can hang me?—were the street of Verdopolis slippery with blood, they'd afford firm enough footing for Charles Townshend, were each member of society a police spy, a law sleuth-dog upon the other Charles Townshend would out-do them all in treachery, in double-dealing, in blood-thirsty hypocrisy. were all the Ladies of Africa transformed into Rolands & Ninon de l'Enclos, Charles Townshend would still find a place in their Saloons & Boudoirs. Con-citoyenne Julia with the Bloodred scarf would as gracefully beckon him to the sofa at her side as Lady Thornton with the vermillion plume & sash & the ruby crosslet & bandeau, & what if the pressure of the fingers was harder in salutation, & what if the dark western eye in lieu of its romantic milesian softness shot the fierceness of a fury? what if the lips, losing their natural music, cheerful & soft with a little, a faint uncertain touch of the accent, were to pour forth the rapid running discords of a Parisienne, what then? change will come in this world & she would be handsome & brilliant still. My Readers know what sort of a day Monday was. All yesterday lord Northangerland's heart was, I know, thrilling high in his bosom, & every pulsation of that energetic & malignant seat of life, beat in the farthest extremities, the suburbs & the environs of Verdopolis. The city, mad & racked with war without & within, woke to the sound of the Tocsin as the world shall hereafter awake to the voice that shall rouse the Dead. & every one in that turmoil & strife knew that Verdopolis did not bound the conflict, that eastward as far as Edwardston, Zamorna—& men's minds are still moved by that name, they still remember how the clouded sun once shone—That Zamorna was struggling for existence. Anxiously beset as themselves were, they inquired how the battle went at Edwardston. Some of the Constitutionalists had

* Northangerland

still a lingering partiality for the Rebel like that of an indulgent father for a prodigal son. But the wish prevailed through the city of annihilation for him & his. Tuesday told them it was granted, that the Angrian army was ruined, the Angrian nation enslaved and the Angrian King disgraced!

JULIA

INTRODUCTION

Julia, *written fourteen months after* Passing Events, *is still rather a collection of loosely-connected episodes than a consecutive narrative. With the same dramatis personae, in the main, for its subject, and the Duke of Zamorna's entourage as its focal point, its novelty rests upon the introduction of two fresh characters, and in the author's increased ability to analyse their feelings. Julia herself makes only a brief appearance. Patently inspired by the types of fashionable women whose portraits appeared in the* Annuals *and whose costumes Charlotte went to great lengths to copy, she first came on the scene in two narratives of 1833 and 1834,* The Foundling *and* The Scrap-Book, *in which she was described as wearing a "diamond aigrette glittering in her hair, surmounted by a stately drooping plume of white ostrich feather". The wife of General Thornton, she had previously been married to Edward Sydney, but the marriage had been annulled.*

The newcomers to the long-established cast of Angrian characters are Captain Henry Hastings and Caroline Vernon as a child. Hastings was originally a creation of Branwell's, dating from 1834. Like all Branwell's prototypes, he was a poet, and figured as the historian and chronicler of the Angrian Establishment in such poems as "History Stood by her Pillar of Fame" (October 1834) and in several fragments recounting the Angrian Wars. After Branwell's failure to gain admittance to the Royal Academy in the autumn of 1835, Hastings became the embodiment of his failure and of his first addiction to drink. In A New Year Story (*January 1836*) *Hastings voiced his growing dissatisfaction with his critics in the home circle, and increasingly assumed a desperado's role which was, in fact, beginning to be Branwell's. Swiftly he took on the characteristic Branwellian qualities of shiftlessness and instability. By the time, in* Julia, *that Charlotte took him over, he was so sufficiently identified with Branwell as to be imbued with all his recognisable traits, such as his social vanity and susceptibility to feminine flattery. His discomfiture at the hands of Lord Hartford in the presence of his lady patronesses, is a penetrating piece of analysis on the writer's part, and affords a pointer to the direction her talent was to take in emotional analysis, which was to become her outstanding quality as a novelist. This narrative serves as an introduction to the later tale,* Captain Hastings, *dated 1839.*

The second character introduced here is that of Caroline Vernon as a child, whose destiny, like that of Mina Laury, so evidently fascinated the young Charlotte Brontë that she came back to it time and again. The sketch of the child Caroline shows a marked advance in the author's ability to touch a subject lightly, and already foreshadows the delectable child-portrait of Paulina Home in Villette. *The situation of Caroline Vernon and that of her mother, Louisa Vernon, the Parisian actress, also foreshadows the situation in* Jane Eyre *of Adèle, Rochester's child by his mistress, Céline Varens. They are the proof of Charlotte Brontë's repeated use of the same material, once the formula had been refined to suit her fastidious taste. The origins of the major figures in her novels will be frequently found to have grown out of the numerous trials and errors of her youthful writings.*

Another episode in Julia *is a satirical account of a service in a Methodist Chapel, whose tone of cynical disillusionment shows the distance Charlotte had travelled since the previous year of her religious crisis, and also shows the hold that Branwell still had on all her thinking.*

The date of composition of this untitled manuscript, June 29th 1837, is only three days later than a diary fragment of Emily Brontë's, written on Branwell's birthday, June 26th, when she describes the family at their favourite avocations—reading and writing—herself and Anne engaged in writing poetry "in the drawing room" and Charlotte "working in aunt's room and Branwell reading Eugene Aram to her".

The manuscript of Julia *is currently in the possession of the Miriam Lutcher Stark Library of the University of Texas, by whose kind permission it is printed here. It has never been previously published.*

JULIA

There is, reader, a sort of pleasure, in sitting down to write, wholly unprovided with a subject. There now lie before me a quire of blank sheets which it is my intention to cover with manuscript, and not a word have I prepared for the occasion, not a scene, not an incident—yet somehow my feelings, far from being uneasy, are similar to those I have often experienced, when with a carpet bag containing two shirts, four pocket-handkerchiefs, a pair of stockings & a suit, I have mounted the Edwardston Mail or the Western Iris, or the Freetown Mercury—& without aim or end allowed myself to be rattled away in the dawn of a June morning, East, West, North or South, as Fate & the Presiding Jehu determined. Supposing myself to be going North—awa', up the Valley—about noon when the sun gets troublesomely hot, and I have exhausted the vivacity & divined the characters of those about me, I drop off just where that shady lane winds away from the high-road between a double row of hawthorn, in a cloud of summer dust. the Mail is in five minutes whirled away from my view—and I am left standing solitary with a cow that has wandered from its pasture feeding quickly beside me—how green the grass is under that white branch of may, and all along what a pleasant bank on both sides fringes the rutty lane—The quadruped, fanning away the flies with her tail, munches up the violets & clusters of primroses most mercilessly—here is the open gate through which she has come. I'll drive her back & fasten the chain to prevent total destruction of the wild flowers—Her way is mine. there is a path through the meadow that leads I well know where—How uneventful at the time and yet how pleasant is the recollection of such idle days—Follow me still, reader, and I will trace further, though generally, the lines in which they have lapsed with me. We are now among the straight stems of a young plantation, skirting the field we have just crossed, it is bounded by a high wall, too-high to overleap—but there is a door, shut fastened—try to open it, you cannot—but I know the secret—press the spring so, it flies apart—What a pleasant landscape! ten to one you never saw it before, at least not from this point of view—but I have twenty times—a large field almost like a park checquered with recumbent herds of cattle—it is too hot to feed—what magnificent creatures they are & lord bless me! theres a Bull—a huge lowering, sullen red Bull, calved & reared I'll be sworn in the pastures of Arundel. he is laid under the shade of an enormous chestnut, with a seraglio of heifers about him. The field descends we know not how far, but dimly rises up—blue with the haze of distance, a vast wood on the other side—& beyond that there are hills of sapphire & the bend of the Bay of Mowbray—in the centre of this park-field, where it swells into a knoll of mossy sward—stands a house large & grey & grand—haply not more than fifty years old, with sash-windows, eight each side & sixteen in the immense front, those in the lower story on each side the entrance open upon the sward like glass-doors—there are no grounds, no gardens round, no shrubbery or flowerbeds, nothing but the daisied & undulating field stretching green as emerald to the very walls of that mansion—with a commanding & bold aspect it seems to gaze upon its domain & ask for neither shelter nor ornament to its Doric proportions—you see at a glance that its masonry is perfect, what blocks of stone—cemented invisibly—what broad slabs for the steps, what casements! what clear, large, panes of glass. How cheerful must be the rooms they light—what a front door! & what a glittering knocker & bell handle. It is afternoon now, I have loitered away two hours in the plantation, it is four o'clock p-m. I begin to want something to eat, come along —here we go down the slope, mind that bull does not follow us—he is stirring—hark! a short roar—but we're safe, we're under the walls. We are at the Kitchen-door—Step in—Well, this is pleasant—what a pavement—white & smooth as marble, what walls—what a ceiling—& look at the fire, clear & bright but without a flame—burnt down to perfection though its the dog-days—you never saw such a hearth, as clean as my hand, & look at that table—scoured the likeness of snow & loaded with new cakes & loaves—they're baking—but there's no bustle here, it's all confined to the back kitchen where you see half a dozen young women—servants as busy as bees—look, to the other side a great arch opening to the passage—such a passage—lofty & wide & long, without carpet, without canvass, floored with the same beautiful white flags as the kitchen—the immense front door is open & the sunshine & the wind are streaming in un-checked. now just stand still a moment & collect the character of the house.

There is evidently company here, you hear a noise of talking from the inner rooms—Gentlemen's voices—& every now & then a step is heard in the passage as they cross from one room to the other. Dogs too rush occasionally to the door, & then bound back again—one enters the kitchen just now, a huge hound muzzled—

I verily believe its master is following it—Aye, striding from the
carpeted dining-room, a spur clinks on the stone pavement, & a
voice changing from the muffled echoes of the throng to the louder
reverbrations of the empty hall—finishes the sentence it has begun.
"Marshall, you are mistaken, they docked the entail before you
were born." The speaker enters the kitchen—a tall & erect gentleman of Juvenile symmetry & aspect—he plants himself with his
back to the fire & calls "Susan, my jewel." a comely little house-
maid appears instanter from the back-kitchen, her neat & trim
dress a little powdered with flour for she has been kneading—
"Sir?" she answers with a smile, keeping at a respectful distance—
"bring me a glass of cold water" is the reply—it is brought &
courteously presented on a little silver tray. "Now, Susan, have
you kept the keepsake I gave you last time I was here?" "Yes, I
carried it home when I went to Howard, but my mother said I
should not have taken it. it was too handsome—may I give it back
again?" "Stuff, no! go away to your baking & remember what I
told you about being steady & good—read your bible every morning & evening—mind you work & be civil to every-body"—the
Gentleman's precepts are interrupted by the entrance of a third
person, an individual of about sixty with a white head & a tremendous hunch on his back—"Please, your reverence" says he
"they want to start—come away—Stewart's swearing at you, so is
my master"—"James, your master will certainly be carried away
bodily." "Not before your reverence, but will you come." "No,
they can easily ride to H–ll without me"—"I must tell my master
so?" "I'll save you the trouble—" the young clergyman, for such
of course he must be by the title given him, strides out of the
Kitchen & is audibly heard dismissing the party with curses—You
are confounded I see, reader, this cheerful large house where
you never where before—the loud mirthful mingling of voices
within—the busy life—like bustle of servants in the Kitchen—
the large silent staircase at the head of the passage where we
now stand, the clock at the top ticking peacefully above the merry
tumult, mirroring in its face the landscape of sunny fields & reposing cattle flung upon it through the open door, all this can
you see but none of it can you understand. However the gentlemen are gone & they have poured down the passage, blocked up
the entrance in a dark body—see, as they stand hatting & glov-
ing, do you know any of them?—too late, they shake hands, they
rattle down the steps & disperse over the field an are vanished.
What silence succeeds—yet listen earnestly & you hear a deep
grand base voice still equably conversing in the dining-room,

but its folding doors are close—pry no further—the whole is a
mystery—

The day had been variable but it closed in a pleasant kind of
evening, such as after a day of close sitting invites one irresistibly
to the open air. "Hill o'Mac!" cried I, rising from my solitary tea-
table "are you disposed for a walk?"—"Why, not particularly
Townshend" answered a voice from the adjoining appartment—
"But, however, as the evening does seem tolerably serene & as one
does require a little change in this dull place—I don't care if you
and I take a turn together"—"Come then, my lad, and mind you
load your pistols—dangerous times these"—"Stuff, Townshend—
we're not men of war you know—the fire-eaters, even if you should
light upon any of them, won't touch us." "May-be aye—may-be
no" said I, and pushing open the door of communication I stepped
into my fellow-lodger's sitting room—he was just rising from the
sofa & languidly drawing on his gloves—"Now I'm ready" said
he, taking up his hat and, as he adjusted it, turning easily to a
mirror over the mantlepiece & parting a lock of light hair from his
forehead—"You're a coxcomb Mac" said I as we gained the outer-
door, and stepped into the street, crowded even at this hour with
soldiers—"A thorough coxcomb—!" he smiled, and touched me
slightly with his slender cane, with a look that intimated "I return
the compliment", I glanced at my puce-brown coat, my straw-
coloured waist-coat & checked pantaloons strapped tight over as
neat a foot as ever effaced the chalk on a ball-room floor, and
answered "well, nobody can deny that we're a genteel though a
dishonest looking pair of bipeds." Macara* slid his arm under mine
and with even and measured tread, we marched down the street,
threading our way through the swaggering uniforms with the utmost ease and nonchalance. erelong we were straying quietly on
the causeway of the East-road—with Evesham just behind us all
smoke & tumult, the canal and the open country on our left hand
—with the ruins of a malt-kiln lately burnt down and blackening
on the green banks of the Cirhala, and on our right the wall
bounding a gentleman's grounds, over shadowed with fruit-trees
in full blossom. Macara pointed significantly to a tall cherry-tree
broken down, which hung over, withered & unsightly—we turned
a corner & stood at the entrance, the iron gates were flung open
and a great stone from the road had been placed to block them
back—a waggon stood within, loaded—its burden was covered
over with oil-cloth & sacking—but we could see the pillar of a

* Lord Macara Lofty

mahogany table and a carpet rolled up. the lawn was trampled to
mire—the groups of shrubs, paled round, were cut down & piled in
faggots—the house looked solitary—"One of Jerry's flittings" remarked Macara with an indifferent glance—"Who lived there?"
I asked—"I hardly know" he said "but I think his name was
Rhodes, one William Rhodes Esqr. I know I heard Sir John cursing him one day—because he had been absurdly contumacious
about some little demand—& the next, Julian Gordon told me he
had seen the pig-headed owner of Orchard-Gate, kick his last in
his own kitchen." "Who was he?" "I don't know, one of the stupid
country-gentlemen here-abouts I suppose. His last dying speech as
reported to me by Gordon indicated a brilliant state of mind."
"what was it—" "He didn't care for no man and he didn't belong
to no party, but his own was his own & he'd die with that word
between his teeth. so Julian even knotted the rope & drew him up
over his bread-flake—he was of Angrian descent I believe"—
The particulars of this relation, though I listened to them as if they
were new, were in reality well known to me before, & much more
which nearly concerned my companion & which I will whisper to
the reader, as it may help him in his calculations of the noble lord's
character—Rhodes—though Macara had mentioned him as a perfect stranger, was a previous acquaintance of his—he had headed
a deputation sent with an address from Evesham during the period
of Ardrah's administration—Lofty, as a member of the Government, received them—and I well remember, when the conference
was over and the deputation retired, entering his office and finding
him in a state of great agitation, with all the marks of livid passion
in his face—I asked him what had happened & though he gave me
no direct answer—I heard afterwards from authentic sources that
Rhodes, who was a rough homely man, had given him to understand in keen tones that of all the then existing base & contemptible
ministry, he was regarded by the country at large as the basest &
most contemptible—Lofty treasured this insult in his heart, Fate
had given him an opportunity of revenging it—& using Gordon
as his tool, he had found means to blot out the taunt with the blood
of him who uttered it.

  "How quiet the road becomes as we walk farther from Evesham"
pursued Macara, glancing towards the shady woods that now
closed in on each side of the broad way—"Who would think that
a beleagured town & two conflicting armies lay so near—" "We
hear them parleying to each other through their Guns" answered
I—"Hark!" I paused, for a peal of artillery broke through the
sultry evening. "Yes" said his lordship "those are our Guns—

MacTerroglen asks the Duke how he feels himself this warm night"—"Be still now" I continued "pause a moment & we shall hear my rampant brother's* reply"—a moment elapsed and further off reverbrated a hoarser & more distant roll—"His grace is sullen" I pursued—"That can only be interpreted "You be ———d Jerry, I'm as well as you wish me to be"."

Silence succeeded, the trees alone rustled to the soft south wind which blew at intervals over them—we could hear the Cirhala too, flowing behind, though it was unseen—a marbled sky canopied us and the sun was setting—"Pity we a'nt two lovers" I remarked —looking up at my dear companion—With what a smile did he pause & fold his arms! We both leaned against the wall—"I never was in love" he murmured—"What, not with the marchioness of Wellesley—?" he closed his eyes & said in a tone of reverie—"A pretty woman was Louisa with a soft expression and pleasant voice—I've seen her look enchanting seated, with her arm resting on a flower-stand, her eyes gazing on some distant object through a window, her dress sweeping the carpet with folds of dark-blue silk all languor & elegance, without a trace of colour on her cheek & a dishevelled grace about her particularly soft & fine hair, called by courtesy auburn—in truth a very light red, but you know, Townshend, she and I had no consumingly ardent love for each other"—"Yet you used to spend many hours in each other's company"—"Aye, it was a nice recreation—the business of the day being over—to repair to that little villa she occupied after her blow-up with Northangerland, on such an evening as this for example—She would be lingering about the door under its porch of roses, or she would be standing by her flower-beds watering her favourite plants—or seated at her work-table within the little drawing-room—she would be trifling over some elegant peice of needle-work—Louisa was never at a loss for some lady-like occupation, calculated to set off her white hands, or to display advantageously her graceful attitudes—her drooping curls, her snowy neck &c. &c. I used to lounge on a sofa by her—and whilst I flattered her Circeian charms she would repay my homage by the communication of two or three pretty little political secrets—no eaves-dropper could have heard us, we spoke so soft & low our voices were scarce louder than the faintest breeze of twilight sighing amongst her roses and acacias—I think I see her now with the look of a Madonna lifting her large blue eyes from the veil of lace she has been embroidering, & strengthening by the appeal of an eloquent glance the suggestion of revenge her lips have just

* Zamorna

uttered—as Talleyrand remarked to me a short time since "Femal—
politicians are always a little *too* blood-thirsty"—Louisa would
have guillotined half the peerage." "Where is her ladyship now?"
I asked—"Arranging her hair at a mirror" he replied, "With the
passion-flowers of Aspen-villa blushing in at her chamber-win-
dows—and thinking as she looks at her pearls & brilliants that she
would give the brightest of them for some enemy's head." "What a
pleasant ingenuous way you have of conversing, Macara" said I.
"I was not aware of it" he replied, taking a diminutive gold box
from his pocket & administering to himself a grain or two of
opium—"One would think" I continued "you were pure as untrodden snow from the faults you see in others"—I am not pure
from Louisa Danci's* faults" he answered. "Her disposition and
my own are so similar we might be brother & sister—" "You
would not have said that, Mac, if you were not conscious that the
same idea was passing through my mind—" he smiled & replied
justly—"You know me, Charles, I confess it, my character is at
your mercy." he passed his wasted & colourless hand over his
brow & looking up to the moon which hung a pale crescent above
us, whispered regretfully—"My frame of mind is not like most
men's, it is perverse, I own it"—checking himself, he hummed a
pensive little air, as if to elude the pressure of unpleasant reflections—then, starting suddenly "we shall be late, Charles, dusk
is approaching—listen, the clocks of Evesham chime nine"—
& stretching to gather a wild rose which bloomed on a briar
above him, he slowly turned townward—I watched him playing
with the blossom & continuing to whistle the melancholy can-
zonette—"There goes the most skilful compound of malignency &
dissimulation in Africa" thought I. "He imagines now that he
has left a favourable impression upon me despite my thorough
conviction of his villainy—but I know him, aye as well as I know
myself."—

What a pretty spot of work—Richton—Warner & Hartford have
made between them!—A dark fit of musing came over my mind
as I laid down the last volume published by Captain Hastings, late
of the 19th—I expected some such catastrophe, the progress of this
affair has been watched by me with a cool eye for some month's
past. credit me, reader, it is no pleasant thing to fall under the
cloud of that trio's ill-will—Each of these illustrious individuals has
a way of crushing his foes with an encroaching gradual tyranny

* Louisa Danci or Dance, formerly Louisa Vernon, Marchioness of Wellesley,
had been Northangerland's mistress and the mother of Caroline

which it paralyses the mind to think of—Hartford never took to Hastings—I remember two years ago when the young soldier was in the blaze of his fame, I chanced one evening to call at Girnington-Hall and I found him seated at Lady Thornton's tea-table between herself & Lady Maria Percy—Thornton had brought him from Zamorna where he was then stationed with his regiment —the group as I saw it then is now clear to my mental vision— amid the daily deeds of strife passing round me, the recollection of domestic scenes is singularly soothing—

Julia, dressed like a queen, was presiding over the porcelain with an urn of pure silver classically moulded, before her—she had a satin robe on with lace sleeves, & through that thin material her arms, round, white & polished, gleamed like ivory—her curls, long & abundant as usual, waved to every movement of the head—& that head, as she distributed her glances of love & light on all sides, was seldom still—Maria,* taller than her sister & of more imperial mien, sat reclined back on her sofa seat. It was hot & her dress was all white, ample open white robe, long sash & scarf of snowy gauze. Her ringlets reposed on her neck—they did not float so luxuriously as Julia's—but shaded her paler cheek & more marble-like temples, with a serene fall of tresses like the wing of a raven—She was laughing, her careless, musical laugh—& railly-ing Hastings for some heroic speech he had just been uttering— Haughty even in her mirth, her eyes looked down upon him through their huge sable lashes—with an expression of scarcely concealed superiority—It was evident she perceived what enthu-siasm her presence, her voice, her beauty inspired—she perceived, enjoyed, but did not share it. The expression on Henry's face indicated a heart rapt in feelings unusual to it—there was a fierce bold excitement in his eye, his cheek was flushed—his hand I could perceive, as he passed the cups to & fro, trembled—he spoke fast and eloquently—not very discreetly or correctly—but at every little slip the ladies laughed again and encouraged him to pro-ceed—General Thornton,† who sat just opposite dallying with some dry toast & apparently reading a newspaper—at last said in a tone that reminded me of his God-father "Henry, my lad, don't ye see they're trying to fool ye?" "Fool me!" exclaimed Hastings, and with a darkened aspect he turned first to one & then to the other, with eyes of uncertain yet threatening meaning—he sought in Julia's face—blooming & sweet—the expression that was to dash

* Both Julia and Maria were Wellesleys and cousins to Zamorna
† Thornton, Julia's husband, is represented as a simple, unvarnished Yorkshire-man

his vanity & freeze his enthusiasm—she was smiling, but very innocently, & her words soon re-assured him. darting a look of vivacity at her husband—she said "The General remembers how I used to fool *him*—aye—Captain. It was my custom to sit with my glass so & to watch him in all his movements through a drawing-room as he shifted about from one group to another, getting more embarassed every moment—from the consciousness of that incessant surveillance—& then, at length, when his annoyance exceeded the bounds of human endurance, he would stride abruptly up to me & whisper with such emphasis "you shall pay for this when you change your name"." Satisfied by the tone & the air of his Hostess—Henry turned to the more formidable Lady of Edwardston—she met his inquiring look without pity—"We fool every-body" she said, curling her beautiful but satirical lip—Hastings was in the act of raising his cup. he put it down untasted—folded his arms & turned moody. The General again looked at him. "All varry grand" he said, and folded the sheets of the newspaper—Lady Julia bent forward, advanced her white hand flashing with rings, to solicit Henry's attention—& whispered "Captain, if we have offended you—you can take your revenge. your pen is a weapon we must all tremble at, even my sister-in-law there who is the proudest of the proud—" "Yes!" replied Hastings, looking up Hardily. "Your ladyship has spoken truth—I know that in my next publication I can make your hearts throb with exultation or sicken with disappointed pride—forgive me for the taunt, I wont retract it, her Royal-Highness drew the bit too tight." Her royal-highness laughed unrestrainedly. "how sensitive you are Captain" returned she "but come, we will chase away the cloud among Julia's flower-borders"—She rose, & stepping through an open door, stood erect in her white robes amongst a flush of foreign shrubs blooming in the garden without—Julia followed, so did Hastings, so did I—The ladies passed along the narrow paths, conversing gaily as they walked, and at intervals, where a rare flower or an opening bud of uncommon beauty attracted their attention, bending to gather it. Hastings, it was evident, felt the scene like enchantment. it was a lovely evening, breathless & cloudless—The green slopes & bowery shades of the garden received the sun's softened smile through vistas of foliage opening to the West. Girnington-Hall, antique & grey, imparted the romance of old time to the hour & the landscape, & words cannot depict the charm added by those two beautiful women—Julia, her hands filled with roses, stood on tip-toes gazing eagerly upwards at a birds-nest half-hid in the glossy leaves of a tall beech. "How I should like to see the young ones!" she exclaimed "they are orioles I believe." "I'll reach the nest for you in a minute" exclaimed Hastings, & before she could prohibit him, he had speeded with the agility of a cat up one tree & dropped from its topmost bough on to the lawn before her—"There it is!" he exclaimed, offering her his prize—"I've not forgotten my Harrow tricks yet." Lady Maria likewise approached to look—Julia then recollected other little curiosities—she had noticed in the plantation below—She condescendingly passed her arm through Henry's & led him down a shady avenue in that direction—Maria followed—a few minutes after I saw them all standing together conversing freely—like a group of children—Hastings unembarassed & animated—was communicating to his two fair auditors a store of sylvan information, then he passed to other things from his boyish knowledge to his mature experience. they sat down on a seat of turf round the roots of an aged elm, his strain of narration flowed on—I heard the words Etrei—Dongola—Gazembo—he was speaking eloquently & they were listening attentively—at this crisis a tall figure strayed slowly up the plantation—it was Lord Hartford—I knew him by his military bearing, his mustachios—& the scar on his forehead— the group arrested his eye, he paused & scanned them with a supercilious smile—advancing, he held out his hand to Julia— "Good evening, my Lady—I was coming as usual to sit by your piano this summer-evening—but I fear my walk from the Hall will be in vain—you seem to be otherwise engaged"—Julia got up. "the story is just finished" said she "& Captain Hastings has told it so well—the martyrdom of Dongola, Colonel—I feel so excited I shall not be able to play for an hour to come—what Demons those Negroes are!" "Shocking bad I dare say" returned his Lordship—& now for the first time he noticed Hastings, who had bowed to him civilly, with the slightest possible nod—Offering an arm to each of the ladies, he continued "But I must have some music—it is the greatest treat a bachelor like me can enjoy—my mother's grand old harp stands in her grand old-drawing-room there, down at Hartford-Hall, & never a finger has swept its strings since the day she was buried—Now the keys of that piano of yours are trembling every day to the touch of its mistresse's fair hands—& you surely won't grudge me, my accustomed half hour of enjoyment at twilight"—by this time he had led her in & seated her at the instrument. He asked for a song, a pretty wild serenade of Spain—Julia shook back her locks, laughed & dashed it off—as animatedly & gracefully as any donna that ever struck the Guitar —Hastings, who stood haughtily aloof, irritated & annoyed by His

Drawing by Charlotte Brontë evocative of her description of Julia
(see page 15)

Colonel's proud demeanour—unconsciously allowed an expression of admiration to escape him—Hartford turned round, regarded him with a studied smile of contempt—& stopping Lady Thornton as she was about to address him, turned her attention to something else—A deep but suppressed oath escaped the captain's lips. His countenance lighted with a strong & almost convulsed expression —which, however, quickly passed away, leaving only a cloud of sullen displeasure—in five minutes after he took his leave—lady Thornton entreated him to stay a little longer—"Thank you, my lady" he said "Lord Hartford thinks you are degraded by the society of a farmer's son—I have stayed too long—I wish your ladyship good evening." He bowed low to both the ladies—defied his colonel by a single fiery glance & left the room. Lord Hartford's laugh followed him—neither by the Superior nor the Subaltern was this scene ever forgotten—it never will be—to Richton— Hartford muttered his Luciferian disdain, it was received with the smile of Belial. I heard them once conversing on the subject as they stood apart from the other individuals composing a large party at the noble Colonel's own house—they were lounging by a lofty window—looking up towards old Hartford-Hall and upon the current of the Olympian—Richton had been saying something about the impressive aspect of the decayed mansion. "Aye" replied Hartford "even plebeians, if you remark Richton, when they look upon an old ruin like that, with its screen of ivy, its grey gables & swallow haunted-stacks of chimney—even dull, fat plebeians—do feel a little reverence towards the family that once owned it. empty & dreary as those chambers now are, they cannot help feeling that they were once as richly decked & as brilliantly peopled as the suite of rooms one can see through those folding-doors—Aristo cracy passes from the Earth, Richton—half a century hence per haps this house will have fallen like that & some staring city mansion of brick will have been reared on its ruins—erected by the wealth of a shop-keeper or the Government Grants to some par venue, soldier of Fortune—or haply the bookseller's meed doled out to some bombastic historian of his own exploits"—Richtons eye shewed that he understood this hit though his lips only answered "The world is easily humbugged—Hartford—" "Aye, & the Directors of the World" was the sullen reply—and Hartford turned his scowling regard towards a recess where a great Per sonage stood leaning upon a lady's harp—Richton nichered & shrugged his shoulders—"Particularly condescending I suppose" he said. "Patronises rising talent, Eh?" "Just so, that plough-boy —that farmer's son, with his broad shoulders & his air en Gascon,

has wonderfully taken the royal taste—" Again Richton laughed—
"He'll supplant you, Hartford, bye & by—we shall see in the Court-
circle, Captain Hastings' shoulder selected for the support of his
Grace's arm—& you, whose wont it has always been to receive that
honour, will be standing behind with all the glooms of all the
passions on your forehead—" "O! no" returned Hartford "I'll
wait at the favourite's elbow & just pick up any little morceau
of slang or profanity he happens to drop from his refined lips &
repeat it by way of making my court—" "But" interrupted Richton, looking round on the glittering throng "I don't see the Hero
of the day among your party—why don't you invite him & give
him an opportunity of paying his respects to the fair & noble of the
land he has contributed so much to exalt both by his pen & his
sword." Hartford answered by a cold sneer—"It is said" pursued
his friend "That the young Gentleman has raised his aspiring eyes
—to yonder fairy-like figure by the book-case." "What! to that
little girl in pink who is pulling down all Shakespeare & scattering
his volumes on the floor?" "The same." "Simple sumph—to commit him then to the tender mercies of our friend the Home-
Secretary—by the bye, Richton, shall we give him a hint, there he
is, take the cue & follow it up." Richton was put upon a task he
delighted in—with easy step he glided towards a couch where Mr
Warner was sitting alone under the shade of a tall exotic—he was
reclined half back, his finger was on his lips, his eyes wandered
with an unquiet gleam over the groups before him—"A tolerably
showy assemblage" began Richton. "Some good heads in the
room tonight, don't you think so, Warner?"—Warner changed his
attitude, folded his arms & sat erect—It is impossible for him to
fall in at once with the simplest opinion. "Your phraseology, lord
Richton, is like that of a Portrait-painter—Good heads? why can't
you say beautiful faces? I won't answer for the heads, Sir—a good
head is no such matter of course, where would you find the brains?
—but I do see some exquisite features, yes exquisite—" Richton
wiped his lips with his delicate cambric handkerchief & looked
askance at Hartford who stood near enough to hear what passed—
"Men's tastes" he continued "differ in nothing so much as in their
opinion of beauty—now for my own part I should say there was
not one really beautiful woman here—I see some fine figures but
no model of perfection." "Model of perfection, Sir" answered
Warner "what do you mean? that is a foolish phrase, amateur
severity is out of place—you come here not to criticise but to
admire." as he spoke, a figure crossed the room just in front of
them, a tall elegantly shaped girl of about nineteen, of slender

proportions but enveloped in very rich & sweeping drapery—The
beauty of her hair struck the spectator at once, it was curling,
golden & profuse. She was very fair, very stately & had eyes of the
sweetest & softest blue—Passing them, she turned, bowed, for she
knew them all, & the smile which accompanied that token of
recognition seemed to repeat "You come here not to criticise but
to admire"—Warner's glance expressed his triumph as he flashed
it upon Richton—"Well" said the Earl, in no wise disconcerted
"That is a lovely creature certainly, beautiful neck, & a hand indicating five hundred years of nobility—high descent? aye, look at
her fingers as she is resting them upon that urn, white, taper delicate—but you see little of that magnificent contour one associates
with an idea of perfection." "Magnificent contour!" repeated
Warner impatiently, and sparing of words on such a subject—he
pointed to an open window, where, suffused by the glow of crimson
hangings drawn before the sunlight, sat a fine woman of about
nine and twenty. She was dark in complexion, not very tall, but in
all her forms round & superb—the natural disdain of her eye & of
her whole haughty but handsome profile seemed such as no smile
could dispel. her features were not aquiline, they were straight,
prominent & Angrian, strikingly similar to Lord Hartford's whose
sister indeed she was. at this moment she was in high good-
humour receiving the homage of a ring of titled & military admirers by whom she was surrounded. her splendid dress—her
jewels costly & profuse, became her—Her attitudes imposing &
regal—her voice rich & full, her dark eyes & intensely black
brows & braids of hair were all in harmony—Richton surveyed her
with a courteous smile, said he feared he must acknowledge himself
vanquished. in truth, lady Emma Arniston's aspect was a demonstration he could not withstand—After a pause, Richton, in low
confidential voice, went on "Poor Hartford, he views this scene
with a less tranquil eye than you or I, Mr Warner." "What do
you mean? the man is in years" answered the Home Secretary, not
at all conciliated by the gossipy tone of the observation—Richton
glanced mischievously at the Baron, who still, though unmarked by
Warner, remained within ear-shot. "Aye, as you say, my noble
friend does begin to pass his climateric, nearer fifty than forty I can
assure you—nevertheless his youth & the feelings of his youth
revive when he thinks of some here present—to speak seriously and
as a friend, I believe he entertains peculiar sentiments towards
Miss Warner"—The home-secretary—looked fretted. "You gossip, Sir," said he, "you gossip—don't trouble me with General
Lord Hartford's tender weaknesses." "Nevertheless you ought to

compassionate him" continued Richton—"He loves but is deterred from declaring his sentiments by the dread of a rival—" Hartford here broke in somewhat annoyed—"D---d you Flower"* he exclaimed "that is just like one of the old tricks you've served me often at school & college—To finish his rhodomontade, Warner, allow me to cut the matter short—that son of one of your tenants, the young author Hastings I think his name is—has, according to popular report, ventured to speak presumptuously of Miss Caroline —I mention this—because—" He could not give his reason, Warner vehemently interrupted him—"What do you mean?" he said. "What do you both mean by accosting me in this way? is any member of my family to be made the subject of an old-woman's —scandal, Lord Richton, or of a Profligate's sneers, Lord Hartford —Gentlemen" he continued "you have ventured too far—too-far—you had better not err so grossly again—" Richton smiled, but Hartford proceeded to ask in what way the Right-honourable Secretary had intended to apply the word Profligate—Warner, irritated extremely, bade him be silent for he was acting like a fool —all this passed in very low and smothered tones of voice, so that it did not attract the general attention of those round—they were not however wholly unnoticed—A low laugh warned Hartford that some one was near—he turned round, it had proceeded from the lips of that very pretty & distinguished Girl, who had crossed the saloon ten minutes since—She was leaning on the arm of a young man extremely like herself in the general cast of his features, but of such imposing stature as to throw her own stately height quite into the shade, her curls of gold fell upon his shoulder as she inclined her head towards him to answer his whispered remark on the group they were watching—Hartford bowed when he saw this pair & fell back a pace or two. "Surely you & Mr Warner are not seriously angry with each other" said the lady. "Yes, yes," was the reply of her companion in a half-displeased tone. "If his Lordship can be jealous even of the Serf, he must be bitterly embroiled with the Liege-Lord." The general coloured, Richton looked surprised, not at all abashed. "The Gift of a supernaturally quick sense of hearing is not exclusively bestowed on Indians, I perceive" he said. "Nor is the propensity of a tattling tongue exclusively confined to elderly ladies" returned the Gentleman severely—Richton, in general not very quick to take offence, was nettled, he bowed & left the circle. The imperious dictator, too, passed on with his beautiful companion—Warner & Hartford said nothing more to

* John, Baron Flower and Viscount Richton. See Branwell Brontë's narrative *The Angrian Adventurer* (June 1834)

each other—but the conversation had left its impression, from that hour Henry Hastings may date his ruin, his Landlord never afterwards lifted a finger to assist him.

When one hears the name of any individual thundered in one's ears incessantly—when one sees it in every print—be it daily newspaper or monthly magazine—we naturally pause, and recalling all we know from observation or have heard from report, ask ourselves "does this man deserve the fame he has earned?"—Some people, however they themselves may be steeped to the lips in villainy—have a knack of always assuming on the stage of public life that part which has a specious show of the right in it. They then in sounding periods declaim on their attachment to their country— their affection for their followers—their devotion to sentiments of chivalry & honour—their abhorrence of every thing that is mean &c. &c. The audience looking on & seeing their great actor, folded in the robe of self-complacency—majestically pacing the boards & with brow of noble resolve & eyes of pure intelligence, maintaining those sentiments which by bonds of faith & kindness cement the fellowship of men, when, I say, they hear him speaking thus & then denouncing with righteous wrath, certain guilty ones that never sinned against his sacred code of morals—the good folk begin to hope that certainly this Mentor has turned from the evil ways of his youth & is now as pure as he seems—Pshaw— can the Leopard cast his spots or the Ethiop change his skin? The majority of mankind may be easily humbugged, for the majority of mankind are fools—but since the days of Elisha there has always been a remnant left in Israel "who have not bowed the knee to Baal".

In the vicinity of Evesham, about three miles out of the town, stands a remarkably pretty little building, quite new, with its pointed front turned towards the road and in the centre a large window—It rises against the sky from a group of old trees, a monument of the successful labours of Mr Bromley—That great apostle of methodism, committing the superintendence of the Verdopolitan circuits to his fellow-labourers in the Gospel—Messr Simpson, Barlow & Chadwick—set out about ten months ago on a mission to that benighted district lying immediately east on the borders of Sine-Gambia. For a full detail of all his persecutions, trials, temptations &c. as well as of his successes & conquests, I refer the reader to the last six numbers of our Magazine from December to June inclusive.—Truly he suffered much—the sword of the flesh was unleashed against him—yet in spite of almost universal opposition, his endeavours finally prevailed for the blessing of the Lord was upon him. I would particularly direct the reader's attention to the last letter received from him by our Superintendent—In the case of the late William Rhodes Esqr of Orchard-Gate, it gives an awful instance of God's judgement upon the wicked. That gentleman was one of the most determined opposers of Methodism in the whole country—The following extract from Mr Barlow's Journal will sufficiently testify the violence of his persecuting spirit.

"Twelve o'clock. midnight. May 18th—"I have had a day of conflicts—but he that brought the three children unharmed out of the fiery furnace, & delivered David safe from the Lions-Den, hath likewise rescued me, his darling, from the power of the Dog." This morning Thomas Dun came to me with the intelligence that we should never be able to hold our meetings—for that Mr Rhodes had threatened Jones, who was his tenant, with expulsion if he lent his wharehouse for that purpose—Direct inspiration from heaven furnished me with an answer to this difficulty—Thomas, said I, fetch the steward & three of the class-leaders—and we will go up to Orchard-Gate & try the power of the word upon that man of sin. Thomas went away and soon returned with John Butler, Reuben Ash, Charles Mitchell & Samuel Clay—After we had sung an hymn & prayed, we set out—I think it might be about two o'clock when we arrived at the house. Knocking civilly at the back-door, I asked of the servant who opened it if Mr Rhodes were at home—he replied "Yes." "Then" said I "Go tell your master that six men stand without desiring to speak with him." The man stared but did as I desired—erelong he returned with the answer that Mr Rhodes was at dinner and could not for the present be interrupted—"We can wait" said I, & each of us taking a chair we sat in a circle round the hall—It was the servant's hall, and they were arranging dinner upon the table—as I watched them bringing in first a tureen of soup and then a leg of pork & then a pie, vegetables &c. a voice came unto me "arise and eat"—"Thy will be done" I answered aloud & getting up I came towards the table. "With your leave" said I to a maid who was standing by "I will take a bason of that broth—" She made no attempt to help me so I took the ladle & served myself—I had no sooner finished this than the voice I had heard before came again & I felt I stood in the situation of Elijah who, as he lay under the juniper tree, was again & again bidden to arise and eat—obeying the supernatural impulse I cut into the pie, & helping myself to greens, took such

sustinence as the body needed—Then whispered my inward
monitor "Give unto the men that are with thee", so shaving a few
slices off the leg of pork and adding turnips I passed it round—The
maid, the only person who stood in the hall, looked greedily at us
& said "She should have to cook another dinner for the servants"
—I made her no answer but falling on my knees, went to prayer—
It was a time of peculiar freedom, I felt priviledged to wrestle
with God and to cry out importunately and insist upon the acceptance of my petitions—"O! Lord!" said I "I will have what I
want—I will take the gates of thy favour by storm—thy great
cause shall prosper, it must—Ride on thou most Mighty & crush
thine enemies before thee—the great oppressor shall be trodden
underfoot, the proud man shall be brought down & choked in his
swollen insolence"—I spoke loud—my words were fervent & so
were the groans & responses of my friends, we drank of the living-
waters flowing from above as we had (which I forgot to mention)
a few minutes before, drank two Gallons of mellow old ale which
stood on the table—Whilst we thus Strove with God in the midst of
footmen & maids who had flocked in from the kitchen & stood
staring at us as if we were wild beasts, a bell rang violently just
above us, a footman ran to answer it. as he opened, an inner voice
we heard, a rough & angry voice exclaim—"What the d———l is
that d———d noise—who's making it?" "The Methodist Preachers,
Sir" answered the man. "They've eat up all our dinner & drank
eight quarts of ale & now they're praying"—"Praying! be
hanged to them" was the answer. "Kick them every one out this
minute, James. Kick them out I say or I'll send you after them."
These brutal words were scarcely out of Mr Rhodes' mouth when
we were set upon by three great, strong men who, I'll take my
oath before any magistrate, attempted to stick us with the knives
they snatched off the table—the steward & the three class-leaders
were hustled out of the house speedily—but I, escaping, rushed
towards the dining-room—I burst open the door and dashed in,
leaning upon the rod & staff which even in this hour of trial continued to comfort me. There I saw one of the dens which Satan
in this world often gives to his worshippers—pampering them
with magnificence here, ere he sends them to lament in the burning vaults of hell hereafter—It was a long room & there were
pictures in gold-frames all down the walls—the side-board groaned
under plate & glass & the large table in the centre glittered with
decanters of cut crystal, full of wine, & plates of gilt china heaped
with fruit. There was Mr Rhodes at the foot, a big pompous man
who by his red face I should conjecture to be half drunk. There

was Mrs Rhodes at the head, in silks & satins & jewels & feathers
—& down the sides were their Sons & daughters with several guests
all dressed in the worldlings flare & frippery. Blessed be my
maker! I was not shaken either by the multitude or the Sodo-
mitish appearance of my adversaries—I calmly advanced &
taking out my pocket-bible & holding it forth in my right hand—I
commenced with a loud clear voice—"Go to now ye rich men!
Howl & cry for your miseries that are come upon you—" Mr
Rhodes broke out violently with a profane oath. "Sacriligeous
Scoundrel" cried he "How dare you come here! the arrogant insolence of your craft is not unknown to me, but it won't tell, sir—it
won't tell—I'll have you washed like wool under the pump
before you leave my house." I opposed his brutality by a mild and
steady demeanour—"William Rhodes" said I "you call yourself a
magistrate, a guardian of the morals of the land—I fine you five
shillings for that oath you have uttered, I shall lay information
against you"—He answered me by some abuse which I do not
think it worth my while to report—I quietly proceeded "You will
not live long, I know you will not—you have nearly filled the
measure of your iniquity—repent then while it is yet day—even at
the eleventh hour there may be hope—I exhort you in all brotherly
kindness, my bowels yearn towards you—The crimes you have
committed are black, are double-dyed—but the Lord's mercy
knoweth no limits—" Mrs Rhodes started up trembling & livid
with rage. "I cannot bear it" she said. "What emboldens this
wretch to speak so to my husband—?" "Woman!" I answered
"part of my mission is also to you—Cover your head with ashes &
sit down & weep—you shall oppress the Lord's saints no longer—&
you young women, the daughters of them that have grown grey in
wickedness—put of that immodest dress & those neck-chains, &
those love-tokens & those rings for the ears & for the hands—&
clothe yourselves with sackcloth & seek the Ditch & the out-
house for your home"—Mr Rhodes' hand was now on my mouth,
he was as white as a sheet, he called as if frantic for his servants
—they came open-mouthed like bulls of Bashan. I was delivered
into their hands, & what I suffered after, it baffles language
to describe. I was scourged, I was dragged through a horse-
pond, I was drowned under a deluge from the pump—Nay, I
have good reason to believe that more than one pistol was dis-
charged at my head—but I survived all, & by the blessing of
God was that night able to make a hearty supper & to sleep as
soundly as ever I did in my life. My master avenged me in his
own good time. about a fortnight after, I saw the dead body of

Rhodes dragged out of his house, & with the rope that he had been hung with still round his neck—I beheld him flung into that very horse-pond where by his orders I had been nearly murdered."

But this digression has led me far astray from the subject with which I commenced—I was speaking of a little chapel, whose white front looks upon a lonely part of the road leading from Evesham west-wards. as I said before—this little sanctuary had sprung up in the wilderness—the first shrine of a new religion and the first memento to the labours of our great Apostle—It was Tuesday evening, on the next day four sermons were to be preached within its walls & four collections to be made to defray the expenses of its erection—Mr Broadbent our Steward had requested me to walk up & see that all was right—I had just completed the survey— seen that the penitential benches were properly placed & that the hamper of wine, spirits, cold meat & bread & cheese &c. had been conveyed into the vestry according to directions given in the morning—for our preachers proposed to work hard the next day & it was necessary that support should be provided for the flesh. I had just, I say, looked to these little matters an was locking the chapel door—when a voice said to me "Townshend, how are you?" I looked round in some surprise—there was a young, slender man in uniform standing still & erect at the bottom of the steps—his back was to the sun, which was near setting, and I could not at once recognise his face, yet his voice sounded familiar— whilst I doubted, another form strolled from behind the trees, whose large arms waved over the chapel-roof—a person in plain clothes, young likewise, dark & thin—he uttered the same greeting "Townshend, how are you?" The sunlight met his features— they were keen, bronzed & foreign. I knew them at once. "Soh, Eugene!* is it you? where in the world have you dropped from?" —"humph, our quarters are not so far off—Clarence-Wood—you know it—?" "Aye, and who's your pal?" "the captain? do you pretend to have forgotten him?"—I looked again, I was nearer now—I acknowledged an old acquaintance—"Oh to be sure" said I "really I beg pardon, Captain—" I held out my hand, the officer put his fore-finger into it—"What the d---l are you doing here, Townshend?" said he. "Taking un tour de promenade as I suppose you are" was my reply. "Humph, I thought you'd been going to prayer in that little conventicle—it belongs to those d---d Wesleyans I suppose—" "Certainly—it is to be opened tomorrow—four sermons, four collections—will you attend?" "No,

* Eugene Rosier, Zamorna's French valet

I'm not at all interested." "You look supremely cold & non-
chalante—what is the matter with you?" "Oh, it's so pleasant to be
dribling away one's time about Evesham—& one feels so completely at liberty, this bivouacking is a nice summer amusement."
"I'm glad you're satisfied. pray write to your brother & tell him
so." "God bless my brother—" "You're very pious." "I am, I
always was, I've had a pious education." "Indeed, who were
your tutors—?" He looked full at me and with a delicious drawl
answered "The fields, the woods, the blue sky & the golden sun—
Nature's temple, nature's ministers you know—" I started at the
sneer with which this was said, it so forcibly recalled to my mind
the recollection of a man—mighty—distant & desolate—"Good
heavens William,* you grow misanthropic—" "Saints forbid—I
wish to live in charity with all men." "Aye, with your mess for
instance" interposed Eugene—"To be sure—I'm blessed if I
don't wish them all a tent pitched in Eden." "Do you ever hear
from your sister,† Percy?" I asked. "O! Lord, my sister is nursing
herself at a watering place." "Well, she might write to you from
thence as well as from any other residence." "She can't, her
health won't admit of stooping—Tut, Townshend, you and I
stand precisely on the same footing with regard to our relations—
Does our Great Gun‡ ever write to you?" "Does he ever write to
his wife?" I retorted. "Eugene, you know, you must see his letters
after they are sealed—" Eugene put his tongue into his cheek.
"The Mogul writes such a crabbed hand one can scarcely read his
directions" he answered—Percy curled his lip. "You see what a
diplomatist our young emigré grows" said he. "He's learnt never
to speak to the point, not by no manner of means—" "Humph!"
said I "if he grows so very prudent—one won't be able to extract
a drop of information from him—Pray, Rosier, what private
letters does your master receive—?" "Precious few, & when
they're brought to him in the mail-bag, he grasps them all so in
one hand—then he stands before the fire reading them each in
turn, most he commits to the flames, & one or two I've seen him
place in his pocket-book—" "You're very stupid Rosier—how do
matters in General proceed up at Clarence-Wood?" "O, there's
nothing but a going & a coming all day-long—this staff-officer
galloping up to the door and that aid-de-camp thundering away
from it, and then his Grace rides off first thing in the morning
with Richton at his back to view the works & the lines & the
entrenchments—& then about noon he'll come back—burnt
brown with the sun, and all dust & sweat & impatience, & stride
_____
* William Percy   † Mary Henrietta, Duchess of Zamorna   ‡ Zamorna

up five-steps at once to his chamber—& then the bell is rung as if
he were going to crack the rope—& then I must go—& I find him
flung into a chair with his head on both his hands & his elbows on
the table—he d–mns me for not coming sooner, though I whipped
into his presence like magic, I pour out the water into a huge
bason—like a china-tub—& he strips his neck & chest & arms &
performs the ablutions of a mahomatan—he swears profanely
concerning the country, and the climate & somebody who has
vexed him during the morning, & meantime dresses himself in the
suit I have laid out, he puts on his morning-gown, throws himself
again into a chair & I shave him—as I pass the razor sweetly over
his chin—I talk of despotic Shahs & Sultans whose wind-pipes
were sliced by their valets. he listens as mild as a lamb, & when I
have finished boxes my ears—a tap comes to the door, it is Lord
Richton or Enara with his hands full of dispatches from the constitutionalists. They are to be read then & there—Whilst Richton is
spluttering them as fast as he can, his Grace stands erect before the
mirror in his shirt sleeves, looking at his curls & sighing to see his
complexion so gone. I take my station about a yard in the back-
ground & begin stropping the razors—meantime I am not so
absorbed in my employment, but that I cast a sheep's-eye at my
master now & then—he unluckily catches a glance reflected in the
mirror & he boxes my ears again. The dispatches are finished—his
Grace sends Fidena & the Constitutionalists to the Great Lord* &
bids Richton help him on with his coat—He walks into the library
& calls for his secretary—Mr Flanaghan comes—his Grace cries
out that he is half-dead with hunger not having tasted that morning, & can't dictate a word till he has got something to eat—I
order biscuits & wine & he takes a glass & a mouthful & then
begins striding through the room & dictating as fast or faster
than Mr Flanaghan's pen can move—He chafes when Flanaghan
cannot keep up with him. Richton recommends coolness & hands
him the biscuits again—he laughed for the first time to-day & looked
for a minute good-tempered, it is only a glimpse. his brow knits
again—he recommences his walk & dictates faster than ever—
Flanaghan swears but he doesn't care, his hand takes the cramp—
the Duke dismisses him with a curse & calls for another secretary
—this work lasts for three or four hours & then the bell is rung for
dinner. If the Duke's in the midst of a document, dinner must
stand & cool till he's done—Then he walks in as grave as a Judge,
takes his place at the head and desires Mr Tennant his chaplain
who sits at his right-hand looking all the time as black as my hat

* The Devil

to ask a blessing—he mutters a few questions to General Enara. Richton pulls up his stock & simpers—he whispers to his neighbour "pray give the Lion something to eat—it's all hunger that makes him so savage". then aloud and as smoothly as possible—"Will your Grace permit me to send you a slice of this Roti, un Gigot dressed à la Venison, I believe?" "No thank you" is the cold reply—and he leans back in his chair & looks as if he were going to eat nothing—meantime his Staff begin the concert of knives & forks very effectively—General Enara, I always remark, plays a most capital one. The Tiger* having appeased the first ferocity of hunger—observes all at once that his master is sitting with his head on his hand quite at leisure—"Head-ache to-day?" he asks. "Yes." "Humph, did your Grace take a reasonable breakfast?" "No." "No wonder then, when a man works all day on an empty stomach—allow me to prescribe for your Grace—Eugene, bring a plate for the Duke." I have one in my hand, I present it—the General deposits thereon two slices of his round—it is received and in ten minutes the trencher is clear—Enara, who has furtively watched his patient, smiles—"Eugene, change your master's plate, he will take some of the currie"—"No Enara, I think not"— "Oh not a doubt of it, rice is a very nourishing thing—Rosier, do as I bid you—" I obey—his Grace makes no bones of the second morceau—his countenance is now cleared, his brows are unbent—he begins, though still in a quiet way, to tease Lord Richton & impede the oily flow of his talk—Enara proposes a glass of Madeira—& gives me a delicate hint to put the milk & water out of my master's reach—The wine is received & sipped with bland condescension—his eye now lights up—it begins to flash in every-body's face—it glances round the table, gathers the subject of conversation on all sides—and he at once dilates into the rules of the Talk—at the first ringing intonation of his voice, telling that he is fully roused & all alive, Richton slides his chair a little back, half-shuts his eyes & begins to watch—The young aid-de-camps at the lower end stop their jabber & listen, Enara gives with his full swing, & when he is in high glee, flushed, mischievous & eloquent—he quietly re-fills his nearly emptied glass—The Duke sips on, he is as sweet now as honey & bright with good-humour, but then in all his glee there's so much of the Devil—nobody that had their senses about them would trust him. I know formerly, when he used to get into these moods, the Duchess was at great pains to humour him—she used to meet him very gaily—but she was so careful never to contradict him, or cross his will in the

* Enara

merest trifle."—"Yes Eugene" interrupted I "and did you ever
notice how she used to woo him to herself—she would glide
to the same sofa, & get hold of his hand, and as she played with his
rings she would look up into his face—so smilingly yet so enviously
at the same time—There was a mortal dread in her mind lest in
such moods, he should take a fancy to amuse himself with some
other lady—She could not spare either a word from his lips or a
glance from his eyes—"Well" said William Percy "Her watch is
over for the present & we'll trust that Eugene there stands sentinel
instead." "Ma foi, Percy, if you'll give me her grace's eyes & her
snowy little hands—& her beautiful curled hair & sweet voice—
I'll undertake to keep the castle three months at least"—"Pray is
any-body laying siege to it at present?" "I can't tell, but there's a
lady at head-quarters"—"Who?" Eugene whispered a name but
so low I could not catch it. "Enara brought her" he continued.
"I never see her—she's said to be ill, she keeps close in one room—"
"Any interviews?" "I'm morally certain not—they could scarcely
meet without my having some inkling—he's impatient at her
stay: she's to quit before active work begins—no-body knows of
her presence except Enara & myself." The conversation was here
interrupted by our arrival at the gates of Clarence-Wood—It
was now dark, I had strolled on without thinking & it was now too
late to return—I therefore gladly accepted an offer of accomoda-
tion for the night made me by Rosier—three or four days elapsed
before I returned to Evesham—during that time my observations
enabled me to concoct the following:

Clarence-Wood is a large, substatial house, the property of Sir
John Clarence, the great conservative of these parts. he yielded it
up at once with all its furniture to the Service of the Angrian
leader on his first arrival here—it is situated on a slope, & over-
looks a vast flat of rich & sultry land, tilled like a garden, &
separated by hedge-rows of briar & hawthorn—Lonely enough in
time of peace, the mansion, now in time of war, over-flowed with
life. The very park, so green & so sequestered, was appropriated as
a spacious pasturage for the horses of the Staff. Within, the rooms,
especially towards night-fall, were thronged—It was pleasant to
walk through the dusky halls, & watch the forms that strode
without cessation from one room to another. Then, if I was in the
mood, I could converse with them for they were all known to me
& none cared to betray my presence where the knowledge of it
could do me harm—though I have no friends, I have few particular
enemies—here was Lord Abercorn—a General now assuming the

importance of command, yet a fop & a coxcomb under all—there was Castlereagh—high in trust, grown grand & great, yet with the same brazen forehead, the same strapped waist, curled hair, & swaggering carriage—There was the thin & pallid William Percy—bearing about him the air of a taciturn man, for though not sparing of speech yet his words were uttered so quietly and with such little change of countenance, you felt them rather as thought than sound—He had a way I noticed—of wandering about, as if he could find no rest for the sole of his foot—no one could fix his place—he was at your elbow when you least dreamed of his presence—He would join a group—stand & gather in silence all the repartees bandied from mouth to mouth—drop a chilling word or two, coldly disabling some argument that had just been uttered & then wander away—if he heard a voice exalted in a loud & blustering tone, he would lift his blue eyes towards the speaker with an ineffable expression of disdain—& say to those near "The man ought to be gagged, why does he bore one so?"—If he chanced to converse with any one who spoke loud—he sank his own voice to a low indolent drawl—(in this way he used ever to meet his brother's hectoring—) the more warmly his antagonist declaimes—the more provokingly inaudible grew William's murmured answers—till at last they would die away in a yawn, & then quietly turning his back he loitered to another apartment— On the first evening of my stay at Clarence-Wood, I was thus engaged in taking observations of those around me—when the outer-door of the Hall in which we were gathered opened, and by a sudden hush I knew that somebody of importance had entered —The fellow was stern enough & held his head high enough—he looked neither to the right hand nor the left—in a minute he had crossed the hall and with long strides had ascended the staircase —he was a dark man & had on a light jacket—"What's to do with the Tiger?" said one "he's in a hurry this evening & mighty high." "That d————l Rosier has been down to fetch him" remarked a second. "Some doings between him & the great-Gun doubtless" —"The Great Gun dined alone to day" said an aid-de-camp. "They say a council of war is to be held to-night, are we going to Storm think you?" A hundred eyes lighted up. "Is Evesham doomed? MacTerroglen they say grows savage—Thornton and Enara—looked very solemn to-day"—"Arundel inspected the 19th himself—what if to-morrow or the day after—" "You find a mare's nest" interrupted Captain Percy. "What excitable imaginations we have—an Italian Desperado can't pass through a room without politely noticing the company present—but you conclude

the world is coming to an end"—"I own if the Gallant General
had bowed & looked civil; I would have made my will." In spite
of this damper, the hum of conjecture continued, but we will leave
them, reader, & make ourselves sure—

The dark man in the light jacket, having as I before said ascended
the staircase, stood in a lobby surrounded by many doors of many
rooms. he opened one of these & entered a large chamber, with a
wide & lofty state-bed—windows shrouded in blinds, crimson
carpets & curtains—& in four niches as many figures of marble,
each holding out a bright candlestick that glittered strongly
through the gloom—he passed on. there was a door at the farther
end, here he stopped & tapped gently—"Come in" said a voice—
The Dark Man entered—it was a small room with a large window
—looking towards the West—and though the sun was set yet the
room was suffused with a ruddy and doubtful glow, a little table
and a chair stood within the imbayed recess—on the table stood a
desk & in the chair sat a man—with a conspicuous nose, a pair of
endless legs—a blue coat & a black stock—this individual appeared
to be writing, but he relinquished his pen as the dark person entered—"Well Henri" he began "You see matters are drawing to a
crisis—our jewel* must be removed—don't you think her whim is
satisfied by this time?" "Certainly not, my Lord Duke, her sole
motive for insisting upon being brought to Evesham was to obtain
an interview with your Grace—you have not complied with her
request yet, I believe"—"Why no, but then she's such a little
viper and I can't be put out of the way by humouring her caprice"
—"Well, I am not going to press the matter further than your
Grace likes—but she'll starve herself to death if she's balked."
"Has she fallen desperately in love with me, Henri?" "I fear I
cannot flatter your Grace's vanity by answering in the affirmative." "There's the puzzle" continued his Grace, the light of such
a smile rising in his eyes as I never saw or imagined before in my
life. "If she were dying for love of me now, I should know how to
manage her—but really one is not prepared to meet such un-
natural crisises at the present—" General Fernando di Enara
blew his nose. "Your Grace is an infernal Fop" said he plainly—
The man with the conspicuous probosis threw back his head matted
with hair of the darkest chestnut & laughed. "I like a love-tryste,
Henri, you know" said he "But as for a hate-tryste—Lord, I don't
understand it." "Then your Grace may unravel it—I've seen you
work out enigmas quite as dark as that—You've had Œdipu's wit

* Louisa Vernon

in such matters ever since you were the height of a lance. I was in the West once, we are not friends of a day. The woods of Lismore Vale, young Douro?" "The woods of Lismore Vale, Fernando—" was the answer, while the eyes of the Duke firmly met those of his councillor—"More magical in breeze, sunshine & storm—than any other woods in the wide world. Do you think, Sir, that to my dying day I shall forget the aspect of their Glades and of their foliage silvered by moonlight?" "No, Lord Douro, you will not. midnight, moonlight & morning dawn—very romantic if you had had a coward to deal with—you might have out watched the stars* by yourself, but I used to wonder at & admire her for her truth—& you a mere boy—with your long hair over your shoulders." "I was a man." "A beardless one—rather different to what I see before me now—your Grace has gathered strength like a Giant. However, let us settle this piece of business. is the bird to fly back to Fort-Adrian without seeing you or not?" "Let her see me, I meant it all the while, but it's as well to speak roughly at the first—Go and fetch her, Enara." "I'll send her. your Grace will not want a third person." Enara left the room, & the Gentleman, rising from his chair, stood erect before the window—with a solemn & excited gaze he looked down towards Evesham, towards the placid Cirhala—bathing the dark fortress as softly, as calmly as if the summer twilight was still closing over it in peace unscared by Danger, by Storm & Annihilation hovering near—far of lay blue & dim the great Barrier of the Gibble-Kumri—& on the brow of the highest peak shone like a gem the Evening—the Western— Star—! I know not what expression disclosed itself like a beam of peculiar light over his face as he looked—something of softness stole away the reckless fire from his eye—he was momentarily subdued—. he watched that solitary star rise—& hang clear large & fixed over the hills—he drew from his breast an oval rimmed with gold—in soft enamel its centre represented a female head—a youthful lady with a white & clear forehead—eyes of full & tender gleam, hazel in colour, shaded away with dark-brown lashes— They looked on the spectator, that is, on the Duke—they sought his soul, his sympathy with serene entreaty—they seemed to say "I have laid on your breast and in your arms—Love me now— Do not forget me". To his mind they spoke so—he was overcome for a minute—"Mary! Mary!" said he "I cannot Forget you—It is useless saying so, you do not hear me, but unless God has designed me for a severe destiny, I will one day seal that assurance on your own lips—One comfort remains to me, the consciousness that

* A direct quote from Byron's *Manfred*

Charlotte Brontë's copy of Finden's engraving representing Marion Hume, Zamorna's first wife

The Countess of Jersey. Engraving by W. Finden after the painting by E. T. Parris

I can, by an hour's ardour, compensate to you for a year's neglect.
I wish that hour were come, I wish you were beside me, sitting
there within the grasp of this hand—utterly in my power—nothing
to sever—nothing to see us." The wish fiercely uttered by his
tongue kindled like a spark in his eyes—One would have thought
their glitter sprang from suppressed fury—and Fury was the feeling
at his heart. he desired something that he could not have, something that Time & distance veiled from his sight, something that
mountains & seas guarded from his grasp—his renown was vain,
his power, his intense passion—he imagined the bliss, but he could
not attain it—Recollection aided the fiend that disturbed him in a
mirror of wondrous truth, it showed him her image as he had seen
it a hundred times—young, pallid, seldom smiling, waiting his
approach in a saloon of gorgeous State—gnawed with Doubt till
his step comes surrounded with the morbid visions of love maddened to jealousy—visions that dissolved to rapture, when the
closing day at last darkened over him at her side. The Duke,
resigning his mind to the illusion, thought he at that hour looked
down on her fair cheek resting on his shoulder, met the adoration
of her eyes, felt the beating of her heart against his circling arm,
saw the pearls flutter on her heaving breast—& beheld the folds of
satin disclosing her exquisite form—with his whole enthusiastic
soul he loved her—it had been to him the delight of his life at times
to satisfy & soothe her intense idolatry—he was in the mood for
that benevolent office now—he had been toiling all day, his young
feelings had known no recreation for many a week—He cursed
War & ambition—Warner, if he had seen him at this moment,
would have gone half-frantic—His troops were arranged, his plans
were laid for an awful crisis. it was at hand and he was sick of it—
All this wild revulse of feeling passed in dead silence, maddened &
baffled—he turned away from the window, sank on to a sofa &
leaning back looked as still & white as a marble image—

Dusk drew softly on, a faint & golden reflection of the window fell
in moonlight on the floor—It fell likewise on something else—a
childish figure, clad in white, a creature with dark hair & Italian
eyes—Standing like a little spirit in the chamber—it had stolen in
noiselessly on as light & slender a foot as ever tripped in Titania's
ring. The apparition saw Zamorna, paused & gazed on him with
wondering solicitude—"Who is it?" she said in a tone awe had
subdued to the softest whisper—His Grace, who had watched her
with interest, answered only by the word "Caroline!"* "He knows

* Caroline Vernon, Northangerland's natural daughter and Zamorna's ward

me" exclaimed the child. "I must have got to the right room. it is the Duke." "Right" said the his Grace. "come here, child"—The little girl needed no second invitation—in trembling excitement she sprang into the tall Officer's arms—Her nature was seen at once—her whole constitutional turn of feeling revealed itself—She cried & shook, & in answer to some soothing endearment clasped him in her childish embrace—"Why Caroline" said he "It is a pity you and I never made acquaintance before—why do you cling to me so, child—I should think you never heard much good of me." "No, mamma hates you—but then I don't believe Papa does—and ever since I can remember I have heard stories about you, and Papa was your prime-minister"—"Yes Caroline, and since he left me, I have never had another—" "Did you like Papa? say you did, I never heard of anybody in my life who liked Papa except some ladies." "Ladies liked him best" replied the Duke smiling—"he never kept his word with men." "Did not he?" answered Caroline doubtfully—then looking up with recovered liveliness into Zamorna's face, she went on "Mamma told me you were a monster and a wicked man—but you have a pretty face, & how large your eyes are, they are like mine—yes, yes! just the same colour—" and she clapped her hands with joy at this discovery. Zamorna seated the lively little thing on his knee. gratified with this notice, she kissed his cheek as confidingly as if she had known him for years—The brightening moonlight, clearly revealed her features. that eye now bent on them, could distinctly trace even in their imperfect symmetry a foreign wildness, a resemblance which stirred sensations in his heart he would have died rather than yielded to—Sensations he had long thought routed out—but "Heat and Frost and Thunder had only withered the stems, the roots still remained". "Do you know where your father is, Caroline?" he asked. Fitful as April in her moods, she shook her head mournfully—"No—I never saw the place—but it is an Island far in the Sea—a very hot country, and Papa's house is in a solitary wood—I wish I might go there—I should so like to see—Papa—again, would not you?" Zamorna bit his lip and—pressed her gently to him—"Your Father and I, never—agree, we should quarrel very fiercely in a week's time." "Then you don't like papa—that's strange—for Lady Greville once told me, that a long while since—when there was a war in Angria, you and Papa were very great friends—and that in dark wet nights when the wind was blowing & the rain falling so fast that it—quenched your fires—you sometimes had to sleep together on moors—and if Papa was so cold that he could not go to sleep—you used to give him your cloak & lie without because you were younger & stronger than he was." "Nothwithstanding that, we quarrelled terribly then, Caroline." "It was very bad of you—you should have done as Papa wanted—but he said once you were as wilful with him as I am with Mamma—I don't do all mamma tells me, you know, because she contradicts herself." "Your Father does not contradict himself—but he contradicts *me*, and that is worse, Caroline." "Yes it is—I don't like to be contradicted—when I am a woman I'll do every thing in my own way." "You will make much such a woman as your half-sister Mary* I fancy—child, I could almost imagine it was her little hand that clasped mine so." "That's your wife—am I like your wife? when I'm old enough I'll marry you— I will, and I often tell mamma so—just to put her in a passion. are you ever angry with Mary?" "Ask herself, Caroline, when you see her—" "O, I should so like to see her, I never did—where does she live?" "She has no home till I come back—her home is just where you are at this moment, she would be happy in no other—" Caroline did not seem quite to comprehend—"Where I am at this moment—I am on your knee?" before her doubts could be solved, the door opened and gave admission to Caroline Vernon's mother—

This singular little woman, magnificently dressed, (indeed her toilet had evidently been elaborated for the occasion) paused at the threshold. "It is dark," she said "I dare not come in." "Why madam?" asked her royal jailer as coolly as if he & she had been acquaintances of a century—She uttered a slight exclamation at his voice—"Oh God—I feel frightened!" "Eh!" cried Caroline delightedly "There's going to be a scene!" "You feel frightened Madam?" replied the Duke. "In that case you may go back to your chamber—I wish to place no restraint on your inclinations." "No!" said she faintly "My courage will revive soon—meantime my conference with your Grace must be without witnesses— Caroline—go—and—ask Elise to put you to bed—" "Indeed ma' I won't—I must see how you and the Duke of Zamorna agree, must I not, Sir?" "My little damsel, your mother & I are so fond of each other we can't bear to be intruded on even by a fly— No, you must go." He attempted to put her off his knee, but she turned her head to his shoulder & began to whine—"Caroline, do as I bid you" said he gravely—the child, subdued by the tone of calm authority to which she was un-used, obeyed though still with reluctance—"I don't thank you, Mamma" said she as she passed

* The Duchess of Zamorna, Northangerland's daughter too

her mother in quitting the room—Lady Louisa with her own hand closed the door—she then glided forward again & stood so that her whole face & person received the radiance of a full & unclouded moon—Zamorna could not help smiling. The little Syren had dressed herself in what she knew suited her best, robes of pure white, that looked spiritual in that cold & silent beam—her hair was parted from her forehead in heavy bows as black as midnight. Her dark eyes were shining with unusual softness, she rolled them on him wet with tears. Zamorna looked—and though acquainted with all the depth of her craft, he could not steel his heart from an impulse of pity—"Lady Vernon" said he "Come here and tell me what you want." "Nothing" said she, approaching however almost close to his side. "What should Louisa want—when all she cares for is divided from her by seas of a thousand miles—a few months since, I had many desires—but captivity has—crushed them." "Humph" said the Duke, a little recovering from his momentary delusion. "So you came here merely to assure me that you were quite satisfied—stood in need of nothing—" "I didn't" said she, piqued exceedingly by his indifferent tone. "I didn't. I've been cruelly used and I'll tell the world so—" "In what respect madam?" "In every respect—That brute, that Enara, in whose— hands you placed me on purpose that I might be maltreated—he has made my life not worth preserving—" "Indeed," was the concise reply. "Yes indeed—I've had to scream out, so as to alarm the whole house, and his savage ferocity has thrown me into fits more than once." "Indeed" said the Duke again—"It's true I tell you" cried the Lady, clenching her little hand—"Do you doubt me—? Yes, you are on his side—you instigated him—I have no protector now my Alexander is taken away—O Percy, why did you leave me behind? what have I suffered since we parted!" "You may follow him Madam—you are at liberty this very evening to set out —I think it would be the best plan, yes, positively you shall go—I'll ring for your maid and order her to prepare"—He stretched his hand to the bell. with a start of unfeigned alarm, Lady Louisa snatched it away—"Surely my Lord—surely you're not jealous— I—I can't bear so long a voyage and the climate would not agree with me, it's scorching hot they say"—"O nonsense! you would be rid of your persecutors, you would be with your adored Percy— advantages I should think—which would amply compensate for any little inroads on your personal comfort—" "Yes, but then I should die—and the sun would burn me so brown, & it's a vile wattled house in a wood." Zamorna laughed aloud—"I've a good mind to make you go notwithstanding" said he. "It would be a

right punishment, madam, for your shrewishness—come, I'll ring
for Elise"—and again his hand touched the bell rope. she eagerly
seized it a second time—clasping it in both her own, she looked up
at him with a wild imploring gaze of terror. "My Lord, you won't
be so cruel, you're young & handsome—and if I have been spiteful
sometimes, I'm only a woman! you will forgive me?" "This prison's
no such bad place after all, Louisa, nor the Jailor so very brutal"
said his Grace, playing with her arts. "No, No, just be kind to me—
and you don't know how faithful and attached I can shew myself."
"Aye, but you hate me" continued the Duke. "Indeed, I don't, I
only said so—the fact is I think you are very—very handsome—"
Lady Vernon spoke for the moment with the fervor of truth—She
felt that his Grace, as he proudly smiled at her, the moonlight half
revealing his splendid features and his curls half shading them—
was indeed marvellously handsome—she felt that his eye, expressing in its large orb such paramount hauteur & yet such youthful fire, such reckless devotion to the sport of the hour—thrilled
her with inexpressible feelings when she met its glance—she hated
him still, she would have been glad to see him stretched a corpse
at her feet, but yet there was an enchaining interest in this moonlight conference, I speak according to nature it could not be otherwise—Now, if The Duke had been John Sneechie he would have
got up & left the room, but the Duke was Augustus Wellesley, so
he sat still & humoured her.

At no pains to conceal his contempt for the Opera-singer, he still
was, or seemed to be, a little taken with her whimsical fascinations
—he laughed when she told him he was handsome, and pushing
away one of the cushions on which he was lounging, made room
for her to sit by his side. "And so Louisa" said he "You don't
favour the scheme of emigrating to Monkey's Island*—what in the
world is it then that you want?" "My liberty, Zamorna, and my
own sweet Eden"—"Aye, the chance of poisoning a few of your
foes & of fermenting a tumult in the North—now don't be sentimental Vernon, don't assume enthusiasm & patriotism—for to tell
you a secret my duck, you know no more of those feelings than a
little Tigress does"—"What! do you say I don't love my country?"
cried she. "Do you say I don't love my beautiful Eden—I would
die to see its Groves again—" "Fudge!" interrupted his Grace,
with such a supreme & abrupt accent of disdain that she started
half-alarmed and wholly piqued at his bluntness—"What" she
asked, "Do you say I'm telling a lie?" "To be sure I do—a flat
* In the Gulf of Guinea, as featured in Branwell's map of the region

lie." "I'll scream" said her ladyship. "I will—you shan't insult me so with impunity." "Scream, Angel, if it will do you any good" returned his Grace—She burst into tears. "You're as hard as a stone" she said "and as cruel as a wild-beast, O what a fate I am doomed to—Oppression, outrage—all I love dead or banished— Alexander—Alexander—I wish you could hear me—!" and she wrung her hands as if in agony—"Too absurd" said Zamorna turning away—with that curl of his lip which expresses more contempt that the Stores of language can supply—"How *could* Northangerland bear such frantic folly?" "He could bear it, he adored it" exclaimed Vernon. "I was his Idol, he thought nothing in the world like me." "I am of the same opinion" remarked his Grace—"You treat me basely" said she, "You've decoyed me here just to torment me—I *must* scream"—She paused and looked at Zamorna to see what effect her words would produce. he seemed to have paid no attention to them—she started to her feet and uttered a frightful cry—it was such a one as from its shrill prolonged wildness could not but strike horror into all who heard it. before Zamorna could stop her, another, and another followed, louder, more urgently agonised—he was infuriated—he seized both her hands with a grasp like a vice—"By—G-d Madam" he said "Squeak again, and I will give you cause for the out-cry, as sure as you are a living woman—What, will you dare?" Silence— She looked, she trembled with rage—the hysterical & fiendish scream rattled in her throat—but she dared not—she swallowed it —she stood white & mute in Zamorna's gripe. Steps now approached, the door opened suddenly & lights & people entered— His Grace was nearly sick with mortification—"A delightful predicament" he muttered, "I wish I were shot—" he dropped Louisa from his arms & turned to the intruders—there were three, one was his own valet Rosier—that he didn't care for—the second —was General Enara, that too was no great matter—The Tiger knew his ways & besides being abundantly indulgent to them, never tattled. But the third—O Horror! was the sly, peering, apologizing, inquisitive figure of Lord Richton—With a bitter curse his Grace turned his back on them all—"The worst card I ever played in my life" he said. "Never was so caught & never was so innocent—" "I do beg your majesty's pardon" began Richton. "Really, 'pon honour, couldn't have imagined it—didn't know— there was a lady about the house—if I had been aware, wouldn't have noticed the exclamation upon any account." "I'll kill you" muttered the Duke without looking at him—"No, surely your Grace won't; it's no fault of mine but I must withdraw—Once

more I beg your majesty's pardon—" The Duke commanded him
to stay where he was—"Certainly, if your Grace requires my
services—but of necessity my presence must be superfluous." His
Grace, colouring high to the temples—broke out into a volley of
oaths—wild and strange—coined from the fury of the instant—this
rhetoric continued for five minutes—It concluded with—"Enara,
I appeal to you—what do you think & be d----d to you—"
Enara, whose brow exhibited an unruffled calm on the occasion,
answered—"Well, in truth your Grace I imagine her ladyship
was just singing out to you as she did to me once—the very first
time I saw her—she was rather put about with being captured &
when I entered the room & bowed to her—she set up such an
Alleluja I could have seen her decapitated without remorse.
General Thornton underwent the same ordeal a day or two after—
I introduced him to her on purpose, for the fact was I wanted a
companion—The poor lad was so hurt—he shed tears about it.
what a tale, he said, some malicious folks might make up & send to
Julia"—Zamorna, in spite of his vexation, could not suppress a
laugh—"Be off—" he said "every one of you. Eugene, say your
prayers, for I shall very likely annihilate you to night—Richton,
stay a moment—if you ever dare to mock at me about this adventure, or to snivel insinuations concerning it to other people—I'll
try the blanket exercise again—as sure as you live, I will—" Richton
bowed, leered with inexpressible significance at the young Duke
and left the room—the others followed—

Thus relieved from their presence—he turned, his cheek still
flushed, his eyes still flashing—to lady Vernon—who had sunk
helpless into a seat nearly fainting with fear—for though always
bringing alarms on herself, nobody yields more impotently than
she does to their pressure—"Well madam" he said "How do you
think I ought to repay you for that nice little exhibition?" "O my
lord, spare me—I won't do it again—but it's my way, I can't help
it, don't—don't hurt me, I'm so afraid of pain—" "Hurt you,
little viper—I have no wish to touch you, I'll send you off to bed
in a minute—only listen—tomorrow you leave Evesham peremp-
torily—you shall go back properly attended & guarded to Fort-
Adrian, & there you shall stay till I return—or—die." She clasped
her hands & held them up as if to avert the sentence. "No—No—
don't send me away—I can't live indeed in that dark castle—
Zamorna—Zamorna hear me!" Zamorna was about to leave the
room, his hand was on the door-lock—her moan of despair arrested
him—he turned back—"Why madam" said he "You cannot stay

here—in less than a week all will be in confusion—I cannot undertake to hamper myself with such a charge as you—if Mac-Terroglen
catches you, he'll eat you up at one mouthful—Look up & speak
rationally." "I'm so miserable" she said, sobbing aloud—"Nobody
in the world cares for me—Nobody wants me to live with them and
I dare not live alone—It's half a year since I've heard a kind word
or seen the face of anybody that wishes me well"—"Is that my
fault?" asked his Grace. "No, but drowning people catch at straws
—In other words, I wish you would be kind to me." "Come here
then" said he, she obeyed him. "Now will you be good? are you
sorry for your possessed conduct this evening—?" "Yes, very."
"Are you sorry for having tormented me when I was a prisoner, a
man in misfortune—detested, broken-down, looking forward to
nothing but death—" "I am, I really am"—"Will you quietly
take your departure tomorrow—without screaming?"—"That's
hard; but if MacTerroglen should take me, it would be dreadful—
yes, yes—I will." "Soh! we're friends, give me a kiss"—Louisa leant
forward, he was sitting; she was—standing by him—She put his
curls from his brow & kissed him as tenderly as if she loved him—
she did love him at that moment—though a quarter of an hour
before she had hated him—"You may write to Percy as often as
you like" continued his Grace in a comforting tone—"And you
may amuse yourself by walking on the terrace at Fort-Adrian—&
looking at the pictures & busts, in my room—you may even
rummage in my cabinet if you will, and my books—there are the
keys—if you've a fancy for a sail, Ryan O'Neil will row you and
Caroline out in the barge—come, no doubt we shall find plenty of
amusement. Keep in a good temper & let politics alone, & you'll
be a clever little shrew enough—Good night—" "Don't go yet"
said Lady Vernon "I begin to like you—" But his Grace was
already gone—and in less than five minutes she was storming at
him in as frantic a paroxysm of resentment—as had ever before
irritated her ungoverned mind. Happily however he could not hear
her for she lay flung on the bed in her own chamber—bathed in the
tears & trembling with the starts of passion—Caroline, roused
from her sleep, tried to console her & so did Elise, but she would
listen to neither—till the body, at last fretted to exhaustion by its
wild & fiery spirit—sank sobbing asleep to repose.

Reader, to-morrow I leave Evesham, it becomes no longer a safe
place for an easy Civillian like me to sojourn in. Lord Macara
Lofty accompanys me—we have booked ourselves at the Union-
Coach-office for two outside places to Verdopolis—What may take

place after our departure I know not—but rumours such as men scarce dare whisper above their breath, are thickening daily— Good bye Reader, 'tis a sweet evening. Can such lovely summer days forebode the advent of a Storm?————————Such a Storm!

C Brontë—June 29th 1837

MINA LAURY

INTRODUCTION

This narrative, left untitled by its author, has tended to be known as Mina Laury II *by cataloguers for the sake of convenience, because of the previous sketch in* Passing Events *in which Mina Laury also figures. She had, as it happens, figured in several previous Angrian sketches written both by Charlotte and Branwell Brontë as far back as 1834, when Zamorna wishing to repudiate his child-wife, Marian Hume, in favour of Mary Percy, committed the care of his son by Marian, Ernest Fitz-Arthur, to Mina Laury. How faithful she was to her charge appears in the present manuscript, when the child is butchered by the King's enemies. Branwell had previously recounted his death in a narrative of 1836, and was followed by Charlotte in two subsequent episodes:* Zamorna's Exile *("And when you left me"—verses dated July 1836) and* Zamorna's Return *(1837–8). When Zamorna sailed into exile, Mina Laury boarded his ship at Marseilles, and though he spurned her in the established Byronic manner, she clung to him in the equally established manner of Claire Claremont, and nursed him through his tribulations. On his clandestine return, she tracked him through France and warned his faithful partisans of his coming, when their support gave him the victory over Northangerland's party and he regained his kingdom. The Duke's leniency towards his father-in-law, despite his past treachery, is the subject of the heated dispute between Zamorna and his prime minister, Howard Warner, in the present narrative.*

The manuscript provides a further example of Charlotte's repeated use of old material from which she felt the maximum effect had not previously been wrung, in the incident of the overturned carriage, which she later elaborated in Villette *in the mortal accident to Miss Marchmont's lover.*

Mina Laury II *was written six months after* Julia, *in the Christmas holidays in January 1838. The author's farewell to her readers at the end of the manuscript marked also the end of her holidays, 17 January, when she had to return to school for another half-year. The work, as it stands, marks the author's advance in technique, especially in narrative flow, as is evident in her greater ability to connect the episodes in her tale, and not use them merely, as heretofore in* Passing Events *and* Julia, *as reportages on a changing theme. Here, though the scene shifts from Alnwick to Hartford House, and thence to Rivaulx and back again, the action is one, and the central interest is the love of Mina Laury for the faithless Zamorna, never lost.*

The author's greatest ability to analyse feeling, and to give it expression,

*is evident also in her treatment of love, which already foreshadows
in penetration and honesty the mature studies of woman's passion in*
Jane Eyre *and* Villette. *Mina's feelings for Zamorna, we read, "were
so fervid and glowing in colour that they effaced everything else—I lost
the power . . . of discerning the difference between right and wrong . . .
Zamorna . . . was sometimes more to me than a human being, he superseded all things, all affections, all interests, all fears and hopes or principles. Unconnected with him my mind would be a blank . . ." This is
language and a state of feeling scarcely inferior to the Brontës at their
best, evocative even of Catherine Earnshaw who realised that she loved
Heathcliff not because he was handsome, but because "he's more myself
than I am. Whatever our souls are made of, his and mine are the same . . ."*

*The tale is told in straight narration, perhaps the first of Charlotte
Brontë's early narratives to be so, and the personality of her busy chronicler
and prototype, Charles Townshend, is dropped.*

The manuscript of Mina Laury II *is currently in the possession of Mr
Robert H. Taylor, by whose kind permission it is printed here. It has
previously been published in its entirety, but with edited spelling, punctuation
and paragraphing, from C. W. Hatfield's transcript of the original manuscript (then in the Law Collection) in F. E. Ratchford's* Legends of
Angria *(Yale University Press, 1933). A short section of the text (again
in edited form) was published in Hatfield and Shorter's* The Twelve
Adventurers *(1925) and also in Phyllis Bentley's edition of* Tales from
Angria *(Collins, 1954).*

MINA LAURY

The last scene in my last book concluded within the walls of Alnwick House*—and the first scene in my present volume opens in the
same place. I have a great partiality for morning pictures—there
is such a freshness about every-body & everything before the
toil of the day has worn them—When you descend from your
bed-room—the parlour looks so clean—the fire so bright—the
hearth so polished—the furnished breakfast-table so tempting—
All these attractions are diffused over the oak-pannelled room—
with the glass-door—to which my readers have before had frequent
admission—The cheerfulness within is enhanced by the dreary,
wildered look of all without—the air is dimmed with snow
careering through it in wild whirls—the sky is one mass of congealed tempest—heavy, wan & icy—the trees rustle their frozen
branches against each other in a blast bitter enough to flay alive
the flesh that should be exposed to its sweep—but hush! the people
of the house are up, I hear a step on the stairs, let us watch the
order in which they will collect in the breakfast room—first by
himself comes an individual in a furred morning-gown of crimson
damask with his shirt collar open and neck-cloth thrown by—his
face fresh & rather rosy than otherwise, partly perhaps with health,
but chiefly with the cold water with which he has been performing
his morning's ablutions, his hair fresh from the toilette—plenty of
it & carefully brushed & curled—his hands clean & white &
visibly cold as icicles—he walks to the fire rubbing them—he
glances towards the window, meantime whistles as much as to say
"it's a rum morning"—He then steps to a side-table, takes up a
newspaper of which there are dozens lying folded & fresh from the
post-man's bag—he throws himself into an arm-chair & begins to
read—Meantime another step & a rustle of silks—In comes the
Countess Zenobia with a white gauze turban over her raven curls
& a dress of grey—"Good morning Arthur" she says in her cheerful
tone—such as she uses when all's right with her—"Good morning
Zenobia" answers the Duke getting up—and they shake hands &
stand together on the rug—"What a morning it is" he continues.
"How the snow drifts—if it were a little less boisterous I would
make you come out & have a snow-balling match with me—just
to whet your appetite for breakfast—" "Aye" said the Countess,

* The home of the Percys

"We look like two people adapted for such childs-play, don't we?" and she glanced with a smile first at the great blethering King of Angria (see Harlaw) and then at her own comely & portly figure. "You don't mean to insinuate that we are too stout for such exercise" said his majesty. Zenobia—laughed. "I am at any rate" said she. "Your Grace is in most superb condition—what a chest!" "This will never do" returned the Duke, shaking his head— "Wherever I go they compliment me on my enlarged dimensions. I must take some measures for reducing them within reasonable bounds—Exercise & Abstinence, that's my motto—"—"No Adrian—let it be Ease & Plenty" said a much softer voice replying to his Grace—a third person had joined the pair & was standing a little behind—for she could not get her share of the fire—being completely shut out—by the Countess with her robes & the Duke with his morning-gown—this person seemed but a little & slight figure when compared with these two robust individuals, & as the Duke drew her in between them—that she might at least have a sight of the glowing hearth, she was almost lost in the contrast. "Ease & Plenty!" exclaimed his Grace—"So you would have a man mountain for your husband at once—" "Yes, I should like to see you really very stout—I call you nothing now—quite slim— scarcely filled up—" "That's right" said Zamorna, "Mary always takes my side—" Lady Helen Percy* now entered—& shortly after her, the earl with slow steps in silence took his place at the breakfast-table. The meal proceeded in silence—Zamorna was reading—newspaper after newspaper he opened, glanced over & threw on the floor—One of them happened to fall over lord Northangerland's foot, it was very gently removed as if there was contamination in the contact. "An Angrian print I believe" murmered the Earl. "Why do they bring such things to the House?"— "They are my papers" answered his son-in-law—swallowing at the same moment—more at one mouthful than would have sufficed his father for the whole repast. "Yours! what do you read them for? to give you an appetite?—if so they seem to have answered their end—Arthur—I wish you would masticate your food better—" "I have not time, I'm very hungry—I eat but one meal all yesterday—" "Humph—and now your making up for it I suppose—but pray put that newspaper away—" "No, I wish to learn what my loving subjects are saying about me." "and what are they saying, pray?" "Why, here is a respectable Gentleman who announces that he fears his beloved monarch is again under the influence of that baleful Star whose ascendancy has already

* Nothangerland's mother

produced such fatal results to Angria—wishing to be witty, he calls it the North Star—another insinuates that their Gallant Sovereign, though a Hector in war, is but a Paris in peace—He talks something about Samson & Delilah—Hercules & the distaff—& hints darkly at the evils of petticoat Government—a hit at you, Mary— a third mutters threateningly of hoary old ruffians who, worn-out with age & excess—sit like Bunyan's Giant Pope at the entrance of their Dens & strive by menace or promise to allure passengers within the reach of their bloody talons—" "Is that me?" asked the earl quietly. "I've very little Doubt of it" was the reply. "and there is a fourth-Print, the War-Despatch, noted for the ardour of its sentiments, which growls a threat concerning the power of Angria to elect a new Sovereign whenever she is offended with her old one—Zenobia, another cup of coffee if you please—" "I suppose you're frightened" said the Earl. "I shake in my shoes" replied the Duke—"However, there are two old sayings that somewhat cheer me—"More noise than work"—"Much cry & little wool", very applicable when properly considered, for I always called the Angrians Hogs & who am I except the Devil that shears them?"

Breakfast had been over for about a quarter of an hour—the room was perfectly still—The Countess & Duchess were reading those papers Zamorna had dropped—Lady Helen was writing to her son's Agent—the Earl was pacing the room in a despondent mood —as for the Duke no one well knew where he was or what he was doing—he had taken himself off however—Erelong his step was heard descending the staircase, then his voice in the Hall giving orders, & then he re-entered the breakfast-room but no longer in morning costume—he had exchanged his crimson damask robe for a black coat & checked pantaloons—he was wrapped up in a huge blue cloak with a furred collar—a light fur cap rested on his brow—his gloves were held in his hands—in short, he was in full travelling costume—"Where are you going?" asked the Earl, pausing in his walk—"To Verdopolis & from thence to Angria" was the reply—"To Verdopolis in such weather" exclaimed the Countess, glancing towards the wild whitened tempest that whirled without—Lady Helen looked up from her writing— "Ab[s]urd, my Lord Duke, you do not mean what you say—" "I do, I must go—the carriage will be at the door directly—I'm come to bid you all good-bye—" "And what is all this haste about?" returned Lady Helen rising—"There is no haste in the business madam—I've been here a week—I intended to go to-day." "You never said anything about your intention." "No, I did not think of mentioning it—but they are bringing the carriage round. Good morning, Madam"—he took lady Helen's hand & saluted her as he always does at meeting & parting—then he passed to the Countess —"Good-bye Zenobia, come to Ellrington House as soon as you can persuade our friend to accompany you—" He kissed her too— the next in succession was the Earl. "Farewell, Sir, & be d———d to you—will you shake hands?" "No—you always hurt me so— Good morning—I hope you won't find your masters quite so angry as you expect them to be, but you do right not to delay attending to their mandates. I'm sorry I have been the occasion of your offending them." "Are we to part in this way?" asked the Duke "& won't you shake hands?"—"No!" Zamorna coloured highly, but turned away & put on his gloves—the Barouche stood at the door, the Groom & the valet were waiting, & the Duke, still with a clouded countenance—was proceeding to join them when his wife came forwards. "You have forgotten me, Adrian—" she said in a very quiet tone—but her eye meantime flashed expressively— He started—for in truth he had forgotten her, he was thinking about her father—"Good bye then, Mary" he said, giving her a hurried kiss & embrace—She detained his hand. "Pray how long am I to stay here?" she asked. "Why do you leave me at all? why am I not to go with you?—" "It is such weather" he answered— "When this storm passes over I will send for you—" "When will that be?" pursued the Duchess, following in his steps as he strode into the hall. "Soon—soon my love—perhaps in a day or two— there now—don't be unreasonable—of course you cannot go to day—" "I can & I will" answered the Duchess quickly—"I have had enough of Alnwick, you shall not leave me behind you." "Go into the room, Mary—the door is open & the wind blows on you far too keenly—Don't you see how it drifts the snow in—" "I will not go into the room—I'll step into the carriage as I am—if you refuse to wait till I can prepare—perhaps you will be humane enough to let me have a share of your cloak—" She shivered as she spoke—her hair & her dress floated in the cold blast that blew in through the open entrance—strewing the hall with snow & dead leaves—His Grace, though he was rather stern, was not quite negligent of her—for he stood so as to screen her in some manner from the draught—"I shall not let you go, Mary" he said "So there is no use in being perverse—" The Duchess regarded him with that troubled anxious glance peculiar to herself—"I wonder why you wish to leave me behind you" she said—"Who told you I wished to do so?" was his answer—"Look at that weather & tell

me if it is fit for a delicate little woman like you to be exposed to?"
"Then" murmured the Duchess wistfully, glancing at the January
Storm "You might wait till it is milder—I don't think it will do
your Grace any good to be out to day—" "But I must go, Mary—
the Christmas Recess is over & business presses—" "Then do take
me, I am sure I can bear it." "Out of the question—you may well
clasp those small, silly hands—so thin I can almost see through
them—and you may well shake your curls over your face—to hide
its paleness from me I suppose—What is the matter? crying?
Good! What the d———l am I to do with her?—Go to your father
Mary, he has spoilt you—" "Adrian, I cannot live at Alnwick
without you" said the Duchess earnestly—"It recalls too forcibly
the very bitterest days of my life—I'll not be separated from you
again except by violence—" She took hold of his arm with one
hand, while with the other she was hastily wiping away the tears
from her eyes—"Well, it will not do to keep her any longer in this
hall" said the Duke, & he pushed open a side-door which led into
a room that, during his stay, he had appropriated for his study—
there was a fire in it & a sofa drawn to the hearth—there he took
the Duchess—& having shut the door—recommenced the task of
persuasion—which was no very easy one—for his own false-play,
his alienations & his unnumbered treacheries had filled her mind
with hideous phantoms of jealousy—had weakened her nerves—
& made them a prey to a hundred vague apprehensions, fears
that never wholly left her except when she was actually in his arms
or at least in his immediate presence—"I tell you, Mary" he said,
regarding her with a smile half expressive of fondness—half of
vexation—"I tell you I will send for you in two or three days—"
"And will you be at Wellesley-House when I get there—you said
you were going from Verdopolis to Angria?" "I am, & probably I
shall be a week in Angria, not more—" "A week! and your Grace
considers that but a short time—to me it will be most wearisome,
however I must submit—I know it is useless to oppose your Grace
—but I could go with you—and you should never find me in the
way—I am not often intrusive on your Grace—" "The horses will
be frozen if they stand much longer—" returned the Duke, not
heeding her last remark—"Come, wipe your eyes & be a little
philosopher for once—There, let me have one smile before I go—
A week will be over directly—this is not like setting out for a campaign—" "Don't forget to send for me in two days" pleaded the
Duchess as Zamorna released her from his arms—"No, No, I'll
send for you to-morrow—if the weather is settled enough—and"
half mimicking her voice "Don't be jealous of me, Mary—unless

you're afraid that the superior charms of Enara & Warner & Kirkwall & Richton & Thornton will seduce me from my allegiance to a certain fair-complexioned, brown-eyed young woman in whom you are considerably interested—Good-bye—" He was gone—she hurried to the window—he passed it—in three minutes the barouche swept with muffled sound round the lawn—shot down the carriage road & was quickly lost in the thickening whirl of the snow-storm—

Late at night the Duke of Zamorna reached Wellesley-House—his journey had been much delayed by the repeated change of horses which the state of the roads rendered necessary—so heavy & constant had been the falls of snow all day that in many places they were almost blocked up—he and his valet had been more than once obliged to alight from the carriage & walk through the deep drifts far above the knee—Under such conditions any other person would have stopped for the night at some of the numerous excellent hotels which skirt the way, but his Grace is well known to be excessively pig-headed—and the more obstacles are thrown in the way of any scheme he wishes to execute—the more resolute he is in pushing on to the attainment of his end—In the prosecution of his journey he had displayed a particular wilfulness—In vain, when he had alighted at some Inn to allow time for a change of horses— Rosier had hinted the propriety of a longer stay—in vain he had recommended some more substantial refreshment than the single glass of Madeira & the half-biscuit wherewith his noble master tantalized rather than satisfied the cravings of a rebellious appetite —at last, leaving him to the enjoyment of obstinacy & starvation in a large Saloon of the Inn—which his Grace was traversing with strides that derived their alacrity partly from nipping cold & partly from impatience—Eugene himself had sought the traveller's room &, while he devoured a chicken with Champagne, he had solaced himself with the muttered ejaculation "Let him starve & be d---d"—Flinging himself from the barouche, the Duke, in no mild mood, passed through his lighted Halls whose echoes were still prolonging the last strokes of mid-night—pealed from the House-bell just as the carriage drew up under the portico— Zamorna seemed not to heed the call to immediate repose which that sound conveyed—for, turning as he stood on the first landing-place of the wide white marble stairs, with a bronze lamp pendant above him & a statue standing in calm contrast to his own figure— he called out "Rosier—I wish Mr Warner to attend me instantly— see that a messenger be despatched to Warner Hotel—" "To night

does your Grace mean?" said the valet—"Yes Sir." Monsieur
Rosier reposed his tongue in his cheek but hastened to obey—
"Hutchinson—send your deputy directly—you heard his Grace's
orders—& Hutchinson, tell the cook to send a tumbler of hot negus
into my room—I want something to thaw me—& tell her to toss
me up a nice hot petit souper—a fricandeau de veau or an omlette,
& carry my compliments to Mr Greenwood & say I shall be happy
to have the honour of his company in my salon half an hour hence
—& above all things, Hutchinson"—here the young Gentleman
lowered his tone to a more confidential key—"Give Mademoiselle
Harriette a hint that I am returned—very ill you may say, for I've
got a cursed sore throat with being exposed to this night air—Ah,
there she is, I'll tell her myself—" As the omnipotent Eugene
spoke—a young lady carrying a china ewer appeared crossing the
gallery—which ran round this inner hall—The French Garçon
skipped up the stairs like a flea—"Ma belle" he exclaimed "per-
mettez moi porte cette cruse-là." "No, monsieur, no" replied the
young lady laughing & throwing back her head which was covered
with very handsome dark hair finely curled—"I will carry it—it is
for the Duke—" "I must assist you" returned the gallant Rosier, &
then "I shall earn a kiss for my services"—but the damsel resisted
him & stepping back shewed to better advantage a pretty foot and
ankle well displayed by a short full petticoat of pink muslin & still
shorter apron of black silk—she had also a modest handkerchief of
thin lace on her neck—She wore no cap, had good eyes & comely
features—had a plump round figure—A very interesting love scene
was commencing in the seclusion of the Gallery—when a bell
rung very loudly—"God! it's the Duke" exclaimed Rosier—he
instantly released his mistress—& she shot away like an arrow—
towards the inner chambers—Eugene followed her very cautiously
—somewhat jealously perhaps—Threading her path through a
labyrinth of intermediate rooms—she came at last to the royal
Chamber & thence a door opened direct to the royal dressing-
room—his Grace was seated in an arm-chair by his mirror—an
enormous one taking him in from head to foot—he looked cursedly
tired & somewhat wan, but the lights & shadows of the fire were
playing about him with an animating effect—"Well Harriet" he
said as the housmaid entered his presence—"I wanted that water
before—put it down & pour me out a glass—what made you so
long in bringing it?—" Harriet blushed as she held the refreshing
draught to her royal master's parched lips (he was too lazy to take
it himself), she was going to stammer out some excuse but meantime the Duke's eye had reverted to the door & caught the dark

vivacious aspect of Rosier—"Ah" he said "I see how it is—well Harriet, mind what you're about—no giddiness—you may go now—& tell your swain to come forwards on pain of having his brains converted into paste—" Eugene strutted in, humming aloud —in no sort abashed or put to the blush—When Harriet was gone, the Duke proceeded to lecture him—the Valet meantime coolly aiding him in the change of his travelling dress, arrangement of his hair, &c. "Dog" began the Saintly Master "take care how you conduct yourself towards that Girl, I'll have no improprieties in my house, none—" "If I do but follow your Grace's example I cannot be guilty of improprieties" snivelled the valet who, being but too well acquainted with many of his master's adventures, is sometimes permitted a freedom of speech few others would attempt. "I'll make you marry her at all risks if you once engage her affections" pursued Zamorna. "Well' replied Rosier "If I do marry her and if I don't like her, I can recompense myself for the sacrifice—" "Keep within your allotted limits, my lad" remarked the Duke quietly—"What does your Grace mean—matrimonial limits or limits of the tongue—?" "Learn to discern for yourself—" returned his master, enforcing the reply by a manual application that sent Monsieur to the other side of the room—He speedily gathered himself up & returned to his employment of combing out the Duke's long and soft curls of dark brown hair—"I have a particular interest in your Harriet" remarked Zamorna benevolently—"I can't say that the other handmaids of the House often cross my sight—but now and then I meet that nymph in a gallery or passage—and she always strikes me as being very modest & correct in her conduct"—"She was first bar-maid at Stancliffe's Hotel in Zamorna not long since" insinuated Rosier—"I know she was, Sir, I have reason to remember her in that station. she once gave me a draught of cold water—when there was not another human being in the world who would have lifted a finger to do me even that kindness—" "I've heard mademoiselle tell that story" replied Eugene—"It was when your Grace was taken prisoner of war before Mac-Terroglen, & she told how your Grace rewarded her afterwards when you stopped six months's ago at Stancliffe's— & gave her a certificate of admission to the Royal household—and into the bargain, if mademoiselle speaks truth, your Grace gave her a kiss from your own royal lips—" "I did & be d———d to you, Sir—the draught of water she gave me & the gush of kind-hearted tears that followed it were cheaply rewarded by a kiss—" "I should have thought so" replied Rosier "but perhaps she did not— Ladies of title sometimes pull each others ears for your Grace's

kisses so I don't know how a simple bar-maid would receive them
—" "Eugene, your nation have a penchant for suicide—go & be
heroic" returned Zamorna—"If your Grace has done with me I
will obey your wishes & immediately seek my quietus in a plate of
ragout of paradise & such delicate claret as the vintages of La belle
France yield when they are in a good humour—" As the illustrious
valet withdrew from the presence of his still more illustrious master,
a different kind of personage entered by another door—A little
man enveloped in a fur cloak—he put it off and, glancing round
the room, his eye settled upon Zamorna—Released from the cum-
brous costume of his journey, Zamorna was again envelloped in
his crimson damask robe—half-inclined on the mattress of a low &
hard couch, his head of curls preparing to drop on to the pillow—
& one hand just drawing up the coverlet of furs & velvet—Warner
beheld him in the act of seeking his nights repose—"I thought your
Grace wanted me on business!" exclaimed the minister "& I find
you in bed!" Zamorna stretched his limbs, folded his arms across
his chest, buried his brow, cheek & dark locks in the pillow, & in a
faint voice requested Warner to arrange the coverlet for he was too
tired to do it—The premier's lip struggled to repress a smile—this
was easily done, for the said lip was unaccustomed to that relaxation—"Has your Majesty dismissed Monsieur Rosier—& have
you sent for me to fulfil the duties of that office he held about your
majesty's person?"—"There—I'm comfortable" said the Duke—
as the drapery fell over him, arranged to his satisfaction—"pray,
Warner, be seated." Warner drew close to his Grace's bedside an
arm-chair & threw himself into it—"What" said he "have you
been doing?—you look extremely pale—have you been raking?
—" "God forgive you for the supposition—no, I have been fagging
myself to death for the good of Angria." "For the good of Angria,
my Lord! Aye, truly, there you come to the point—& it is, I
suppose, for the good of Angria that you go to Alnwick & spend a
week in the sickroom of lord Northangerland." "How dutiful of
me, Howard! I hope my subjects admire me for it." "My lord
Duke, do not jest—the feeling which has been raised by that ill-
advised step is no fit subject for levity—what a strange mind is
yours—which teaches you to rush headlong into those very errors
which your enemies are always attributing to you—it is in vain that
you now & then display a splendid flash of talent when the
interstices, as it were, of your political life are filled up with such
horrid bungling as this—" "Be easy Howard—what harm have I
done?" "My lord, I will tell you—has it not ever been the bitterest
reproach in the mouth of your foes that you are a weak man liable

to be influenced & controlled—have not Ardrah & Montmorenci
a thousand times affirmed that Northangerland guided, ruled, infatuated you? They have tried to bring that charge home to you—
to prove it—but they could not—& you, with all christian charity,
have taken the trouble off their hands—you have proved it beyond
dispute or contradiction." "As how, my dear Howard?" "My
lord, you see it, you feel it yourself—in what state was Angria last
year at this time? you remember it, laid in ashes—Plague & famine
& slaughter struggling with each other which should sway the
sceptre that disastrous war had wrested from your own hand—and
I ask my lord, who had brought Angria to this state?" "Northangerland!" replied Zamorna promptly—"Your Grace as spoken
truly—& knowing this, was it weakness or was it wickedness which
led you to the debauched Traitor's couch & taught you to bend
over him with the tenderness of a son to a kind father?" Warner
paused for an answer, but none came—he continued "That the
man is dying I have very little doubt—dying in that premature
decay brought on by excesses such as would have disgraced any
nature—aye, even that of an unreasoning beast—but ought you
not to have let him meet Death alone—in that passion of anguish
& desolation which is the just meed for crime, for depravity like
his?—What call was there for you to go and count his pulses? can
you prolong their beat? Why should you mingle your still pure
breath with his last contaminated gasps—can you purify that
breath which Debauchery has so sullied? why should you comit
your young hand to the touch of his clammy nerveless fingers? can
the contact infuse vitality into his veins or vigour into his sinews?
Had you not the strength of mind to stand aloof & let him who has
lived the slave of vice, die the victim of Disease?—" The Duke of
Zamorna raised himself on his elbow—"Very bad language this,
Howard" said he "And it won't do—I know very well what the
Reformers and the Constitutionalists & my own opinionated &
self-complacent Angrians have been saying because I chose to
spend my Christmas recess at Alnwick—I knew beforehand what
they would say—& above all I knew in particular what you would
say—Now it was not in defiance of either public or private opinion
that I went—neither was it from the working of any un-controllable
impulse—no, the whole matter was the result of mature reflection
—My Angrians have certain rights over me—so have my ministers
—I also have certain rights independent of them, independent of
any living thing under the the firmament of Heaven! I claim the
possession of my reason—I am neither insane nor idiotic, whatever
the all-accomplished Harlaw may say to the contrary—& in two

or three things I will, whilst I retain that valuable possession, judge for myself—one of these is the degree of intimacy which I choose to maintain with lord Northangerland—In a public sense I have long done with him—the alienation cost me much—for in two or three particular points his views & mine harmonized, & neither could hope to find a substitute for the other in the whole earth beside—However, though it was like tearing up something whose roots had taken deep hold in my very heart of hearts—the separation was made—& since it was finally completed, by what glance or look or word have I sighed for a reunion?—I have not done so & I cannot do so—My path I have struck out & it sweeps far away out of sight of his—The rivers of blood Angria shed last year & the hills of cold carnage which she piled up before the shrine of Freedom—effectually, eternally divide Northangerland's spirit from mine—But in the body we may meet—we shall meet—till death interposes—I say, Warner, no sneers of my Foes nor threats for my friends—no murmurs from my subjects shall over-rule me in this matter—Howard, you are a different man from Northangerland, but let me whisper to you this secret—you also love to control & if you could, you would extend the energies of that keen haughty mind—till they surrounded me & spell-bound my will & actions within a magic circle of your own creating—it will not do, it will not do!—hate Northangerland if you please—abhor him, loathe him, you have a right to do so—he has more than once treated you brutally—spoken of you grossly. if you feel so inclined & if an opportunity should offer, you have a right to pistol him—but, Sir, do not dare to impose your private feelings on me—to call upon me to avenge them—do it yourself—in you the action would be justifiable—in me dastardly—Neither will I bend to Ardrah or to the defiled Cuckold Montmorenci—I will not, at their bidding, give up the best feelings of a very bad nature—I will not crush the only impulses that ennable me to be endured by my fellow-men. I will not leave the man who was once my *comrade*—my *friend*—to die in unrelieved agony because Angria mutinies & Verdopolis sneers—my heart, my hand, my energies belong to the Public—my feelings are my own—talk no more on the subject—" Warner did not—he sat & gazed in silence on his master who, with closed eyes & averted head, seemed composing himself to slumber—At last, he said aloud "A false step, a false step, I would die on the word—" Zamorna woke from his momentary doze—"You have papers for me to sign & look over, I dare say Howard—give me them—I wish to despatch arrears to-night as it is my intention to set-off for Angria—I wish to ascertain in person

the state of feeling there & to turn it into its legitimate channel."
Warner produced a green bag well filled—the Duke raised himself
on his couch &, collecting his wearied faculties, proceeded to the
task—a silence of nearly an hour ensued—broken only by occasional monosyllables from the King & minister as papers were
presented & returned—at length Warner locked the padlock with
which the bag was secured, & saying "I recommend your Majesty
to sleep"—rose to reassume his cloak—"Warner" said the Duke
with an appearance of nonchalance—"Where is lord Hartford?
I have seen nothing of him for sometime—" "Lord Hartford? my
lord! lord Hartford is a fool & affects delicacy of the lungs—his
health, forsooth, is in too precarious a state to allow of any attention to public affairs & he is withdrawn to Hartford-Hall there to
nurse his maudlin folly in retirement—" "What? the maudlin
folly of being ill? you are very unsparing, Howard—" "Ill, Sir—
the man is as strong & sound as you are—all trash. It is the effects
of his ruling passion, Sir, which will pursue him—to hoary age I
suppose—Lord Hartford is love sick, my lord Duke—the superannuated Profligate." "Did he tell you so?" "No—indeed he
dared not—but lord Richton insinuated as much in his gossipy
way—I will cut lord Hartford, Sir—I despise him, he ought to be
sent to Coventry—" "How very bitter you are, Warner—be more
moderate. meantime—Good-night—" "I wish your Grace a very
Good-night—take care that you sleep soundly & derive refreshment—from your slumbers." "I will do my best" replied the Duke
laughing—Warner, having clasped on his cloak, with-drew—Could
he have watched unseen by the couch of his master for two hours
longer—he would have repined at the hidden feeling that prevented the lids from closing over those dark & restless eyes—Long
Zamorna lay awake, neither Youth, nor health, nor Weariness
could woo sleep to his pillow—he saw his lamp expire—he saw the
brilliant flame of the hearth settle into ruddy embers—then fade,
decay & at last perish—he felt silence & total darkness close around
him—but still the unslumbering eye wandered over images which
the fiery imagination pourtrayed upon vacancy—thought yielded
at last & sleep triumphed—Zamorna lay in dead repose amidst the
hollow darkness of his chamber — — —

Lord Hartford sat by himself after his solitary dinner with a
decanter of Champagne & a half filled glass before him—there
was also a newspaper spread out on which his elbow leaned and
his eye rested—The noble lord sat in a large dining-room—the
windows of which looked out on a secluded part of his own grounds

—a part pleasant enough in summer leafiness & verdure, but dreary now in the cold white clothing of winter—Many a time had this dining-room rung with the merriment of select dinner parties —chosen by the noble Bachelor from his particular friends—& often had the rum physionomies of Richton, Arundel, Castlereagh & Thornton been reflected in the mirror-like surface of that long dark polished mahogany table at whose head Edward Hartford now sat alone—Gallant & Gay & bearing on his broad forehead the very brightest & greenest laurels Angria had gathered on the banks of the Cirhala—he had retired with all his blushing honours thick upon him—from the Council, the Court, the Salon—he had left Verdopolis in the height of the most dazzling season it had ever known, & gone to haunt like a ghost his lonely Halls in Angria—most people thought the noble General's brain had suffered some slight injury amid the hardships of the late campaign —Richton, among the number, found it impossible to account for his friend's conduct upon any other supposition——As the Dusk closed & the room grew more dismal, Hartford threw the news-paper from him—poured out a bumper of amber-coloured wine & quaffed it off to the memory of the vintage that produced it— according to books, men in general soliloquise when they are by themselves & so did Hartford—"What the d---l" he began "has brought our lord the King down to Angria?—that drunken Editor of the War Despatch gives a pretty account of his progress—hissed it seems in the streets of Zamorna & then, like himself, instead of getting through the town as quickly as he could—bidding the postillions halt before Stancliffe's & treating them to one of his fire & gunpowder explosions! What a speech, beginning "My lads, what a d---d set you are—unstable as water. you shall never excel!" It's odd, but that Western Dandy knows the genius of our land—"take the bull by the horns", that's his motto—Hitherto his tactics have succeeded, but I thought it said somewhere, either in Revelations or the Apocalypse, the end is not yet—I wish he'd keep out of Angria." Here a pause ensued & Hartford filled it up with another goblet of the golden wine—"Now" he proceeded "I know I ought not drink this Guanache, it is a kindling sort of draught & I were better take to toast & water—but Lord bless me, I've got a feeling about my heart I can neither stifle nor tear away, & I would fain drown it—They talk of optical delusions—I wonder what twisting of the nerves it is that fixed before my eyes that image—which neither darkness can hide nor light dissipate— Some demon is certainly making a bonfire of my inwards—the burning thrill struck through all my veins to my heart—with that last touch of the little warm soft hand—by heaven, nearly a year ago, & it has never left me since—It masters me—I'm not half the man I was, but I'm handsome still!—" He looked up at a lofty mirror between the two opposite windows—it reflected his dark, commanding face with the prominent profile—the hard forehead —the deep expressive eye—the mass of raven hair, whisker & moustache—the stately aspect & figure—the breadth of chest & length of limb—in short, it gave back to his sight as fine a realisation of soldier & patrician majesty as Angria ever produced from her ardent soil—Hartford sprung up—"What should I give up hope for?" he said—rapidly pacing the room—"By G–d I think I could make her love me—I never yet have told her how I adore her—I've never offered her my title & hand & my half-phrenzied heart—but I will do it—Who says it is impossible she should prefer being my wife to being *His* mistress—The world will laugh at me— I don't care for the World—It's inconsistent with the honour of my house—I've burnt the honour of my House & drunk its ashes in Guanache—It's dastardly to meddle with another man's matters— another man who has been my friend—with whom I have fought & feasted—suffered & enjoyed—By G–d it is, but I know it is— if any man but myself had dared to entertain the same thought I'd have called him out—But Zamorna leaves her & cares no more about her except when she can be of use to him—than I do for that silly Christmas rose on the lawn, shrivelled up by the frost— Besides, every man for himself—I'll try & if it don't succeed I'll try again & again—She's worth a struggle—perhaps meantime Warner or Enara will send me an invitation to dine on bullets for two—or perhaps I may forget the rules of the drill & present a fire not from, but at, myself—in either case I get comfortably provided for & that torment will be over which now frightens away my sleep by night & my sense by day—" This was rather wild talk, but his lordship's peculiar glance told that wine had not been without its effect—We will leave him striding about the room & maddening under the influence of his fiery passions—A sweet specimen of an Aristocrat—!

Late one fine, still evening in January the moon arose over the blue summit of the Sydenham Hills—& looked down on a quiet road winding from the hamlet of Rivaulx—The earth was bound in frost, hard, mute & glittering—The forest of Hawkscliffe was as still as a tomb, & its black leafless wilds stretched away in the distance & cut of, with a harsh serrated line, the sky from the country—That sky was all silver blue—pierced here & there with a

star like a diamond, only the moon softened it, large, full, golden—
the by-road I have spoken of received her ascending beam on a
path of perfect solitude—Spectral pines & great old beech trees
guarded the way like Sentinels from Hawkscliffe—farther on, the
rude track wound deep into the shades of the forest, but here it was
open & the worn causeway bleached with frost ran under an old
wall—grown over with moss & wild ivy—Over this scene the sun
of winter had gone down in cloudless calm—red as fire & kindling
with the last beams the windows of a mansion on the verge of
Hawkscliffe—to that mansion the road in question was the shortest
cut from Rivaulx—& here a moment let us wait, wrapped, it is to
be hoped, in furs, for a keener frost never congealed the Olympian
—Almost before you are aware, a figure strays up the causeway—
at a leisurely pace, musing amid the tranquillity of evening—
Doubtless that figure must be an inmate of the before-mentioned
mansion—for it is an elegant & pleasing object—Approaching
gradually nearer you can observe more definitely—you see now a
lady of distinguished carriage—straight & slender, something in-
ceding & princess-like in her walk, but unconsciously so—her ankles
are so perfect & her feet—if she tryed she could scarcely tread otherwise than she does, lightly, firmly, erectly—the ermine muff—the
silk pelisse—the graceful & ample hat of dark beaver—suit & set off
her slight youthful form—She is deeply veiled—you must guess at
her features—but she passes on & a turn of the road conceals her.
Breaking up the silence—dashing in on the silence was a horseman*—fire flashes from under his steed's hoofs—out of the flinty
road—he rides desperately—now & then he rises on his stirrups &
eagerly looks along the track as if to catch sight of some object that
has eluded him—He sees it & the spurs are struck mercilessly into
his horse's flanks—Horse & rider vanish in a whirlwind—

The lady passing through the iron gates—had just entered upon
the Demesne of Hawkscliffe—She paused to gaze at the moon
which now, fully risen—looked upon her through the boughs of a
superb elm—a green lawn lay between her & the House, & where
its light shimmered in gold—Thundering behind her came the
sound of hoofs—& bending low to his saddle to avoid the contact
of oversweeping branches—That wild horseman we saw five
minutes since, rushed upon the scene—harshly curbing the charger, he brought it almost upon its haunches close to the spot where
she stood—"Miss Laury! good evening!" he said—the lady threw
back her veil—surveyed him with one glance & replied—"Lord

* Cf. *Jane Ayre*, Chapter 12

Hartford!—I am glad to see you, my lord—you have ridden fast—
your horse foams—any bad news?" "No—!" "Then you are on
your way to Adrianopolis I suppose—you will pass the night
here—?" "If you ask me, I will—" "If I ask you—yes, this is the
proper half-way house between the capitals—the night is cold, let
us go in—" They were now at the door—Hartford flung himself
from his saddle—& servants came to lead the over-ridden steed to
the stables & he followed Miss Laury in—It was her own drawing-
room to which she led him—just such a scene as is most welcome
after the contrast of a winter evening's chill—not a large room,
simply furnished—with curtains & couches of green silk—a single
large mirror—a Grecian lamp dependent from the centre—softly
burning now & mingling with the warmer illumination of the fire
—whose brilliant glow bore testimony to the keenness of the frost
—Hartford glanced round him—he had been in Miss Laury's
drawing-room before—but never as her sole guest—He had, before
the troubles broke out, more than once, formed one of a high &
important trio—whose custom it was to make the lodge of Rivaux
their occasional Rendezvous—Warner, Enara & himself had often
stood on that hearth—in a ring round Miss Laury's sofa, & he
recalled now her face looking up to them with its serious, soft
intelligence that blent no woman's frivolity with the heartfelt
interest of those subjects on which they conversed—He remembered
those first kindlings of the flame that now devoured his life—as he
watched her keenly—& saw the earnest enthusiasm with which
she threw her soul into topics of the highest import—She had often
done for these great men what they could get no man to do for
them—she had kept their secrets & executed their wishes as far
as in her lay—for it had never been her part to counsel. with
humble feminine devotedness she always looked up for her task to
be set—& then not Warner himself could have bent his energies
more resolutely to the fulfilment of that task than did Miss Laury—
Had Mina's lot in life been different, she never would have interfered in such matters—she did not interfere now—she only served
—nothing like intrigue had ever stained her course in politics—
she told her Directors what she had done & she asked for more to
do—grateful always that they would trust her so far as to employ
her—grateful too for the enthusiasm of their loyalty—in short,
devoted to them heart & mind because she believed them to be
devoted as unreservedly to the common Master of all—The consequences of this species of deeply confidential intercourse between
the Statesmen and their beautiful Lieutenant had been intense &
chivalric—admiration on the part of Mr Warner—strong attach-

ment on that of General Enara—& on Lord Hartford's the burning brand of passion—His Lordship had always been a man of
strong & ill-regulated feelings & in his youth (if report may be
credited) of somewhat dissolute habits—but he had his own ideas
of honour—strongly implanted in his breast, & though he would
not have scrupled if the wife of one of his equals, or the daughter of
one of his tenants had been in the question—yet, as it was, he stood
beset & nonplussed—Miss Laury belonged to the Duke of Zamorna—She was indisputably his property as much as the Lodge of
Rivaux or the stately woods of Hawkscliffe, & in that light she
considered herself—All his dealings with her had been on matters
connected with the Duke—& she had ever shewn an habitual,
rooted, solemn devotedness to his interest—which seemed to leave
her hardly a thought for anything else in the world beside—She
had but one idea—Zamorna, Zamorna—! it had grown up with
her—become part of her nature—Absence—Coldness—total
neglect—for long periods together—went for nothing—she could
no more feel alienation from him than she could from herself*—
She did not even repine when he forgot her—any more than the
religious Devotee does when his Deity seems to turn away his face
for a time & leave him to the ordeal of temporal afflictions—It
seemed as if she could have lived on the remembrance of what he
had once been to her without asking for anything more—All this
Hartford knew, & he knew too that she valued himself in proportion as she believed him to be loyal to his sovereign—her friendship
for him turned on this hinge—"we have been fellow-labourers &
fellow-sufferers together in the same good cause"—These were her
own words which she had uttered one night—as she took leave of
her three noble colleagues—just before the storm burst over
Angria. Hartford had noted the expression of her countenance as
she spoke—& thought what a young & beautiful being, thus
appealing for sympathy with minds scarcely like her own in
mould. However, let us dwell no longer on these topics—suffice it
to say that lord Hartford, against reason & without hope, had
finally delivered himself wholly up to the guidance of his vehement
passions—& it was with the resolution to make one desperate
effort in the attainment of their end that he now stood before the
lady of Rivaux—.

Above two hours had elapsed since lord Hartford had entered the
house—tea was over—& in the perfect quiet of evening he & Miss
Laury were left together—He sat on one side of the hearth, she on

* Cf. Cathy in *Wuthering Heights*, Chapter 9

the other—her work-table only between them—& on that her little hand rested within his reach—it was embedded on a veil of lace—the embroidery of which she had just relinquished for a moment's thought—Lord Hartford's eye was fascinated by the white soft fingers—his whole heart at the moment was in a tumult of bliss—to be so near—to be reclined so benignly, so kindly—he forgot himself—his own hand closed half involuntarily upon hers—Miss Laury looked at him, if the action had left any room for doubt of its significance—the glance which met hers filled up the deficiencies—a wild fiery glance as if his feelings were wrought up almost to delirium —Shocked for a moment, almost overwhelmed, she yet speedily measured her motions—took her hand away, resumed her work— & with head bent down—seemed endeavouring to conceal embarassment under the appearance of occupation—The dead silence that followed would not do—so she broke it—in a very calm—self-possessed tone—"That ring, Lord Hartford, which you were admiring just now belonged once to the Duchess of Wellington—" "And was given you by her son?" asked the General bitterly— "No, my lord, the Duchess herself gave it me a few days before she died—It has her maiden name, Catherine Pakenham, engraved within the stone—" "But" pursued Hartford "I was not admiring the ring when I touched your hand—no, the thought struck me if ever I marry I should like my wife's hand to be just as white & snowy & taper as that—" "I am the Daughter of a common soldier, my lord, & it is said that ladies of high descent have fairer hands than peasant-women." Hartford made no reply, he rose restlessly from his seat & stood leaning against the mantle-piece— "Miss Laury, shall I tell you which was the happiest hour of my life?"—"I will guess, my lord—perhaps when the bill passed which made Angria an independent kingdom." "No" replied Hartford with an expressive smile. "perhaps, then, when Lord Northangerland resigned his seals—For I know you & the Earl were never on good terms." "No, I hated his lordship—but there are moments of deeper felicity even than those which see the triumph of a fallen enemy—" "I will hope, then, it was at the Restoration—" "Wrong again—why Madam, young as you are, your mind is so used to the harness of politics that you can imagine no happiness or misery unconnected with them—You remind me of Warner—" "I believe I am like him" returned Miss Laury— "He often tells me so himself—but I live so with men & statesmen —I almost lose the ideas of a woman—" "Do you?" muttered Hartford with the dark sinister smile peculiar to him—"I wish you would tell the Duke so the next time you see him—" Miss

The Fall of Babylon. Engraving by John Martin

Laury passed over this equivocal remark & proceeded with the conversation—"I cannot guess your riddle, my lord, so I think you must explain it—" "Then Miss Laury—prepare to be astonished—you are so patriotic, so loyal, that you will scarcely credit me when I say that the happiest hour I have ever known fell on the darkest day in the deadliest crisis of Angria's calamities—" "How, lord Hartford?" "Moreover, Miss Laury, it was at no bright period of your own life—it was to you an hour of the most acute agony, to me one of ecstasy—" Miss Laury turned aside her head with a disturbed air & trembled—she seemed to know to what he alluded —"You remember The First of July—36?" continued Hartford—She bowed—"You remember that the evening of that day closed in a tremendous storm—" "Yes, my lord—" "You recollect how you sat in this very room by this fire-side—fearful of retiring for the night lest you should awake in another world in the morning—the country was not then so quiet as it is now—you have not forgotten the deep explosion which roared up at midnight—& told you that your life & liberty hung on a thread—that the enemy had come suddenly upon Rivaux & that we who lay there to defend the forlorn hope were surprised & routed by a night attack—Then Madam, perhaps you recollect the warning which I brought you at one o'clock in the morning to fly instantly—unless you chose the alternative of infamous captivity in the hands of Jordan—I found you here sitting by a black hearth without fire, & Ernest Fitz-Arthur lay on your knee asleep—You told me you had heard the firing & that you were waiting for some communication from me—determined not to stir without orders lest a precipitate step on your part should embarass me—I had a carriage already in waiting for you, I put you in & with the remnant of my defeated followers escorted you as far as Zamorna—What followed after this, Miss Laury—?" Miss Laury covered her eyes with her hand —she seemed as if she could not answer—"Well" continued Hartford "In the midst of darkness & tempest, & while the whole city of Zamorna seemed changed into a hell peopled with fiends & inspired with madness—my lads were hewed down about you and your carriage was stopped—I very well remember what you did—how frantically you struggled to save Fitz-Arthur, & how you looked at me when he was snatched from you—as to your own preservation, that I need not repeat—only my arm did it—you acknowledge that, Miss Laury?"—"Hartford, I do—but why do you dwell on that horrible scene?" "Because I am now approaching the happiest hour of my life—I took you to the house of one of my tenants whom I could depend upon—& just as morning dawned, you & I sat together & alone in the little chamber of a farmhouse—you were in my arms, your head upon my shoulder & weeping out all your anguish on a breast that longed to bleed for you—" Miss Laury agitatedly rose, she approached Hartford— "My Lord, you have been very kind to me—and I feel very grateful for that kindness—perhaps sometime I may be able to repay it —we know not how the chances of fortune may turn—the weak have aided the strong—I will watch vigilantly for the slightest opportunity to serve you, but do not talk in this way—I scarcely know whither your words tend." Lord Hartford paused a moment before he replied—gazing at her with bended brows & folded arms, he said "Miss Laury, what do you think of me?" "That you are one of the noblest hearts in the world" she replied unhesitatingly—she was standing just before Hartford looking up at him —her hair in the attitude falling back from her brow—shading with exquisite curls her temples & her slender neck—her small sweet features, with that high seriousness deepening their beauty, lit up by eyes so large, so dark, so swimming—so full of pleading benignity—of an expression of alarmed regard—as if she at once feared for and pitied the sinful abstraction of a great mind— Hartford could not stand it—he could have borne female anger or terror—but the look of enthusiastic gratitude softened by compassion—nearly unmanned him—he turned his head for a moment aside—but then passion prevailed—her beauty when he looked again struck through him a maddening sensation—whetted to acuter power by a feeling like despair—"You shall love me!" he exclaimed desperately. "Do I not love you—would I not die for you & must I in return receive only the cold regard of friendship? —I am no platonist, Miss Laury—I am not your friend—I am, hear me Madam—your declared Lover—nay, you shall not leave me, by heaven! I am stronger than you are—" She had stepped a pace or two back, apalled by his vehemence—he thought she meant to withdraw & determined not to be so balked—he clasped her at once in both his arms—& kissed her furiously rather than fondly. Miss Laury did not struggle—"Hartford" said she, steadying her voice though it faltered in spite of her effort—"this must be our parting-scene—I will never see you again if you do not restrain yourself—" Hartford saw that she turned pale & he felt her tremble violently—his arms relaxed their hold—he allowed her to leave him—She sat down on a chair opposite—& hurriedly wiped her brow which was damp & marble-pale—"Now, Miss Laury" said his Lordship "no man in the world loves you as I do—will you accept my title & my coronet?—I fling them at your feet—" "My

Lord, do you know whose I am?" she replied in a hollow, very suppressed tone—"Do you know with what a sound those proposals fall on my ear?—how impious & blasphemous they seem to be? Do you at all conceive how utterly impossible it is that I should ever love you? the scene I have just witnessed has given a strange wrench to all my accustomed habits of thought—I thought you a true-hearted faithful man—I find that you are a traitor—" "And do you despise me?" asked Hartford—"No, my lord, I do not"—she paused & looked down—the colour rose rapidly into her pale face—she sobbed—not in tears—but in the over-mastering approach of an impulse born of a warm & Western heart—again she looked up—her eyes had changed—their aspect burning with a wild bright inspiration—truly, divinely Irish—"Hartford" said she "had I met you long since, before I left Ellibank & forgot St Cyprian & dishonoured my father—I would have loved you. O my lord, you know not how truly—I would have married you & made it the glory of my life to cheer & brighten your hearth—but I cannot do so now—never—I saw my present master when he had scarcely attained manhood—do you think, Hartford, I will tell you what feelings I had for him?—no tongue could express them— they were so fervid, so glowing in their colour that they effaced everything else—I lost the power of properly appreciating the value of the world's opinion, of discerning the difference between right & wrong—I have never in my life contradicted Zamorna— never delayed obedience to his commands—I could not! he was sometimes more to me than a human being—he superseded all things—all affections, all interests, all fears or hopes or principles— Unconnected with him my mind would be a blank—cold, dead, susceptible only of a sense of despair. How I should sicken if I were torn from him & thrown to you! Do not ask it—I would die first—No woman that ever loved my master could consent to leave him—There is nothing like him elsewhere—Hartford, if I were to be your wife—if Zamorna only looked at me I should creep back like a slave to my former service—I should disgrace you as I have long since disgraced all my kindred—think of that, my lord, & never say you love me again—" "You do not frighten me" replied Lord Hartford hardily. "I would stand that chance, aye & every other—If I might only see at the head of my table in that old dining-room at Hartford-Hall, yourself as my wife & lady—I am called proud as it is, but then I would shew Angria to what pitch of pride a man might attain—If I could, coming home at night, find Mina Laury waiting to receive me—If I could sit down & look at you with the consciousness that your exquisite beauty was

all my own—That that cheek—those lips—that lovely hand might
be claimed arbitrarily & you dare not refuse me—I should then
feel happy." "Hartford, you would be more likely when you came
home to find your house vacant & your hearth deserted—I know
the extent of my own infatuation—I should go back to Zamorna—
& entreat him on my knees to let me be his slave again—"
"Madam" said Hartford frowning "you dared not if you were my
wife! I should guard you." "Then I should die under your guardianship—but the experiment will never be tried—" Hartford came
near—sat down by her side & leaned over her—She did not shrink
away—"Oh!" he said "I am happy—there was a time when I
dared not have come so near you—one summer evening two years
ago—I was walking in the twilight—amongst those trees on the
lawn—& at the turn I saw you sitting at the root of one of them
by yourself—you were looking up at a star which was twinkling
above the Sydenham's*—you were in white, your hands were
folded on your knee—& your hair was resting in still shining curls
on your neck—I stood and watched—the thought struck me, if
that image sat now in my woods—if she were something in which
I had an interest—if I could go & press my lips to her brow &
expect a smile in answer to the caress—If I could take her in my
arms & turn her thoughts from that sky—with its single star—&
from the distant country to which it points (for it hung in the
West & I knew you were thinking about Senegambia—), if I
could attract those thoughts & centre them all in myself—how
like heaven would the world become to me—I heard a window
open & Zamorna's voice called—through the silence "Mina!"
The next moment I had the pleasure of seeing you standing on
the Lawn close under this very casement—where the Duke sat
leaning out, & you were allowing his hand to stray through your
hair & his lips——!" "Lord Hartford!" exclaimed Miss Laury,
colouring to the eyes—"This is more than I can bear—I have not
been angry yet—I thought it folly to rage at you—because you
said you loved me—but what you have just said is like touching a
nerve—it overpowers all reason—it is like a stinging taunt which
I am under no obligation to endure from you—Every one knows
what I am—but where is the woman in Africa who would would
have acted more wisely than I did if under the same circumstances
she had been subject to the same temptations?—" "That is" returned Hartford, whose eye was now glittering with a desperate
reckless expression—"Where is the woman in Africa who would
have said no to young Douro—when amongst the romantic hills

* The Sydenham Hills

of Ellibanks—he has pressed his suit on some fine moonlight summer night—& the Girl & Boy have found themselves alone in a green dell—here & there a tree to be their shade, far above the stars for their sentinels, & around the night for their wide curtains—" The wild bounding throb of Miss Laury's heart was visible through her satin boddice—it was even audible as for a moment Hartford ceased his scoffing to note the effect—he was still close by her & she did not move from him—she did not speak. the pallid lamp-light showed her lips white, her cheeks bloodless— he continued unrelentingly & bitterly—"In after times doubtless the woods of Hawkscliffe have witnessed many a tender scene when the King of Angria has retired from the turmoil of business & the teazing of matrimony to love & leisure with his Gentle Mistress—" "Now, Hartford, we must part" interrupted Miss Laury—"I see what your opinion of me is—it is very just—but not one which I willingly hear expressed—You have cut me to the heart—Good bye, I shall try to avoid seeing you for the future"—She rose— Hartford did not attempt to detain her—she went out—as she closed the door he heard the bursting convulsive gush of feeling which his taunts had wrought up to agony—.

Her absence left a blank—suddenly the wish to recall, to soothe, to propitiate her rose in his mind. he strode to the door & opened it—There was a little hall or rather a wide passage without in which one large lamp was quietly burning. nothing appeared there nor on the staircase of low broad steps in which it terminated—She seemed to have vanished—Lord Hartford's hat & horseman's cloak lay on the side slab—there remained no further attraction for him at the Lodge of Rivaux—The delirious dream of rapture which had intoxicated his sense broke up & disappeared—He strode out into the black & frozen night—burning in flames no ice could quench—he ordered & mounted his steed, & dashing his spurs with harsh cruelty up to the rowels into the flanks of the noble war-horse which had borne him victorious through the carnage of Westwood & Leyden—he dashed in furious gallop down the road to Rivaux.

The frost continued unbroken, & the snow lay cold & cheerless all over Angria—It was a dreary morning—large flakes were fluttering slowly down from the sky—thickening every moment—the trees around a stately hall lying up among its grounds at some distance from the road-side—shuddered in the cutting wind that at intervals howled through them. We are now on a broad public road—A great town lies on our left hand—with a deep river sweeping under the arches of a bridge—this is Zamorna, & that house is Hartford-Hall—the wind increased, the sky darkened, & the bleached whirl of a snow-storm began to fill the air—Dashing at a rapid rate through the tempest, an open travelling carriage swept up the road—four splendid greys & two mounted postillions gave the equipage an air of aristocratic style—It contained two Gentlemen—one a man of between thirty or forty—having about him a good deal of the air of a nobleman shawled up to the eyes & buttoned up in at least three surtouts, with a water-proof white beaver hat—an immense mackintosh cape & beaver gloves—his countenance bore a half rueful, half jesting expression—he seemed endeavouring to bear all things as smoothly as he could—but still the cold east wind & driving snow evidently put his philosophy very much to the test—The other traveller was a young high-featured Gentleman—with a pale face & accurately arched dark eyebrows—his person was carefully done up in a vast roquelaire of furs—a fur travelling cap decorated his head which, however, Nature had much more effectively protected by a profusion of chestnut ringlets—now streaming long & thick to the winds—he presented to the said wind a case of bared teeth firmly set together &, exposed in a desperate grin, they seemed daring the snow-flakes to a comparison of whiteness—"Oh!" groaned the elder traveller "I wish your Grace would be ruled by reason—what could possess you to insist on prosecuting the journey in such weather as this?—" "Stuff, Richton, an old campaigner like you ought to make objections to no weather—it's d———d cold though —I think all Greenland's coming down upon us—but you're not going to faint are you Richton?—What are you staring at so? do you see the d———l?" "I think I do—" replied lord Richton "& really, if your Grace will look two yards before you—you will be of the same opinion—"

The carriage was now turning that angle of the park-wall where a lodge on each side—overhung by some magnificent trees—formed the supporters to the stately iron gates opening upon the broad carriage-road which wound up through the park—The gates were open & just outside, on the causeway of the high-road, stood a tall well-dressed man—in a blue coat with military pantaloons of grey, having a broad stripe of scarlet down the sides—his distinguished air—his handsome dark face & his composed atti-tude—for he stood perfectly still with one hand on his side—gave singular effect to the circumstance of his being without hat—had it been a summer day one would not so much have wondered at it though even in the warmest weather it is not usual to see gentlemen parading the public roads uncovered. Now, as the keen wind rushed down upon him through the boughs of the lofty trees arching the park-portal—and as the snow-flakes settled thick upon the short raven curls of his hair—he looked strange indeed Abruptly stepping forwards, he seized the first Leader of the chariot by the head & backed it fiercely—the postillions were about to whip on—consigning the hatless & energetic gentleman to that fate which is sought by the worshippers of Juggernaut— when Lord Richton called out to them "for God's sake to stop the horses". "I think they are stopped with a vengeance" said his young companion—Then leaning forward with a most verjuice expression on his pale face—he said "Give that gentleman half a minute to get out of the way & then drive on forward like d———ls—" "My lord Duke" interposed Richton "do you see who it is? permit me to solicit a few minutes forbearance—Lord Hartford must be ill—I will alight & speak to him—" Before Richton could fulfil his purpose, the individual had let go his hold & stood by the side of the chariot—holding out his clenched hand with a menacing gesture—he addressed Zamorna thus—"I've no hat to take off in your majesty's presence so you must excuse my rustic breeding—I saw the royal carriage at a distance so I came out to meet it something in a hurry—I'm just in time, God be thanked!—will your Grace get out & speak to me?—By the Lord, I'll not leave this spot alive without an audience—" "Your lordship is cursedly drunk" replied the Duke, keeping his teeth as close shut as a vice. "Ask for an audience when you're sober—Drive on Postillions!" "At the peril of your lives!" cried Hartford, & he drew out a brace of pistols, cokked them & presented one at each postillion— "Rosier! my pistols!" shouted Zamorna to his valet who sat behind—& he threw himself at once from the chariot & stood facing lord Hartford on the high-road—"It is your Grace that is intoxicated" retorted the nobleman—"And I'll tell you with what —with wine of Cyprus or Cythera—your Majesty is far too amorous, you had better keep a Harem—!" "Come, Sir" said Zamorna in lofty scorn "this won't do—I see you are mad— postillions seize him, & you Rosier go up to the Hall & fetch five or six of his own domestics—tell them to bring a strait waistcoat if they have such a thing—" "Your Grace would like to throw me into a dungeon" said Hartford—"but this is a free Country & we will have no Western despotism—Be so good as to hear me, my lord Duke, or I will shoot myself—" "Small loss" said Zamorna, lifting his lip with a sour sneer—"Do not aggravate his insanity"

whispered Richton. "Allow me to manage him, my lord Duke—
you had better return to the carriage & I will accompany Hartford
home—" then, turning to Hartford, "take my arm Edward & let
us return to the house together—you do not seem well this morning—" "None of your snivel—" replied the gallant Nobleman—
"I'll have satisfaction, I'm resolved on it, his Grace has injured me
deeply—" "A good move" replied Zamorna. "then take your
pistols, Sir, & come along—Rosier, take the carriage back to the
town—call at Dr Cooper's & ask him to ride over to Hartford
Hall—D––n you Sir, what are you staring at?—do as I bid
you—" "He is staring at the propriety of the monarch of a kingdom fighting a duel with a madman" replied Richton. "If your
Grace will allow me to go, I will return with a detachment of
police & put both the sovereign & the subject under safe ward—"
"Have done with that trash" said Zamorna angrily—"Come on—
you will be wanted for a second—" "Well" said Richton "I don't
wish to disoblige either your Grace or my friend Hartford, but it's
an absurd & frantic piece of business—I beseech you to consider a
moment—Hartford, reflect what you are about to do—!" "To get
a vengeance for a thousand wrongs & sufferings" was the reply—
"His Grace has dashed my happiness for life—" Richton shook his
head—"I must stop this work" he muttered to himself. "What
Demon is influencing Edward Hartford—& Zamorna too—for I
never saw such a fiendish glitter as that in his eyes just now—
strange madness!" The noble Earl buttoned his surtout still closer
& then followed the three other Gentlemen who were already on
their way to the House—the carriage meantime drove off according to orders in the direction of Zamorna—

Lord Hartford was not mad, though his conduct might seem to
betoken such a state of mind—he was only desperate—the disappointment of the previous night had wrought him up to a pitch
of rage & recklessness—whose results, as we have just seen them,
were of such a nature as to convince Lord Richton that the doubts
he had long harboured of his friend's sanity were correct—so long
as his passion for Miss Laury remained unavowed & consequently
unrejected, he had cherished a dreamy kind of hope—that there
existed some chance of success—when wandering through his
woods alone he had fed on reveries of some future day when she
might fill his Halls with the bliss of her presence and the light of
her beauty—all day her image haunted him, it seemed to speak to
& look upon him with that mild friendly aspect he had ever seen
her wear, & then, as imagination prevailed, it brought vividly back

that hour when, in a moment almost of Despair—her feminine weakness had thrown itself utterly on him for support, & he had been permitted to hold her in his arms—take her to his heart—he remembered how she looked when torn from danger & tumult— rescued from hideous Captivity—he carried her up the humble stair-case of a farm-house—all pale & shuddering—with her long black curls spread dishevelled on his shoulder & her soft cheek resting there as confidingly as if he had indeed been her Husband— from her trusting gentleness in those moments he drew blissful omens now, alas, utterly belied. No web of self-delusion could now be woven, the truth was too stern—& besides he had taunted her, hurt her feelings & alienated for ever her grateful friendship— having thus entered more particularly into the state of his feelings, let me proceed with my narrative—

The appartment into which Lord Hartford shewed his illustrious guest was that very dining-room where I first represented him sitting alone & maddening under the double influence of passion & wine—His manner now was more composed & he demeaned himself with lofty courtesy towards his sovereign—There was a particular chair in that room which Zamorna had always been accustomed to occupy when in happier days he had not unfre- quently formed one of the splendid dinner-parties given at Hart- ford-Hall—The General asked him to assume that seat now—but he declined, acknowledging the courtesy only by a slight inclination of the head—& planted himself just before the hearth—his elbow leaning on the mantle-piece & his eye looking down. in that position the eye-lids, like the long fringes, partly concealed the sweet expression of vindictiveness lurking beneath—but still aided by the sour curl & pout of the lip, the passionate dishevellment of the hair & flushing of the brow—there was enough seen to stamp his countenance with a character of unpleasantness more easily con- ceived than described—Lord Hartford, influenced by his usual habits, would not sit whilst his monarch stood—so he retired with Richton to the deeply embayed recess of a window—. That worthy & prudent personage, bent upon settling this matter without com- ing to the absurd extreme now contemplated—began to reason with his friend on the subject. "Hartford" he said, speaking soft & low so that Zamorna could not overhear him "let me entreat you to consider well what you are about to do—I know that the scene which we have just witnessed is not the primary cause of the dispute between you & his Grace there which is now about to terminate so fatally—I know that circumstances previously existed which gave

birth to bitter feelings on both sides—I wish, Hartford, you would
reconsider the steps you have taken—all is in vain, the lady in
question can never be yours—" "I know that, Sir, & that is what
makes me frantic—I have no motive left for living, & if Zamorna
wants my blood, let him have it." "You may kill him" suggested
Richton "and what will be the consequences then?" "Trust me"
returned Hartford "I'll not hurt him much—though he deserves
it—the double-dyed infernal Western profligate—but the fact is
he hates me far more than I hate him—look at his face now, reflected in that mirror—God! he longs to see the last drop of blood I
have in my heart—" "Hush! he will hear you" said Richton—"He
certainly does not look very amiable—but recollect you are the
offender—" "I know that" replied Hartford gloomily—"But it is
not out of spite to him that I wish to get his mistress—& how often
in the half-year does he see her or think about her?—grasping
dog! another King, when he was tired of his mistress would give
her up—but he!—I think I'll shoot him straight through the head
—I would if his death would only win me Miss Laury." That
name, though spoken very low, caught Zamorna's ear & he at
once comprehended the nature of the conversation. It is not often
that he had occasion to be jealous, & as it is a rare, so also is it a
remarkably curious & pretty sight to see him under the influence
of that passion. It worked in every fibre of his frame & boiled in every
vein—dark blush after dark blush deepened the hue of his cheek, as
one faded, another of darker crimson followed (this variation of
colour resulting from strong emotion has been his wonted peculiarity from childhood), his whiskers twined & writhed & even the
very curls seemed to stir on his brow—Turning to Hartford, he
spoke—"What drivelling folly have you got into your head, Sir,
to dare to look at anything which belonged to me?—Frantic
Idiot! to dream that I should allow a coarse Angrian Squire to
possess anything that had ever been mine—as if I knew how to relinquish—G–d d––n your grossness!—Richton, you have my
pistols—bring them here directly—I will neither wait for Doctor nor
anybody else to settle this business—" "My lord Duke!" began
Richton— "No interference, Sir!" exclaimed his Grace, "bring
the pistols!" The earl was not going to stand this arbitrary work—
"I wash my hands of this bloody affair" he said, sternly placing the
pistols on the table, & in silence he left the room. The Demon of
Zamorna's nature was now completely roused—Growling out his
words in a deep & hoarse tone almost like the smothered roar of a
Lion—he savagely told Hartford to measure out his ground in this
room, for he would not delay the business a moment—Hartford

did so without remonstrance or reply—"Take your station!" thundered the Barbarian—"I have done so" replied his lordship "and my pistol is ready—" "then Fire!" The deadly explosion succeeded the flash & the cloud of smoke—!

While the room still shook to the sound, almost before the flash had expired & the smoke burst after it—the door slowly opened—Lord Richton reappeared—wearing upon his face a far more fixed & stern solemnity than I ever saw there before—"Who is hurt?" he asked—there was but one erect figure visible through the vapour, & the thought thrilled through him "the other may be a corpse"— Lord Hartford lay across the doorway still & pale—"my poor friend" said lord Richton, & kneeling on one knee he propped against the other the wounded nobleman—from whose lips a moan of agony escaped as the earl moved him—"Thank God he is not quite dead!" was Richton's involuntary exclamation, for though a man accustomed to scenes of carnage on gory battle-plains, & though of enduring nerves & cool resolution—he felt a pang at this spectacle of fierce manslaughter amid scenes of domestic peace—the renowned & gallant soldier who had escaped hostile weapons & returned unharmed from fields of terrific strife—lay as it seemed dying under his own roof—blood began to drip on to Richton's hand & a large crimson stain appeared on the ruffles of his shirt. the same ominous dye darkened Lord Hartford's lips & oozed through them when he made vain efforts to speak, he had been wounded in the region of the lungs—A thundering knock & a loud ring at the door-bell now broke that appalling silence which had fallen—it was Dr Cooper.* he speedily entered, followed by a Surgeon with instruments &c.—Richton silently resigned his friend to their hands & turned for the first time to the other actor in this horrid scene—

The Duke of Zamorna was standing by a window—coolly buttoning his surtout over the pistols which he had replaced in his breast—"Is your majesty hurt?" asked Richton—"No Sir—may I trouble you to hand me my gloves—" they lay on a side-board near the Earl— he politely complied with the request, handing over at the same time a large shawl or scarf of crimson silk, which the Duke had taken from his neck—in this he proceeded to envelope his throat & a considerable portion of his face, leaving little more visible than the forehead, eyes & high Roman nose—then, drawing on his gloves, he turned to Dr Cooper—"Of what nature is the wound,

*A character inspired by Sir Astley Cooper, the royal physician.

Sir? Is there any likelihood of Lord Hartford's recovery?"—"A possibility exists that he may recover, my lord Duke—but the wound is a severe one—the lungs have only just escaped—" The Duke drew near the couch on which his General had been raised—looked at the wound, then under the operation of the surgeon's probing knife, & transferred his glance from the bloody breast to the pallid face of the sufferer—Hartford, who had borne the extraction of the bullet without a groan & whose clenched teeth & rigid brow seemed defying pain to do its worst—Smiled faintly when he saw his monarch's eye bent upon him with searching Fierceness—in spite of the surgeon's prohibition, he attempted to speak. "Zamorna" he said "I have got your hate, but you shall not blight me with your contempt—This is but a little matter—why did you not inflict more upon me that I might bear it without flinching? —you called me a coarse Angrian Squire—ten minutes since—Angrians are men as well as Westerns—" "Dogs, Brutes rather" replied Zamorna "Faithful, gallant, noble Brutes—" & he left the room, for his carriage had now returned and waited at the door—before lord Richton followed him, he stopped a moment to take leave of his friend—"Well" murmured Hartford, as he feebly returned the pressure of the Earl's hand—"Zamorna has finished me, but I bear him no ill-will—my love for his mistress was involuntary —I am not sorry for it now—I adore her to the last—Flower, if I die, give Miss Laury this token of my truth"—he drew the gold ring from his little finger & gave it into Richton's hand. "Good God!" he muttered, turning away "I would have endured Hell's tortures to win her love—my feelings are not changed, they are just the same—passion for her, bitter self-reproach for my treachery to her Master—but he has paid himself in blood—the purest coin to a Western—farewell Richton—" they parted without another word on either side—Richton joined the Duke—sprung to his side in the carriage & off it swept like the wind—

II

Miss Laury was sitting after breakfast in a small library, her desk lay before her & two large ruled quartos filled with items & figures which she seemed to be comparing—behind her chair stood a tall, well made, soldierly young man with light hair—his dress was plain & gentlemanly—the epaulette on one shoulder alone indicated an official capacity—he watched with a fixed look of attention the movements of the small fingers which ascended in rapid calculation the long columns of accounts—it was strange to see the

absorption of mind expressed in Miss Laury's face—the gravity of
her smooth white brow shaded with drooping curls—the scarcely
perceptible & unsmiling movement of her lips—though those lips
in their rosy sweetness seemed formed only for smiles—Edward
Percy at his Ledger could not have appeared more completely
wrapt in the mysteries of Practice & Fractions—An hour or more
lapsed in the employment—the room meantime continuing in
profound silence—broken only by an occasional observation
addressed by Miss Laury to the Gentleman behind her—concerning the legitimacy of some item or the absence of some stray
farthing wanted to complete the necessary of the sum total—In the
balancing of the books she displayed a most business-like sharp-
ness & strictness—the slightest fault was detected and remarked
on in few words but with a quick searching glance—however,
the accountant had evidently been accustomed to her surveillance
for on the whole his books were a specimen of mathematical
correctness—"Very well" said Miss Laury as she closed the
volumes "Your accounts do you credit Mr O'Neill—you may tell
his Grace that all is quite right—your memoranda tally with my
own exactly—" Mr O'Neill bowed—"Thank you Madam—this
will bear me out against Lord Hartford—his lordship lectured me
severely last time he came to inspect Fort-Adrian—" "What
about?" asked Miss Laury, turning aside her face to hide the
deepening of colour which overspread it at the mention of Lord
Hartford's name. "I can hardly tell you, madam, but his Lordship
was in a savage temper—nothing could please him—he found
fault with everything & everybody. I thought he scarcely appeared
himself, that has been the opinion of many lately—" Miss Laury
gently shook her head—"You should not say so, Ryan" she
replied in a soft tone of regret. "Lord Hartford has a great many
things to think about, and he is naturally rather stern. you ought
to bear with his tempers." "Necessity has no law, Madam"
replied Mr O'Neill with a smile—"& I must bear with them—but
his Lordship is not a popular man in the army—he orders the lash
so unsparingly. We like the Earl of Arundel ten times better—"
"Ah!" said Miss Laury smiling—"You & I are Westerns, Mr
O'Neill—Irish, & we favour our Countrymen—but Hartford is a
gallant Commander—his men can always trust him—Do not let us
be partial—" Mr O'Neill bowed with deference to her opinion—
but smiled at the same time as if he doubted its justice—Taking up
his books, he seemd about to leave the room. before he did so,
however, he turned & said "The Duke wished me to inform you,
Madam, that he would probably be here about four or five o'clock

in the afternoon—" "To-day?" asked Miss Laury in an accent of surprise. "Yes Madam." she paused a moment, then said quickly "Very well Sir—" Mr O'Neill now took his leave with another bow of low & respectful obeisance—Miss Laury returned it with a slight abstracted bow—her thoughts were all caught up & hurried away by that last communication—for a long time after the door had closed, she sat with her head on her hand—lost in a tumultuous flush of ideas, anticipations awakened by that simple sentence "The Duke will be here to-day—" The striking of the time-piece roused her—she remembered that twenty tasks waited her direction—always active—always employed, it was not her custom to while away hours in dreaming—She rose, closed her desk & left the quiet library for busier scenes—

Four o'clock came & Miss Laury's foot was heard on the staircase descending from her chamber—She crossed the large light passage, such an apparition of feminine elegance & beauty—She had dressed herself splendidly—the robe of black satin became at once her slender form, which it envelloped in full & shining folds—& her bright blooming complexion which it set off by the contrast of colour—glittering through her curls there was a band of fine diamonds, & drops of the same pure gem trembled from her small, delicate ears—These ornaments, so regal in their nature, had been the gift of royalty—& were worn now chiefly for the associations of soft & happy moments which their gleam might be supposed to convey—She entered her drawing-room & stood by the window— from thence appeared one glimpse of the high-road visible through the thickening shades of Rivaux—even that was now almost concealed by the frozen mist in which the approach of twilight was wrapt—All was very quiet, both in the House & in the wood—A carriage drew near, she heard the sound. She saw it shoot through the fog—But it was not Zamorna—no, the driving was neither the driving of Jehu the son of Nimshi, nor that of Jehu's postillions— She had not gazed a minute before her experienced eye discerned that there was something wrong with the horses—the harness had got entangled, or they were frightened—The coachman had lost command over them, they were plunging violently—She rung the bell—a servant entered, she ordered immediate assistance to be despatched to that carriage on the road—Two grooms presently hurried down the drive to execute her commands—but before they could reach the spot, one of the horses, in its gambols, had slipped on the icy road & fallen. the others grew more unmanageable & presently the carriage lay overturned on the road-side—One of

Miss Laury's messengers came back—She threw up the window that she might communicate with him more readily—"Any accident?" she asked "anybody hurt?" "I hope not much, Madam." "Who is in the carriage?—" "Only one lady, and she seems to have fainted—she looked very white when I opened the door—What is to be done, Madam?—" Miss Laury, with Irish frankness, answered directly—"Bring them all into the house—let the horses be taken into the stables & the servants—how many are there?" "Three, Madam, two postillions & a footman. it seems quite a gentleman's turn-out—very plain but quite slap-up— beautiful horses—" "Do you know the liveries?" "Can't say, Madam. Postillions grey & white, footman in plain-clothes— horses frightened at a drove of Sydenham oxen they say—very spirited nags—" "Well, you have my orders. bring the lady in directly & make the others comfortable—" "Yes Madam"—The groom touched his hat & departed—Miss [Laury] shut her window, it was very cold—Not many minutes elapsed before the lady, in the arms of her own servant, was slowly brought up the lawn—& ushered into the drawing-room—"Lay her on the sofa" said Miss Laury—she was obeyed—the lady's travelling cloak was carefully removed, & a thin figure became apparent in a dark silk dress— the cushions of down scarcely sunk under the pressure, it was so light—

Her swoon was now passing off—the genial warmth of the fire, which shone full on her, revived her—opening her eyes, she looked up at Miss Laury's face who was bending close over her & wetting her lips with some cordial—recognising a stranger, she shyly turned her glance aside—& asked for her servants—"they are in the house, Madam, & perfectly safe—but you cannot pursue your journey at present, the carriage is much broken"—The lady lay silent—she looked keenly round the room & seeing the perfect elegance of its arrangement—the cheerful & tranquil glow of its hearthlight—she appeared to grow more composed—Turning a little on the cushions which supported her, & by no means looking at Miss Laury but straight the other way—she said "To whom am I indebted for this kindness—Where am I?" "In a hospitable country, Madam—the Angrians never turn their backs on strangers—" "I know I am in Angria" she said quietly—"But where? What is the name of the House & who are you?"—Miss Laury coloured slightly, it seemed as if there was some undefined reluctance to give her real name—that she knew she was widely celebrated—too widely—most likely the lady would turn from her in contempt if she heard it—& Miss Laury felt she could not bear

that—"I am only the housekeeper" she said. "This is a shooting
Lodge belonging to a Great Angrian proprietor—" "Who?"
asked the lady, who was not to be put off by indirect answers—
Again Miss Laury hesitated, for her life she could not have said
"His Grace the Duke of Zamorna—" She replied hastily "A
Gentleman of Western extraction, a distant branch of the Great
Pakenhams—so at least the family records say, but they have been
long naturalised in the east—" "I never heard of them" replied the
lady—"Pakenham?—that is not an Angrian name!" "Perhaps,
Madam, you are not particularly acquainted with this part of the
Country—" "I know Hawkscliffe" said the lady— "& your House
is on the very borders within the Royal Liberties—is it not?" "Yes
Madam—it stood there before the great Duke bought up the
forest Manor—& his majesty allowed my master to retain this
Lodge & the privilidge of sporting in the chase—" "Well, and
you are Mr Pakenham's housekeeper—?" "Yes Madam—" the
lady surveyed Miss Laury with another furtive side-glance of her
large, majestic eyes—those eyes lingered upon the diamond ear-
rings—the bandeau of brilliants that flashed from between the
clusters of raven curls—then passed over the sweet face, the
exquisite figure of the young housekeeper—& finally were reverted
to the wall with an expression that spoke volumes—Miss Laury
could have torn the dazzling pendants from her ears, she was
bitterly stung—"Every body knows me" she said to herself.
" "Mistress" I suppose is branded on my brow—" In her turn she
gazed on her Guest—the lady was but a young creature, though
so high & commanding in her demeanour—She had very small &
feminine features—handsome eyes—a neck of delicate curve, &
had fair, long, graceful little snowy aristocratic hands & sandalled
feet to match—It would have been difficult to tell her rank by her
dress—None of those dazzling witnesses appeared which had
betrayed Miss Laury—any Gentleman's wife might have worn the
gown of dark blue silk—the tinted gloves of Parisian kid & the fairy
sandals of black satin in which she was attired—"May I have a
room to myself?" she asked—again turning her eyes with something like a smile toward Miss Laury—"Certainly, Madam, I wish
to make you comfortable—can you walk upstairs?" "Oh yes!"
She rose from the couch, & leaning upon Miss Laury's offered arm
in a way that shewed she had been used to that sort of support—
they both glided from the room. Having seen her fair but somewhat
haughty guest carefully laid on a stately crimson bed in a quiet &
spacious chamber—having seen her head sink with all its curls on
to the pillow of down, her large shy eyes close under their smooth

Drawing by Charlotte Brontë evocative of Zenobia Ellrington,
Countess of Northangerland

eyelids & her little slender hands fold on her breast—in an attitude of perfect repose, Miss Laury prepared to leave her— She stirred. "Come back a moment" she said—She was obeyed, there was something in the tone of her voice which exacted obedience—"I don't know who you are" she said "but I am very much obliged to you for your kindness—if my manners are displeasing, forgive me—I mean no incivility—I suppose you will wish to know my name—it is Mrs Irving—my husband is a minister in the Northern Kirk—I came from Sneachiesland—now you may go—" Miss Laury did go. Mrs Irving had testified incredulity respecting her story & now she reciprocated that incredulity—Both ladies were lost in their own mystification—

Five o'clock now struck—it was nearly dark—a servant with a taper was lighting up the chandeliers in the large dining-room where a table spread for dinner received the kindling lamp-light upon a starry service of silver—it was likewise magnificently flashed back from a splendid side-board—all arranged in readiness to receive the Great—the expected Guest—Tolerably punctual in keeping an appointment when he meant to keep it at all— Zamorna entered the House—as the fairy-like voice of a musical-clock in the passage—struck out its symphony to the pendulum. The opening of the front-door, a bitter rush of the night wind—& then the sudden close & the step advancing forwards were the signals of his arrival—Miss Laury was in the dining-room looking round & giving the last touch to all things—she just met her master as he entered—His cold lip pressed to her forehead & his colder hand clasping hers brought the sensation which it was her custom of weeks & months to wait for, and to consider, when attained, as the single recompense of all delay & all toil, all suffering—"I am frozen, Mina" said he "I came on horseback for the last four miles and the night is like Canada—" Chafing his icy hand to animation between her own warm & supple palms—she answered by the speechless but expressive look of joy, satisfaction— idolatry which filled & overflowed her eyes. "What can I do for you, my lord?" were her first words—as he stood by the fire raising his hands cheerily over the blaze—he laughed—"Put your arms round my neck, Mina, & kiss my cheek as warm & blooming as your own—" if Mina Laury had been Mina Wellesley she would have done so—& it gave her a pang to resist the impulse that urged her to take him at his word, but she put it by and only diffidently drew near the arm-chair into which he had now thrown himself, & began to smooth & separate the curls which were matted on his temples. She noticed, as the first smile of salutation subsided, a gloom succeeded on her master's brow—which, however he spoke or laughed afterwards, remained a settled characteristic of his countenance—"What visitors are in the house?" he asked. "I saw the groom rubbing down four black horses before the Stables as I came in—they are not of the Hawkscliffe stud I think?" "No my lord—A carriage was overturned at the Lodge-Gates about an hour since—& as the lady who was in it was taken out insensible, I ordered her to be brought up here & her servants accommodated for the night—" "And do you know who the lady is?" continued his Grace. "The horses are good—first rate—" "She says her name is Mrs Irving & that she is the wife of a Presbyterian minister—in the North but—" "You hardly believe her?" interrupted the Duke— "No" returned Miss Laury. "I must say I took her for a lady of rank—she has something highly aristocratic about her manners & aspect, & she appeared to know a good deal about Angria." "What is she like?" asked Zamorna. "Young or old—handsome or ugly?" "She is young—slender, not so tall as I—& I should say rather elegant than handsome—very pale & cold in her demeanour— She has a small mouth & chin & a very fair neck—" "Humph—a trifle like lady Stuartville" replied his Majesty—"I should not wonder if it is the Countess, but I'll know—perhaps you did not say to whom the house belonged, Mina?" "I said" replied Mina smiling "the owner of the House was a great Angrian Proprietor— a lineal descendant of the Western Pakenhams, & that I was his Housekeeper." "Very good, she would not believe you—you look like an Angrian country Gentleman's Dolly—give me your hand, my Girl—are you not as old as I am?—" "Yes, my lord Duke—I was born on the same day an hour after your Grace." "So I have heard, but it must be a mistake—you don't look twenty & I am twenty-five—my beautiful Western—what eyes!—look at me, Mina—straight & don't blush—" Mina tryed to look but she could not do it without blushing—She coloured to the temples— "Pshaw!" said his Grace, putting her away—"Pretending to be modest—my acquaintance of ten years cannot meet my eye unshrinkingly—have you lost that ring I once gave you, Mina?" "What ring, my lord, you have given me many—" "That which I said had the essence of your whole heart & mind engraven in the stone as a motto—" "FIDELITY?" asked Miss Laury, & she held out her hand with a graven emerald on her forefinger— "Right" was the reply. "Is it your motto still?" And with one of his haughty, jealous glances he seemed trying to read her conscience— Miss Laury at once saw that late transactions were not a secret confined between herself & lord Hartford—She saw his Grace was unhinged & strongly inclined to be savage—She stood & watched him with a sad fearful gaze—"Well" she said, turning away after a long pause—"If your Grace is angry with me, I've very little to care about in this world " The entrance of servants with the dinner prevented Zamorna's answer—As he took his place at the head of the table, he said to the man who stood behind him "Give Mr Pakenham's compliments to Mrs Irving and say that he will be happy to see her at his table if she will honour him so far as to be present there—" The footman vanished—he returned in five minutes—"Mrs Irving is too much tired to avail herself of Mr Pakenham's kind invitation at present, but she will be happy to join him at tea—" "Very well" said Zamorna, then looking round "Where is Miss Laury?" Mina was in the act of gliding from the room, but she stopped mechanically at his call. "Am I to dine alone?" he asked—"Does your Grace wish me to attend you?" he answered by rising & leading her to her seat. he then resumed his own—Dinner commenced—It was not till after the cloth was withdrawn & the servants had retired that the Duke, whilst he sipped his single glass of Champagne, recommenced the conversation he had before so unpleasantly entered upon—"Come here, my girl" he said, drawing a seat close to his side—Mina never delayed nor hesitated through bashfulness or any other feeling to comply with his orders—"now" he continued, leaning his head towards hers—& placing his hand on her shoulder "Are you happy Mina—do you want anything?" "Nothing, my lord." she spoke truly—all that was capable of yielding her happiness on this side of eternity was at that moment within her reach—The room was full of calm—the lamps hung as if they were listening—the fire sent up no flickering flame, but diffused a broad still glowing light over all the spacious saloon—Zamorna touched her—his form & features filled her eye—his voice her ear—his presence her whole heart—she was soothed to perfect happiness—"My Fidelity" pursued that musical voice—"If thou hast any favour to ask, now is the time—I'm all concession—as sweet as honey, as yielding as a lady's glove—Come, Esther, what is thy petition & thy request?— even to the half of my Kingdom it shall be granted"—"Nothing" again murmured Miss Laury—"Oh my lord, nothing—what can I want?" "Nothing!" he repeated. "What, no reward for ten year's faith & love & devotion, no reward for the companionship in six month's Exile—no recompense to the little hand that has so often smoothed my pillow in sickness—to the sweet lips that have many a time in cool & dewy health been pressed to a brow of fever, none to the dark Milesian eyes that once grew dim with watching through endless nights by my couch of delirium?—need I speak of the sweetness & fortitude that cheered sufferings known only to thee & me, Mina—of the devotion that gave me bread when thou wert dying of hunger, & that scarcely more than a year since?—for all this & much more must there be no reward?" "I have had it" said Miss Laury "I have it now—" "But" continued the Duke "what if I have devised something worthy of your acceptance—look up now & listen to me—" She did look up, but she speedily looked down again—her master's eye was insupportable—it burnt absolutely with infernal fire—"What is he going to say?" murmured Miss Laury to herself, she trembled—"I say, love" pursued the individual, drawing her a little closer to him—"I will give you as a reward a husband—don't start now—& that husband shall be a nobleman & that nobleman is called lord Hartford—! Now Madam—stand up & let me look at you—" he opened his arms & Miss Laury sprang erect like a loosened bow—"Your Grace is anticipated!" she said "that offer has been made me before—lord Hartford did it himself three days ago—" "And what did you say, Madam? speak the truth now—subterfuge won't avail you—" "What did I say? Zamorna, I don't know—it little signifies—you have rewarded me, my lord Duke, but I cannot bear this—I feel sick." with a deep short sob, she turned white, & fell—close by the Duke—her head against his foot—This was the first time in her life that Miss Laury had fainted—but strong health availed nothing against the deadly struggle which convulsed every feeling of her nature when she heard her master's announcement—She believed him to be perfectly sincere—she thought he was tired of her and she could not stand it. I suppose Zamorna's first feeling when she fell was horror, & his next, I am tolerably certain, was intense gratification—People say I am not in earnest when I abuse him—or else I would here insert half a page of deserved vituperation—deserved & heart-felt—as it is I will merely relate his conduct without note or comment—He took a wax taper from the table & held it over Miss Laury—hers could be no dissimulation—she went white as marble & still as stone. In truth then, she did intensely love him with a devotion that left no room in her thoughts for one shadow of an alien image—Do not think, reader, that Zamorna meant to be so generous as to bestow Miss Laury on lord Hartford—no, trust him—he was but testing in his usual way the attachment which a thousand proofs daily given ought long ago to have convinced him was undying—while he yet gazed, she began to recover—her eyelids stirred, & then slowly dawned from beneath, the large black orbs that scarcely met his before they filled to over-flowing with sorrow—not a gleam of anger, not a whisper of reproach—her lips & eyes spoke together no other language than the simple words "I cannot leave you"—She rose feebly & with effort—the Duke stretched out his hand to assist her—he held to her lips the scarcely-tasted wine-glass—"Mina" he said—"are you collected enough to hear me?" "Yes, my lord." "Then listen—I would much sooner give half—aye, the whole of my estates to lord Hartford than yourself—What I said just now was only to try you." Miss Laury raised her eyes, sighed like awaking from some hideous dream—but she could not speak— "Would I" continued the Duke, "Would I resign the possession of my first love to any hands but my own? I would far rather see her in her coffin—and I would lay you there as still, as white, & much more lifeless than you were stretched just now at my feet—before I would for threat, for entreaty, for purchase, give to another a glance of your eye, a smile from your lip—I know you adore me now, Miss Laury, for you could not feign that agitation, & therefore I will tell you what a proof I gave yesterday of my regard for you—Hartford mentioned your name in my presence & I revenged the profanation by a shot which sent him to his bed little better than a corpse—" Miss Laury shuddered, but so dark & profound are the mysteries of human nature, ever allying vice with virtue, that I fear this bloody proof of her master's love brought to her heart more rapture than horror. She said not a word—for now Zamorna's arms were again folded round her, & again he was soothing her to tranquillity—by endearments & caresses that far away removed all thought of the world, all past pangs of shame, all cold doubts, all weariness, all heart-sickness resulting from Hope—long-deferred—She [He] had told her that she was his first Love, & now she felt tempted to believe that she was likewise his only love—Strong-minded beyond her sex—active, energetic & accomplished in all other points of view—here she was as weak as a child—she lost her identity—her very way of life was swallowed up in that of another—

There came a knock at the door—Zamorna rose & opened it. His valet stood without—"Might I speak with your Grace in the Ante-room?" asked Monsieur Rosier in somewhat a hurried tone— the Duke followed him out—"What do you want with me, Sir? anything the matter?"—"Ahem" began Eugene, whose coun- tenance expressed much more embarassment than is the usual characteristic of his dark sharp physiognomy—"Ahem! my lord

Duke, rather a curious spot of work—a complete conjuror's trick, if your Grace will allow me to say so—" "What do you mean, Sir?" "Sacre! I hardly know—I must confess I felt a trifle stultified when I saw it—" "Saw what? speak plainly Rosier—" "How your Grace is to act I can't imagine—" replied the valet "Though indeed I have seen your majesty double wonderfully well when the case appeared to me extremely embarassing—but this I really thought extra—I could not have dreamt—" "Speak to the point Rosier or—" Zamorna lifted his hand—"Mort de ma vie!" exclaimed Eugene "I will tell your Grace all I know—I was walking carelessly through the passage about ten minutes since, when I heard a step on the stairs—a light step as if of a very small foot—I turned, & there was a lady coming down. my lord, she was a lady!" "Well, Sir, did you know her?" "I think, if my eyes were not bewitched, I did—I stood in the shade screened by a pillar & she passed very near without observing me—I saw her distinctly, & may I be d———d this very moment—if it was not—" "Who Sir—?" "The Duchess!!" there was a pause which was closed by a remarkably prolonged whistle from the Duke—he put both his hands into his pockets & took a leisurely turn through the room—"You're sure, Eugene?" he said. "I know you dare not tell me a lie in such matters—because you have a laudable & natural regard to your proper carcass—Aye, it's true enough I'll be sworn —Mrs Irving—wife of a minister in the North—a satirical hit at my royal self by G–d—pale, fair neck—little mouth & chin— Very good! I wish that same little mouth & chin were about a hundred miles off—what can have brought her? Anxiety about her invaluable husband? could not bear any longer without him— obliged to set off to see what he was doing?—It's as well that turn-spit Rosier told me, however—if she had entered the room un-expectedly about five minutes since—God! I should have had no resource but to tie her hand and foot—It would have killed her— What the d———l shall I do? Must not be angry, she can't do with that sort of thing just now—Talk softly—reprove her gently— swear black & white to my having no connection with Mr Paken-ham's housekeeper—" Closing his soliloquy, the Duke turned again to his valet—"What room did her Grace go into?" "The drawing-room, my lord—she's there now—" "Well, say nothing about it, Rosier, on pain of sudden death—do you hear, Sir—?" Rosier laid his hand on his heart & Zamorna left the room to commence operations—

Softly unclosing the drawing-room door, he perceived a lady by the

hearth—her back was towards him—but there could be no mistake
—the whole turn of form—the style of dress—the curled auburn
head—all were attributes of but one person—of his own unique,
haughty, jealous little Duchess—he closed the door as noiselessly as
he had opened it and stole forwards—Her attention was absorbed
in something, a book she had picked up as he stood unobserved behind her—he could see that her eye rested on the fly leaf where
was written in his own hand—

> Holy St Cyprian! thy waters stray
>   With still & solemn tone,
> And fast my bright hours pass away
> And somewhat throws a shadow grey,
> Even as twilight closes day,
>   Upon thy waters lone.
>
> Farewell! if I might come again,
>   Young as I was & free,
> And feel once more in every vein
> The fire of that first passion reign
> Which sorrow could not quench nor pain,
>   I'd soon return to thee,
> But while thy billows seek the main
>   That never more may be!

This was dated "Mornington—1829"—The Duchess felt a hand
press her shoulder & she looked up—The force of attraction had
its usual result, & she clung to what she saw—"Adrian! Adrian!"
was all her lips could utter—"Mary! Mary!" replied the Duke,
allowing her to hang about him—"Pretty doings!—what brought
you here? are you running away, eloping, in my absence?"
"Adrian, why did you leave me, you said you would come back
in a week & its eight days since you left me—do come home—"
"So you actually have set off in search of a husband" said Zamorna
laughing heartily "& been overturned & obliged to take shelter in
Pakenham's shooting box—!" "Why are you here Adrian?"
enquired the Duchess, who was far too much in earnest to join in
his laugh—"Who is Pakenham & who is that person who calls
herself his housekeeper, & why do you let anybody live so near
Hawkscliffe without ever telling me?"—"I forgot to tell you" said
his Grace—"I've other things to think about—when those bright
hazel eyes are looking up at me—as for Pakenham, to tell you the
truth—he's a sort of left-hand cousin of your own—being Natural

son to the old Admiral, my uncle, in the South, & his housekeeper
is his sister—Voila tout—kiss me now—"—the Duchess did kiss
him, but it was with a heavy sigh—the cloud of jealous anxiety
hung on her brow undissipated—"Adrian, my heart aches still—
why have you been staying so long in Angria?—O, you don't care
for me!—you have never thought how miserably I have been
longing for your return—Adrian—" she stopped & cryed—"Mary,
recollect yourself" said his Grace—"I cannot be always at your
feet—you were not so weak when we were first married—you let
me leave you often then without any jealous remonstrance—" "I
did not know you so well at that time—" said Mary—"& if my
mind is weakened—all its strength has gone away in tears &
terrors for you—I am neither so handsome nor so cheerful as I once
was—but you ought to forgive my decay because you have caused
it." "Low spirits!" returned Zamorna—"Looking on the dark side
of matters—God bless me! the wicked is caught in his own net—I
wish I could add "yet shall I withal escape"—Mary, never again
reproach yourself with loss of beauty till I give the hint first—
believe me now—in that & every other respect, you are just what I
wish you to be—you cannot fade any more than marble can—at
least not to my eyes—& as for your devotion & tenderness—though
I chide it's excess sometimes, because it wastes & bleaches you
almost to a shadow—yet it forms the very firmest chain that binds
me to you—Now cheer up—to-night you shall go to Hawkscliffe,
it is only five miles off—I cannot accompany you because I have
some important business to transact with Pakenham which must
not be deferred—to-morrow I will be at the castle before dawn—
the carriage shall be ready, I will put you in, myself beside you—
Off we go straight to Verdopolis, & there for the next three months
I will tire you of my company, morning, noon & night—Now, what
can I promise more? if you choose to be jealous of Henri Fernando,
baron of Etrei, or John, Duke of Fidena, or the earl of Richton,
who, as God is my witness, has been the only companion of my
present perambulation—why, I can't help it—I must then take to
soda-water & Despair—or have myself petrified & carved into an
Apollo for your dressing-room—Lord! I get no credit with my
Virtue—" By dint of lies & laughter—the individual at last
succeeded in getting all things settled to his mind—the Duchess
went to Hawkscliffe that night. keeping his promise for once, he
accompanied her to Verdopolis the next morning—

Lord Hartford still lies between life & death—his passion is
neither weakened by pain—piqued by rejection, nor cooled by

absence—on the iron nerves of the man are graven an impression which nothing can efface—Warner curses him—Richton deplores—

For a long space of time, Good-bye Reader—I have done my best to please you—& though I know that through Feebleness, Dullness & Iteration my work terminates rather in Failure & [than] triumph—yet you are bound to forgive, for I have done my best—

Haworth 1838   C. Brontë Jany 17th

CAPTAIN HENRY HASTINGS

INTRODUCTION

The following narrative, again untitled by its author, was written at a time when Charlotte Brontë was unemployed and at home for a longer period than at any time since her twentieth year. She dated the two parts into which she divided her tale February 24th and March 26th, 1839, and the manuscript's length can, therefore, be attributed to the author's greater leisure.

Written fourteen months after Mina Laury, *it also marks a further command of her medium since the earlier tale. This is to be noted in its wider range of situation and character, and for its psychological insights. The gain is not without its corresponding loss: the tenderness and poetry of* Mina Laury *are absent, and are replaced by an overall cynicism which no longer appears, as in the earlier tales, to be an assumed swagger on the part of the inexperienced author. In* Captain Hastings, *the cause of the cynicism lies in the very subject of which she treats—the degradation of Captain Hastings and his sister's complete involvement in his ruin. It is a bitter tale, born of who knows what fresh disillusionment with Branwell's conduct. That Henry Hastings continues to be the prototype of Branwell there can be no doubt; that Elizabeth Hastings reflects Charlotte's own loyalty and devotion to him, despite her loss of hope in his ability to amend, is equally evident. The passages dealing with the brother/sister relationship are among the very first from the pen of Charlotte Brontë to reflect real experience as distinct from dream-experience, and are admirable for their truth and dignity. They are also biographically revealing. Though completely disillusioned about her brother, Elizabeth Hastings can say of him: "It was very odd but his sister did not think a pin the worse of him for all his Dishonour. It is private meanness, not the public infamy, that degrade a man in the opinion of his relatives . . . he was the same brother to her he had always been, still she beheld him acting through a medium peculiar to herself . . . Natural affection is never rooted out . . ."*

The honesty in the portrayal of the character of Elizabeth, whose physical and mental likeness to herself Charlotte Brontë was at no pains to hide, is a first step towards those prototypes of herself, Jane Eyre and Lucy Snowe, who are the crowning achievement of her maturer work. Elizabeth, we are told, had "a sharp irritable temper which rendered her wholly unfit" for teaching small children. She also felt herself—and knew herself to be—superior to her surroundings, and far more intelligent than the young women, like Jane Moore, upon whom she had to wait. But the main revelation made on Elizabeth's behalf was her longing for love, and the repeated frustration of her passion. We read that she "lingered over the recollection of his [her lover's] look and language, with an intensity of romantic feeling that very few people in this world can form the remotest conception of". Here, already at this early stage in the author's development, she showed herself capable of plumbing the depths of passion, not the yielding passion of a Mina Laury or of the Caroline Vernon to come, but of the girl Charlotte Brontë herself was, a girl too proud to accept happiness at the price of her self-respect. When Sir William Percy proposes to Elizabeth to make her his mistress, she refuses him, just as Jane Eyre later refuses Rochester. The character of Elizabeth Hastings looks, therefore, forward *in her author's evolution, and is the first, among the innumerable train of Zamorna's easy loves, to stand by her principles. The resultant truth of the characterisation is an immense advance even on such a sharply-analysed creation as Mina Laury, since it was* drawn from life.

It is a matter of biographical interest that, at the very time Charlotte Brontë was writing Captain Hastings, *she received a first proposal of marriage from the brother of her closest friend, Ellen Nussey. He was the Rev. Henry Nussey, and the total unsuitability of his character and temperament to attract such a girl as Charlotte, and her immediate refusal of him, did not, however, leave her untouched by the experience. Love, even in such unromantic habiliments as Henry Nussey, had come her way, and she had been forced to spurn it. She was realist enough even then to judge that her chances of a renewal of such an offer were very tenuous. It is evident that the incident, which occurred in March 1839, set her thinking very seriously on the question of the alternatives open to women without fortune, like herself: loneliness, or a life without love in the company of an uncongenial mate. The third alternative, illicit pleasure, she squarely rejected. It may be that she introduced the incident of Rosamund Wellesley here as a foil to Elizabeth's own more resolute conduct under temptation. That Charlotte claims no prodigies of virtue for her heroine is seen in her honest confession, under pressure from Sir William Percy, that "I am afraid of nothing but myself".*

In the present manuscript Charlotte Brontë reverted to her pseudonym, Charles Towns(h)end, temporarily abandoned in Mina Laury. *As a consequence, the dialogue gains in raciness and, at the same time, in ease. The slang, though an obvious reflection of Branwell's way of talking, carries conviction in the creation of Hastings himself. Except for a single appearance in the final sketch, Zamorna himself is absent from the tale, a proof of how keenly the author was absorbed at the time in the brother/sister theme.*

The character of Henry Hastings was a prototype of Branwell, a poet and historian created in his image. He was the "Chronicler of the Angrian Wars" and the composer of the Angrian National Anthems "History Stood by her Pillar of Fame" (1834) and "Sound the Loud Trumpet o'er Afric's Dark Seas" (1834). As seen in Julia, *Charlotte took over the character and introduced him into Verdopolitan society. He continued to figure in*

Branwell's own narratives, however, and notably in Percy *(c.1840) where he assumed the role of commentator as well as narrator, without reference being made to his destiny as previously reported by Charlotte here.*

The plot of Captain Hastings *is not as desultory as appears at first sight; there is a link binding the separate episodes in the pursuit, capture and trial of Hastings, and in his sister's intervention on his behalf. Only the author's love of mystification at this period of her writing, makes a secret of Elizabeth's identity as the unkown female passenger in the coach, whose journey to the city of Zamorna to plead for her brother's life opens the narrative.*

The manuscript of Captain Hastings *is currently in the possession of the Harry Elkins Widener Collection in Harvard College Library, by whose kind permission it is printed here. It has never been previously published.*

CAPTAIN HENRY HASTINGS

A young man of captivating exterior, elegant address and most gentlemanlike deportment, is desirous of getting his bread easy & of living in the greatest possible enjoyment of comfort & splendour —at the least possible expense of labour & drudgery—to this end he begs to inform the public that it would suit him uncommon well to have a fortune left him, or to get a wife whose least merit should not be her pecuniary endowment. The advertiser is not particular as to age—nor does he lay any stress on those fleeting charms of a merely personal nature—which, according to the opinion of the best-informed medical men of all ages, a few days sickness or the most trivial accident may suffice to remove. On the contrary, an imperfect symmetry of form—a limb—laterally—horizontally or obliquely bent aside from the line of rigid rectitude, or even the absence of a feature—as an eye too few, or a row of teeth minus— will be no material objection to this enlightened & sincere individual—provided only satisfactory testimonials be given of the possession of that one great & paramount virtue—that eminent & irresistible charm C–A–S–H! address C T.—care of Mr Graeme Ellrington, No 12 Chapel Street, Verdopolis. P.S. None need apply whose property—personal—landed & funded, amounts to less than 20,000 £ sterling. the Advertiser considers himself a cheap bargain at double this sum—He would have no objection to enter into an immediate negotiation with Miss Victoria Delph of Brunswick Terrace or Miss Angelica Corbett of Melon Grove. These ladies or any others who may feel disposed to try their luck at this noble lottery—are referred for character &c. to the most noble Viscount Macara Lofty, Sir W. Percy, Bart., Mr Steaton Esqr—Rev G. Bromley—Revd W. Stephens, Revd Mr Chambers &c. &c.

Such was the advertisement that lately appeared in the columns of a metropolitan paper—being the last resource of an unoffending & meritorious individual who, pennyless & placeless, found himself driven upon the two horns of a hideous dilemma, & all attempts to raise the wind by less desperate methods having failed—compelled either to write or to wed—for the last six months I have been living on, as it were, on turtle-soup & foie grasse—I have been rowing & revelling & rioting to my heart's content—but now, alas, my pockets are empty & my pleasures are gone—I must either write

a book or marry a wife, to refill the one & to recall the other—
which shall I do? Hymen with a waving torch invites me—But no,
I am beloved by too many to give up my liberty to one. Fascinating
as a pheasant, I will still be free as an eagle—Wail not then, O
dark-eyed Daughters of the West—Lament not, ye ruddy virgins
of the east—Sit not in sackcloth soft maids of the sunny South, nor
weep upon the hill-tops proud damsels of the North—nor yet send
the voice of mourning from afar, O ye mermaids of the island
realm—Charles Townsend will not marry—he is yet too young—
too frisky, too untamed, to submit to the sober bonds of matrimony—Charles Townshend will still be the handsome Bachelor,
the cynosure of neighbouring eyes, the tempting apple of Discord
to the African fair—Charles Townshend, therefore, gets pen, ink &
paper & sits down to write a book—though his charming noddle
is about as empty of ideas as his pocket is of pence—"Regardez
comme nous allons commencer—"

I have clean forgotten what day of the month it was—or even what
month in the year—whether the last week in September or the
first week in October—that I, comfortably seated—in an Angrian
stage-coach—found myself comfortably rolling up from Adrianopolis—& [*illegible*] towards the mighty Megatherian—the Old
Capital of the country. However, it was Autumn—the woods were
turning Brown. It was the season of partridge shooting—for the
popping of guns was continually to be heard over the landscape &,
as we whirled past Meadowbank, the seat of John Kirkwall Esqr.
M.P., I recollect catching a glimpse from the coach window of
three or four young gentlemen in green shooting-jackets—followed
by a yelling train of pointers & a brassy-browed gamekeeper. These
sparks were just issuing from the Park-gate—& as one of them
hailed our equipage with an impressive oath—& another sportively directed his fowling piece toward a young girl on the outside
—thereby causing her to ejaculate a scream of exemplary shrillness,
a Gentleman opposite to me observed "that is Mr Frank Kirkwall".
at the same time he smiled significantly, as good as to add "a
scoundrelly young blade". "And I believe" he continued "the
other with the gun is no other than Lord Vincent James Warner, the
youngest brother of the premier." "Indeed!" exclaimed a voice at
my side—& at the same moment a person I had not before observed
[*illegible*] forward & almost rudely pushed past me to get a look
from the window—The person was a lady & therefore I could not
well resent her want of ceremony—so I waited patiently till she
chose to sit down again—& then I said with a jocular smile—"You

seem interested ma'am in the lieutenant—" "Why" she answered "I don't often see celebrated men—" "I am not aware that that young chap is particularly celebrated" was my reply—"Yes, but his brother you know" responded the lady with [*illegible*] clearness of expression—"and I believe the lieutenant himself is an officer of the illustrious nineteenth." "Illustrious ma'am! a parcel of blackguards!" exclaimed the gentleman who had spoken before —"Yes, they are" said the lady, who seemed not strongly inclined to dispute any opinion uttered by another—"They are certainly very wild & reckless according to all accounts—but then, after all, they have performed gallant exploits—Evesham would never have been won but for them." "Fit for nothing but storming towns" answered the gentleman "And thats dirty work after all—bloody work ma'am." "Yes, it is" again assented she "But if we have war, there must be bloodshed—& then the nineteenth have other things to do than that, & they have never failed—at least the newspapers say so—" "They always prime so well before they explode—" "I've understood ma'am that that honourable regiment mostly drinks up de trop in time of action." I expected the lady would turn enthusiastic & indignant at this, but she only smiled. "Indeed Sir! well then they do their duty much better than most men do sober"—"I can tell you ma'am on the best authority that at Westwood, half an hour before General Thornton put himself at their head to make the final charge—every officer & almost every private of the nineteenth were as drunk as they could sit in their saddles—" "Very plucky!" said the lady, still not at all roused. "Yet that charge was most noble & successful—was it not said that Lord Arundel thanked them on the field of battle for their gallantry?" "Don't know" said the gentleman coldly "& if he did, madam, his lordship is very little better than they are—" "No, certainly" said she "I should think his courage to be much of the same order—" "Very likely" said the gentleman, whom by this time I more than suspected to be a millowner of Zamorna or Hartford Dale, & now, taking a newspaper from his pocket, he leant back in the coach & immersed himself in the perusal of a long speech which had been made by Edward Percy Esqr. M.P. at a dinner lately given him by his constituents. The lady leant back too and was silent—

Until the commencement of the little dialogue above recorded— I had not been sufficiently attracted by my fellow-passenger to give her more than the slightest cursory glance imaginable—but I now scrutinised her a little more closely—I remembered indeed that early that morning as, after travelling all night, our vehicle was traversing a wild tract of country in the Douro—its speed had suddenly been checked by a cry of "Coach! Coach!"—& on looking out I perceived that we had neared a little Inn just where a branch-path winding down from among the loneliest hills formed a junction with the great high-road—& by the grey light was just discernible a female figure in a shawl—bonnet & veil— waiting at the Inn-Door & a woman-servant standing guard over certain pharophernalia of boxes—packages &c. The luggage was hoisted onto the top of the coach & the lady was helped inside, were, being but little & thin, she was easily stowed away between myself & a stout woman in a plurality of cloaks. I just saw her shake hands with her attendant. She said something which sounded like "Good bye Mary"—or "Martha"—or "Hannah"—& then as the coach dashed off—she sat well back behind my shoulder—& comfortably hid in her veil & shawl, gave herself up to most unsocial & unfascinating taciturnity.

One can't feel interest in a person that will neither speak nor look—so, after the lapse of nearly four mortal hours silence, I had completely forgotten her existence & should never have remembered it again if that sudden push of hers towards the window, in which she disarranged my hair with the contact of her shawl, had not reminded me of it. The few sentences she subsequently uttered prevented her from sinking again into immediate oblivion, & though no-one could have deducted a character from them—yet they were sufficiently marked to make me feel a little curiosity as to what & who she might be—I had already made two or three attempts to get a view of her face, but in vain—her bonnet & veil effectually shaded it from observation—besides, I thought she intentionally turned from me, & though she had talked freely enough to the crusty middle-aged manufacturer opposite—I had not yet been able to draw a syllable of conversation from her—By her voice I concluded she must be a young person—though her dress was of that general simple nature that almost any age might have adopted it. a dark silk gown & heavy chenille shawl—a straw bonnet plainly trimmed, completed a costume unpretending but not unladylike—Thinking at last that the best way to get a look at her was to begin to talk—I turned rather suddenly towards her for the purpose of commencing a conversation—Meantime, while I had been thinking of her, she, I found, had also been thinking of me—and as she sat shrinking behind me, she had taken the opportunity of my seeming abstraction to scrutinise my physiognomy most closely— consequently, when I made the unexpected movement of turning my head—I saw her veil thrown back & her eyes fixed full on me with a gaze of keen sharp observation—I protest I felt almost flattered by the discovery—however, I soon recovered my wonted self-possession sufficiently to take revenge by an answering stare of, I flatter myself, at least equal intensity—The lady exhibited some command of countenance, she only coloured a little—& then, looking towards the window, remarked "It was a beautiful country we were entering upon". It was, for we were now in the province of Zamorna, & the green & fertile glades of March were unfolding on either side of the noble road—had the lady been very old & very ugly I would have said no more to her —had she been young & extremely handsome I would have commenced a series of petits soins & soft speeches—Young indeed she was—but not handsome—she had a fair, rather wan complexion, dark hair smoothly combed in two plain folds from her forehead— features capable of much varied expression & a quick wandering eye of singular & by no means common-place significance.

"You are a native, madam, I presume of Angria?" "Yes" said she—"a fine thriving nation yours—no doubt you're very patriotic?" "O, of course" was her answer, & she smiled—"Now I shouldn't wonder if you take a great deal of interest in politics—" continued I. "people who live in retired places often do" she returned—"You are not from any particular district then, ma'am —?" "No, a solitary hilly country on the borders of Northangerland —" & as she spoke, I remembered the place where she had been taken up—just at the corner of a bye-path winding away amongst untrodden hills—"You must find a pleasant change in visiting this busy—stirring region" said I "were you ever in Zamorna before?" "Yes, it is a splendid province—the most populous & wealthy of all the seven—" "I dare say, now, you think it is worthy of giving a title to your gallant young monarch—eh Madam —you Angrian ladies are all very loyal I know—" "Yes" she said "I suppose the women of Angria have that character—but I understand it is not peculiar to them—most African ladies admire his Grace, don't they?" "They make a great profession of doing so, ma'am, & of course you are not an exception—" "O no!" she said with extreme coolness—"I never had the happiness of seeing him, however." "Perhaps that is the reason you speak so indifferently about him—I am quite astonished, all his fair subjects with whom I have conversed on the topic before—speak in raptures—" she smiled again. "I make a point of never speaking in raptures, especially in a stage-coach." "except about the gallant 19th" I interposed significantly—then, with my most insinuating air—

"perhaps some hero of that heroic corps is honoured with your especial interest—?" "All of them are, Sir—I like them the better because they are so abused by the cold Whiggish Ardrahians—I could even worship the Bloodhounds for the same reason—" "Humph" said I, taking a pinch of snuff—"I see how it is, madam —you don't scruple to admire in general terms any body of men— but you decline coming to individuals—" "Just so" said she gaily— "I'm not free to condescend on particulars—" "Do you travel far on this road, ma'am—?" "No, I get out at the Spinning Jenny in Zamorna—the Inn where the coach stops"—"then you are going to visit some friend in that city?"—"I expect to be met there"— this was an answer so indirect that it was as good as a rebuff—it was evident this young woman did not intend to make anybody the confidant either of her opinions or plans. "She may keep her secrets to herself then," thought I, a little huffed at her reserve, & folding my arms I resumed my former silence & so did she hers—It was about noon when we got into Zamorna—the bustle of a market day was throughout all the streets of the thriving commercial city—As the coach stopped at the Spinning Jenny—I saw my fellow-traveller give an anxious glance from the window as if in search of those she expected to meet her—I thought I would keep an eye upon her movements for my curiosity was a little piqued concerning her— the door being opened, I was just stepped out into the Inn-yard & was offering my hand to assist her in alighting, when a man in livery pushed up & forestalled me in that office—touching his hat to the lady, he enquired what luggage she had. She gave him her orders & in five minutes after I saw her enter a handsome travel- ling carriage, & the trunks & portmanteaus being stowed away in the same conveyance, & a touch being given to the horses, the whole concern rolled lightly off & in a twinkling had vanished like a dream. Surely she can't be anybody of consequence, thought I—"She has little of the bearing or mien of an Aristocrat—that quiet aspect & plain demure dress scarcely harmonize with so splendid an equipment—"

I always like to be in time for the opening of the sessions, the commencement of the grand political season—When the mustering of forces begins—when the carriages roll in daily, hourly, from the country—when Town-houses fill—& manors—Halls & castles are left to the dreariness of December-rains—Then it is that you meet country-gentlemen—walking the broad pavès of Verdopolis— Then do Angrian members swarm in the club-rooms of the capital —then do you hear the designations of eastern officials bandied from mouth to mouth like watch-words—& with the broad accent of that polished land—the clan-names of their chiefs—Warner, Stuartville—Thornton [*one line illegible*] at every turn & every corner—in all the squares & streets within three miles of Parliament Street—you hear a Mr Howard calling to a Mr Kirkwall—and a Captain Fala shouting recognition to a Major Sydenham—and a counsellor Hartford hailing a Sergeant Warner—while the Warners, the Westfields—the Stancliffes—the Binghams—the Moores—the Pighills—the Steatons—the Naylors & the Bugdens swarm like midges in the summer Hayfields of their own Arundel. Then, too, the North sends over its St Clairs—its Dinards—its Gordons & its Gildereys—while bearing up full sail from the South —the great men of war's men—Elphinstone—Ilcomkill—Wilson & Macauley cast anchor in neat commodious lodging-Houses kept by canny Scotch landladies. At this time, too, Newspapers become interesting—leading articles are piquant, parliamentary intelligence—spicy, prime-ministers wax wild—ministerial supporters are troubled with cholera-morbus, while the opposition professes piety & patriotism. Pleasant then is it after a good dinner at a friend's house with just as much wine in a man as will float his spirits off the quick-sands of despondency into the open sea of bliss —to sally forth—not in a carriage & four, but rejoicingly six abreast—if the night is wet & wild, so much the better—thus to seek Parliament-Street, to repair to the gallery, & seated there—to view the legislators come forth upon the arena. above the candle-light, when the war of words has waxed warm, what an exulting sight it is—the world shut out—candle-light—closed-doors—a hell of hate & rage, an agony of attention & suspense within, around— the members of the House—bench behind bench—with grim faces —young & old—they have forgotten to be handsome—Beauty— smiles & softness is the incense offered to pleasure—these are now sacrificing to ambition, & even such a fop as lord Stuartville has dashed his curled locks into bristling confusion—with one spas-modic movement of phrenzy—while the shade of a tall peer is standing opposite, looking at him like a devil & speaking of him words that make him less than man—In the other house, one man speaking amid the silence of many—turns upon you a thin flushed face & an eye with the glitter of fever in its pupil—he stands in the centre of the floor by the table, & on the other side is another man leaning over to him, asking him in a steady low tone questions which he can hardly answer—not for a moment does the hard-browed but pallid inquisitor spare his victim—he hears the stam-mer, the word uttered and then recalled—he turns to the house with a smile—the Devil's smile, for that is Macara Lofty—skinning alive a poor eel—a young Member who has been making a maiden speech in favour of the constitutionalists—Just look now at that individual on the Angrian side of the house, a leader, for he sits on the front-bench, a worn, delicate man, watching the combatants— he is smiling and curling his thin upper lip—not with hate at Macara, but with scorn at his baffled prey—he coldly admires that fiend's quick firm hand in the operation—his subtlety—his un-relenting pursuit of the rash Greenhorn—it is a trick in his own trade well executed—it pleases him though performed by an enemy —Bravo Mr Warner—you are a saintly premier after all.

Yet what ninnies all these are! Upon my Christian d---n---n, I do think a man who is really interested in politics the greatest fool the sun looks on—unless, indeed, as a simple matter of gain, ministers do right to hold hard on by their places—opposition members do right to try to—to supplant them—but as to oratorical fame or party prejudices—all I can say is, I don't understand that sort of thing—the above—concerning the agony of flayed eels—the attention of breathless lookers-on—the ferocity of infernal operators —I wrote merely as a specimen of a certain style—my dear reader, when you are inclined to grow enthusiastic about such things— just recall my image—leaning over the gallery with my hat on & alternately squeezing & sucking a remarkably fine madeira orange —& meantime cocking my eye at the honourable gent on his legs with an expression sufficiently indicative of the absorbing interest I take in his speechifications—there is but one individual whom it refreshes me to look at—that lengthy-limbed young member in the stiff black stock half-reclined on that bench—with a white pocket-handkerchief judiciously arranged over his face—so as to leave you in doubt as to whether that ardour & attention may not be suffi-ciently expressed by his veiled features—which the admirable nonchalance of his figure denies—That gentleman, as you may perceive, is on the Angrian side of the House, & you may derive edification from noticing the conscientious manner in which he acts with his party—Sir Marmaduke Howard is on his legs, & consequently astounding cheers are the order of the day—at every thundering peal—this worthy individual, without rising, lifts his fine eyes & utters an huzza like the dying fall of a jews-harp— Presently, when Mr Macombich rises to answer, he will roar hot contempt like any sucking dove—I respect that man—When he speaks himself, which he does as seldom as he can possibly help —though, being closely connected with the Angrian Government—he is obliged now & then to answer questions & make statements—he saunters forward to the table—says what he has to say in language that exhibits all the burning glow of an icicle—all the figurative eloquence of a well-kept Ledger—his Grace the Duke of Wellington never was more imaginative—diffusive & poetic in his most inspired moments—He seems now & then to take a sort of pleasure in rising to answer such a man as Lindsay— especially when the pulse of the house is beating quick after the outpouring of some torrents of hot rabid eloquence—Dry & cold are the answers he gives to the indignant questioning of most, for he spares his invective—his satire—his scorn—turns an icy eye of wonder on him—goes on telling his own plain quiet tale to the house—concludes with a compliment to Lindsay on his calm dispassionate demeanour—deliberately sits down & takes snuff—

As I was coming out of the house rather late one night and as several of the members were leaving it at the same time, I got mixed amongst them—Something light as a glove or handkerchief tapped my shoulder—and on turning I saw a figure somewhat taller than myself close at my shoulder—the light of a street-lamp near was brilliant enough to reveal the identity at a glance—no one could mistake the cloak with standing-up collar closely drawn about the wasted person—the black silk kerchief folded again & again round the throat—the hat with ample brim pulled over the eyes—throwing the pale forehead & strange eyes underneath into shade— implying the habitual half-hidden features of one always suspecting & always shrinking from any notice. "A cold night, Townshend" said my friend, as he and I eagerly commingled our gloved hands. "Infernally so, my Lord, but you have your carriage? you're not going to walk in this." "O yes, it does not rain I think—come, give me your arm—I'm almost finished with these late sittings of the house" —the shivering Lord leant upon me as we descended the steps & walked away up Parliament Street—"How do you like the style in which our ardent dear Baronet comes out this Sessions?" said he, meaning the Gentleman above alluded to—" "O very good, Viscount—a trifle too warm as usual—pray have you seen anything of him of late in a private way—?" "No, he has been very much about the Angrian Court ever since his return from Paris— but you, Townshend, are in correspondence with him of course—?" "Not I, indeed, the Colonel is very fitful in his friendships—he has none of your constancy, my dear Lord—" "Ah! Townshend, you and I know each other's worth—yet I thought I saw Percy move to you the other night when you & he met in the Lobby—" "Just so, he did move & passed on—though we were so close that I had an opportunity of nabbing the delicate cambric handkerchief which hung [*illegible*] from his coat-pocket—the gift of some Parisian divinity no doubt, for it had a coronet in black hair embroidered on the corner, and the word "Agathe" underneath—" "Pathètique —and really, Townshend, he did not speak to you—?" "Not a syllable, though it was the first time of our meeting for a quarter of a year"—"Aint you very low about such faithlessness—?" "Au desespoir" said I, directing my forefinger to my heart—The Viscount and I expressed our mutual grief in a low sympathetic laugh —"And what" said Macara "What can it possibly be, dear Townshend, that has expelled your loved image from his breast—?" "Ah!" returned I "There are thoughts that breathe & words that burn—Sir William has of late been in climes where softer feelings than those of friendship float from the pastile-perfumed bowers of the South—" "You grow poetic, Townshend. its your opinion then that our friend—frigid as he seems—is not altogether proof against temptation?"—"Did your lordship think he was?" "Why, I don't know—he's very philosophique"—"Your lordship, I perceive, judges from your own unsunned snow—you know yourself innocent, & you believe others to be the same—" "Will you take a pinch of snuff, Townshend—?" "I'm obliged to you, my lord—yet in this matter I believe you're somewhat too charitable—The baronet's a remarkably sly hand—depend on it, he's taken pleasure & business together during his late diplomatique excursion—" "I've heard so much hinted before" said Macara—"By whom—?" "An individual not to be doubted in such things—our illustrious friend the earl—I met him the other day at a dinner-party—he was seated between lady Stuartville & Georgina Greville, and talking in as low a voice as you please—just like a turtle cooing to his mates—I heard something about Sir William & a certain marquise of Franceville —now I think on it, her name was Agathe—I heard the word duel, too—has the Colonel been fighting do you think?" "Very likely— However, here we are at your lodgings—Good-night, give me love to Louisa* when you see her—" "I will, good-night—Stay a moment Townshend" calling me back as I was turning from the door where his lordship stood with his hand on the half-handle— "You will come and take a quiet cup of tea with me to-morrow?— I'll ask our friend to meet you if you like—" "With pleasure, I'll be punctual at eight o'clock." His lordship rung the bell and was admitted—I moved away.

* Louisa Vernon

Lord Macara's apartments are in a street of splendid lodging-houses mostly let to M-P-s towards the West end—The evening of the next day being very wet and the wind besides being high—I called a hackney coach, and at the appointed hour was set down under the imposing portico of his Hotel—His valet let me in and I was shewn through a well-lighted hall and up a handsome flight of stairs to a drawing-room of small size but tasteful arrangement, cheerfully shining in the light of a good fire & of four tall wax candles burning on the table—I perceived at once that Macara had been thoughtful enough to provide female superintendence —Her ladyship was there, seated in a low chair by the hearth & playing with the silken ears of a little spaniel—A lady, if there be but one in an apartment, always rivets the attention first, and I did not look for other visitors—until I had satisfactorily scanned Louisa's easy figure—"Down, Pepin, down" she was saying as she tantalized the pigmy [illegible] with a bit of biscuit—then again, changing her tone "Poor thing—come" and she laid her slim hand lightly on its head and soothed it till the reclining creature sprang into her lap—there it was caressed for a while—still with the same aristocratic hand whose touch seemed lighter than foam—shaking her head meantime in affected rebuke—so as to produce a pretty waving motion in her big curls—and cause them to stray readily upon her cheeks & neck—this charming pantomime having been acted a due length of time, she saw fit to start & acknowledge my approach. "Dear Mr Townshend—how you frighten me with stealing into the room! pray, how long have you been standing at the door watching me & Pepin?" "Perhaps five minutes, Madam— it's rude I know—but you must excuse me—the picture was such a pretty one—" "Now" said she, turning to a person in another part of the room whom I had not noticed before—"we'll have no flattery to-night, will we, Sir?" "Not from me at least, ma'am" answered a voice from a dark corner—"You never flatter, I know" she continued—"I've not done lately" was the reply "my tongue is out of practice—" "Perhaps you disdain all soft nonsense" said she—"I'm a novice—a novice—" answered the Unseen hastily. "I don't understand it"—"Come & learn then" interposed I. "At Louisa Dance's feet, who would be a novice in Love's worship long?" "Curse it—I'm cold—!" ejaculated the gentleman, & rising hastily from the sofa where he had been lounging—he strode forward on to the hearth. The Gentleman, as he spread his hands over the fire, regarded me from top to toe with a rapid sharp glance —that implied in its sidelong scrutiny anything rather than an open comfortable shade of mind. I pretended not to look at him, but yet from one corner of my eye I took a sufficiently scrutinising survey of his person & demeanour—He was a man of a muscular & powerful frame, though not tall—of a worn & haggard aspect though not old or even middle-aged—his hair had no gloss upon it though it was jet-black & thick—little care had been bestowed upon its arrangement—it crossed his forehead in disordered flakes, & yet his dress was good & fashionable—judging by the man's face, he must have been blessed with a devilish temper—I never saw such a mad, suspicious irritability as glinted in his little black eyes —His complexion, of a dark sallowness, aided the effect of a scowl which seemed habitual to his hard, beetling brow—leaning on the mantle-piece, he looked at Louisa—what a contrast was there between him & her—"I've not seen his lordship, Madam, where is he?" "O, he'll be down soon—but the viscount's health is really so very indifferent now—during the last week he has never left his bed till it was time to go to the house"—"Hum!" said the gentleman— then after a pause of some minutes during which he looked ferociously into the fire—he added "Dash it—I feel a want!" the marchioness was now playing with her dog—& her attention being wholly taken up with its gambols—the dark stranger turned to me—& putting his thumb to his nose-end said with felicitous politeness— "Do you?" "Can't say" was my response. "'Cause" he continued "If your case is a similar one to my own, I know the whereabouts & we'll apply a remedy—" I thanked him for his civility but said "I was well enough—& for the present at least would dispense with his medicine"—"you Don't take" returned he. "However, please yourself—every man to his mind—as the man said &c. but I must corn or it's no go—" He walked towards a door & opened it— there was a room within—I watched him walk up to the far end —where was a lamp hanging over a side-board—Decanters & glasses stood there. he filled a glass & drank it—another—again —again—again—even to the mysterious number of seven times— he returned wiping his lips with a handkerchief—just then the door opened & a figure in slippers & dressing-gown came bending into the apartment—"Glad to see you, my lord" said the stranger, advancing very brusquely—"I've come according to invitation you see—I hope your lordship's well"—"Indifferent, Mr Wilson —indifferent—I've made an effort to rise on your account— Louisa, will you lend me your arm to a seat—I don't feel strong this morning—" "Certainly, my dear Viscount" said the marchioness—& rising, she supported her friend to an easy chair set by the hearth—He leant back on the cushions & thanked her with a placid patient smile—To look at him now a stranger might have

thought him a saint—he was as white as a sheet—every feature
expressed extreme exhaustion—but his eye glittered with temporary excitement—"What have you been doing with yourself since
last night?" asked I with surprise. "O, I took cold" he answered
—"cold always weakens me so   but I shall be better soon, Townshend—you & Mr Wilson don't know each other I believe—let me
introduce you—Townsend, Mr Wilson—Wilson, Mr Townshend
—" Wilson bowed to me with an assured impudent air—& then
he sat down immediately in front of the fire, folded his arms on his
broad chest—& favoured me with one or two of his pleasant
ingenuous glances. "My lord" he said, addressing Macara— "I
hadn't expected to meet company here when I [*illegible*]"—"O,
Mr Townshend is a friend" returned lord Macara. "I hope you &
he will soon be on the best terms"—"have you ever been in the
army, Sir?" asked Mr Wilson turning to me—it was evident the
man was too mad or too muddy to have any perception of my real
identity—So I answered calmly—"No"—though I had a large
circle of military friends. "Humph! I suppose among the constitutional troops—old stiff-backs of the Fidena school—your
friends, I have no doubt—distinguished themselves in the retreat
before Massena of 1833—?" "I believe not" returned I, lighting a
cigar. "It strikes me that most of them were at that time lying snug
with Squire Warner—who, you will remember, hopped about with
his ragamuffins—keeping wide of both armies, always hiding from
danger—in those confounded dirty marshes of theirs—up in the
nice Angrian hills"—"I know—I know" returned Mr Wilson,
"that's a nasty country that Angria—I never was there but once
when I was commercial traveller to the House of Macandlien &
Jamieson—& I left the situation on that very account that they
sent me & my gig through sich a Hell—" "Indeed!" said I with
some surprise—"then you're not a native of the country—?" "A
native!" roared Mr Wilson, his little eyes fixing upon me with
tiger-fury—& an inexpressible searching gleam of distrust—"A
native! what d'ye mean Sir—? Blast the country! I, a native! that
never slept but one night within its frontiers—which I remember
by the same token that it was in that grand hotel of theirs at
Zamorna—Inchcliffe's—Ratcliffe's—Stancliffe's—what d'ye call
it—where I was brutally bitten by bugs and had such a face in the
morning that I was forced to borrow the chambermaid's shawl—
to fold about it up to the eyes—Now Sir, what do you say to that
—?" "O, I beg a thousand pardons—I merely hazarded the supposition from the circumstance of your having a strong twang of
the Angrian accent—" "It's the Scotch accent!" exclaimed he.

"I'll stand to it—its the Scotch accent—I was born in Ross-town & brought up in Ross-town—behind the counter—I took a trifle from the till & was consequently expunged to Stumpsland— Frederick's town, where I went into the House of Macandlien & Jamieson as I told you before—and I'll break any man's bones who shall dare—" "Mr Wilson, take some coffee" interposed the voice of Miss Dance, and that lady stood before him in a bending attitude with the cup in her hand & the smile of persuasion on her lips—Almost as lavish of her fascinations to the Commercial Traveller as she could have been to her high & aristocratic lover— the fastidious Earl of N———.* Wilson looked at her—& taking the cup she offered him—said "Were it poison I'd drink it—" "I hope it will act as a sedative" said she smiling gently. "No madam, as a fiery stimulant—this draught, given by you, makes me a soldier again—" he swallowed the coffee—"now" he continued, flashing at her with a glance of fierce sentiment—"I've done what you bid me—I wish it were a harder task—" "I can impose one you will think harder" returned she. "Restrain that haughty temper of yours—be quiet for at least five minutes—see, I seal your lips—" she sportively touched his mouth with her finger—& laughing returned to her seat. "There" said lord Macara "you cannot break a prohibition so delivered." Who can account for the strange association of ideas in the human mind?—During the brief operation of the silent spell that Louisa Dance had thrown over her visitor—I looked round me & the tout-ensemble of what I saw recalled to me another picture—like this, but yet how different! Here was a room in the heart of a great Town—closed—curtained & lighted up. by a table, with silver & china before her, sat a lady —an elegant form in thin meritricious robes—with a face a little faded by time, a little wasted by dissipation—but still lovely in softening lamplight—the Syren look in her rolling blue eyes—the loose dishevellement of her hair—the studied languor of every glance & movement—told plainly enough her character, the un-principled—the insincere—the heartless—the unchaste—but still the seductive—by the fireside, that image in a dressing-gown—that man with a face like clay—& hands like cold white fleshless bone— all the spirit of health & youth evidently gone from him—a lassitude suffering, quickened with Devilishness left—then the other, Wilson, calling himself a Scotch trader—evidently from bearing, mien & aspect—some scoundrelly broken officer—some skulking debauchee, military miscreant—who dared not own his country & had blotted out his family name with stains of infamy.

* Northangerland

This picture, as I gazed on it, suggested to my mind another—a parlour in an old Hall—a summer evening shining over a glorious park—near the open window, a table—surrounded by a circle of lovely women, young & unfaded with vice—& one bold handsome hardy soldier admitted amongst them by the passport of fame*—but the scene is no longer vivid—I have forgotten it—its healthy hues will not stand in the vitiated atmosphere of this other tableau, & even on that I will dwell no more—it is enough to say that I saw Wilson put into Warner's carriage that night blind-drunk—where it took him I do not know—for the night was so cold & tempestuous I could not be at the pains to follow him—The viscount I left sitting in his easy-chair very still, with a leering vacant simper fixed on his lips. Miss Dance had driven home to Azalia Bower some hours before—after lavishing the softest attentions on the intoxicated Wilson—I thought I could discern that Macara had employed her to act the basilisk, & lure, by her dangerous charms, the reckless ruffian into his power. During the conversation of the evening, when wine removed restraint, I heard hints of political machinations—Wilson spoke of his associates, of his pals, a short time before he fell under the table—he drank in a brimming bumper d--mn--n to the Soldan† & his satellites—he insisted that I should pledge him, to which I made no objection—I knew nothing who the Soldan might be—I did not even know, though perhaps I might guess—but n'importe.

Surena & I had just had a quarrel concerning the quantity of coal to be consumed in the back-parlour-grate—I had conquered & was enjoying the results of my triumph in a charming good fire which I effectually monopolised by sitting full in front—with a foot on each hob. Surena had retreated after his defeat to the shop—whence his voice—softened by distance & the intervening pannels of a double door—was heard at intervals—swearing away his precious soul to attest the fact that he was now selling his goods at a lower price than he bought them—tea was over—Hannah Rowley had closed the shutter & drawn the curtain of our single window—I was the sole occupant of the parlour—& as I sat in the elegant position above described & leant back in my chair—I saw in the fitful firelight my gigantic shadow wavering wide on the ceiling—It chanced that I had made a capital good bet—much to the disquietude of my Landlord, & all being sufficiently tranquil about me & my stomach in a state of comfortable & not over-loaded repletion, I felt inclined to reverie if not to drowsiness—the

* See *Julia* for the origin of this scene   † Zamorna

influence of a soft opiate seemed diffused over my brain—already my eyes were closed & thick-coming fancies were condensing into gentle dreams—I was very far from Verdopolis—I was in the presence of something fair & poetic—a silken sleeve and a fair white hand resting on my arm—& She & I were wandering in a moonlight lane—She—aye, what was her name?—what were her features?—I was just about to hear her name pronounced & the face was turning towards me when something stirred—a tinkle—a clang—"the fire-irons!" thought I—& the conviction darted into my mind that Surena had entered the room & meanly seizing the advantage my somnolent state afforded him, had commenced the process of taking off the fire with the tongs. "Hillo!" I shouted, starting up—"let the fire alone will ye—or I'll shiver your skull with the poker—" Somebody laughed—and as I opened my eyes & woke up—I perceived that the flame was ascending the chimney more brilliantly than before, & that fresh fuel had been added within the last few minutes—A dusk form was bending over the hearth in the very act of replacing the poker against the support— "Who are you?" I demanded. "Look!" was the concise answer— I did look & not small was my astonishment to discern—an individual attired in the dress, & bearing all the insignia of a policeman—there was no mistaking the dark blue uniform faced with red, the white gloves—the staff & sword-stick—"Who sent you & what do you want?" I again interrogated—"Only your company for a short distance—" returned the man. "My company! where to?" "No need to alarm yourself, Mr Townsend —its only a trifle—the nobs want a word or two of you—Meantime, if you'll use your eyes you'll see I'm a friend—if it were not for previous acquaintance, I should not have made bold to come upon you so sudden-like—" In fact, the man's features did seem familiar to me when I examined them nearly, & at length I recognized an old pal whom under the name of James Ingham I have mentioned in some of my former works—"Sure it's not you, Jimmy!" I exclaimed. "But it is, Sir, & I mean to use you genteel—so I've got a cab at the door ready waiting for you." "But what for, Jim? what have I done?" "Don't know, your honour was always a gentleman of spirit— however we must go & here's my warrant—" "Is it a case of murder?" I demanded. "or of bigamy? or of Arson or of burglary or what—?" "Don't know. your honour will soon find out— come—" & come I did, for just then stept in two other chaps —in the same blue coats & white gloves, & placing me between them I was walked out through our kitchen & the back-

door—placed in a hackney-coach & nolens volens driven off—the
d———l knows where.

We had scarcely proceeded the length of three streets when one of
the policemen put his head out of the window & ordered the driver
to stop as the Gen'leman would get out here—accordingly I
alighted at the door of a good-sized house which, being presently
opened, admitted me to a passage lighted with gas—where were
sundry great-coats dangling from pins & sundry hats lying on a
slab—a servant in a striped jacket was waiting there—"You'll
show this gentleman upstairs—" said my friend Ingham—"Yes
Sir—follow me if you please—" I did follow him up a staircase
into a gallery. he opened one of a row of doors along the side—I
was ushered into a moderate-sized, neatly-furnished library—at a
round table in the middle of the room two gentlemen were sitting—
one with a desk before him, the other leaning his head on his hand
—the latter rose as I entered. "How do you do, Mr Townshend—
be seated will you—I am sorry to have given you this trouble, but
we will explain matters presently—Jenkins—place Mr Townshend
a chair—" Jenkins, the individual behind the desk—briskly rose—
placed a chair for me just opposite his superior & resumed his own
seat—the manner in which this trifling movement was executed at
once informed me that he occupied the situation of clerk—the other
person I conjectured to be a magistrate—he was a professional-
looking, middle-aged man—with a cold shrewd eye—a pale face
& dark hair turning grey—a gas-lamp burning just above the
table clearly shewed his features—too clearly, indeed, for every
line, every muscle—every furrow was revealed in the chilly-white
light, & as I looked, methought this was not the first time I had
seen that hard—man of the world physiognomy—I was sure such
a face had met my gaze often in electioneering crowds—in public
dinners & political meetings—yet I could not recall his name—
"Mr Townshend" he began "a gentleman such as I know you to
be—will not require apology for a mode of procedure which seems
harsh but which legal formalities require should be adopted—you
will recognize me as a member of the Angrian magistracy—& I
have summoned you hither to give information concerning certain important matters which now occupy the attention of the
government of which I am an unworthy servant—" "Really, Sir"
I replied—effectually puzzled by this preamble, "I feel very much
at a loss to imagine in what way I can be of use to you—may I know
on whose authority besides your own the warrant of my arrest was
issued—?" "You shall presently be satisfied that I do not act

without authority" replied the magistrate. "meantime, my clerk will administer to you the oath & I will then proceed to take your testimony—" A bible being brought, I commenced the prescribed ceremony—I had nearly completed it when an inner door opened & a third person appeared upon the scene—an individual in a surtout entered the appartment unbuttoning his coat with a cool self-possessed air—he advanced to the fire-place—"Good evening, Mr Moore" said he, bowing to the magistrate, & Mr Moore rose & returned his bow with a suppleness that shewed he considered the new-comer no small shakes—"Hope you're well, Mr Townshend" continued the person in question—inclining his body again with the slight bend of a poplar in a calm—& then he threw the breast of his surtout open, inserted his thumbs in the armholes of his waistcoat, erected himself before the fire & looked at me with the air of some Almighty Nabob to whom I had formerly been shoe-black—"Go it, my boy!" thought I, "I'm not the chap to play off these airs upon—I'll give you change for your notes." So, having duly kissed the book &c., I resumed my seat opposite Mr Moore—took out my snuff-box &, while deliberately taking a pinch between my finger & thum, I pretended to scrutinise the two-legged fire-screen with a sidelong glance of keen observation—Small need was there for my eye to linger long on the young face—with thin but unmarked features, the light hair brushed into curls on the temples—the martial moustaches & whiskers—the sinewy but very slight figure invested with the carriage of a ramrod—Curse him!—was he not as fully known to me as my own heart?—& there he stood like an icicle!—however, the dramatis personae being assembled, we'll now go on with the play—

"The witness is just about to commence his deposition, I presume" began the young Dragoon—"He is" returned Mr Moore. "Will you question him, Sir William,* or shall I?" "I will begin if you please" was the answer, & wiping his mouth with a cambric handkerchief—he put the usual interrogation. "Your name is Townshend, I believe?" "It is—" "Have you another name—or do you sometimes use an alias?" "I frequently use an alias—" "What other names then are you known by?" "Gardiner—Jones—Collier & Wellesley." "On what grounds do you base your claim to that last name?" "I don't know." "Perhaps you have relations who bear it?" "Perhaps I have—" "Have you been living long in Verdopolis?" "About twenty one years." "What is your age?"

* Sir William Percy

"One & twenty." "Remember, witness, you are upon your oath—
I again ask you what is your age—" "Twenty-one—" "Indeed!"
& the examiner paused as if in great doubt—in a minute he
recommenced "are you a married man or a bachelor?" "I don't
know." "Will you be kind enough to explain that last answer—"
"I never was married that I know of, but I've often wished to be—"
"What business do you carry on—?" "a very thriving one." "what
is it?" "I'm a Jerrey—" "What species of conveyance do you
drive—an omnibus or Cab?" "neither." "What then?" "A quill"
—"If I were to require a character of you—do you think you
could procure respectable testimonials?" "No." "that's a strange
admission—to what circumstances of your life do you ascribe the
loss of so valuable a thing as reputation?" "to the circumstances of
my having been at one time connected with a rascal of the name of
Clarke—William Clarke—a Private in the Angrian army." "Soh!
well now, to come to the point—where were you last Thursday?"
"In Verdopolis"—"Where were you on the evening of that day?"
"I'm cursed if I can recollect." "Perhaps in that case I may be able
to refresh your memory—you know Clarges Street?" "Yes." "Is it
not chiefly occupied by lodging-houses?" "Very likely." "Can you
recall the names of any individuals to whom these lodgings are let?"
"Perhaps I might by to-morrow night at this time—" "You were
there last Thursday evening." "Was I?" "Mr Moore, undertake
the Witness—" The magistrate obeyed. "Lord Macara Lofty
occupies apartments in that street, Mr Townshend, & you were
there as a guest of his lordship's last Thursday evening—now you
are required on your oath to say what visitors you met on that
occasion—" Hum! thought I, here's some enquiry—I paused, I
rapidly ran over in my own mind the state of the business, I calculated whether I had any interest in concealing names & screening
the noble Viscount—I weighed the affair & adjusted the balance
as evenly as I could—& as, after due consideration, I could not
discern that one atom of advantage would accrue to me by telling
a lie, I resolved to speak the truth. "I was at Clarges Street last
Thursday" said I "& I saw Lord Lofty & the honourable Miss
Dance—I took tea with them—" "You were alone then in their company—?" "No, there was a sort of lap-dog, a poodle or spaniel of
the name of Pepin—" Sir William interposed a word—"You &
the poodle then were invited to meet each other I presume, Mr
Townshend—& the noble Viscount had not troubled himself to ask
a third person—?" "Yes, a very respectable Bag-man—" "Of the
name of Wilson?" added Mr Moore— "Just so—" "Will you
describe the person of this gentleman. Was he tall?" "he was, in

comparison of the poodle—" "Mr Townshend, this won't do"
said Mr Moore. "I must demand proper answers to my questions—
I request you again to give me a description of Mr Wilson"—
"I will then" said I "& it shall be done con amore. He was a
middle-sized man with a deep open chest—a very dark skin—
strong black hair & Whiskers—a dissipated prof[l]igate look,
a kind of branded brow hanging over his eyes with a scowl—a
remarkably bass voice for a man under thirty—which I should
judge him to be—though strong-drink & bad courses had ploughed
lines in his face which might better have suited three score. He
called himself a Scotchman, but had none of the Scotch physio-
gnomical characteristics—" "Did he talk much?" "No." "Had you
any wine in the course of the evening?" "Just a drop—" "Did Mr
Wilson profess tee-totalism?" "Hardly." "Was he quite sober
when he left the house?"—"I daresay he would be by next day at
noon—" "Was he carried out or did he walk—?" "something
between the two. He walked to the top of the stairs—fell to the
bottom & was carried to Lord Macara's carriage"—"who went
home with him—?" "No one except the coachman"—"Did you
see the carriage drive off?"—"Yes, for that matter I saw two
carriages—at the moment I was labouring under the complaint
called second sight"—"In what direction did it drive? up Clarges
Street or down—?" "On my oath I can't say—I was in a kind of
mist, & to speak truth—one vision of it seemed to go one way & the
other another—I was a little carried in liquor myself—" "Were the
Viscount & Mr Wilson apparently on friendly terms?"—"Yes, but
Wilson & Miss Dance were on still friendlier—especially after
Wilson's tenth tumbler—" "Did Miss Dance take glass for glass
with Wilson?" asked Sir William gravely—"I didn't observe that
she mixed herself any gin & water, but she certainly allowed lord
Macara to help her from the Decanter very freely—" "Did the
conversation at all turn on political subjects?"—"Wilson blasted
out once or twice about that d—nd Turk* in the east—but whenever he did so Miss Dance drew her chair nearer to him—& by
touching his hand & looking into his face got him off onto some
other subject"—"Did you infer from any part of Mr Wilson's
conversation that he had lately been abroad—in France for
instance, or any foreign country—?" "He talked much to Miss
Dance about the beauty of French women & recommended her to
drape her hair in the Parisian style—he was beginning a story to[o]
with the words "When I was last in the Palais Royal—" but lord
Macara stopped him & turned the conversation another way—"

* Zamorna

"On your oath, Mr Townshend, have you seen or heard anything of Wilson since the night in question?"—"On my oath I have not"—"Well" said Mr Moore, turning to the baronet "I think we have now got from Mr Townshend all the information on the subject he is capable of communicating—there can be no doubt of Wilson's identity & for the rest, time & vigilance will be our best assistants—" "Mr Townshend is at liberty to depart—" observed Sir William—I got up—a nod of the most distant civility was interchanged between me & the baronet—I turned to the door—Mr Moore followed me—in the gallery he apologised again for the seemingly harsh measures which the law had obliged him to adopt, assured me he should consider my future acquaintance as an honour & that he could not help being glad of an occasion which had brought him into contact with a man of so much literary eminence—Of course I bowed acknowledgement & we parted on the best mutual terms possible. Perhaps before closing this chapter I should say a word about Mr Moore—my readers will not need to be told where they have seen him before—not in Verdopolis, but in the streets of mercantile Zamorna—which he cannot walk without hearing on all sides the whispered sentence "there goes Hartford's main man." An eminent Barrister—& wealthy landholder, he is still the tool of a most haughty task-master—yet I had just found him acting in close coalition with his superior's bitterest enemy—hiring himself out to be the instrument of that government which had spurned the Baron from amongst them—truly I now began to wonder who this Wilson was—that could occasion the junction of two such hostile powers—They must be on the scent of blood, thought I—or that implacable Percy would not hunt in couples with Hartford, even by proxy.

Where the Olympian crept along—slow, deep & quiet—after escaping from the rushing mill-dams of Zamorna—a thin ice was beginning to crisp upon its surface—A frost was setting in that evening which already had hardened the road down Hartford Dale to such iron-firmness that when any solitary carriage passed up at that late hour—the sound of its wheels tinkled among the dusk woods as if they had rolled over metal—Ascending above the dimness of the valley, a full moon filled the cloudless & breathless winter twilight with a sort of peace the largest star could but have faintly typified—Yet here was no summer softness—it was cold, icy—a night of marble, & fast beneath its influence did Bagmen urge their gigs, & rejoicingly did mail-coach guards wind their horns—when the lights of Zamorna flashed in the distance—&

the vision of a tankard of hot ale & rum flashed upon their inward
eye—

A man in a cloak came over the Bridge of Zamorna and, turning
down the dale—held a straight course along the causeway of that
noble road—he walked on foot with his cloak gathered about him—
his head & chest erected—& his hat so set on his brow that the
brim rested very near on the bridge of his nose—Hartford Woods,
unfolding on each hand, shewed in a fissure between their dark
sweep of shade—the sky filled with the glorious rising moon—
which moon looked intently upon the traveller with that melancholy aspect it has always worn since the flood—The man
stinted his stride a moment when on his right hand he passed the
great gates of Hartford-Hall—& beheld far within, towering amid
the stretch of grounds—the wide front & wings of that lordly seat—
While you gaze, reader—on those long windows shining in moonlight, on those stately & turret-like chimneys—& that gleaming
roof—the traveller has hurried on—where is he?—not on the road—
has he vanished—? follow me & we shall see—he crossed a style
in that hedge—the field beyond was steep—green & wide—he
skirted it quickly & then, with a faster stride than ever, he threaded
the broad far stretching Ings of the Olympian. Distant now from
the main road, he pursued a lone track through the silence of lanes
& fields—not a creature crossed his path—flocks & herds were
folded—the farms here are vast & the farm-houses far asunder—
this was lord Hartford's land, let in long leases half a century ago.

Well, he was now four miles away from Zamorna, & the bells of a
church were heard far away chiming nine at night—that was from
Massinger, & he stopped till they had ceased ringing, perhaps to
listen, perhaps to draw breath—At last he came to a field with a
very noble row of magnificent old trees down the sides, & close
along their trunks a broad gravelled foot-path which their boughs
overhung like arches—Following this road, he came soon to the
house called Massinger Hall—an ancient spacious Dwelling—
situated all alone in those wide fields, very solitary & impressive—
with a sombre rookery frowning behind it—The pillars of the
garden-gate were crowned with stone-balls—as also were the
Gables of the house—& in the garden, on the lawn, there was a
stone pillar & a time-stained Dial-plate—Massinger-Hall was as
silent as the grave, all the front was black—except where the moonlight shone on the masses of ivy clustered around every casement—
Yet it was not ruined—a calm, stately order pervaded the scene—It

was only antique—lonely & grey. The man in the cloak roamed backwards & forwards before the front of the Hall—pausing sometimes as if to listen—& when no sound was audible & no light streamed from the many closed & frost-wrought casements—wandering on again with the same measured stride—at length from within the house a sound was heard of the deep bark of some large dog—not near at hand, but in a remote room away at the back —Fearful evidently of discovery, the Traveller started at the noise—in a moment he had turned the corner of the house & stood sheltered under the more retired gable—here at last his eye met some sign of habitation—The Gable had but one large window almost like that of a church—long & low, opening upon the turf of the lawn—& from this window glowed a reflection of warm light upon all the garden-shrubs about it—Every one knows how distinctly the interior of a lamp-lit room can be seen at night when there is no shutter or blind to screen the window, & as the stranger knelt on the ground behind a large laurel whose branches were partly shot over the lattice—he could see into the very penetralia of the grim house as distinctly as if he had been actually within its walls—

About the Window there hung the festoons & drapery of a heavy moreen curtain—deep crimson in coulour—these, looped up, showed a long room—glittering on all sides with the reflection of firelight from the darkest pannels of oak—the room was carpeted & in the middle was a massive table having the raven-gloss of ebony—there were no candles, no lamps burning—but a glowing hearth—this might have been a cheerful room when filled with company—but to-night it wore, like the rest of Massinger-Hall, an air of proud gloom almost too impressive to the imagination. A figure came towards the window & then paced back again & was almost lost in the shadow of the opposite end—again it appeared, drawing near slowly—as slowly, it withdrew to the dusk of distance—To & fro it paced with the same measured step down the whole length of the large old parlour, & there was nothing else visible—A single person walking about there in that remote mansion embosomed amid boundless fields.

This person was a woman—rather a girl of about nineteen. She looked like one who lived alone—for her dress shewed none of the studied arrangement & decorative taste by which women—young women especially, endeavour to please those with whom they associate—She looked also like one who lived too much alone—

for the expression of her face as she roamed to & fro, was fixed & dreamy. Whether at this moment her thoughts were sad or bright, I cannot tell—but they were evidently very interesting, for she had forgot heaven above & earth beneath & all things that are thereon, in the charm that they wrapped about her—No doubt it was to excite in her mind these feverish Dreams that she had left the curtains of the great window undrawn—So that whenever she looked towards it there was the moon gliding out into a broad space of blue sky—from behind the still tall spire of a poplar—& under her beams spreading to the horizon—there were wide solitary pastures—with the noblest timber of the province along their swells. At last she is waking, & it's time, for a clock somewhere in the house struck ten five minutes ago—She shakes off her trance with a short sigh, walks to the fire, stirs it, & then thinks she'll let down the window-curtains—Being not very tall, she stept on to a chair for this purpose—but she quickly jumped down again—for as she was stretching her hand to loose the crimson rope, a man rose from behind the Laurel-branches & stood straight up with his foot on the very sill of the window—The young woman gave back & looked towards the door—considerable dismay & amazement were at first depicted in her face—but before she had time to run away—the apparition had passed the thin barrier of the glass door & stood in her very presence—Most considerately, he closed the lattice behind him & also let down the curtains, a feat his stature ennabled him to perform much more conveniently than the lady could have done—then he took off his hat &, while he ran his fingers through his thick hair, said in an ordinary masculine voice "Now Elizabeth, I suppose you know me?" But this greeting, easy as it was, seemed for a while to produce no answering token of recognition—the young woman looked again & again in complete astonishment—at last, some conviction seemed fastening on her mind—it excited strong feeling—she lost the very little colour which had tinged her complexion before—and at last she said in a peculiar voice, a voice flesh & blood human beings never use but when the strongest & strangest sensations are roused—"Henry! can it be you?" Smiling as well as he could in a kind of way that shewed he was not used to that sort of thing, the man in the cloak offered his hand—it was clasped in two that together were not as large as that one—& wrung & pressed with wild & agitated eagerness—The Girl would not speak till she had cleared her voice so as to be able to utter her words without making hysterical demonstrations, & then she said her visitor was cold & drew him towards the fire—"I shall do, Elizabeth—I shall do—" said the man "only you get a trifle calmer—come, come, I don't know that I've exactly deserved much of a welcome—" "No, but I *must* give it you when I can't help it" she answered sharply. "Sit down—I never thought you were alive—according to the newspapers you were in France—why have you left it for a country where you can't be safe? Do you think the police have a glimpse of suspicion which route you have taken?—how cold you are, Henry—it is two years to-night since I saw you, Sit down." There was a large antique arm-chair on each side of the hearth, & he threw himself into one with the abandonment of a weary man—"I've not had two hours sleep for the last three nights" said he. "How their d–n–d police have dogged me since they got fairly on the scent—" "What! officers are in pursuit of you now!" exclaimed the girl in a tone of dread—"Yes—yes—but I think I've shown them a trick in coming here—they'd think Angria would be the last cover the Fox would take—Give me a draught of wine, Elizabeth, I'm almost done"— She went out of the room hurriedly, looking round at his harrassed, pallid face as she closed the door—In her absence, he dropped his head upon the arm of the chair & gave expression to his sufferings in a single groan—the language of a strong man's distress—when her step was heard returning, he started up—cleared his countenance & sat erect—She brought wine which he took from her hand & swallowed eagerly—"Now" said he "All's right again—come, you look sadly scared, Elizabeth—but with regard to you I'm just the same Harry Hastings that I always was—I daresay by this time you've learnt to think of me as a kind of ogre—" He looked at her with that kind of mistrust born of conscious degradation— but his suspicions were allayed by the expressive glance with which she answered him—it said more convincingly than words—"Your faults & yourself are separate existences in my mind, Henry". Now reader, how were those two connected? they were not lovers— they were not man & wife—they must have been, a marked resemblance in their features attested it, brother & sister—Neither were handsome, the man had wasted his vigour & his youth in vice—there was more to repel than charm in the dark fiery eye sunk far below the brow—an aspect marked with the various lines of suffering, passion & profligacy—yet there were the remnants of a strong and steady young frame—a bold-martial bearing in proud, confident & ready action—which in better days had won him smiles from eyes he adored like a fanatic. but you remember, reader, what I said of Wilson—I need not paint his portrait anew— for this was Wilson—just the same dark reprobate in the lonely oak-parlour of Massinger-Hall—as he had been in Lord Lofty's elegant drawing-room at Verdopolis. His sister was almost as fair as he was dark—but she had little colour—her features could lay no claim to regularity—though they might to expression—yet she had handsome brown eyes—and a lady like & elegant turn of figure. had she dressed herself stylishly & curled her hair, no one would have called her plain—but in a brown silk frock—a simple collar & hair parted on her forehead in smooth braids—she was just an insignificant—unattractive young woman wholly without the bloom—majesty or fullness of beauty—She looked like a person of quick perceptions & dexterous address, & when the first tumult of emotion consequent on the adventure of the night had subsided —she spoke to her brother with an assumed tone of cheerfulness— as if desirous to avert from his vigilant jealousy those pangs of anguish which his changed appearance—his dreadful & death-struck prospects, must have forced into her heart—He had gone away a young soldier full of hope, & what career of life must that have been which had brought him back a Cain-like Wanderer with a price upon his blood—

"I am not as bad as you think me" said Henry Hastings suddenly. "I'm a man that has been atrociously wronged—I'll tell you, Elizabeth, a black tale about Adams & that Gutter-blood, that Fiend of Hell, lord Hartford—they envied me—but I suppose you're on their side, so it's no use talking—" "You think I care more about Hartford & Adams than I do about you—do you Henry? and I know so little of you as to suppose you would shoot a man dead without a galling & infamous provocation?" "Aye— but besides that, I'm a deserter & no doubt at Pendleton* everybody is very patriotic & it's ultra-Heterodox to hate an Angrian renegade one whit less than the Devil—my Father, for instance, would he see me, d'ye think?" "No." the answer was short & decisive—but Hastings would not have tolerated evasion—the truth was a bitter pill, but he swallowed it in silence—"Well, I don't care!" he exclaimed after a pause—"I'm a man yet—& a better man & a better man than most of those that hate me too—& don't think I've been spending the last two years in puling & whining, either, Elizabeth—I've lived like a prince at Paris, a good life, & feasted so well on pleasure that a little pain comes in conveniently to prevent a surfeit—then this pursuit will soon blow over—I'll keep close with you at Massinger till the hounds are baffled—& then I'll slip down to Doverham—take ship & emigrate to one of the Islands—I'll make myself rich there, &

* Pendle Hill is a landmark near Haworth

when I've built a good house & got an estate full of slaves, I'll stand for a Borough—then I'll come back. after seven years absence they can't touch me—I'll speak in Parliament—I'll flatter the people—I'll set hell burning through the land—I'll impeach half the peerage for their brutal corruptions & tyrannies—if Northangerland be dead, I'll Apotheize his memory—Let my bloodyhanded-foes remember that

> If we do but watch the hour,
> There never yet was human power
> That could evade, if unforgiven,
> The patient search & vigil long
> Of him who treasures up a wrong."

Instead of softening the renegade's excited ferocity, & reasoning against his malignant vindictiveness—Miss Hastings caught his spirit & answered in a quick excited voice—"You have been basely persecuted—you have been driven to desperation—I know it & I always did know it—I said so on the day that Mr Warner came to Pendleton & told my father you were broken by a court-martial for desertion. My father took out his will &, while Mr Warner looked on, drew a long line through your name & said he disowned you forever—Our landlord said—He had done right, Sir—but I told him he had done wrong & unnaturally—my father was then scarcely himself, & he is always quick & passionate as his son—he knocked me down—in Mr Warner's presence—I got up & said the words over again—Mr Warner said I was an undutiful daughter, & was adding by my obstinacy to my father's misery—I cared nothing for his reproof, & I left Pendleton a few weeks after —I've been earning my bread since by my own efforts"—"So I heard" returned Hastings "& that is the reason you are at Mas-singer, I suppose." "Yes, the house belongs to the Moores. old Mr Moore died lately, & his son, the barrister, is going to reside here—I am keeping it for him while he & his daughter are in Ver-dopolis—Miss Moore pretends to have a great regard for me & says she can't live without me—because I flatter her vanity & don't rival her beauty—& I teach her to speak French and Italian— which of course is a convenience." "Well Elizabeth, can you keep me here in safety for a day or two?" "I'll do my best—there are only two or three old servants in the house. But Henry, you are sick with weariness—you must have something to eat & go to bed directly—I'll order a room to be prepared for you—"

While Elizabeth Hastings [*illegible*] the parlour to find her way through dark passages to the distant kitchen, we also will turn for a time from the contemplation of her & her brother—my candle is nearly burnt out & I must close the chapter—

Sir William Percy's Diary

Lay long abed this morning—couldn't get up because I was engaged with one of those pleasant dreams that sometimes fill the night with the joy of a lifetime—I wonder what I'd give to realize for one half hour the events of that trance—my hand, I think, or else my two front-teeth—hardly though, teeth are precious things. I shan't soon forget what Monsieur Adams said about false ones— "les trois maisons dans la bouche". Well, but the dream—I think I was a God—or something quite as irresistible, & I just had in my power what I'd lose a chance of promotion to-morrow to obtain— that's saying a great deal—We sometimes see very beautiful eyes in dreams—those were resplendent—& the whole face just the living woman as she is—If I were a fool I might hang myself; knowing as I do that this dream is a false lie from hell—but I made a good breakfast as soon as I got up, & consoled myself by looking at the Marquise's miniature in the lid of my snuff-box. Bah! what was the made-up artificial French face to *Hers*! But Agathe has dark eyes I think & that's the reason I flattered her. it's mighty convenient to be in love with Frenchwomen—one's passion never interferes with one's comfort—I think I'll never marry, but spend my life in finding out resemblances to the single Shape I glorify—& when I'm very love-sick, I'll remember that my Idol is altogether terrestrial & so far from perfect that the other day a modest young lady blushed when, in turning over a volume of portraits, she chanced to come to hers—& perceived at the same moment that my eye had caught the name—Heaven's but it told tales—

Just given audience to Ingham—my police Inspector. he tells me that he has quite ascertained that Wilson has left his haunts— about town—my lads had smoked every hole where he could hide with such strong fumes of brimstone that he's been forced into flight—an important object gained—it's easier to chase the Fox over an open campaign—than in the broken ground & pits & holes of a rabbit warren like Verdopolis—aye, or Paris either. Drove to York Place to communicate the intelligence to Moore. the oily-tongued, smooth-faced toadie of a Blackguard Cut-throat was sly enough to see the advantage at once—he rubbed his hands & said, chuckling "We have him now, Sir William—only a little patience, a little time, & we'll all be in at the Death—'' Well, when Hastings is down, there's a wild-boar chase to come on, & then a wolf-hunt, & after that a bull-baiting—Simpson & Montmorenci & Macara are every one marked—we'll keep on their track, their

> Long gallop shall never tire
> The hound's deep hate & hunter's fire.

Moreover I must not forget an afterpiece to be performed under the special patronage of royalty—the tiger hunt—the great striped Animal of Kings turned loose, & Colonel Adrian Augustus O'Shaughnessy at his heels—Lord! the Gladiatorial wild-beast fights of the Romans were nothing to these!—But what tack has Hastings taken—! my lads must disperse far & wide.

I've ordered some to Edwardston to watch the east-road, & some to Alnwick to guard the west, & some to Free-town to bestride the North—if he does escape me—he's a devil & not a man—yet he has skill in baffling pursuit—again & again, when the hounds were on his very haunches, he has doubled & slipped. I wonder what charm the miserable ruffian can find in life to make him stick to it so?—in Paris, I more than once so hemmed him in & harrassed him—so crushed him to the wall—that he must have been at the verge of absolute starvation—the man would have cut his throat long since if he had been left alone—but while others seek his life to take it, his obstinate nature will lead him to defend the worthless possession to the last—to-day, while thinking about him, I recollected a little incident which I may hereafter turn to account in discovering his lair—Some months since I chanced to go to the opera one night—while I was sitting in my box & thinking myself in my full-dress uniform an uncommonly killing sight, I observed a sort of sensation commencing round me, & heard, amidst many whispers & a rising hum of admiration, the words often repeated "It is the beautiful Angrian!" Translate me—if I didn't at first think they were alluding to myself!—the words "Spare my blushes" were at my tongue's end, and I was beginning to consider whether it would or would not be necessary to acknowledge so much polite attention by a grateful bow—when I perceived that the heads & eyes of the ninnies were not turned towards me, but in a clean opposite direction—to a box where a tall young woman was sitting in the middle of a crowd of most respectable-looking masculine individuals who one & all wanted nothing but a tail to make the prettiest counterfeit monkeys imaginable—the young woman shone in blond & satin—with plumes enough on her head to waft

an ostrich from Arabia to [?Sagalecon]—the liberal display of neck
& arms showed plainly enough that she knew both were as white
& round & statuesque as if Phidias had got up from the dead to
chisel them out of the purest marble he could find from the quar-
ries of Paros, & the pearls circling them round showed that she had
taste enough to be aware how effective was the contrast between
the dazzling living flesh & the cold gleaming gem—She'd a nose like
Alexander the Great's, & large blue imperial eyes—bright with the
sort of ecstacy that a woman, flattered with conviction of her own
divinity, must feel glowing at her heart—Nature had given her a
profusion of hair, & Art had trained it into long silky ringlets
bright as gold—She was a superb animal, there's not a doubt of it
—& I hardly know a face or form in Africa that would not have
looked dim by her side—and a dim dusk foil she had indeed to her
diamond lustre—a little shade just at her elbow, hustled backwards & forwards by the men—Pagans that were crowding to the
shrine of this idol. While I was looking at her, Townshend came
into my box—"D'ye see how triumphant Jane Moore is looking to-
night?" said he. "Yes" I answered "she's poisoning half the female
Peerage with envy—but who in heaven's name has she got at her
side, Townsend? Who can that little blighted mortal be? somebody she's hired at so much a night to keep near her for the purpose
of shewing her off—?" Townshend took a sight with his opera-
glass—"D'ye mean that pale undersized young woman dressed as
plainly as a Quakeress in grey—with her hair done à la Victoria
Delph—small credit to her taste for that same—I think a few curls
wouldn't have been amiss—to relieve her singular features a trifle
—& yet I don't know—there's something studied about her dress
—everything suits—white scarf—plain silver ribbon in her hair—"
I interrupted "D'ye know who she is, Townshend—is she some—
Heiress—that has sufficient attractions of purse to dispense with
those of person—?" "Hardly, I think, for if you observe—she has
not a single man in her train—if she'd had brass now, half that raff
of young Angrian scamps that are pressing their attentions upon
Miss Moore, would have turned their thoughts to the Holder of the
money-bags—it strikes me now, as that Girl looks towards us, I've
seen her face before—I have—I'm sure it was in a stage coach on
the Angrian road—I travelled with her some distance & I remember, from what she said, I thought her a sharp shrewd customer
enough—" "Did you hear her name—?" "No." here the conversation dropped—for I could take no particular interest in a
person of that sort—But a day or two after—I went to dine at
Thornton's—it was a blow-out for the Angrians on the occasion

of their omni-gathering at the commencement of the Verdopolitan season, & I was a trifle late, as is my way occasionally—& when I entered the drawing-room they were already marshalling themselves for dinner—Jane Moore was the first person I saw, & three Gentlemen were offering her their arms at once—the earl of Stuartville—Captain Frank Kirkwall & the omnipotent lord Arundel. of course the last carried her off—while I was watching their manoeuvres, all the other ladies had found conductors— & lo, I was last in the long train of plumes & robes, & to my horror & consternation nothing left for me to patronise—but the same little dusk apparition I had seen at the opera—the plain—pinched protegè of Miss Moore's. "Well" thought I "she may go by herself before I offer her my arm" & pretending not to see her, I carelessly followed the rest & took my place, with all the ease & coolness of my natural habits, at the very bottom of the table. She came stealing after—there was a single chair below mine & into this, being the only seat vacant, she was obliged to induct herself. However, I'd a pleasant pretty girl on the other side of me, an Augusta Londsdale, & one of the stately Ladies Seymour being opposite to me. So, having formed the determination not to notice my left-hand neighbour by word or look—I made myself very comfortable. Your Angrians have always a deal of laughing & conversation over their meals, & the party were exceedingly merry—looking up the table, I saw a great many handsome women & much glittering of jewellry & sparkling of bright eyes—invitations to take wine were also passing from lip to lip, & bows were interchanged across the table with infinite suavity—Ladies were leaning their heads to hear the flatteries of the men at their sides—& for my part I was cajoling Miss Augusta Lonsdale with the finest possible compliments on the bloom of her complexion & the softness of her smile— when all this flow of enjoyment was at its height, I chanced to look round for the purpose of taking some vegetables a footman was handing, & my eye unfortunately fell on the little individual I had resolved not to see—She was eating nothing—listening to nothing —not a soul had addressed a word to her, & her face was turned towards a large painting of a battle between the windows which, in that room by lamplight, had a peculiar aspect of gloom & horror—I can't pretend to say what thoughts were in her mind— but something she beheld in the rolling clouds of smoke—in the tossed manes & wild eyes of charging horses & in the bloody forms of men trampled beneath their hoofs—which had filled her eyes with tears—more likely, however, she felt herself solitary & neglected. there is no bitterness the human heart knows like that of being alone & despised—while around it hundred hundreds are lorded & idolized—I think I should have spoken to her—but something suggested to me "every body has their own burdens to bear—let her drink the chalice fate commands to her lips"—besides, there was something that suited my turn of mind in the idea of a neglected human being—turning from the hollow world, glittering with such congenial & selfish splendour before her—to the contemplation of that grim vision of war, & finding in the clouds of battle-dust & smoke there melting into air—something that touched her spirit on the quick—I would not break the charm by trying to remove the sorrow—& when a tear trickled from her eyelash to her cheek, & she hastily lifted her handkerchief to wipe it away—& then, roused to recollection, called into her face an indifferent expression &, turning from the picture, looked like a person without an idea alien from those she was with—I took good care to seem engaged in deep discourse with Augusta Lonsdale—that she might not suspect what scrutiny she had been the subject of a moment before. After dinner, when the ladies had retired to the drawing-room, I was, as I always am, one of the first to follow them—I hate sotting over the decanters—it's a vulgar beastly habit—the whole of that evening I watched the protegè very closely, but she evinced no other habit that took my fancy—She got a little more notice, several ladies talked to her—& she entered into conversation with a good deal of fluency & address—She assented & gave up her opinion & listened with becoming interest to whatever others had to say—She asked Miss Moore to sing just when Miss Moore wanted to be asked—she ran over the list of her finest songs where Jane's grand show-off voice is most efficiently displayed—& when the lady had fairly commenced, she retired from the Piano & left room for her admirers to crowd about her—in two hours, she had grown quite a favourite with the female part of the company, the men she never looked at nor seemed once desirous of attracting their attention—yet the creature, on a close examination, was by no means ugly—her eyes were very fine & seemed as if they could express anything—she'd a fair smooth skin & a hand as fine as a fairy's, & her feet & ancles were like those of a crack-dancer in an Opera-ballet corps—but her features were masked with an expression foreign to them—her movements were restrained & guarded—she wanted openness—originality—frankness—Before the evening was over, I contrived to learn her name & family—It was Elizabeth Hastings, the sister of that Devil Henry—I have never seen her since—till to-day I had forgotten her—but it struck me all at once that if I could find her out I might, by proper

management, get some useful intelligence respecting her brother—
I'll call on Miss Moore & ask her a few careless questions about her
protegè, taking care to throw in deprecating remarks & a general
air of contempt & indifference. A careful gleaner finds corn of good
grain where a fool passes by & sees only stubble.

Feb 10th*—Dedicated the whole of this morning to an easy lounge
in Miss Moore's boudoir—How much wisdom there is in taking
things quietly—Instead of ferreting like Warner in dismal Government Offices, I carry on my machinations amidst the velvet &
down of a lady's chamber—Jane Moore certainly knows how to
fascinate. she is what the world calls exquisitely sweet-tempered—
a sweet-temper in a beautiful face is a divine thing to gaze on—&
she has a kind of simplicity about her—which disclaims affectation
—She does not know human nature—she does not penetrate into the
minds of those about her—She does not fix her heart fervently on
some point which it would be destructive to take it from—She has
none of that strong refinement of the senses which makes some
temperaments thrill with undefined emotion at changes or chances
in the skies or the earth, in a softness in the clouds, a trembling of
moonlight in water—an old & vast tree—the tone of the passing
wind at night—or any other little accident of nature which contains in it more botheration than sense—Well, & what of that?
Genius & enthusiasm may go & be hanged. I did not care a d--n
for all the Genius & enthusiasm on earth—when Jane rose from
her nest by the fire—& stood up in her graceful height of stature—
with her hand held out to welcome me, and "Good morning, Sir
William" those fresh lips said with such a frank smile—I liked my
name better for being uttered by her voice. "Sit down, close to the
fire, you must be very cold—" So I did sit down, & in two minutes
she & I were engaged in the most friendly bit of chat imaginable.
Jane asked me if I was getting warm, & rang for some more coal
for my special benefit—then she enquired when I thought of going
down into Angria—for she hoped whenever I chanced to be
about Zamorna I would be sure to pay them a visit—provided
only they were at home—"you've never been to our new house"
said she—"you know we've left Kirkham Lodge since my Grandfather died—" "Indeed" said I "but you live in the neighbourhood still, I suppose—?" "O yes, it's the family place near
Massinger—an old queer sort of house—but papa intends to pull
it down & build a proper seat—I'm rather sorry, because the

* A typical example of how Charlotte Brontë suits the climate and landscape
of her tales to the actual period of the year in which she is writing

people at Zamorna will be sure to say it is pride—" "O, you shouldn't mind envy" I returned, & then by way of changing the conversation I made a remark on the beauty of an ornamental vase on the mantle-piece—the sides of which were exquisitely painted with a landscape of Grecian ruins & olives—& a dim mountain back-ground—"Is it not beautiful!" she said, taking it down, "& it was done by the sister of poor Captain Hastings—by the bye, Colonel, it is very cruel of you to hunt young Hastings as they say you do—he was such a clever, [*illegible*]—high-spirited fellow—" "Aye, he shewed high spirit in that bloody murder of Adams" I returned. "Adams was not half as nice a man as he" returned Jane. "He was very arrogant—I daresay he insulted poor Hastings shamefully—Adams was just like lord Hartford—I once met him at Hartford-Hall when Papa & I dined there—& I told papa when I came home, I thought he was a very proud disagreeable man." "Then you think his Subaltern did right to shoot him through the brain—?" "No, not right—but it is a pity Hastings should die for it—I wish you knew his sister—Colonel, you would be very sorry for her—" "His sister, who is she? not that very plain girl I saw with you one night at the Opera?" "You wouldn't call her plain if you knew her, Colonel" said Jane—with the most amiable earnestness of manner—"She is so good & so clever—She knows everything very nearly & she's quite different to other people—I can't tell how—" "Well" said I "she's not a person, my dear Miss Moore, to attract my attention much—is she really a friend of yours—?" "I won't tell you, Colonel, because you speak so sneeringly of her—" I laughed. "and so I suppose this paragon bothers you a great deal about her murdering brother—tells you tales of his heroism & genius & sorrows?" "No" said Jane "there's one very odd thing I've often wondered at—she never mentions him—& somehow I never dare to talk on the subject—for she has her peculiarities &, if she happened to take offence, she'd leave me directly—" "Leave you! what! does she live with you?" "She's my governess in a sense" said Miss Moore. "I learn French & Italian of her—she went to school at Paris—& she speaks French very well—" "Where do the Hastings come from?" I enquired—"From Pendleton up in Angria, quite a rough, wild country—very different to Zamorna—there's no good society there at all, & the land is very little cleared—I once rode over to the neighbourhood on horse-back when I was on a visit to Sir Markham Howards—& I was quite astonished at the moors & mountains, you've no idea—hardly any green fields & no trees & such stony bad roads—I called at old Mr Hastings' house—they don't live like us there—he's considered a gentleman & his family is one of the oldest in that part of the country, & he was sitting in his kitchen —what they call the house—it was wonderfully clean, the floor scoured as fair nearly as this marble—and a great fire in the chimney such as we have in our halls—still, it looked strange, & Mr Hastings was roughly dressed—& had his hat on. he spoke quite with an Angrian accent, far broader than General Thornton's— but I liked him very much, he was so hospitable—he called me a bonny lass & said I was as welcome to Colne-Moss Tarn as the day—" "Was Captain Hastings at home then?" I enquired. "No, it was soon after he had entered the army & when every-body was talking in his praise, & his songs were sung at public dinners & meetings—but Elizabeth Hastings was at home, & she did look such an elegant—lady-like being, in that homely place—but though she's quite fastidious in her refinement, I really believe she likes those dreary moors & that old-manor-house far better than Zamorna or even Verdopolis—isn't it odd—?" "Very—" said I— Jane continued "I often wonder what it was that made her leave Pendleton & go out into the world as she has done—Papa thinks it is for something her father has said or done against Henry—for old Mr Hastings is an exceedingly obstinate passionate man, & indeed all the family are passionate.* Elizabeth has never been home for two years—& now she's living by herself at our old place, Massinger-Hall—such a lonely situation & such gloomy old rooms—I wonder she can bear it—" This last sentence of Miss Moore's comprised the information I wished to obtain, so it was not necessary I should prolong my visit much further. after a few minutes further, I took a final gaze on her kind—handsome face—shook hands, made my parting bow & exit—Man, when I got home, I found Ingham waiting for me with an important piece of intelligence—he had succeeded in ascertaining that the Dog Wilson had certainly gone in an easterly direction—Angria is the word then— I'll set off to-morrow—& as to this Massinger-Hall, I mean to see the interior of it before two more suns set—

[End of Sir William Percy's Diary]

The stillest time of a winter's day is often the afternoon—especially when the desolation of snow & tempest without seem to give additional value to the comfort of a warm hearth & sheltering roof within—Near the close of a wild day—just before twilight's shadows began to fold over the world, Captain Hastings & his

* The whole of this description clearly applies to Haworth and the Brontë family

sister were sitting by the hearth of the oak-parlour at Massinger-Hall—Hastings watched the dreary snow-storm careering past that large Gothic casement, & after a long silence he said—"There will be deep drifts on Boulshill*—" The man was in a gloomy mood & so was his sister—for neither of them was the brightest, mildest or gentlest of human beings—& one had the horror of a violent Death always before him—& the other had the consciousness that the murderer, an outlaw—a deserter & a traitor, were all united in the person of her only brother—"And you think no intercession on your behalf would be listened to at court?" said Elizabeth Hastings, recurring to a conversation they had engaged in some minutes previously—"I think they are all unhanged villains at court" replied Henry in a deep rough voice—

Before proceeding with my narration, I would pause a minute for the character of Captain Hastings—The 19th regiment, of which the renegade had once been an officer, had lost from its bold bad ranks a man so well calculated to sustain the peculiar species of celebrity which that corps have so widely earned—He was, at the outset of his career, just what a candidate for distinction there—ought to have been—before vice fired her canker in him, he was a strong, active, athletic man—with all the health of his native hills glowing in his dark cheeks—with a daring ferocity of courage always awake in his eyes—with an arrogance of demeanour that bore down weaker minds & which, added to an intellect strong in the wings as an eagle, drew round him wherever he went—a train of besotted followers. But the man was mutinous & selfish & accursedly malignant—His mind was of that peculiarly agreeable conformation—that if anyone conferred a benefit upon him—he instantly jumped to the conclusion that they expected some act of mean submission in return—& the consequence was he always bit the hand that caressed him—then his former patrons looked coldly at him—shrugged their shoulders & drew off in disgust—while Hastings followed their retreat with a howl of hate & a shout of defiance—Thus he ruined his public prospects—for the Bashaws whom he insulted, the Richtons & Hartfords & Arundels—were already in possession of the high places—& they stood on the lofty steps of preferment, & with pride & tyranny, more demoniac even than his own, shook their lordly fists at the baffled lion below & swore, till the bottom of hell was moved by their oaths, that they'd go bodily to Beelzebub before Hastings should rise an inch—no doubt these Aristocratic vows will be fulfilled all in good time—but meanwhile

* There is a landmark on Haworth Moors called Boulsworth Hill

the Captain, like a wise man, thought he'd be beforehand with them—Ambition would not carry him fast enough to Pandemonium —so he harnessed the flying steeds of pleasure to aid it—His passions were naturally strong, & his Imagination was warm to fever—the two together made wild work, especially when Drunken Delirium lashed them up to a gallop, that the Steeds of the Apocalypse thundering to Armageddon would have emulated in vain—He was talked of everywhere for his excesses—people heard of them with dismay, the very Heros of the 19th held up their saintly hands & eyes at some of his exploits & exclaimed "Dang it! that beats every-thing!" One day, during the campaign of the Cirhala—Hastings was on Duty somewhere—when a man in an officer's cloak rode by on horseback—He reined up & said "Hastings, is that you?" "Yes" said the Captain, not looking up from the but-end of his rifle on which he was leaning—for he knew the voice & the figure too, & it galled him that anything should come near him whose approach it would be necessary to recognise by an act of homage—However the horseman was alone—so, as there were no witnesses of the humiliation, Hastings at last condescended to lift his military cap from his brow—"Your going to the Dogs I understand, Hastings" continued the other. "What the D---l do you think your con-stitution's made of, man—?" "Devilment, if I may judge from what I feel" answered the suffering profligate with the air of a rated bull-dog. "D'ye mean to stop?" continued the interrogator. "I've no present intention of that sort, my lord Duke"—"Well, perhaps you're in the right" continued the horseman, coolly managing his restless charger which fretted impatiently beneath the restraint of the rein—"Perhaps you're in the right, lad—it would be hardly worth your while to stop *now*, you're a lost worn-out broken-up scoundrel—" the Captain bowed. "Thank you, my lord—that's God's truth however"—"I once had a pleasure in looking at you" added his adviser—"I thought you a fine promising fellow that was fit for anything—you're now just a poor d---l—nothing more"— "And that's God's truth too" was the answer—The horseman stooped a moment from his saddle—laid his hand on Hastings' shoulder & with a remarkably solemn air ejaculated "D--n you Sir!" the horse was then touched with the spur & it sprang off as if St Nicholas had ridden it—It was evening when this interview took place & the next morning Hastings shot Colonel Adams—I will now return to Sir William Percy's diary.

Feb 18th—Stancliffe's is a real nice comfortable Inn—I always feel as content as a King when I'm seated in that upper room of theirs

what looks out on the Court-house—I'd a wretchedly cold journey
from Verdopolis down to Zamorna—very wet & dreary day, got in
just about noon & felt very philanthropic & benevolent when I was
shewn into the aforesaid upper-room with a good fire—& as pretty
a little luncheon as eye could wish to see, set out on the table—
having appeased the sacred rage of hunger, I began to consider
whether I should order fresh horses to my barouche—& drive
forward to Massinger—but a single glance towards the window
settled that matter—Such driving, pelting rain—such a bitter dis-
consolate wind—such sunless gloom in the sky—& streets brown &
shining with wet, clattering with pattens* & canopied by umbrellas
—"no, it's no go" I said to myself—"I'll give anybody leave to cut
off my ears that shall catch me romancing in search of old halls to-
day"—so I just laid me down easy on the sofa—that stood convenient to the fire-side—& with the aid of the last number of "Rook-
wood's Northern Magazine" & a glass of pleasant Madeira placed
on a little stand within the reach of my arm—I proposed spending
an afternoon at once rational & agreeable—Well, for two hours all
went uncommon well—the fire burnt calm & bright—the room
was still—the elements without gibbered more infernal moans than
ever—& I, hanging over the pages of a deliciously besotted tale—
entitled "Leasehold-Beck"—was just subsiding into a heavenly
slumber when, knock—knock—knock—some fiend of Tartarus
tapped at the door—I know how to punish intruders—I pretended
not to hear—tap—tap—tap—no answer—rap—rap—rap—no go
—Bang—bang—bang—"Come in" said I, with the most gentlemanly languor of tone imaginable—a Ghoul in the likeness of a
waiter appeared at the invitation—"A note for you, Sir" said he,
poking a silver salver into my face—"A note?—I hope it's a billet-
doux" thought I, taking up the missive—& lingering over the seal
as if breaking it would dissolve a charm—"I believe it's from
Hartford-Hall" continued the Ghoul. "A tiger in their livery
brought it." "A tiger!" I repeated. "aye, it's all the work of magic.
pray, is the wild-beast waiting for an answer?"—"Wild-beast,
Sir! it's a tiger—a boy—no, Sir, he's gone." "Very-well—do me
the favour then to follow his example." thus rebuked, the Ghoul
vanished. Having opened the note, I found its contents to run
as follows. "Lord Hartford having learnt that Sir William Percy
is at Stancliffe's Hotel, requests the favour of his immediate
attendance at Hartford-Hall—as Lord Hartford has important
intelligence to communicate—he hopes Sir William will not
delay complying with the solicitation contained in this note. P.S.

* The villagers in Northern regions commonly wore pattens in rough weather

Lord Hartford is momently expecting the arrival of Ingham with the detachment of Police stationed by Sir William's orders at Edwardston."

Having achieved the perusal of this dispatch, I found myself giving utterance to a whistle & at the same instant the spirit moved me to ring the bell & order a horse—In about a quarter of an hour after I had been dreaming on a couch under the dozy influence of a stupid tale—I found myself perched-up in a saddle, dashing over the bridge of Zamorna like a laundrymaid heading a charge of cavalry —When I got to Hartford-Hall I found a carriage drawn up at the entrance—& four of my own police ready-mounted in the disguise of postillions—One of them was Ingham. he doffed his cap— "Scent's as strong as stink, Sir" says he. encouraged by this agreeable hint, I alighted & hastened into the house to obtain more precise information—passing through the hall I perceived the door of the dining-room was open so I walked in—The Great Creole* had just concluded his dinner & was in the act of helping himself to a glass of wine when I entered—his gloves & his hat lay on a sidetable, and a servant stood with his cloak over his arm waiting to assist him on with it—"Well Percy" he began with his growling bass voice as soon as ever his eye caught me—"I hope the rascal is about to be disposed of at last—Fielding, is my cloak ready?" "Yes, my lord—" "Will you take wine, Sir William?—Fielding, the carriage is at the door I suppose?" "Yes, my lord—" "You have nothing to detain you I presume, Sir William—time is precious— Fielding, have the police had the whisky I ordered?" "Yes, my lord." "I got upon the train only this morning, Sir William—I laid my plans instantly—Fielding, did you load my pistols?" "Yes, my lord." "A desperate scoundrel like that ought to be guarded against —by G–d, if he resists, if he proves troublesome—a small thing will make me blow his brains out—Fielding, my cloak—help me on with it"—"yes, my lord"—"By G–d, I wish he may only give me sufficient pretext. I'll provide for him handsomely—ha! ha! I'm more than half in old Judge Jeffrey's mind. provided he'll save me the trouble of a trial, I'll put him out of pain a little quicker. Sir William, you're ready?" "yes, my lord"—So the Baron swallowed another bumper of his claret & then drew on his gloves & pulled his hat over his broad-black eye-brows—so as half to shade the orbs, flickering underneath, with an unaccustomed smile kindled partly by wine—& partly by the instinct of blood-hound exultation—Out he strode into the Hall & I followed—I wonder if that

* Hartford

man knows how intensely I hate him—sometimes I think he has a
dim consciousness that sound-creeping-thrills of abhorrence steal
along my veins whenever he & I look into each other's eyes—At
other times, I imagine, he lives in stolid ignorance of the fact—I
promise myself the pleasure of enlightening his mind on the subject
sometime—when a fair opportunity offers—till then I'll conceal—
Before getting into the carriage, I just stepped up to my two inno-
cents & inquired how they were off for soap, alias fire-arms—for I
know the Stag would gore when brought to bay—the dear babes
shewed me each a couple of chickens nestling in his bosom—I was
satisfied & took my seat calmly by the side of my noble friend. how
my heart warmed towards him in the close proximity of our relative
positions, especially when I looked at his visnomy & saw him dis-
severing his lips with a devilish grin & setting his clenched teeth
against the wild sheets of rain that, as we whirled down his park,
came driving in our faces—Evening was now setting in, & all the
woods of the dale were bending under the gloom of heavy clouds
& rushing to the impetus of the tremendous wind—as we swept out
at the town-gates which swung back at our approach with a heavy
clang—lights glanced from the Porter's lodge—they were gone in a
moment—& on we thundered through rain & tempest & mist—
Hartford cursing his coachman every five minutes & ordering him
to make the horses get over the ground faster—I shall not soon
forget that ride—my sensations were those of strange blood-thirsty
excitement—& woods & hills rolled by in dusky twilight—spangled
with lights from the scattered houses of the valley—while rain drove
slanting wildly over everything—& the swollen & roaring Olympian seemed running a mad race with ourselves. Hartford, between
his oaths, at last contrived to give me some sort of explanation of the
errand we were going upon. His game-keeper, he said, had been
that morning down at Massinger, and while he was setting some
springes in a wood near the old place called Massinger-Hall—He
had seen a fellow come out of the Garden Gate whose appearance
exactly answered to the handbill description of Henry Hastings,
Gent. & says Hartford "I know a sister of the man's is residing there
as a housekeeper or housemaid or something of that sort—& this, in
conjunction with the track Ingham has succeeded in tracing out—
justifies me in supposing that we have unkennelled the right fox at
last—Drive on, Jhonson! D--n the villain, he crawls like a
tortoise!" Though it was now getting very dark, I could perceive
that we had for some time left the high-road & were following the
course of a bye-path whose windings led us down into some region
of fields & solitude where hardly the twinkle of a single window

could be seen through the gloom—The first intimation we had of a near approach to the hall was the rushing of trees above us & the vision of vast dusky trunks—lining the road with a long colonnade of timber—Hartford now countermanded his former orders to Jhonson & desired him to drive softly—a mandate easily obeyed— for the path was carpeted with a thick bed of withered leaves never cleared since last Autumn—& over these the wheels passed with a dead, muffled sound—scarcely heard at all through the confusion of wind & rain & groaning branches. The carriage suddenly stopped & when I looked up theire was the dim out-line of a gate with balls upon the pillars—& beyond—rising above trees, I saw a stack of chimneys & a Gable-end—"Here we are!" said Hartford, & he jumped out as eager & impatient for his prey as the most un- reclaimed tiger of the Jungle—"Have you got the manacles?" I asked—quietly bending over to Ingham—"Yes, Sir, & a strait- waistcoat"—"Come Sir William—you lose time" growled blood- hound. "I'll not be hurried by you" was my internal resolution— while I stood up in the carriage & buttoned my surtout—comfort- ably over my chest—& then I felt if my handkerchief was in my pocket—chance I should find it necessary to shed any tears on the occasion of the poor d----l's capture—I also ascertained that a vinaigrette I usually carry about me was safe in its place—for I considerately thought of Miss Hastings & imagined it was not impossible she might faint in the course of the scene about to go off —especially if there was any puffing of gunpowder. my waistcoat was then to pull down & a shawl I had about my neck was to adjust more conveniently—lastly I felt I could not live without priming with a pinch of snuff—During the settlement of these small but essential preliminaries, my noble friend stood on the wet grass before the gate fuming—cursing—& ejaculating in a most exem- plary way—first it began "Sir William, surely your ready—what the d----l can you be about? Jhonson—Ingham, Jones, can't ye assist Sir William—the whole affair will be spoiled by this accursed dawdling—precious time passing away & nothing done—G-d d--n—blast such folly! cursed conceited Humbug! infernal— petticoat perverseness! fated foppery!—Are you ready—I say, Sir?" this interrogation was put in the harshest [*illegible*]—of savage, arbitrary insolence---"I shall be by & bye" said I, & having now perfectly arranged myself, I proceeded to alight from the carriage with the care & deliberation of a lady—fearful of soiling her silk gown by contact with the wheels. "Your lordship looks somewhat hurried" I remarked in an indifferent sort of way. "take your time —no fear"—& in a consolatory whisper—"perhaps the fellow may not have fire arms". I heard something about a d————d impertinent puppy! & his lordship turned his ferocity on our assistants. "What are you all standing gaping there for?—to your stations—every one—Jhonson, you idiot, take the carriage to the back-way & have it ready—do you hear, Sir?" And now serious work commenced— there were four policemen—one of them was to be stationed behind, one in front of the house to bar all egress—the two others were destined for the business of the interior. I now led my men to their posts—all the garden-paths were dark & wet—the house was silent—all the windows closed & not a beam of light streaming from their panes—it seemed an old pile—& had something of haunted & romantic gloom about it—my lads having received their orders & commenced their sentinel march in the yard & on the lawn, I stole round to join lord Hartford—He was waiting for me on the front door steps—I could just discern his dusk cloaked figure standing there like a Goblin—"Is all right?" said he. "All's right" I answered —He turned to the door—lifted the knocker, & to the sound of his summons a long desolate echo answered from within. In the inter- val that followed, how utterly I forgot that drenching-rain—wild wind & utter darkness envelloped me round. a door opened—& a very light but very rapid step was heard to run quickly up the passage —then another step & a hollow treading sound as of one ascending oaken stairs—then a pause—a silence of some minutes—Hartford began again with his growling solo of oaths—"Hustling the lumber into concealment, I suppose" said he—he gave another louder rap & in two minutes more the withdrawing of a bolt & the rattling of a chain was heard—the heavy front-door turned grating on its hinges —& a woman-servant stood before us with a light. the look with which she scanned us said plainly enough "Who can be making such a noise at this time of night?" "Is Miss Hasting at home?" I asked. "Yes, Sir." "Can we see her?" "walk forward, Sir—" & still with a perplexed air, the woman led the way through a long passage, & opening a door in the side asked us to step in—she left her light on the table of the room into which she shewed us & closing the door went away—It was an appartment with the chill of a vault on its atmosphere—furnished in drawing-room style—but without fire in its bright steel grate—without light in its icy chandelier whose drops streamed from the ceiling like a cold crystal stalactite. the mirror between the windows looked as if it had never reflected a human face for ages—the couch—the chairs—the grand-piano all stood like fixtures never to be moved. Over the piano was a large picture, the only one in the room—I could see by the dim candle on the table that it was a portrait painted by some eminent hand—

for the coulours were flesh-like & brilliant—it was a girl of about twelve years old with the lips & the eyes & the soft shadowy hair that that flattering villain Lawrence bestows on all his portraits. the image, smiling all by itself in this frozen-dreary room, reminds one of that legendary lady who pricked her finger—& having fallen into a trance, was enshrined in a splendid chamber where she sat twenty years in all the stillness of death & all the beauty of life—I was still looking at this picture & had just ascertained in the features an indubitable likeness to Jane Moore—when the turning of the door-handle caused me also to turn, & having so done I saw a young female enter the room—curtsy to myself & Lord Hartford & then stand with her fingers nervously twined in a watch-chain round her neck—& her eyes fixed on us with a look of searching yet apprehensive enquiry. "We shall want a few minute's conversation with you, Miss Hastings" said Hartford, shutting the door & handing a chair —while the stern arrogance of the dissipated old rake instantly softened to gentle condescension at the sight of a petticoat—"I believe I am speaking to Lord Hartford" said she, summoning a kind of high-bred composed tact into her manner—though the lady-like trembling of her thin white hands let me into the secret as to the reality of that composure—"Yes, madam, & I wish to treat you as considerately as I can—now come, be under no alarm—sit down—" "now for my vinaigrette" thought I—for already the nervous being had lost her front of calmness & was beginning to look sick—She took the chair Hartford brought her—"I am only surprised at your lordship's visit—I am not alarmed—there is nothing to alarm me —" & a respectful air of reserve was assumed. "I can trust to your sense" said his lordship politely—"You will receive the communication I have to make with proper fortitude I am sure—It grieves me that you happen to be the sister of a man proscribed by the law— but Justice must have its course, Madam, & it is now my painful duty to tell you that I am here to-night for the purpose of arresting Captain Henry Hastings on a charge of murder—desertion & treason—" "Will she swoon now" thought I—but humph—no—up she got like a Doe starting erect at the sound of horns. "But Henry Hastings is not here" said she, & she stood within a pace or two of Hartford looking up into his face as if she were going to challenge him—His lordship—still drawing it mild—shook his head. "It won't do, Miss Hastings—It won't do—" said he. "Very natural that you should wish to screen your brother—but my information is decisive—my plans are laid—there are four policemen about the house, your doors are guarded—so now compose yourself—stay here with Sir William Percy—I am going to execute my warrant, &

in two minutes the thing will be done—" Sparks of fire danced in Miss Hastings' eyes—there was very little resemblance between what now stood before me & the submissive-dexterous-retiring individual I had seen at Verdopolis. "Dare your lordship intend to search the house" said she. "Yes, Madam—every cranny of it from the Hall to a rat-hole"—"and every cranny of it from the Hall to a rat-hole is free for your lordship's inspection" she rejoined. Hartford moved towards the door—"I shall certainly attend your lordship" she pursued—& turning sharply to the table she took up the candle & walked after him, thus leaving me very unceremoniously in the dark. I heard Hartford stop in the passage. "Miss Hastings, you must not follow me." there was a pause—"I must lead you back to the drawing-room." "No, my lord—" "I must—" "Don't" in an intreating tone "I'll show you every room." but Hartford insisted—she was obliged to retreat—still she did not yield —she only backed as the Baron advanced—a little overawed by his towering stature & threatening look—She made a stand at the drawing-room door. "will you compel me to use coercive measures?" said his lordship. he laid a hand on her shoulder—one touch was enough—she shrunk away from it into the room— Hartford shut the door & she was left standing, her eyes fixed on the vacant pannels. mechanically she replaced the candle on the table —& then she wrung her hands & turned a distressed wild glance on me. It was now my turn to address her, & my knowledge of her character shewed me in what way to proceed—Here, I saw, was little strength of mind—though their was a semblance of courage— the result merely of very overwrought & ardent feeling. here was a being made up of intense emotions—in her ordinary course of life always smothered under the diffidence of prudence & a skilful address, but now when her affections were about to suffer almost a death-stab—when incidents of strange excitement were transpiring around her—on the point of bursting forth like lava—still she struggled to keep wrapt about her the veil of reserve & propriety— She sat down at a distance from me & turned her face from the light to evade the look with which I followed all her movements. I walked towards her chair—"Miss Hastings—you look very much agitated—If it would be a relief to you, you shall accompany the officers on their search—I have authority to give you permission— I am sorry for you, my poor girl—" She turned more & more away from me as I spoke—[? She leant] her eyes & forehead on her hand & when I uttered [? those last] words, there was a short irrepressible sob—every part of her frame quivered—& she gave way to the bitter [*illegible*] of despair—She got over it as soon as she could—

[*illegible*] & thanked me for my compassion in a [*illegible*] that shewed all caution & disguise were [*illegible*] impulse & imagination were now in full & unguarded [? possession] "I may go?" she said—I gave her leave &, as quick as thought, she was gone.

"But I must follow" thought I—& it required my fastest stride to overtake her—the lower-rooms had been clearly examined. we heard the policemen's tramp in the lobby overhead—she was speeding up the old staircase as if her feet had been winged— Hartford confronted her at the top of the stairs—he frowned prohibition & stretched out his arm to impede passage, but she darted under the bar—sprang before Ingham, who was just in the act of opening a chamber door—darted in before him, exclaiming "Henry, the window!" & clapping the door to, tryed with all her strength to hold it & to bolt it—till the Murderer should have time to escape—"The vixen!" thought I "the witch!" that's the consequence of minding female tears—I sprang to Ingham's assistance —in her agony she had had strength to hold it against him for a fraction of time—I put my foot & hand to the door—the inefficient arm within failed—she was flung to the ground by the force of the rebound—I & my myrmidons rushed in—the room was dark—but there, by the window, was the black outline of a man—madly tearing at the stanchons & bolt by which the old lattice was secured—It was a night-mare. "Seize him!" thundered Hartford— "Man, your pistols!—shoot him dead if he resists—" There was a flash through the dark chamber—a crack—somebody's pistol had exploded—another louder crash—the whole frame-work of the lattice was dashed in, bars—glass & all—the cold howling storm swept through the hollow—Hastings was gone—I gave a glance to see if I could follow, but there was an unfathomed depth of darkness down below—I thought of legs jammed into the body like a telescope—To the outside I shouted—I cleared the stairs at two bounds—made for the front-door &, followed by I know not what hurly-burly of tramping feet—rushed onto the front—the contest was already begun—there was a grass-plat in front of the house, & in the middle of it I saw a huddled struggle of two figures in deadly grips—Hastings & the Sentinel that had been stationed outside—God bless me! there sprung a flash of fire between them— & the ringing crack of a pistol split the air again—the mass of wrestling mortality dissolved, the arms of one were loosened from the body of the other & a heavy weight fell on the grass—off sprang one survivor, bounding like a panther—but he was surrounded, he was hemmed in—the three remaining policemen cut

across the lawn, interrupted his flight—he was too stunned to
struggle more—& while two held him down on his knees, the third
fixed his hands in a pair of bracelets more easily put on than taken
off—Just as this ceremony was completed, the moon for the first
time that night came rolling out of a cloud—She was in her wane—
but the decayed orb gave light enough to shew me the features I
longed to see—he was in the act of rising up—his head was bare—
his face lifted a little—a gloom, cold, wan & wild, revealed the
aspect, the expression of the man I had followed for eighteen
months & hunted down in blood at last—of that daring, desperate
miscreant—Henry Hastings the Angrian!

C. Townshend Feby 24th 1839

*

*Although the narrative that follows (again untitled by Charlotte Brontë) is
now known as* Henry Hastings Part II, *it is immediately obvious from
the opening words that it does not directly follow* Part I. *The intervening
narrative, however, has unfortunately not been located, but it must presumably
have told of further desperate steps taken by Hastings on his downward path.
In what follows, Hastings is on trial, but it is not for the murder of Colonel
Adams. In the missing "volume" he must somehow have escaped, and his
subsequent actions must have culminated in an attack on Zamorna's life.*

My last volume, I believe, terminated at the ringing of the
Duchess's bell—which bell, acting like a charm on the dramatis
personae of the narrative—all at once sealed their lips—& sent
the curtain rolling "down" like midnight loosed at noon over her
Grace's ante-room—This, no doubt, was a providential interference—for if my readers recollect—an angry parle was then in
progress—which—from the pitch at which it had arrived at,
seemed likely to terminate in nothing less than a duello between
the Premier of Angria and one of his lease-holder's daughters.
W. H. Warner Esqre. had just ordered Miss Hastings to stop—&
Miss Hastings was just asking herself what right any living creature
had to give her any orders whatever—& in dim perspective was
making up her mind to leave Verdopolis instanter—committing
herself & her fortunes to the first Angrian coach which should be
ready to start—to return to Zamorna & there, doggedly to wait
whatever luck should befall her martyr-brother—then to sit down
with a consolatory & lasting hate at her heart towards all & sundry,
the Judge—jury—King—Court & Country—who had tryed—
condemned—& suffered the execution of that notorious & in-

effable saint—such, I say, was the tenor of Miss Hastings' embryo-resolves—when that bell from within rang its short call—when the inner-door opened & in spite of herself—the young woman found that she was compelled to finish the adventure she had commenced—

How quietly & defferentially—with what a studied look of awe, she would under other circumstances have crossed that hallowed threshold! She would have considered only how best to prove her deep innate sense of her own inferiority—of the transcendant supremacy of the royal Lady she was about to petition—She would have called up all her tact, all her instinctive knowledge of human nature, especially of the human nature of the beautiful & titled woman—she would have laid by her scorn—shut up out of sight—the trifling property of pride—which, after all, gave the little woman the power of valuing to their full extent her own acute perceptions & mental gifts. She would have said—"here I am, dust & ashes, and I presume to speak to a Queen." But the hazing Mr Warner had very properly administered was still burning at her heart. it had raised her Dander—& had quickened in her mind divers calculations as to the relative value of patriotism & plebeian flesh & blood—now, these calculations it had ever been her wont occasionally to indulge in by her own fireside—but she had never before attempted to solve the problem under the roofs of royalty or even of aristocracy. the effort consequently threw her into some sort of agitation, & when she stepped into the imperial breakfast-room—the tears were so hot & blinding in her eyes—she could scarcely discern into what a region of delicate splendour her foot had intruded—

She saw however a table before her, & at the table there was a lady seated—& when she had cleared the troublesome mist from her vision—she perceived that the Lady was engaged with some loose sheets that looked like music &, as she turned them over, conversing with a person who stood behind her chair—that person was Sir William Percy—and when Miss Hastings entered, as his royal sister did not appear to notice her approach, he observed coolly—"the young woman is in waiting—will your Grace speak to her—?" her Grace raised her head—not quickly as your low persons do when they are told an individual is expecting their attention—but with a calm deliberate movement—as if it was a thing of course that somebody should be waiting the honour of her notice—Her Grace's eyes were very large & very full—she turned them on Miss Hastings—let them linger a moment over her figure & then withdrew them again—"A sister of Captain Hastings, you say" she remarked, addressing her brother—"Yes" was the answer—her Grace turned the leaves of a fresh sheet of music—put it quietly from her—& once more regarded the petitioner—Now, her royal Highness's glance was not penetrating —that is, the brown eyes had not that quick arrowy flicker which darts to the heart in a minute—but it seemed to dwell quietly & searchingly—it had the effect of sinking through the countenance to the mind. it was grave, & the darkness of the eye-lashes—the langour of the lids, made it seem pensive—However, Miss Hastings stood that gaze—& her temper so refractory at the time she could almost have curled her lip in token of defying it—yet, as she stood opposite the fair princess, she felt by degrees the effect of that beautiful eye—changing her mood—awakening a new feeling—& her heart confessed, as it had a thousand times done before, the Dazzling omnipotence of beauty—the Degradation of personal insignificance. "Come forward" said the Duchess. Miss Hastings barely moved a step—still she would hardly endure the tone of Dictation—"Explain to me what you wish in your present circumstances & I will consider if I can serve you"—"I presume" returned Miss Hastings—looking down—& speaking in a low, quick voice— not at all supplicatory—"I presume your Royal Highness is aware of the situation of Captain Hastings. my present circumstances are to be inferred from that situation—" And so she abruptly stopped—"I do not quite comprehend you" returned the Duchess —"I understand you came as a Petitioner—" "I do" was the answer—"But perhaps I have done wrong—perhaps your royal highness would rather not be troubled with my request—I know what seems of importance to private individuals—is often trivial to the great." "I assure you I regard your brother's case with no unconcerned eye—perhaps I may have already done all that I can to obtain a remission of his sentence—" "In that case, I thank your Grace—but if your Grace has done what you can—it follows that your Grace can do no more—so it would be presumption in me to trouble your Grace further—" The Duchess seemed rather puzzled—she looked at the little stubborn sight before her with a perplexed air & then she turned her inquiring glance to Sir William, as good as to say—"What does she mean?"—Sir William was stuffing a pocket-handkerchief into his mouth by way of stifling an incipient laugh—he stooped to his sister's ear & said in a whisper—"She has an odd temper—something has occurred to ruffle it—your Grace will excuse it—" but the Duchess hardly looked as if she would. at any rate she did not condescend to continue the conversation till Miss Hastings should choose to explain. That individual in the meantime, liable always to quick & strong revulsions of feeling, began to recollect that she was not going the right way to work—if she intended to make an impression in favour of her brother. "What a fool I am" she thought to herself. "To have spent the best part of my life in learning how to propitiate the vices & vanity of these Aristocrats—& now, when my skill might do some good—I am on the point of throwing it away for the sake of a pique of offended pride—Come, let me act like myself, or that Beautiful Woman will order her lackey to shew me to the door directly—" So she came a little nearer to the chair where the Queen of Angria was seated—& looking up, she said with the emphatic earnestness of tone & manner peculiar to her "Do hear the few words I have to say—" "I said before I would hear them" was the haughty reply—a reply intended to show Miss Hastings that Great People are not to be wantonly trifled with—"Then" continued the Petitioner "I have nothing to urge in extenuation of my brother—his crimes have been proved against him. I have only to ask your Grace to remember what he was before he fell—how warm his heart was towards Angria—how bold his actions were in her cause —It is not necessary that I should tell your royal highness of the energy that marks Captain Hasting's mind—of the powerful & vigorous talent that distinguished him above most of his contemporaries—the Country rung with his name once, & that is proof sufficient—" "I know he was a brave & able man" interposed the Duchess "but that did not prevent him from being a very dangerous man." "Am I permitted to reply to your Royal Highness?" asked Miss Hastings—The Duchess signified her permission by a slight inclination of the head. "Then" said Miss Hastings "I will suggest to your Grace that his courage & his talents are the best guarantee against dishonourable meanness—against treachery—& if my brother's Sovereign will condescend to pardon him, he will by that gracious action win back a most efficient subject to his standard—" "An efficient subject!" repeated the Duchess. "A man free from treachery! you are aware, young woman, that the King's life has been endangered by the treasonable attempt of the very man whose cause you are pleading—you know that Captain Hastings went near to become a regicide—" "But the attempt failed" pleaded she. "And it was in distraction & despair that Hastings hazarded it—" "Enough!" said the Duchess—"I have heard you now—and I think you can say nothing more to me which can throw fresh light on the subject—I will give you my answer—Captain Hastings' fate will be regarded by me with

regret—but I consider it inevitable—you seem shocked—I know
it is natural you should feel—but I cannot see the use of buoying
up your expectations with false hopes—To speak candidly, I have
already used all the influence I possess in Hastings' behalf——
reasons were given me why my request should meet with a denial—
reasons I could not answer & therefore I was silent—if I recur to
the subject again, it will be with reluctance because I know that
the word passed will not be revoked—However, I promise to try—
you need not thank me—you may go—" & she turned her head
quite away from Miss Hastings—the hauteur of her exquisite
features expressed that if more was said she did not mean to listen
to it—Her humble subject looked at her a moment—it was difficult
to say what language was spoken by her dark glowing eyes—
indignation, disappointment, & shame seemed to be the prevailing
feelings—She felt that somehow she did not take with the Duchess
of Zamorna—that she had hit on a wrong tack, had made a false
impression at first—that she had injured her brother's cause,
rather than benefitted it—above all she felt that she had failed thus
signally before the eyes & in the presence of Sir William Percy—
she left the room quite heart-sick—

"Do you know much of that young woman?" asked the Duchess,
turning to her brother—"I've seen her a few times" was Sir
William's reply—"Well, but do you know her—are you acquainted with her character?" "Not much—she's a warm-hearted Girl"
returned the Baronet—& he smiled with an expression meant to be
very inexplicable and mysterious—"Where has she lived & what
are her connections?" "Till lately she was a sort of Governess in
the Barrister Moore's family"—"What, the father of Miss Moore—
Jane, Julia—or what is her name?" "just so—the beautiful
Angrian, your Grace means—" "Aye—well this Miss Hastings is
not very pleasing—I don't like her"—"Why, please your Grace
—?" "She's odd—abrupt—I would rather not grant another
audience—you'll remember that—" "Very well—by the bye—I'm
tired of standing—will it be lesè majestè to sit down in your Grace's
presence—?" "No Sir—draw a chair to the table." Sir William
left his station behind the royal sofa & took a seat near his sister's—
They looked a rather remarkable pair & seemed too on rather
remarkable terms—their conversation was short & terse—their
looks at each other were quick, not very sentimental, but still such
as indicated a sort of mutual understanding—The Duchess did not
forget her rank—she addressed her relative with a regal freedom &
brusquerie. "What have you been about lately?" she asked—

regarding with a half-frown—half-smile—the random scamp who now rested his elbow on her sofa-arm—"Could not justly tell you, Madame—been breathing myself a trifle after the hard race I ran lately—" "But where have you been?—I assure you I have heard nothing but complaints of your absence from Town—the Premier has more than once expressed himself very warmly on the subject" —"Retirement is necessary now & then your Grace knows—to give a man an opportunity for thought—the hurry & bustle of this wicked world is enough to drive him distracted—" "Retirement William!—Stuff—retirement gets you into mischief, I know it does—I wish you'd keep in action—" "What! is your Grace going to trouble yourself about my morals—?" "Don't sneer William—your morals are your own concern—not mine—but tell me what you've been doing—?" "Nothing—Mary—as I'm a Christian—I tell you I've been in no mischief whatever—what makes you suspect me so?"—"Well, keep your confession to yourself then, & now inform me what you're going to do—can I further any of your intentions—?" "no, thank you, my work is set for the present—I'm after Montmorenci & Simpson"—"Have you any idea where they are, William?—" "Scarcely—but I think they've left Paris"—"I imagined so from what I heard last night—" "What did you hear?" "Why, the Duke & my father were talking about them—& my father said he thought they were nearer home than France." "Was that all?" asked Sir William, looking at his sister keenly—"Yes, I heard nothing more. they stopped talking when I came into the room—" "Do you suppose" continued the Baronet "that our respected & illustrious Parent has any connection with his old friends now?" "Not the least, I should think—he seldom alludes to politics—O William, I do wish he would keep out of them!" "O Mary—I don't care—the smallest pearl in that brooch of yours whether he does or not—but its very blackguardly of him to give his quondam associates the slip in that way—" "Come, I'll have none of Edward's slang" rejoined the Drover's daughter—"I'd say the same to his face" answered that Drover's son. "I've often thought, Mary, that a more peculiarly strange—insane Scoundrel than the man who begot me never existed—as to Edward's coarse abuse, it's all fudge—& I've no irresistible natural impulse to hate our Noble Sire—" "Then be silent, Sir—!" broke in Queen Mary. "Nay, I've a right to speak—" was the answer. "The man's a monomaniac—I'll swear to it—God bless me, I'd never marry if I thought I should inherit the wild delusion of believing that all the male children who might be borne to me were devils." "He never said or believed that you & Edward were devils—he'd have been near the truth if he had—" "No, the Gentleman dare'nt say such a thing—it's too horrible a supposition to be expressed in words—in his hypochondria dread he must darkly have concluded that he himself was not altogether human—but a something with a cross of the fiend in it—that's just the lunatic's idea, & he thinks his sons take after their Demon father—& his Daughter is the pure offering of her pleasant human mother—pray, Mary, have you any such notions about your children? there would be some sense in it if you had, for no doubt their father is a demon—" "William, what a strange scoffing sneerer you are—I've been angry with you once or twice e'er now for talk of this kind—but it's of no use, I'll dismiss you Sir, & have as little to do with you as I have with Edward—" "Do madam—deny me an audience once when I ask for it—& I'll just take revenge by rushing head-foremost into a little scrape I've been contemplating for the last two years. a single insult either from you or the Great Cham—Chi Thaung-Gru—will make me come out on to the stage of publicity & turn out my fool like a good 'un." "Do as you will, I'll not be threatened" answered the Duchess—"Your dark hints are all nonsense—you've a bad temper, William." "So have you, Mary—& if you'd been married to a decent man like Sir Robert Pelham—instead of the individual who now blesses you with his faithful love, you'd have shewn it 'ere now—" "Happily I was *not* married to Sir Robert Pelham—let him thank his stars for it" answered the Duchess—"He does, I have no doubt—" was the quiet rejoinder—"William, you're exceedingly disagreeable this morning" continued her Grace. "And you were most encouraging kind & agreeable to that poor wretch who came to ask a favour of you half an hour since—" "O, I vexed you, did I? how you smoothed over your anger till it could explode with the best effect—" "That's a quality natural to our family—& peculiarly derived from our Satanic parentage—" "William, your character is an odd one—I confess myself sometimes puzzled with it—Sometimes you will come & sit in my appartment for an hour—stupidly silent—but with a placid smile of satisfaction on your quizzical face—as if you were the gentlest—most contented creature in the world—if the children are here you'll play with them & seem rather fond of them than otherwise—then again you'll walk in when I don't want you, looking as sour as cynical as—nay, I know no figure of speech that will express an adequate comparison—you sit down & begin a series of taunts & innuendoes—whose bitterness would lead me to conclude that you hated & envied me worse than Edward does—how am I to account for this inconsistency? Does it arise from the mere love of wantonly exercising the sort of influence which your relationship gives you? Do you think I am in Danger of being too happy—if I am not occasionally reminded of my mortal state—by the intrusion of a haughty capricious brother—who tries to convert himself into a sort of phantom to haunt me always with secret gnawing uneasiness—" "Why, bless my life! what have I done, what have I said to call forth all this tirade?" cried Sir William. "Secret gnawing uneasiness!" he repeated sarcastically. "No—no, Mary—the great Cham spares me the trouble of all that sort of thing—you know his last foible—I suppose—" "No, but you may tell it me, I'll believe it or not as I please—" "O, of course your too good a wife to believe it—but the town believes it notwithstanding—he went to a soirèe at Clarence-House two nights ago did he not—?" "Yes, what of that?" "Nothing, only that the lady you mentioned a while since—the Beautiful Angrian was there too—" "Go on William, say your worst—" "Nay, I've nothing to say—except that the King & Miss Jane were closeted together for nearly an hour in that little cabinet opening to the drawing-room, you may remember it—" "Alone?" asked the Duchess—"Aye, alone—but don't look so exceedingly concerned—perhaps there was no harm done after all—" "Who told you of it—?" "I saw it—I was at the Soirèe & I used my eyes—I saw Richton take Miss Moore into the Cabinet—I heard him tell her that the Duke was there—I noticed how long she stayed & I observed her come out." The Duchess looked at her brother narrowly—his face was pale & had something very envenomed in its expression. "What are you telling me this for, William?" said she. "for a very good reason, Madam, & I'll confess my motive candidly—I rather liked that Miss Moore— I thought her a handsome—good-natured girl—& as I mean to marry before long, I had some faint intention of asking her to be Lady Percy, but when I saw that delectable transaction & saw her allow Richton to lead her behind the curtain of a recess—heard a mock struggle that ensued between them—was aware afterwards of her admittance into the cabinet—& witnessed the heated face & flurried manner with which she left it—I felt such a stunner of disgust I could have insulted her before the whole party—however I determined to punish her in a safer & more effectual way. I thought I'd communicate the business quietly to my royal sister, & she might act as she pleased—my advice is—nay, what are you going to do?—stop a moment—humph, she's off—well I was in a very bad temper this morning, but I feel much easier in my mind now—Mary took fire in the right style—how will she act?—is she gone to attack him instanter—? I don't care whether she does or not—am I going to cut my throat for disappointed love—? no, nor even drop a tear—I find I did not love her, the buxom—hearty—heartless—laughing brainless jilt—what in the world do I care for her with her snivelling simplicity? but I've had my revenge. I'm quite comfortable—now let's drop heroics—& go home & take our luncheon—I'll call on Townshend to-day, I think, & we'll flay the world alive—"

CHAPTER I

"Will ye tell Major King I want to speak to him" said Lord Hartford, opening his dressing-room door—& addressing a house-maid who was dusting the gilded picture frames in the Gallery—"Yes, my lord" &, with her brush in her hand, the smart house-maid bustled down the great wide staircase as far as the last landing. there she stopped—"Wood" she called to a man-servant crossing the hall with a tray in his hand on which were some silver egg-cups & some toast—"Wood, are the Gentlemen at breakfast?"—"Yes, but they'll have done soon. What for, Susan?" "You're to tell Major King my lord wants him & be sharp." the house-maid ran up the stair-case to return to her work & the footman passed on to the breakfast-room.

Major King—Captain Berkley & Lieutenant Jones, being visitors at Hartford-Hall—had come down a little after ten o'clock & were sitting in a handsome appartment engaged in the discussion of a capital good breakfast—"How d'ye feel this morning, Berkley, my cock?" said Major King—"is that a chicken's wing your picking? your appetite seems only delicate to-day." "As good as yours. I've a notion I've not seen you take anything but a mouthful of dry toast—& there's Jones is lingering over his coffee as fondly as if it were poison—" "I wonder what breakfasts were made for—" grumbled Jones—"You can't see the use of them, can you?" inquired Major King "especially when your head & stomach are in the condition they are just now—conscientiously, Jones, how many bottles do you think you decanted last night—?" "I forgot to count after the fourth" answered Jones. "And where did you sleep, my buck?" "I don't know—I found myself amongst a lot of flowers when I awoke"—"A lot of flowers—yes, when you framed to steal out of the dining-room, instead of making for the door like a Christian—you took a grand tack to one side & went crash through the glass of the conservatory—Hartford swore he would make you pay for damages—"

"If you please, Sir, you're wanted" said the footman, addressing

Major King—"Who wants me, Wood?" "My lord—he's in his dressing-room—" "O" said the Major, rising from the table with a wink "I suppose he's done—can't come down this morning—I'll recommend bleeding & if the Doctor'll prick him in the jugular there's a chance for me—take away the breakfast, Wood. Captain Berkley & Mr Jones are Roman-Catholics & they mean to fast to day—Bring the liqueur-case, Wood—& a bottle or two of soda-water & fetch Mr Jones a box of cigars—& a novel from the library or something light to amuse him"—"D––n you, King—I wish you'd order for yourself" said Mr Jones—Major King laughed as he looked askance at the Lieutenant's feckless face—& while laughing he left the room.

The excellent Major went up the stair-case & came with swing-ing stride along the gallery—looking as little like a rakish raff as any officer of the nineteenth could be expected to do, on the morning succeeding a deep debauch—Susan, the housemaid mentioned before, was still at her work—still whisking her light brush & dusters over the burnished frames of all the dark Salvators & Carracis & Corregios which frowned along that lengthened wall—Major King seemed to have something particular to say to her—he stopped & was for commencing a conversation—which he would fain have preluded with a salute—but Susan slipped away & took refuge in a neighbouring appartment of which she bolted the door—On then marched Major King—& at last made a halt before a door at the far-end of the Gallery—he knocked. "Come in, d––n you" growled a voice as of one either in the gout or the colic. Major King sucked in his cheeks & obeyed orders. Lord Hartford's dressing-room was somewhat dark—the blinds being down & the curtains half drawn—however, a freer admittance of light was scarcely to be desired—seeing that both the room & its occupant were in what may be called "a mess". The toilet was scattered over with shaving materials—with brooches & rings—a loose miniature shut up in a case & a magnificent gold repeater—A Great Cheval mirror was standing in the middle of the room with an arm-chair placed before it and a damask dressing-gown, like a musoulman's robe, thrown untidly over the back thereof—the rich carpet was ruffled up & a foot-stool lay by the door—as if it had been hurled missive-wise in some access of patrician furor. full in front of the fire there was a chair & seated therein was a man of savage, hirsute aspect, unwashed, uncombed, unshaven—with hands plunged to an unknown depth in his pockets—& long legs widely sundered so that one morocco-slippered foot rested upon one hob & the other on the corresponding pedestal opposite. He

was a charming figure—especially as his eyes were fixed steadfastly on the back of the chimney, with a smothered cholor of
expression rather to be imagined than described—

"Well, what's the bulletin for to day, Colonel" inquired Major
King, swaggering up to his superior. "Will ye shut the door" said
Hartford, with as little amenity of tone as is expressed in the growl
of a sick tiger—King walked back & kicked the door to with his
foot—"Will ye read them documents" continued the first Gentleman in Angria—at the same time reluctantly drawing one hand
from the pocket of his inexcusables & directing his thumb towards
a brace of letters which, with their envellopes, lay open on the
table—the Major obeyed orders. "Will ye read up" pursued the
ornament of the Peerage—King cleared his throat—flourished
the letters & in the tone of a sentinel singing out the watch-word
began as follows.

Victoria Square—Verdopolis—March 18
To Lord Hartford—Colonel of the 19th regiment of infantry—
Judge of the Court-Martial at Zamorna—My lord—I have
received his majesty's commands to lay before you the following
decision sanctioned by his majesty in council concerning the
Prisoner Hastings—now in your Lordship's custody in the County-
Jail of Zamorna—It is desired that your Lordship shall proceed
forthwith to lay before him the following articles, on agreeing to
which the Prisoner is to be set at liberty with the reservations hereafter stated—

firstly—he is to make a full confession as to how far he was connected with the other individuals included with himself in the
sentence of outlawry—

Secondly—he is to state all he knows of the plans & intentions of
those individuals.

Thirdly—he is to give information where he last saw Hector
Mirabeau Montmorenci—Jeremiah Simpson—James Macqueen
—George Frederick Caversham & Quashia Quamina Kashna—
also where he now supposes them to be—also how far they were
concerned with the late massacre in the east & the disembarkation
of French arms at Wilson's creek—also whether these persons are
connected with any foreign political incendiaries, with Parvas—
Dupin & Bernadotte—also, & this your Lordship will consider an
important question, whether the Courts of the Southern States have
maintained any secret correspondence with the Angrian renegades,
whether they have given them any encouragement directly or
indirectly.

Should Hastings consent to give such answers to these questions as his Majesty & the Government shall deem satisfactory—his sentence of Death will be commuted to degradation from his rank as an Officer in the Angrian army—expulsion from the 19th regiment, & compulsory service as a private soldier in the troops commanded by Colonel Nicholas Balcastro.

Should Hastings decline answering all or any of these questions after being allowed half an hour for deliberation—Your Lordship will cause his sentence to be executed without reserve—His Majesty particularly requests that your Lordship will not delay complying with his commands on these points as he thinks it is high time the affair were brought to a conclusion—in order that your Lordship may be relieved from the anxiety of having the whole responsibility of this matter—The Government have given orders that Sir Wm. Percy shall be in attendance at the next sitting of your Lordship's court.

I have the honour to remain
Your Lordship's Obedient humble servant
H. F. Etrei

Secretary at War—Verdopolis March 18th—39

Major King, have[ing] finished the perusal of this despatch, was about to make his comment on it—he had already began "G–d d––n" when he was stopped by the stormy uprising of the man in the morocco slippers with the black unshaven beard & the grizzled uncombed head—"There" roared Hartford—striding down the length of his dressing-room—"there—that's what you may call black-bile—that's something to stink in a man's nostrils—till the day of his eternal Death—that's a court-insult—they'll pardon the hound, they'll give him a fair chance—the fellow that should have been shot when caught—as you'd shoot a dirty grinning wolf—and all to spite me—and they'll set their snivelling Government agent, their hired spy—their toadie—their loathsome lickspittle—to watch my actions—to relieve me from anxiety forsooth—to hector & bully the court-martial of the 19th & I'm to have Sir Wm. Percy stink at my elbow & I'm to have every look & movement watched by him & every word reported by his befouled hireling pen—curse me— Curse the Globe!" this last anathema was uttered with a perfect yell—for just then, the irate nobleman, happening in his furious promenade to come in contact with the great Cheval-Glass in the middle of the floor—he kicked his foot through it, thereby shivering to atoms the noble reflect it was affording of his own tall dark muscular shape & of his swarthy strong-featured & most choleric physiognomy—Having performed this exploit, his lordship began calling upon several fiends by their names—as nobody seemed to answer, unless indeed Major King might be considered as the representative of the infernal muster-roll, the noble Lord at last cooled down so far as to resume his seat before the fire, & having verbally consigned the King & Court of Angria to the custody of the infernal agents he had invoked—he fetched a deep sigh & through mere exhaustion was silent—Now, it so happened that Major King did not at all sympathise with this explosion of the noble Colonel's furor—it seemed to him that no better or more exquisite revenge could be devised than that Hastings should be cashiered from his sublime post as Captain in the 19th & forced, on the most degrading conditions, to enter the ranks of the Blood-hounds & put his neck under the grinding yoke of Colonel Nicholas Belcastro—"It's the best card that's turned up for many a day" thought he—"We can make the rascals wince again with telling them how they're forced to take our dirtiest leavings—to be sure they may give us tit for tat by replying that what is good enough for an officer in the 19th will only do for a private in the blood-hounds. bah! that's bad, but if any of them dare say such a thing, there's always one remedy, pistols & six paces." The Major was amusing himself with these pleasing reflections when Hartford interrupted him by a request that he would read the other letter—It was short.

General Sir Wilson Thornton is desired by his Majesty to intimate to Lord Hartford that as there is some prospect of the army being called into active service erelong—it will be necessary that all the regiments should be effectively efficient. General Sir Wilson therefore has received directions to inquire whether Lord Hartford considers himself in a condition to take the field along with his troops in case the 19th should be called out—or whether the state of his health & spirits will not render such a mode of procedure unadvisable—In case Lord Hartford should be of the latter opinion—it will be considered necessary to appoint a substitute for his lordship—even though, by so doing, his Majesty should have to report the permanent loss of Lord Hartford's valuable services. an immediate answer is requested—signed W. Thornton.

"There's for you" said Lord Hartford, & for the space of ten minutes he said no more, but at the expiration of that period of silence he, in a faint voice, bade Major King take a pen & a sheet of paper & write what he should dictate—"Begin" said he "Hartford-Hall

—Hartford-Dale, Zamorna—I'll remind them I have a house to shelter me in at any rate—have you written that?" "Yes." "Now put March 18th 1839—I'll shew them I've sense enough to know what day of the month it is & what year of the century—you've written that?" "Yes." "Now then, Hearken & jot away as fast as you can—Sir—mind I'm addressing farmer Thornton—Sir—Allow me, through your medium, to thank his Majesty with all the warmth & sincerity his Majesty's unprecedented kindness deserves —for the touching & philanthropic interest his Majesty has condescended to take in my welfare—It affords me matter of self-congratulation that, through the blessing & protection of an Omnipotent Providence, I am ennabled to return a most satisfactory answer to his Majesty's benignant enquiry—His Majesty's kind & generous heart will be rejoiced to hear that I never in all my life have been favoured with a state of more perfect, sound & uninterrupted health than what I at present enjoy—that my spirits are consequently light, free & even at times exuberant—that so far from shrinking from active service with my regiment, I feel pleasure amounting to exultation at the thought of setting my foot in the stirrup again —His Majesty may rest assured that whenever his Majesty shall be pleased to summon the 19th to the field, not an officer or a soldier in that well-tried regiment will respond more cheerfully to the call than I shall do—I am ready for anything—the post of honour & the post of Danger—I have been faithful to my country so far, & I mean to die with that quality untarnished—Report my allegiance to his Majesty & my heartfelt gratitude for all the Honourable—justifiable attentions I have lately received.

I am Yours &c. Edward Hartford

"Now then, you'll ring the bell & send that letter off directly, King—& then you'll take horse & ride to Zamorna to order & prepare matters for the sitting of the Court-Martial to-morrow. As for me, I'm going to bed & I shall keep it for the rest of the day— as I'm exceedingly sick—G-d d--n." and with these words Lord Hartford passed from his dressing-room to his chamber—When he was gone, Major King nearly suffered strangulation in a silent fit of laughter.

CHAPTER II

The City of Zamorna is a very pleasant place—in fine sunny weather—The public buildings are all new, of very handsome architecture—& constructed of white gleaming stone—the principal streets are broad—the shops look busy & affluent—the ladies walking on the pavements are richly dressed like the wives & daughters of wealthy merchants, & at the same time they have a stylish air about them, for the province of Zamorna is highly aristocratic. There is almost the appearance of an Ant-hill, one moving mass of animation. The grand focus of bustle is Thornton Street, with Stancliffe's Hotel on one side of the way & the Court-House on the other.

It was March, the 19th day of the month, & Tuesday by the week*—the day was fine—the sky bright blue with a hot sun, & far on the horizon those silver-piled towering clouds that foretell the rapid showers of spring—there had been rain an hour ago, but the fresh breeze had dried it up—& only here & there a glittering pool of wet remained on the bleached street pavement—One could tell that in the country the grass was growing green, that the trees were knotty with buds & the gardens golden with crocuses. Zamorna, however, & the citizens of Zamorna thought little of these rural delights—Tuesday was Market-day—the Piece-Hall† & the Commercial Buildings were as throng as they could stand —The Stuartville Arms, the Wool-Pack and the Rising Sun were all astir with the preparations for their separate Market dinners, & the waiters were almost run off their feet with answering the countless calls for bottoms of brandy, glasses of gin & water—& bottles of North-Country-Ale—

Serene in the Majesty of Aristocracy, Stancliffe's Hotel stood aloof from this commercial stir—Bustle there was however even there, & that of no ordinary kind—To be sure, the Gentlemen passing in & out of its great Door had a different air & different ton—to the red-whiskered travellers—the swearing brandy-drinking manufacturers crowding the inferior inns—servants in military & aristocratic liveries, too, were to be seen lounging in the passages—& had you gone into the stable-yards, you would have found a dozen grooms busily engaged in brushing down & corning some pairs of splendid carriage-horses as well as three or four very grand-looking chargers, proud pawing beasts who looked conscious of the glories of Westwood & the bloodier triumphs of Leyden.

No doubt there is some affair of importance transacting at the Court-House opposite—for the doors are besieged with a gentlemanly crowd of black & green & brown velvet collared frock-

* The actual day and date are correct by the calendar for 1839
† A central feature of northern wool-manufacturing towns, where the woven pieces of cloth were exhibited for sale

coats & black & drab beaver hats, & moreover, every now & then, the doors open & an individual comes out—turns hastily down the steps across the way to Stancliffe's—there calls impatiently for wine, & having swallowed what is brought him, runs with equal haste back again—a lane being simultaneously opened for him by the crowd through which he passes with absorbed important gravity, looking neither to the left-hand nor the right. the door is jealously closed as he enters—allowing you but one glimpse of a man with a constable's staff standing inside.

On the morning in question, I was myself one of the crowd about the Court-house-doors, & I believe I stood four mortal hours at the bottom of a flight of broad steps, looking up at the solid & lofty columns—supporting the portico above—ever since nine o'clock the Court-martial had been assembled within—& it was known throughout all Zamorna that Henry Hastings the renegade was at this moment undergoing a rigid examination on the result of which hung the issues of life & death. yes—just now the stern Hartford occupied his seat as Judge—the crafty Percy sat by, watching every transaction—ferreting out every mystery—urging relentlessly the question that would fain be eluded—insinuating his sly acumen like the veriest Belial that ever clothed himself in flesh. all round are ranged the martial Jury—whose character shall be their names alone—King—Kirkwall—James—Dickens—Berkley—Paget &c. etceterorum—while the few Gentlemen privileged to be spectators sit on benches near, & then the prisoner Hastings—imagine him, at this instant the mental torture is proceeding—a broad gleam of sunshine rests on the outside walls of the Court-House—the pillared front & noble roof rise against the unclouded sky—But if Judas Hastings is selling his soul to about a score of Devils sitting upon him in judgement—what thought has he to spare for the cheerful daylight—?

The Town-Clock & the Minster Clock struck twelve—"Bless my life, do they never mean to have done to day?" I said to a chap standing near, & when I turned I recognized the peculiar phiz of the Sydenhams—it was John Sydenham, the eldest son of Wm. Sydenham Esqre. of Southwood—"How d'ye do, Mr John." "Haven't the pleasure of knowing you, Sir" replied he with true Angrian politeness—"My name's Townshend—you may remember meeting me in Sir Frederick Fala's box in the Theatre at Verdopolis." "O so, I believe I do—Charles Townshend—really beg your pardon—we went to a chop-house after the play—& had a night of it—I remember perfectly—hope your well, Mr Townshend." "Quite well thank you—rather tired of standing though—

you've not heard anything of what's going on inside there I suppose, Mr John." "Not a shiver—they're laying bets at Stancliffe's about the result—some say Hastings'll sign terms & some say he'll stand pepper—" "What's your own opinion—?" "O, I judge of others according to myself—not a doubt he'll tip King's evidence—I'd do it if I were him—" "Why, the man that turned his coat once will turn it again, I suppose—" "Yes—yes, it's only the first move that's awkward—you get used to it after that." "They say they've nearly wound up" said a third person joining us. "indeed Midgley, who told you?" "Paget—he's just been out—& they're reporting it in Stancliffe's that the Prisoner has turned stupid. every-body there says he won't peach—" "Why, some of the articles come it very strong, I suppose—" "Very, they hold him tight—" "And the execution's to take place directly if he declines conditions." "Yes, this afternoon"—"He's to be shot on Edwardstone Common—Orders have been sent to the Barracks that the soldiers are to be in readiness by three o'clock they say." "Then that's a sure sign he's stupid"—"I should think so—they'd press him very hard no doubt & serve him right—" "Paget said the Judge was swaggering bloodily—" "What about?" "Some interference of the Government Agents." "What, Sir Wm. Percy?" "Yes." "Does Percy want to save the prisoner?" "No—God knows—Paget said he pushed all ways & seemed to have eyes both before & behind—" "I say, what are they doing at that end of the crowd—?" "Don't know, they seem to be making a kind of sign—" "D'ye think the Court's rising?"—"Shouldn't wonder, they've sat four hours I believe—" "There's Mackay coming on to the steps." "Yes, & they're drawing up the blinds—" "Now for it then—let's push to get a bit nearer the steps—" With these words, Messrs Sydenham, Midgley & Townshend made a bold plunge into the throng & by dint of elbowing, pushing & kicking succeeded in obtaining an advantageous position very near the Court-House door—

That door being now opened—the occupants of the Magistrate's room began to issue from the interior—First came Mr Edward Percy in the act of blowing his nose—& then, thrusting his silk handkerchief into his coat-pocket—he descended the steps at two strides & went straight across the way to Stancliffe's—no intelligence was to be had from him—so far from speaking to any one in the passage, he did not so much as vouchsafe a look either to right hand or the left—Next came some officers, four abreast, with spurs on their heels jingling as they trod the stone-pavement—Then a professional-looking man with a grey head and a pallid-thoughtful face—that was Mr Moore—he raised his hat to me as he passed—

these all disappeared into Stancliffe's—Now a policeman or two turned out onto the broad sumit of the steps & stood erect by the pillars—Mackay came down into the crowd & began to clear a way with his official staff—a hackney-coach came wheeling out of the hotel-yard & drew up just before the door—Just then Midgley said in a low voice "There's Hastings"—& when I looked up there was a man emerging from the shade of the portico—dressed in black— with his single-breasted coat buttoned close over his broad chest, & his hat drawn down on his brow. I can hardly say that I saw his face—& yet one glimpse I caught—as he raised his head for a moment & threw a hurried glance over the crowd—the expression of that glance was one to be soon caught & long retained. it denoted the jealous suspicion of a bad man who expects others to hate, & the iron hardihood of a vindictive man who resolves to hate others in return—his teeth were set, his countenance was one dark scowl—he seemed like one whose mind was troubling him with the gall of self-abhorrence—A policeman got into the hackney-coach. Then Hastings entered it & a second policeman followed him—the vehicle drove away—not a sound followed its departure, neither cheer nor hoot—"He's Judas—I'll lay my life on it" said I, turning to John Sydenham—John nodded assent—

"Sir William Percy's coming out" said a voice near me, & in the door-way appeared the thin Hussar in his blue & white dress, settling his hat on his brow & looking straight before him at no object in particular—with that keen quiet unsmiling aspect he always wears when he's really busy about something important & has no time for his usual sneers of superciliousness or airs of non-chalance—He passed by us on his easy, leisurely way—I had a full view of his face—for he always carries his head very erect. His forehead, the only regularly handsome part of his phiz, had a trace of shade on its smoothness not often seen there—I believe just then he was burning with venom against somebody—perhaps his brother or Lord Hartford—yet how calm he looked! I lost sight of him in the all absorbing abyss of Stancliffe's passage.

"Make way for Lord Hartford's carriage—" cried a voice from the yard—& out thundering upon us came a dashing barouche with four fiery Greys. Last but not least the Judge appeared when his vehicle was announced—a Grand Judge he looked in an Officer's cloak with boots & a travelling-cap. this last article of dress suited his strongly-marked face, swarthy skin & bushy black whiskers. amazingly—it gave him very much the air of a gigantic Ourang-Outang—I'm sure he might have passed for that sort of Gentleman in any menagerie in the Kingdom—arm in arm with his Lordship appeared a fine personage in a Mackintosh & light drab Castor—of course nobody was at a loss to recognise the ubiquitous earl of Richton—who, no doubt grudging to lose so charming an amusement as was to be afforded by the spectacle of Hastings' final Degradation—had come down for the day, & too proud to accept the princely accommodations of Stancliffe's was now about to accompany his noble friend to the Hall—the two entered the carriage—one looking as black as midnight—the other all smiles & suavity—in five minutes they had swept up Thornton Street & were far on the Hartford road.

Two hours had not elapsed before the result of the days proceedings was known all over Zamorna—Hastings had accepted conditions—had delivered a mass of evidence against his quondam friends, whose purport, as yet a secret, would erelong be indicated by the future proceedings of Government—had yielded his captain's commission—had taken the striped jacket & scarlet belt of a private in Belcastro's bloodhounds—& in recompense had received the boon of life—Life without Honour, without Freedom, without the remnant of a character. So opens the new career of Henry Hastings—the young hero, the soldier Poet of Angria! "How are the mighty fallen!"

CHAPTER III

Sir William Percy, like his Father, is very tenacious of a favourite idea, any little pet whim of his fancy—and the less likely it is to be productive of good either to the individual who conceived it or to others, the more carefully it is treasured and the more intently it is pursued—Northangerland has all his life been a child chasing the Rainbow—& into what wild abysses has the pursuit often plunged him! how often has it seduced him from his serious aims—called him back when ambition was leading him to her loftiest summit—when the brow was nearly gained & the kingdoms of the world & the glory of them were lying in prospect below—how often at this crisis has Alexander Percy turned because the illusion of Beauty dawned on his imagination—& down the steep that cost him days & nights of toil to climb—sprung like a maniac to clasp the Dream in his arms, when it mocked him & melted into mist—he never awoke to reason—still he saw those soft hues chasing the clouds before him—& still he followed—though the clouds & their arch faded into nothingness.

Sir William, being of a cooler & less imaginative temperament than his father, has never yielded to delirium like this—compared

The Duke of Zamorna. Pen and ink drawing by Branwell Brontë

to Northangerland he is a man of marble—but still marble under a strange spell—capable of warming to life like the Sculpture of Pygmalion—he is a being of changeful moods—now the loveliest face will call from him nothing but a sneer on female vanity—and again an expression flitting over ordinary features—a transient ray in an eye neither large nor brilliant—will fix his attention & throw him into romantic musing—merely because it chanced to harmonize with some preconceived whim of his own capricious mind— yet having once caught an idea of this kind—have[ing] once received the seeds of this sort of partiality—inclination—fondness— call it what you will, his heart offered a tenacious soil likely to hold fast—to nurture long, to cultivate secretly, but surely, the unfolding germ of what might in time grow to a rooted-passion. Sir William, busied with the debates of cabinet-councils—in posting to & fro on political errands—holding the portfolio of a trusted & heavily responsible Government attachè—consequently living in an atmosphere of turmoil—still kept in view that little private matter of his own—that freak of taste—that small soothing amusement—his fancy for Miss Hastings. She had dropped out of his sight, he hardly knew where—after that audience with his royal sister, he had never troubled himself to inquire after her—the last view he had of her face was as it looked, flushed with painful feeling, when she retired from the presence-chamber—The warm-hearted young man chuckled with internal pleasure at the recollection of the cold indifferent mien he had assumed as he stood behind the royal chair—he knew at the time she would apply to him no more—that she would thenceforth shun his very shadow—fearful lest her remotest approach should be deemed an unwelcome intrusion. he knew she would leave Verdopolis that very hour if possible —& he allowed her to do so without a parting word from him. Still Miss Hastings lingered in his recollection—still he smiled at the thought of her ardour—still it pleased him to picture again the quick glances of her eye when he spoke to her, glances in which he could read so plainly—what she imagined buried out of sight in her inmost heart—Still, whenever he saw a light form, a small foot, an intelligent thin face, it brought a vague feeling of something agreeable, something he liked to dwell on. Miss Hastings therefore was not by any means to be given up—no, he would see her again sometime—events might slip on—one thing he was certain of—he need be under no fear of the impression passing away—No,

> His form would fill her eye by night,
> His voice her ear by day,

The touch that pressed her fingers slight
Would never pass away.

So, when he came again to Zamorna, having ascertained that she was still there, he began to employ his little odds & ends of leisure-time in quiet speculations as to how, when & where he should reopen a communication with her. It would not do at all to conduct the thing in an abrupt straight-forward way—he must not seem to seek her—he must come upon her sometime as if by accident—then too, this business of her brothers must be allowed to get out of her head—he would wait a few days—till the excitement of his trial had subsided—& the renegade was fairly removed from Zamorna & on his march to the quarters & companions assigned him beyond the limits of civilisation—Miss Hastings would then be very fairly alone in the world, quite disembarassed from friends & relations—not perplexed with a multitude of calls on her atten-tion—In such a state of things an easy chance meeting with a Friend would, Sir William calculated, be no unimpressive event. He'd keep his eye then on her movements & with care he did not doubt he should be able to mould events so as exactly to suit his purpose.

Well, a week or two passed on, Hasting's trial—like all nine-day's wonders, had sunk into oblivion—Hastings himself was gone to the D———l or to Belcastro, which is the same thing—he had naturally marched bodily out of Zamorna in the white trousers—the red sash—the gingham jacket of a thorough-going blood-hound—as one of a detachment of that illustrious regiment under the command of Captain Dampier—To the sound of fife, Drum & Bugle—the Lost Desperado had departed—leaving behind him the recollection of what he had been, a man—the reality of what he was, a Monster—It was very odd but his sister did not think a pin the worse of him for all his Dishonour—it is private mean-ness—not public infamy that degrade a man in the opinion of his rela-tives—Miss Hastings heard him cursed by every mouth—saw him denounced in every newspaper. still he was the same brother to her he had always been—still she beheld his actions through a medium peculiar to herself—She saw him go away with a trium-phant Hope (of which she had the full benefit, for no one else shared it) that his future actions would nobly blot out the calum-nies of his ennemies—yet after all she knew he was an unredeemed villain—human nature is full of inconsistencies—natural affection is a thing never rooted out where it has once really existed.

These passages of excitement being over—Miss Hastings very

well satisfied that her brother had walked out of Jail with the breath of life in his body—& having the aforesaid satisfactory impression on her mind that he was the finest man on the top of this world—began to look about her & consider how she was to make out life—most persons would have thought themselves in a very handsome fix—majestically alone in the midst of trading Zamorna—however, she set to work with the activity of an emmet—summoned her address & lady-manners to her aid—called on the wealthy manufacturers of the city & the aristocracy of the seats round—pleased them with her tact—her quickness—with the specimens of her accomplishments, & in a fortnight's time had raised a class of pupils sufficient not only to secure her from want, but to supply her with the means of comfort & elegance—She was now settled to her mind, she was dependent on nobody—responsible to nobody—She spent her mornings in her drawing-room surrounded by her class, not wearily toiling to impart the dry rudiments of knowledge to yawning, obstinate children—a thing she hated & for which her sharp-irritable temper rendered her wholly unfit—but instructing those who had already mastered the elements of education—reading, commenting, explaining, leaving it to them to listen—if they failed, comfortably conscious that the blame would rest on her pupils, not herself. The little dignified Governess soon gained considerable influence over her scholars, Daughters many of them of the wealthiest families in the city—she had always the art of awing young ladies minds with an idea of her superior talent, & then of winning their confidence—by her kind sympathizing affability. She quickly gained a large circle of friends—had constant invitations to the most stylish houses of Zamorna—acquired a most impeccable character—for ability—accomplishment—obliging disposition—& most correct & elegant manners—of course her class enlarged, & she was as prosperous as any little woman of five feet high & not twenty years old need wish to be. She looked well—she dressed well—plainer if possible than ever, but still with such fastidious care & taste—she moved about as brisk as a bee—of course, then, she was happy.—

No—advantages are equally portioned out in this world—she'd plenty of money—scores of friends—good health—people making much of her everywhere—but still the exclusive proud being thought she had not met with a single individual equal to herself in mind, & therefore not one whom she could love—besides, it was respect not affection that her pompous friends felt for her, & she was one who scorned respect—she never wished to attract it for a moment, & still it always came to her—she was always burning for warmer, closer attachment—she couldn't live without it—but the feeling never woke & never was reciprocated—O for Henry, for Pendleton—for one glimpse of the Warner Hills—Sometimes when she was alone in the evenings—walking through her handsome drawing-room by twilight—she would think of home & long for Home till she cried passionately at the conviction that she should see it no more. So wild was her longing that when she looked out on the dusky sky—between the curtains of her bay-window—fancy seemed to trace on the horizon the blue outline of the moors—just as seen from the parlour at Colne-moss—the evening star hung over the brow of Boulshill—the farm-fields stretched away between—& when reality returned, Houses, lamps & streets, she was phrenzied— again, a noise in the house seemed to her like the sound made by her father's chair when he drew it nearer to the kitchen hearth— something would recall the whine or the bark of Hector & Juno, Henry's pointers. again, the step of Henry himself would seem to tread in the passage—& she would distinctly hear his gun deposited in the house-corner. All was a dream. Henry was changed, she was changed, those times were departed for ever. She had been her Brother's & her fathers favourite—she had lost one & forsaken the other—at these moments her heart would yearn towards the old lonely old man in Angria—till it almost broke. But Pride is a thing not easily subdued—she would not return to him.

Very often too—as the twilight deepened & the fire, settling to clear red, diffused a calm glow over the papered walls—her thoughts took another turn—the enthusiast dreamed about Sir William Percy. She expected to hear no more of him—she blushed when she recollected how for a moment she had even dared to conceive the presumptuous idea that he cared for her—but still she lingered over his remembered voice & look & language—with an intensity of romantic feeling that very few people in this world can form the remotest conception of—all he had said was treasured in her mind, she could distinctly tell over every word—she could picture vividly as life his face, his quick hawk's eye—his habitual attitudes—it was an era in her existence to see his name or an anecdote respecting him mentioned in the newspapers—she would preserve such paragraphs to read over & over again when she was alone—there was one which mentioned that he was numbered amongst the list of officers designed for the expected campaign in the East—& thereupon her excitable imagination kindled with anticipation of his perils & glories & wanderings—she realized him in a hundred situations—on the verge of battle—in the long weary march—in the halt by wild river banks—she seemed to watch his slumber under the Desert-moon—with large-leaved jungle plants spreading their rank shade above him. Doubtless she thought the young Hussar would then dream of someone that he loved—some beautiful face would seem to bend over his rough pillow, such as had charmed him in the Saloons of the capital.

> And with that thought came an impulse
>   Which broke the dreamy spell,
> For no longer on the picture
>   Could her eye endure to dwell.
> She vowed to leave her visions
>   And seek life's arousing stir,
> For she knew Sir William's slumber
>   Would not bring a thought of her.
>
> How fruitless then to ponder
>   O'er such dreams as chained her now,
> Her heart should cease to wander
>   And her tears no more should flow.
> The trance was over—over,
>   The spell was scattered far,
> Yet how blest were she whose lover
>   Would be Angria's young Hussar!
>
> Earth knew no hope more glorious,
>   Heaven gave no nobler boon,
> Than to welcome him victorious
>   To a heart he claimed his own.
> How sweet to tell each feeling
>   The kindled soul might prove!
> How sad to die concealing
>   The anguish born of love!

Such were Miss Hastings musings—such were almost the words that arranged themselves like a song in her mind—words, however, neither spoken nor sung—She dared not so far confess her phrenzy to herself—only once she paused in her walk through the drawing-room by the open piano—laid her fingers on the keys—& wakening a note or two of plaintive melody—murmured the last lines of the last stanza—

> How sad to die concealing
>   The anguish born of love!

and instantly snatching her hand away—& closing the instrument with a clash—made some emphatic remark about unmitigated

Folly—then lighted her bed-candle &, it being now eleven at night—hastened up-stairs to her chamber as fast as if a night-mare had been behind her.

CHAPTER IV

One mild still afternoon—Miss Hastings had gone out to walk— she was already removed from the stir of Zamorna—& slowly pacing along the causeway of Girnington Road—the high wall & trees enclosing a Gentleman's place—ran along the road side—the distant track stretched out into a quiet & open country—now & then a carriage or a horseman rolled or galloped past—but the general characteristic of the scene & day was tranquillity—Miss Hastings, folded in her shawl & with her veil down—moved leisurely on—in as comfortable a frame of mind as she could desire— inclined to silence & with no one to disturb her by talking—dis- posed for reverie, at liberty to indulge her dreams unbroken—the carriages that passed at intervals kept her in a state of vague expec- tation—She always raised her eyes when they drew near—as if with the undefined hope of seeing somebody, she hardly knew whom, a face from distant Pendleton perhaps. Following a course she had often taken before, she soon turned into a bye-lane with a worn white causeway running under a green hedge &, on either hand, fields. The stillness now grew more perfect as she wandered on, the mail-road disappeared behind her—the sense of perfect solitude deepened—that calm afternoon sun seemed to smile with a softer lustre—away in a distant field a bird was heard singing with a fitful note—now clear & cheerful—now dropping to pensive silence—She came to an old Gate—the posts were of stone, mouldering & grey—the wooden paling was broken—clusters of springing leaves grew beside it—it was just a fit subject for an artist's sketch—this Gate opened into a large & secluded meadow— or rather into a succession of meadows—for the track worn in the grass led on through stiles & gates from pasture to pasture to an unknown extent—here Miss Hastings had been accustomed to ramble for many an hour—indulging her morbid propensity for castle-building—as happy as she was capable of being except when now & then scared by hearing the remote & angry low of a Great Girnington Bull which haunted these parts—

On reaching the Gate she instinctively stopped to open it—it was open & she passed through—She stopped with a start. by the Gate-Post lay a Gentlemanly-looking hat & a pair of Gloves— with a Spaniel coiled up beside them—as if keeping Guard. the creature sprung forward at the approach of a stranger & gave a short bark—not very furious. its instinct seemed to tell it that the intruder was not of a dangerous order—a very low whistle sounded from some quarter—quite close at hand—yet no human being was visible from whom it could proceed—the Spaniel obeyed the signal—whined & lay down again. Miss Hastings passed on—She had hardly set her foot in the field when she heard the emphatic ejaculation "Bless my stars!" distinctly pronounced immediately behind her—Of course she turned—there was a hedge of hazels on her right hand under which all sorts of leaves & foliage grew green & soft—stretched full-length on this bed of verdure—with the declining sun resting upon him, she saw a masculine figure—without a hat & with an open book in his hand—which it is to be supposed he had been perusing—though his eyes were now raised from the literary page—& fixed on Miss Hastings—It being broad daylight & the individual being denuded as to the head—features, forehead—hair, whiskers, blue eyes &c. &c. were all distinctly visible—Of course my readers know him, Sir William Percy & no mistake, though what he could possibly be doing here ruralizing in a remote nook of the Girnington Summerings I candidly confess myself not sufficiently sagacious to divine.

Miss Hastings being, as my readers are aware, possessed with certain romantic notions about him—got something of a start at this unexpected meeting—for about five minutes she'd little to say—& indeed was deeply occupied in collecting her wits & contriving an apology for what she shuddered to think Sir William would consider an unwelcome intrusion. Meantime the baronet gathered himself up—took his hat & came towards her with a look & smile that implied anything rather than annoyance at her presence. "Well, you've not a single word to say to me—how shocked you look & as pale as a sheet—I hope I've not frightened you—" "No—no—" with agitation in the tone "but it is an unusual thing to meet anybody in these fields—" & she feared she had perhaps disturbed Sir William—she was sorry—she ought to have taken the spaniel's hint & retreated in time—"Retreated—what from? were you afraid of Carlo? I thought he saluted you very gently—upon my word I believe the beast had sense enough to know that the newcomer was not one his master would be displeased to see—had it been a Great Male Scare now in Jacket & continuations he'd have flown at his throat." The tone of Sir William's voice brought back again like a charm the feeling of confidence Miss Hastings had experienced before in conversing with him. it brought back, too, a throbbing of the heart & pulse, & a kindling of the veins which soon flushed her pale face with suffusing colour. but never mind that, let us go on with the conversation. "I was not afraid of Carlo" said Miss Hasting. "What then were you afraid of, surely not me?" She looked up at him—her natural voice & manner—so long disused, returned to her—"Yes" she said quickly—"you & nothing else—it is so long since I had seen you, I thought you would have forgotten me & would think I had no business to cross your way again—I expected you would be very cold & proud." "Nay, I'll be as warm as you please—& as to pride I calculate you are not exactly the sort of person to excite that feeling in my mind." "I suppose then I should have said contempt—you are proud no doubt to your equals or superiors. however, you have spoken to me very civilly—for which I am obliged as it makes me unhappy to be scorned." "May I ask if your quite by yourself here?" inquired Sir William—"Or have you companions near at hand?"—"I'm alone—I always walk alone—" "Humph—& I'm alone likewise, & as it's highly improper that a young woman such as you should be wandering by herself in such a lot of solitary fields—I shall take the liberty of offering my protection whilst you finish your walk & then seeing you safe home—" Miss Hastings made excuses—she could not think of giving Sir William so much trouble—she was accustomed to manage for herself—there was nothing in the world to be apprehended, &c. The baronet answered by drawing her arm through his. "I shall act authoritatively" said he. "I know what's for the best—" Seeing she could not so escape, she pleaded the lateness of the hour, it would be best to turn back immediately—"No." Sir William had a mind to take her half a mile further. She would be able to get back to Zamorna before dark & as he was with her she needn't fear—On they went then—Miss Hastings hurriedly considering whether she was doing any thing really wrong & deciding that she was not, & that it would be sin & nonsense to throw away the moment of bliss Chance had offered her. besides, she had nobody in the world to find fault with her—nobody to whom she was responsible—neither father nor brother—she was her own Mistress—& she was sure it would be cant & prudery to apprehend harm.

Having thus set aside scruples & wholly yielded herself to the wild delight fluttering at her heart—she bounded on with so light & quick a step Sir William was put to his mettle to keep pace with her—"Softly—softly" said he at last—"I like to take my time in a ramble like this—one can't walk fast & talk comfortably at the same time—" " The afternoon is so exceedingly pleasant" returned Miss Hastings "and the grass is so soft & green in these fields—my spirits feel cheerier than usual—but however, to please you I'll draw in." "Now" continued the baronet "Will you tell me what your doing in Zamorna & how you're getting on?" "I'm teaching & I have two classes of twelve pupils each—my terms are high— first-rate—so I'm in no danger of want—" "But have you money enough—are you comfortable?" "Yes, I am as rich as a Jew—I mean to begin to save for the first time in my Life, & when I've got two thousand pounds I'll give up work & live like a fine lady—" "You're an excellent little manager for yourself—I thought now, if I left you a month or two unlooked after—just plodding on as you could—you'd get into straits or difficulty & be glad of a friend's hand to help you out, but somehow you contrive provokingly well—" "Yes, I don't want to be under obligations." "Come, let me have no proud speeches of that sort—Remember, Fortune is ever changing & the best of us are not exempt from reverses—I may have to triumph over you yet—" "But if I wanted a sixpence you would be the last person I should ask for it" said Miss Hastings— looking up at him with an arch expression—very natural to her eyes—but which seldom indeed was allowed to shine there— "Should I young lady?—take care—make no rash resolutions—if you were compelled to ask, you would be glad to go to the person who would give most willingly—& you would not find many hands so open as mine would be. I tell you plainly it would give me pleasure to humble you—I have not yet forgotten your refusal to accept that silly little cross."

"Nay" said Miss Hastings "I knew so little of you at that time I felt it would be quite a shame to take presents from you—" "But you know me better now—& I have the cross here—will you take it?" he produced the green box from his waistcoat pocket—took out the jewel & offered it. "I won't" was the answer. "Humph!" said Sir William "I'll be revenged sometime—Such nonsense!" He looked angry—an unusual thing with him—"I don't mean to offend you" pleaded Miss Hastings "but it would hurt me to accept anything of value from you—I would take a little book—or an autograph of your name or a straw or a pebble—but not a Diamond—" the attachment implied by those words was so very flattering & at the same time expressed with such utterly un- conscious simplicity that Sir William could not suppress a smile— his forehead cleared—"You know how to turn a compliment after all, Miss Hastings" said he—"I'm obliged to you—I was beginning to think myself a very unskilful general—for, turn which way I would, & try what tactics I chose—the Fortress would never give me a moment's advantage—I could not win a single outwork.

however, if there's a friend in the Citadel, if the heart speaks for me, all's right—" Miss Hastings felt her face grow rather uncomfortably hot—she was confused for a few minutes & could not reply to Sir William's odd metaphorical speech. The Baronet squinted towards her one of his piercing side-glances &, perceiving she was a trifle startled, he whistled a stave to give her time to compose herself—affected to be engaged with his spaniel—& then, when another squint had assured him that the flush was subsiding on her cheek, he drew her arm a little closer & recommenced the conversation on a fresh theme.

"Lonely, Quiet meadows these" said he. "And all this country has something very sequestered about it—I know it well—every lane & gate & style."

"You've been here before then?" returned Miss Hastings. "I've often heard that you were a Rambler."

"I've been here by day & by night, I've seen these hedges bright as they are now in sunshine, & throwing a dark shade by moonlight—if there were such things as fairies I should have met them often—for these are just their haunts—fox-glove leaves & bells—moss like green velvet—mushrooms—springing at the roots of oak-trees—Thorns a hundred years old grown over with ivy—all precisely in the fairy-tale style."

"And what did you do here?" enquired Miss Hastings—"what made you wander alone early & late—? Was it because you liked to see twilight gathering in such lanes as these—& the moon rising over such a green swell of pasture as that, or because you were unhappy—?"

"I'll answer you with another question" returned Sir William. "Why do *you* like to ramble by yourself? it is because you can think, & so could I—it never was my habit to impart my thoughts much, especially those that gave me the most pleasure—so I wanted no companion—I used to dream indeed of some nameless being— whom I invested with the species of mind & face & figure that I imagined I could love—I used to wish for some existence with finer feelings and a warmer heart than what I saw round me—I had a kind of idea that I could be a very impassioned lover—if I met with a woman who was young & elegant & had a mind above the grade of an animal."

"You must have met with many such" said Miss Hastings, not shrinking from the conversation, for its confidential tone charmed her like a spell.

"I've met with many pretty women, with some clever ones, I've even seen one or two that I thought myself in love with for a time

but a few days or at most weeks tired me of them—I grew enuyè
with their insipid charms & turned again to my ideal Bride—Once
indeed I plunged over head & ears into a mad passion with a real
object—But that's over."

"Who was she?"

"One of the most beautiful & celebrated women of her day—
unfortunately she was appropriated—I could have died to win
that woman's smile—to take her hand & touch her lips I could
have suffered torture. & to obtain her love, to have the power of
clasping her in my arms & telling her all I felt—to have my ardour
returned—to hear in her musical earnest voice the expression of
responsive attachment—I could, if the D——l had asked me, have
sold my redemption & consented to take the stamp of the hoof on
both my hands."

"Who was she?" again asked Miss Hastings—

"I could not utter her name without choking—but she is one
you have often heard of—a woman possessed of a singular charm—
I never knew a man of strong & susceptible feelings yet who came
near her without being more or less influenced by her attractions—
she's beautiful in form & face & expression, most divinely so—she's
impassioned too—her feelings are concentrated & strong—& this
gives a tone to her looks, her manners—her whole aspect—that no
heart can resist—sorrow has made her grave—the recollection of
important & strange events in which she has been deeply concerned have fixed a character of solemnity on her brow. She looks
as if she could never be frivolous, seldom gay—She has endured a
great deal & with the same motive to animate her now, she would
endure it all again."

"Does she live in Angria?"

"Yes—now ask me no more questions for I'll not answer them.
Come, give me your hand & I'll help you over this style—there!
we're out of the fields now—were you ever so far as this before—?"

"Never" said Miss Hastings looking round—the objects she saw
were not familiar to her—they had entered upon another road,
rough, rutty & grown over—not a house or a human being was to
be seen—but immediately before them stood a church with a low
tower & a little churchyard—scattered over with a few head-stones
& many turf mounds. about four miles off stretched a line of hills
darkly ridged with heath—now all empurpled with a lovely sunset
—Miss Hastings' eye kindled as she caught them.

"What moors are those?" she asked quickly.

"Ingleside & the Scars" replied Sir William.

"And what is that church?"

"Scar-Chapel". "It looks old—How long do you think it is since it was built?"

"It is one of the earliest date in Angria—what caps me is why the d———l any church at all was set down in a spot like this where there is no population."

"Shall we go into the churchyard?" "Yes, if you like—& you'd better rest there for a few minutes for you look tired—"

In the centre of the enclosure stood an ancient Yew—gnarled, sable & huge—the only raised tomb in the place rested under the shadow of this grim old sentinel—"You can sit down here" said Sir William, pointing to the monument with his cane—Miss Hastings approached, but before she took her seat on the slab, something in its appearance caught her attention—It was of marble not stone—plain & unornamented—but gleaming with dazzling whiteness from the surrounding turf—at first sight it seemed to bear no inscription—but . . . looking nearer, one word was visible "RESURGAM"—nothing else, no name, date or age—

"What is this?" asked Miss Hastings. "Who is buried here?" "You may well ask" returned Sir William "but who d'ye think can answer you?—I've stood by this grave many a time when that church clock was striking twelve at midnight—sometimes in rain & darkness, sometimes in clear quivering starlight—& looked at that single word—& pondered over the mystery it seemed to involve—till I could have wished the dead corpse underneath would rise & answer my unavailing questions."

"And have you never learnt the history of this tomb?"

"Why, partly—you know I've a sort of knack of worming out any trifling little secret that I get it into my [head] I should like to discover—& it's not very likely that a slab like this should be laid down in any church-yard without somebody knowing something about it."

"Tell me what you know then" said Miss Hastings—raising her eyes to Sir Williams with a look that told him how magical was the effect—how profound was the interest of all this sweet confidential interchange of feeling. it was more bewitching even than the open language of love—She had no need to blush & tremble—she had only to listen when he spoke to feel that he trusted her—that he deemed her worthy to be the depository of those half-romantic thoughts he had never perhaps breathed into human ear before—These sensations might all be delusive, but they were sweet &, for the time, Doubt & Apprehension dared not intrude their warnings.

"Come, sit down" said the baronet "and you shall hear all I can tell you—I see you like anything with the savour of romance in it."

"I do" replied Miss Hastings. "And so do you, Sir William—only you're rather ashamed to confess it."

He smiled & went on—"Well, the first clue I got to this business was by a rather remarkable chance. I had been shooting on Ingleside there—one day last August—& towards afternoon, as it was very hot, I got tired, & so I thought I would take a stroll down to Scar-Chapel & rest myself a while—under this old Yew, proposing to make & meditate & perhaps concoct a poem over the economic grave-stone with one word on it—By the bye, Elizabeth, it has just struck me what a capital economist the individual must have been who ordered the inscription—you know—stone-cutters always charge so much a letter—he couldn't have had much to pay*—On my life, I'll mention that notion to my brother Edward next time I see him—it will suit him to a hair—but excuse me, you don't like practical remarks of that sort—it interferes with the romance—To proceed, I was just opening the little gate yonder &, as it stuck against a stone, I had bestowed upon it an emphatic kick—to make it fly back more sharply. When I saw to my horror that the churchyard was not empty. You can't conceive how aggravated I was. I had come here so often & had always found it so utterly lonely that I had begun to imagine somehow that it was my own property & that nobody ever came near it but myself—However, I now perceived that this idea was an egregious mistake. A Chap in a shooting-dress was standing by this very tomb—my own blank tablet of mystery—leaning with both his hands on a long fowling-piece, & about a yard off, on that mound of turf, two pointers were laid stretched out with their tongues lolling from their jaws, panting after a long day's run on the summer Hills. I was on the point of levelling my rifle at the interesting group when Prudence checked me by two considerations—firstly that the fellow's head might be of too leaden a consistency to be susceptible of injury from a bullet, & secondly that there were such things as Coroner's Inquests & verdicts of Wilful Murder—so I thought I'd stand & watch—The Sportsman had his face turned from me, but he was a tall-strapping specimen of mortality—with a contour of form that, when I looked hard at him for five minutes on end, seemed to me particularly familiar to my eye—He stood a long time still as a statue, till I began to think he must be the victim of sentiment—this idea was confirmed by seeing him once or twice take a handkerchief from his pocket & apply it to his eyes—I had placed my

* John Brown, the Haworth sexton, was a stone-cutter for whom Branwell often obtained commissions

thumb to the side of my nose & was on the point of calling out in a loud clear voice to know how he was off for soap—when he used his handkerchief for the last time—thrust it hastily into his pocket & calling Dash & Bell—came striding down towards the Gate with his Dogs at his heels. My God—here was a kettle of Fish! I knew his face as well as I know yours—it was one I had seen under the rim of a crown—in short it was our Sovereign Lord—Adrian Augustus—himself.

"The Duke of Zamorna!" exclaimed Miss Hastings—

"Yes"—"and did he see you?" "See me—the D———l no!—I cut the moment I recognized his Satanic Majesty—& ran—my stars, how I did run!"

"Well, & what had he to do with the grave stone—why did he cry?"

"O, because one of his women is buried under it, a Woman very much talked of five years ago—Rosamund Wellesley—she died at a house somewhere between here & Ingle-side—where she had lived for some months under a feigned name—from what I have heard I should think she gave nature a lift, helped herself out of the world when she was quite tired of it—"

"Killed herself! do you mean? why?"

"Because she was ashamed of having loved his majesty not wisely but too well—I remember seeing her, she was very beautiful —not unlike your friend Jane Moore in features—figure & complexion—very tall & graceful—with light hair & fine blue eyes— very different to Miss Moore in mind, though—clever, I daresay, & sensitive. The Duke undertook to be her Guardian & Tutor—He executed his office in a manner peculiar to himself—Guarded her with a vengeance & tutored her till she could construe the Art of Love at any rate—She enjoyed the benefit of his protection & instructions for about a year—& then somehow she began to pine away. awkward little reports were spread—she got to hear them. her relations insisted upon it that she should leave her Royal Mentor—He swore she should not, they persisted in claiming her, so his Majesty sequestered her in one of his remote haunts out of their reach. then he dared them to come into the heart of his kingdom & fetch her out—She did not give them the chance. Shame & Horror, I suppose, had worked her feelings into Delirium & she died very suddenly—whether fairly or not Heaven knows. Here she was interred, & this is the Stone Her Lover laid over her. Now, Elizabeth, what do you say to such a business as that?"

"It seems the Duke of Zamorna never forsook her & that he remembered her after she was dead" remarked Miss Hastings.

"Oh! & that's sufficient consolation! as the Duke of Zamorna is a very fine, proud God incarnate I suppose. G–d d––n!"

"The Duke of Zamorna is a sort of scoundrel from all that ever I heard of him—but then most men of rank are from what I can understand—"

"Were you ever blessed with a sight of his Majesty?" inquired Sir William.

"Never"—"but you've seen his portraits—which are one & all very like—do you admire them—?"

"He's handsome—no doubt".

"O, of course, killingly—infernally handsome—such eyes & nose—such curls & whiskers—& then his stature! magnificent! & his chest two feet across—I never knew a woman yet who did not calculate the value of a man by the proportions of his inches—" Miss Hastings said nothing, she only looked down & smiled.

"I'm exceedingly nettled & dissatisfied" remarked Sir William.

"Why?" inquired Miss Hastings, still smiling.

Sir William, in his turn, gave no answer, he only whistled a stave or two—After a moment's silence he looked all round him with a keen, careful eye—he then turned to his companion.

"Do you see" said he "that the sun is set & that it is getting dark?" "Indeed it is" replied Miss Hastings, & she started instantly to her feet. "We must go home, Sir William—I had forgotten—how could I let time slip so."

"Hush" said the young baronet—"and sit down again for a few minutes—I will say what I have to say." Miss Hastings obeyed him—

"Do you see" he continued "that everything is still round us—that the twilight is deepening, that there is no light but what that rising half-moon gives?"

"Yes."

"Do you know that there is not a house within two miles & that you are four miles from Zamorna—?"

"Yes."

"You are aware then that in this shade & solitude you & I are alone?"

"I am."

"Would you have trusted yourself in such a situation with any one you did not care for?"

"No."

"You care for me then?" "I do." "How much?" There was a pause—a long pause—Sir William did not urge the question impatiently—he only sat keenly & quietly watching Miss Hastings & waiting for an answer—at last she said in a very low voice:

"Tell me first, Sir William Percy, how much you care for me."

"More than at this moment I do for any other woman in the world."

"Then" was the heart-felt rejoinder—"I adore you—& that's a confession death should not make me cancel."

"Now Elizabeth—" continued Sir William "listen to the last question I have to put—& don't be afraid of me. I'll act like a gentleman whatever your answer may be—You said just now that all men of rank were scoundrels—I'm a man of rank—Will you be my mistress—?"

"No." "You said you adored me." "I do, intensely—but I'll never be your mistress—I could not without incurring the miseries of self-hatred."

"That is to say" replied the Baronet "you are afraid of the scorn of the world."

"I am—the scorn of the world is a horrible thing, & more especially I should dread to lose the good opinion of three persons —of my father—of Henry & of Mr Warner—I would rather die than be despised by them. I feel a secret triumph now in the consciousness that though I have been left entirely to my own guidance, I have never committed an action or narrated a word that would bring my character for a moment under the breath of suspicion! My father & Mr Warner call me obstinate & resentful—but they are both proud of the address I have shewn in making my way through life—& keeping always in the strictest limits of rectitude— Henry, though a wild wanderer himself, would blow his brains out if he heard of his sister adding to the pile of disgrace he had heaped so thickly on the name of Hastings."

"You would risk nothing for me then?" returned Sir William. "You would find no compensation for the loss of the world's favour in my perfect love & trusting confidence—it is no pleasure to you to talk to me—to sit by my side as you do now—to allow your hand to rest in mine—?"

The tears came into Miss Hastings' eyes—"I dare not answer you" she said "because I know I should say something frantic. I could no more help loving you than that moon can help shining. If I might live with you as your servant I should be happy—but as your mistress! it is quite impossible."

"Elizabeth" said Sir William—looking at her & placing his hand on her shoulder—"Elizabeth, your eyes betray you—they speak the language of a very ardent, very imaginative temperament—

Alexander Percy, Earl of Northangerland. Drawing by
Branwell Brontë

they confess not only that you love me, but that you cannot live without me—yield to your nature & let me claim you this moment as my own—"

Miss Hastings was silent—but she was not going to yield—only the hard conflict of passionate love—with feelings that shrank horror-struck from the remotest shadow of infamy compelled her for a moment to silent agony.

Sir William thought his point was nearly gained—"One word" said he—"will be sufficient, one smile or whisper—you tremble, rest on my shoulder—turn your face to the moonlight & give me a single look."

That moonlight shewed her eyes swimming in tears—the baronet, mistaking these tears for the signs of resolution fast dissolving, attempted to kiss them away—She slipt from his hold like an apparition—"If I stay another moment God knows what I shall say or do" said she—"Good-bye Sir William—I implore you not to follow me—the night is light—I am afraid of nothing but myself—I shall be in Zamorna in an hour. Good bye, I suppose, for ever!"

"Elizabeth!" exclaimed Sir William—She lingered for a moment—she could not go—a cloud just then crossed the moon—in two minutes it had passed away—Sir William looked towards the place where Miss Hastings had been standing—she was gone—the church-yard gate swung to—he muttered a furious curse but did not stir to follow. There he remained where she had left him for hours, as fixed as the old Yew whose black arms brooded over his head—He must have passed a quiet night—church & graves & tree, all mute as Death—Lady Rosamund's tomb alone proclaiming in the moonlight "I shall rise".

CHAPTER V

You must now, Reader, step into this library where you shall see a big man sitting at a table with a long swan-quill pen in his hand—& an ink-stand before him—behind the big man's chair stands a little man holding a green bag from which he hands papers for the big man to sign. The scene is a silent one—when you have looked awhile you begin to imagine that both performers are dummies—it reminds you of the wise allegories shewn by the Interpreter to Christian or of the old Dutch Groups of Ghosts who play dice & ninepins a hundred years after they are dead. At last the profound taciturnity of the scene is relieved by an audible sigh heaved from the deep chest of the big man—"I think" he says "there's no bottom to that d———d bag—" "Patience" replies the little man "some persons are soon tired, I think—where is the labour of affixing a signature?" "Another pen" demands the big man, throwing away his swan-quill—"There is a loss of time in changing the pen often" replies the little man. "Cannot your Grace make that do?" "Look at it" was the answer—the quill was split up in some emphatic dash or down stroke—"Strange mismanagement" says the little man—handing over another pen—the pantomime again proceeded. In a while its monotony was broken by a gentle knock at the library-door—"Come in" said the big man—"Absurd interruption of business" muttered the little man—the door opened, the person entering closed it again & crossed the soft carpet without much sound—a lady approached the table of tall & dignified appearance. She wore a hat with black feathers & a veil thrown back—"How d'ye do" said she, placing her hand on the table. "How d'ye do" responded the signer of documents, & that was all the interchange of words that took place—Him of the green bag bowed, with an air of mixed respect & annoyance, & the lady said something that sounded like "a good morning". She stood a moment by the table looking half-abstractedly at what was trans-acting there—She then moved away to the hearth & stood for about five minutes, turning over the coins & shells laid on the mantle-piece—& surveying the features of three bronze busts that stood there as ornaments. Finally she loosened the strings of her hat—removed a fur boa from her neck & having thrown that & her shawl on a sofa that stood near the fire—she seated herself there also & remained perfectly still.

"All things must have an end" and so at long last the green bag & its contents were exhausted. "I have given your Grace the last Paper" said Mr Warner—When his Master, now broken into the service, looked round with the patience of despair, expecting another document & yet another. "God be thanked for all his mercies" replied the King solemnly—Mr Warner, who was in a ruinous temper—did not vouchsafe a reply—he merely locked his bag—with particular emphasis—drew on his gloves & bowing stiffly said "I wish your Majesty a very good morning". another silent bow to the lady followed—& then the premier of Angria formally backed out of his master's presence.

The Duke of Zamorna now crossed his legs—leant his arm on the back of his chair & turned half-round to his stately visitor. "The little man's cursedly peevish to-day" said he smiling—The lady uttered a scarcely articulate monosyllable of assent—& continued to sit gravely gazing at the window opposite—the Duke reached out his arm & drew from under a pile of books & papers an immense folio—"You've seen these new Maps, I suppose" said he opening the vast boards. "They're the pride of my life, so beautifully accurate." The lady got up—stood behind him & stooped over his shoulder as he turned the leaves—"The first military Chartists in Angria have been employed to get up these" he continued. "I daresay they're good" replied the lady—"Good—they're exquisite!" exclaimed the Monarch. "And the engraving is first-rate love—look there & there—how distinct." he traced his ringed forefinger along certain ridges of mountains & courses of rivers & markings of sand-hills & boundaries of trackless wildernesses. "Very clear" said the lady. "And correct, that's the point" added her companion—"No guessing here—no romancing—One can depend on such stuff as this—My word, if the fellows had given rope to their imagination here—Etrei would soon have twisted it into a halter for their own necks—but bring a chair, Zenobia, & I'll shew you the whole thing & all my pencil-marks—" Zenobia brought a chair—she leant her arm on the table—& inclined her head to look & listen while the Maps were shewn & their bearings explained—"Take your hat off first" began his Majesty "the feathers throw a shade on the paper so that you cannot see"—She complied in silence, removed her hat & let it drop onto the floor beside her. The process of demonstration & elucidation then began, in other words his Majesty proceeded to make a famous bore of himself. He was listened to with exemplary patience—a patience the more remarkable as the Royal Lecturer, like all very formidable Bores, exacted the most rigid attention from his hearer—& every now & then, to convince himself that she comprehended what he said—required prompt answers to very botheracious questions— One of his interrogations not being readily replied to—he got vexed—"Now Zenobia, I wish you would attend more closely— Why, I explained all that only five minutes ago—" "Well, just repeat it once more"—So, in a deliberate doctrinal tone his Majesty proceeded to lay down the law again—in about a quarter of an hour another bungle occurred—Zenobia requested some explanation which seemed to produce the effect of an electrical shock in her Royal Instructor. He dropped his pencil—raised his eyes to the ceiling in rapt astonishment—& turning his chair completely round from the table to the fire—gave the important information that "since she didn't understand *that*, the Game was up". In a while he seized the poker & having made an emphatic assault on the already blazing coals, he read on thus: "What the D———l you're thinking about this morning I can't tell—I never knew you so stupid before—never—When I've spent the last hour in explaining to you the finest system of tactics that ever a d———d infernal, sand-hill & jungle warfare was conducted on—& proved to a moral certainty that if I can only have my own way, not a black piccaninny will be left to cheep between this & Tunis—all at once you pose me with a question that shews you no more heard or understood a word of my argument than the babe unborn."

"Well Zamorna" said the Countess "you know that sort of abstruse reasoning is not my forte—you always said I never could deduce an inference." "Yes, I know that—Mathematics & Logic are Chaos & Confusion in your estimation I'm perfectly aware— but this caps the Globe—as they say in Angria—I tell you, Zenobia—if I'd spent as much time over my Frederick in teaching him the facts of the case, & he'd cut me short with such a speech as that, by the Lord I'd have whipt him." "Well, I'll do better another time" continued the Countess. "But the truth is, Zamorna, my thoughts were running on something else all the time you were speaking—I'm downright unhappy." "O, that's another thing" returned the Duke—"You should have told me so at once—but what's the matter?" "Percy vexes me so—I shall have to leave him." "What—his vagaries are not over are they?" "No indeed, worse than ever—I feel persuaded he will not settle till he has done something very wild & outrèe." "Come, you're looking on the dark side Zenobia, cheer up! has he done anything very extraordinary lately—?" "He seems so strange & fitful" returned the Countess. "every evening he goes into the Red-Saloon—& plays on the Organ for hours together—if I happen to be there not a single word does he speak. he seems altogether absorbed in the music—he looks up in that inspired kind of way he has when he feels excited—then he takes his fingers from the keys & sits silent with his head on his hand—if I ask him a question he says "I don't know"—or "I can't tell"—nothing can draw him into conversa- tion—at last he'll get up & ring for his hat & set off God knows where—I understand he often goes to Lady Georgina Greville's* or Lady St Jame's—sometimes even to that little insignificant wretch Miss Delph's—but I *will* not bear it, & I solemnly declare to you, Zamorna, that if he does not change soon I'll leave him & go away to the West."

"No, Zenobia" returned his Grace. "Take my advice & make no public move of that sort, nothing to cause eclat—it will only hurry on some frantic catastrophe, besides you know you'll only hurry back to him as soon as he chooses to coax you—refuse to see him if

* Charlotte Brontë originally wrote 'Vernon', but then crossed it through

you like—confine yourself entirely to your own suite of rooms & give him to understand that you're appartments are forbidden ground—then shut your eyes & let him go to the D———l his own way—he'll sit down quietly enough in a while."

"What!" exclaimed the Countess—"then I'm to let him follow a score of Mistresses—waste all his love on Greville & Lalande who, by the by, like a dirty French Demi-rep as she is—has actually come over from Paris & taken up her quarters at Dèmrys Hotel that she may make hay while the sun-shines—I'm to endure all this tamely, am I—? no, Augustus—that's a trifle too much to require of me—you know I could not do it—" "Then box his ears, Zenobia, he deserves it—invite all his ladies to a good dinner—feed them well, give them a few glasses of wine & then flog them all round—I wouldn't hesitate to back you against any ten of them—one down & another come on—"

"It would do me good" replied the Countess, half-crying & half-smiling. "I should like to chastise some of them, especially that Delph & that Lalande—I say again, Augustus, it's too bad when I love him so well & for himself alone—that he should refuse to give me so much as a word or look & lavish all his affection on these nasty, mercenary wretches."

"Yes, men are cursed animals" replied Zamorna. "That's a fact & it won't deny—& your Alexander is a charming specimen of the worst of a bad set. but, Zenobia, you may exaggerate a little, you may be misinformed—there's such a thing you know as ladies being jealous without reason—I happen just now to be acquainted with a case in point &, as you & I are on the subject of matrimonial grievances, I'll tell you what it is in order that we may condole with each other."

"O Zamorna" interrupted the Countess "You're going to turn the whole affair into ridicule in your usual way."

"No indeed—I was merely about to tell you that I've quite a weight on my mind at present on account of the freezing distance at which her Grace the Duchess has thought proper to keep me lately, & the unaccountable coolness & frigidity which has marked her whole manner towards me for this fortnight last past—I've thought every day that I'd request an explanation—but somehow I felt a sort of impulse to let matters take their own course & look as if I was not greatly concerned about the business—when I do so, she makes a point of crying—yes, actually shedding tears & looking considerably heart-broken, & I declare before Heaven I can't guess what it's all about—" The Countess shook her head. "You're a Nathaniel without guile, all the world knows that" said she. "But

I see you'll not consider my distresses in a serious light—& yet I'm such a fool I can't help complaining to you—"

"Well" returned his Grace. "I complain to you & you won't pity me & so we're even—Come Zenobia—& dismiss sad thoughts from your mind—it's precisely three o'clock by my repeater, I've had a very hard morning's work & am just in tune for an hour or two's relaxation—go & put on your riding habit & beaver—I'll order a pair of my Hunters to be saddled & we'll have a gallop on the Alnwick Road—in the old style, neck & neck."

The Countess rose, wiping her eyes & smiling in spite of herself. "Mercurial as ever" said she. "Care does not cling to you, Augustus."

"Nor to you either" was the answer. "In half an hour, as soon as you've inhaled a draught of fresh air & got fairly into the country —you'll be as fresh as a lark & thinking only how to beat me in the hard trot & sharp canter—but the chances are not as equal as they used to be, Zenobia—though you are magnificently round, my height & bone will outweigh you now—"

"Well" said the Countess "I suppose I must humour you—I shall not be long in preparing. do you mean to ride till dinner time—?" "Yes. we shall only have two hours & a half, so make haste, it's a glorious day—bright & breezy. Hey, what's that passing the window? Zenobia—just come & look."

Zenobia approached the casement where his Grace was standing —two elfish figures rode by—mounted on diminutive & shaggy ponies & followed by a tall & stately footman in splendid scarlet livery, mounted on a glossy black steed—The first Cavalier's were little fellows in blue dressed with tassled caps—they sat in their saddles as erect as arrows & looked about them with an air of shy proud consequence, truly aristocratic—"Not bad riders are they?" said the Duke—gazing after them with a grin of complacency that displayed all his white teeth. "They manage their chargers wonderfully well" replied the Countess "& the ponies look spirited too —you must have begun to teach them in good time"—"Only half a year ago—the lads took to their saddles well—look at Frederick —d--n the little toad, he's laying it into his nag most viciously—" At this moment one of the Shelties turned somewhat restive—& the slim rider, a pale light-haired boy of between four & five— lifted his switch &, setting his teeth, laid on about the ponies head like a savage—the creature kicked & reared &, if the footman had not interfered, a drawn battle might have ensued—with his aid, the matter was at last settled—both the little chaps then started into a canter—& sweeping across Victoria Square entered Fidena

Park—"There go the Hopes of Angria" said Zamorna laughing—
"that was a touch of the Grand-father—he looked very like him at
the moment—he deserves licking."

CHAPTER VI

Evening being come on—the time for closing curtains & rousing
fires, I will introduce my readers to a domestic scene in Wellesley-
House—all very innocent & homely—The daylight perhaps is not
quite drawn in—for winter, you must remember, is past & the
sunset of a fine day leaves a long glimmer behind it—However, it is
dusk enough to bring out the full glow of a good fire—& in this
Drawing[-room] which I wish you now to imagine, there is more of
red reflection from the hearth than of pale gleam from the windows.

Don't suppose you are about to witness a scene of unalloyed
peace—on the contrary, the room is full of talk & noise—or rather
their are two divisions in the place—calm reigns on one side, chaos
on the other—By some tacit regulation, nothing tumultuous dare
approach the region of the rug & mantle-piece. A sofa covered with
crimson occupies one side of the hearth—the further end of this
sofa comes against a window—through which the shrubs of a
garden are seen dimly clustered in twilight—& above them
ascends a half-moon—softening a sky of clear, cold azure. This
moon directs a very pale beam on to the brow of a gentleman who
sits on the sofa & gazes serenely at vacancy—without proffering a
word to man or beast. now a person of slim, genteel stature &
mellow years, with a bald smooth lofty brow glistening in moonlight & bust-like features fitted—must needs look very poetical,
especially when he is dressed in an angelical blue swallow-tail coat,
a pallid primrose vest & pantaloons which are a sight to see—not
speak of—nor was there wanting to give full effect to this said
picture the force of contrast. Behold, at the feet of this celestial
form, this heavenly thought embodied in marble, sat or crept or
rolled a human infant—yea, an absolute child—small & plump—
with a white frock & round face—features as yet invisible—& a
pair of saucer eyes a shade darker than jet in their hue. This child
seemed to hold the territory of the rug with undivided sway—& it
crept from end to end of its dominions with an unwearied & cease-
less vigilance of surveillance not easily accounted for on any known
principal of Government—now & then it laid its minute fingers on
the rim of the tarnished brass fender which formed the boundary
to one side of its realm, & seemed inclined to overpass this formidable barrier & make an incursion into the fiery district beyond—

Whenever these signs of a rising spirit of discovery occurred—the tall pensive Gentleman would bend down & with a gentle hand remove the Adventurer to its own limits—just as he would put back a white mouse convicted of attempting to escape from its cage. These transactions took place in silence—neither God-like Man nor impish child seemed gifted with the faculty of speech.

Individuals of a different calibre peopled the other end of the room—there, three boys were making a furious clatter—chairs & foot-stools were hurled about with small regard to decorum, & a yelp of voices was kept up much like what you might expect to hear in a kennel of pointer puppies. Two of the lads were pale slight fellows—with curling light hair—the other was a rounder rosier animal with a dimple in his cheek & with hair a shade darker, more thickly curled—large brown eyes seemed a family peculiarity common to them all.

The uproar they were keeping up seemed partly controlled, partly excited by a powerful-built Gentleman who sat on a music-stool in the midst of them—At the identical moment we speak of he had them in a half-circle before him & appeared to be asking them some questions.

"Frederick, did you & Edward say your lessons this morning before you rode out?" "Yes, Papa." "All of them?" A pause—"I did, but he didn't" exclaimed Edward—"And why didn't he, Sir—?" "Because he wouldn't." "Wouldn't—what's the meaning of that, Frederick? I said you were not to come down in the evening next time you missed your lessons." "I did all but spelling" said the accused. "And why didn't you do your spelling too—?" "'Cause Dr Cook wanted me to say G–– & I wanted to say J––" "A pretty reason, Sir, truly—I hope Dr Cook will lick you soundly next time you take that whim—Do you know, Sir, what Solomon says on the subject of flogging?" Silence was the expressive answer to this question—"Spare the rod & spoil the Child" pursued the paternal monitor—"& moreover, Frederick my lad, let me tell you —that the very next time I see that switch of yours laid on in the way it was this morning, I'll take the pony from you & you shall ride no more for a month to come." "It wouldn't go right" said Frederic "and Edward did just the same only worse when we got into the park." "Very well, Gentlemen, I'll speak to your Groom—& you shall walk out with Miss Clifton to-morrow like little Girls. now Arthur, what are you looking so eager about?" "I want to ask you something, Papa"—the rosy wretch—sitting a stool—proceeded rumbustiously to climb on to his Father's knee. having seated himself en cavalier, he began "I've said all my lessons to-day—"

"Well, that's a fine lad—what then?" "May I have a pony?" "He neither read yesterday nor the day before" interposed Edward—who, with his brother, had been struck with chill dismay on hearing the sentence pronounced that they were to walk out with Miss Clifton like little Girls.—"And he cried & screamed all the time we were out this morning because he mightn't ride too" added Frederic—The Duke shook his head at hearing this—"Bad account, Arthur." Arthur knew how to manage. instead of crying, he eyed his father with a twinkling merry glance out of the corner of his roguish dark eye & repeated "let me have a pony, Ma-ma says I ought," "Mamma spoils thee, my lad" said Zamorna "because thou happenest to have a cheek like an apple & a vile dimple mark upon it—with sundry tricks of smiles & glances that, judging by my own experience, are never likely to win thee a share in saving grace." "A pony—a pony" persisted the petitioner—"well—well, be a good boy for three days & then we'll see about it—" "I suppose Maria is to have a pony next"—muttered Frederic, regarding the diminutive thing on the rug with a look of lordly scorn—& then turning a displeased eye on Arthur—happily His father did not hear this remark or it would probably have been rewarded by a manual application on to the auricular organs. Edward, retreating a little behind his Father, expressed his feelings on the subject in the more delicate language of signs—applying his thumb to his nose, he took a sight thereby, meaning to intimate "Never mind, Fred. let Arthur have his pony—he'll never sit in the saddle & what fun the tumbling will be"—Frederic, being a trifle in the sullens, strayed away to the quiet region of the fireplace & stood looking into the embers—for some time—his noble Grand-Sire, opposite to whom he had planted himself—noticed his proximity only by an uncertain glitter of the eye with which he surveyed him at intervals. at last Northangerland made a movement as if he were going to speak, though reluctantly—"Where's your mother?" said he abruptly—at the same moment directing a singular squint at the young heir of Angria—& withdrawing his gaze instantly— The pale sharp lad looked up. "What did ye say, Sir?" he asked with the quick utterance that seemed natural to him. " I asked you where your mother was" replied the earl somewhat sternly. "Mamma's in her room, Sir." "And why doesn't she come down?" "I don't know, Sir." "Go & ask your father then"—"Ask him what, Sir?" "Blockhead!" said Northangerland—scowling. "Ask your father why your mother is not here." "Very well, Sir—" Frederic whipt of—

"Please papa—my Grandfather wants to know why mamma is

not come down"—"Tell your Grandfather" replied his Grace "that I have been asking myself the same question—& that I had just screwed my courage up to the exploit of ascertaining the reason in propria persona—" "In what, papa?" "In my own august person, Frederic"—The ambassador returned—"Papa's screwed up his courage to go & ask in his own august person." Northangerland curled his upper lip—"I've done with you, Sir" he said, nodding to Frederic. But the imp, like a true Angrian, would not take a hint—he continued to stand by the fender—& shew to his annoyed progenitor the small correct features & pale auburn curls of the house of Percy—gleaming in firelight. Zamorna drew near—a tower of strength. "Frederic" said he "go to the other side of the room—" "What for, papa—Maria's always let to be on the rug & we never are—" "To the right-about instantly" said the Duke. "No words from you, my lad" & placing a hand on the slim malcontent's shoulder, he impelled him some yards on his way. "If you return here while I am out of the room—I shall send you to bed directly" said his Grace, & with these words he opened a side-door & departed.

The Duchess of Zamorna was sitting in a room as beautiful as jewelled work but without a fire & therefore chilly & ungenial in spite of its splendour. One taper was shining on the toilet—& by the light it shed, her Grace, seated in an arm-chair, seemed reading —at least she had an open book in her hand & her eyes were fixed on the page—though the fair slight finger resting between the leaves was not often raised to turn them over. Her dress was all elegant & queenly—& her hair, divided from her forehead in a silken braid—separated into wavy curls on the temples & relieved her rounded cheek & delicate features with its soft shade. She looked somewhat proud & somewhat sad—but most perfectly, most picturesquely, lovely. what could be imagined fairer? De Lisle's pencil could not add a charm & Chantry's chisel could not remove a defect.

A rather smart rap at the door roused her—she lifted her cheek from the hand of ivory on which it rested—& seemed to consider a moment before she replied—it was not like the rap of her attendants—their summons was usually more gentle & subdued, & the one other person who had a right to enter this room always claimed his full privilege of appearing unannounced—while she doubted, the rap was repeated with a still smarter, more prolonged application of the knuckles. "Come in" she said—with a stately composure of tone & mien which seemed to rebuke the impetuosity of the summons.

The door unclosed—"I hope I've done right" said the Duke of Zamorna, stepping forward & shutting himself in—"I'd be sorry to be too bold & hurt anybody's notions of delicacy—even if they were a little fastidious—or so." "Your Grace wishes to speak to me perhaps" returned the Duchess, laying down her book & looking up with an aspect of some attention. "Yes, merely to speak, I pledge my word, nothing more—in surety whereof I'll take a chair here just by the door—which will leave at least four yards between your ladyship & me." accordingly he placed a chair with its back against the door & there seated himself. The Duchess looked down & something stole into her eye which made it glisten with a more humid shine than heretofore. "Your Grace will be cold there I think" said she—& a half smile lit the incipient tear—"Cold? aye, it seems to be a hard frost to night I think, Mary—Pray, if I might presume to put the question—will you be kind enough to tell me why you prefer sitting here reading a homily or a sermon by yourself—instead of coming down into your drawing-room & looking after the children—Frederic has been bothering his Grandfather again, & little Maria has kept him engaged all the evening." "I'll come down if you wish me" replied the Duchess "But my head ached a little after dinner—& I thought perhaps if I sat in the room & looked out of spirits, you would think me sullen—"

"Why, you've been looking out of spirits for the last fortnight & therefore I should most likely never have noticed what I am now grown so much accustomed to—but if you'll favour me with the reason of it all—I'll consider myself obliged to you." Her Grace sat silent—she reopened her book & turned over the leaves—"Are you going to read me a sermon?" asked his majesty. the Duchess turned her head aside & wiped away the single tear now starting down her cheek. "I can't talk to you at that distance" said she. "Well" returned Zamorna "I would wish always to observe the strictest proprieties—but if you'll give me an invitation, perhaps I may venture a yard or two nearer"—"Come" said the Duchess—still engaged with her handkerchief. His Grace approached—"You'll perhaps faint if I stir another step" said he—pausing half-way between the door & the toilet. the Duchess held out her hand, though still her head was turned away—Thus encouraged, his Diffident Grace drew nearer by degrees, & at last cast anchor with his chair alongside of his Royal Consort—he possessed himself to, of the hand which had not been withdrawn & then with his peculiar smile sat waiting for the sequel.

"You haven't been to Flower-House lately, have you?" asked the Duchess. "Not very—but what of that? do you suspect a growing friendship between me & the Countess?" "No—no—but Adrian—" a pause—"Well, Mary?" "You were at Flower-House a few weeks ago." "I believe I was" said his Grace, & he blushed to the eyes. "And you forgot me, Adrian—you saw some one you liked better—" "Who told you that snivelling lie?" returned his Grace, "did Richton?" "No." "Warner?" "No." "the Countess or some other busybody in petticoats?" "No." "Who then—?" "I dare not tell you who, Adrian—but a person I was forced to believe." "Well, what more—what Goddess was it that I liked better than you —?" "It was a lady I have heard you praise yourself—you called her the most Beautiful Woman in Angria—Miss Moore"—His Grace laughed aloud. "And that's all, Mary, is it" said he "that's what you've been pining over for two mortal weeks—& I like Miss Moore better than you, do I? I've a strange taste—Miss Moore?" he continued, as if endeavouring to recall the lady's identity — "Miss Moore—? aye, I recollect—a tall girl with light hair & a somewhat high coulour—I believe I did once say that she was a fine specimen of the Angrian female—& on second thoughts I re- member now that the last time I was at Flower-House, Richton brought her into the room where I was taking off my coat—& she bothered me a little with some kind of request about Henry Hast- ings—all in a very modest way though—she was not intrusive. I told her I was sorry I could not oblige her & gave her a little serious advice about not being too ready to take up the causes of scoundrelly young red-coats—as it might subject her to unpleasant imputations—She blushed with due propriety & there the matter ended—now Mary, there's the naked truth—" "Is it all the truth, Adrian?" "All—upon my Christian d---n--tion—" The Duchess looked willing & yet afraid to believe—"I wish I could feel convinced" said she—"A heavy weight would be removed from my mind." "Dismiss it instantly" said his Grace "its all imaginary—a mere nervous affection—you inherit your father's turn for hypochondria, Mary."

"But" pursued her Grace "I am sure, Adrian, you have been very cold to me for some days past—I have hardly had an oppor- tunity of exchanging a word with you." again Zamorna laughed— "Well, the inconsistency of woman!" exclaimed he "reproaching me with the effects of her own caprice! have you not been shrinking from me like a sensitive plant—? answering my questions in monosyllables—crying when I spoke to you kindly—& contriv- ing to slip away whenever by any chance you happened to be left alone with me?" "You exaggerate" said the Duchess. "Not in the least—& pray, what was I to make of all this?" "Of course I imagined you had taken some kind of odd whim into your head—had perhaps begun to entertain scruples regarding the lawfulness of matrimony, & in fact every day I expected formal application for a dissolution of the conjugal tie—& an intimation that it was your purpose to seek some sacred retreat where the follies of carnal affection might beset you no more—"

"Adrian!" said the Duchess, smiling at his taunts while she deprecated their severity—"you know such ideas never crossed your mind—while you talk in that way, your eyes are full of triumph—yes, Adrian, from the very first moment you saw me six years ago, you perceived your own power, you perceive it now—it's of no use resisting, I'll believe all you tell me—I've acted foolishly—forgive me & don't retaliate—" "Then you drop the idea of a convent, do you Mary? you think there will be time enough to turn devout some thirty years hence—when that pretty face is not quite so fair & smooth, & those eyes are not altogether so subduing—& moreover when your husband's head has grown a little grizzled & his brow has a furrow or two across, deep enough to give him the air of a stern old fire-eater as he will be.—then you'll refuse him a kiss"—but now, two or three kisses were offered & received & warmly returned. Duke & Duchess then rose —The candle remained burning on the toilet—the two chairs stood vacant before it—the splendid little room reflected around its fairy beauty—but the living figures of the scene were gone— Solitude & silence lingered behind them. the candle burnt soon to its socket, the flame flickered, waned—streamed up in a long tongue of light, sank again—trembled a moment & finally vanished in total darkness. Then a piano was heard playing in the drawing-room below—& when the first notes had stifled the clamour of children, a voice sung.

> Life, believe, is not a scene
>   So dark as sages say,
> Oft' a little morning rain
>   Will bring a pleasant day.
> Sometimes there are clouds of gloom,
>   But these are transient all,
> If the shower will make the roses bloom,
>   O why lament its fall?
>   Merrily—rapidly
>   Our sunny hours flit by,
>   Then gratefully—cheerily
>   Enjoy them as they fly.

What, though Death at times steps in,
   And calls our best away?
What, though sorrow seems to win
   O'er Hope a heavy sway?
Yet Hope again elastic springs
   Unconquered, though she fell.
Still buoyant are her golden wings,
   Still strong to bear us well.
     Then manfully, fearlessly
   The day of trial bear,
     For gloriously, victoriously
   Can Courage quell Despair!

Charles Townshend—March 26th 1839

CAROLINE VERNON

INTRODUCTION

The introductory remarks with which the author opened the present narrative, indicating her resolve "to write no more till I had something to write about", are symptomatic of an altogether more critical approach to her work, and it is this that distinguishes Caroline Vernon *from the preceding narratives. It is, in all respects, a more mature work and is marred by fewer blemishes of taste and execution.*

Though the MS was not dated, internal evidence can confirm the clues which biographical data supply. From May to 20 July 1839, Charlotte Brontë was away from home, engaged as governess in the Sidgwick family of Stonegappe, Lothersdale, an interval which accounts for the "three months lapse of time" mentioned in her introductory remarks. Caroline Vernon, evidently begun on her return home, falls into two parts, following a further interruption during August and September when Charlotte was on holiday on the East Coast. As indicated by occasional dating of incidents in the plot itself, it was not finished until November or even December 1839. It was a habit of Charlotte's, as previously noted, to situate her tales in the actual time of year when she was writing them, a choice dictated by her interest in climatic conditions and in the growing place she gave to natural description. Thus, Quashia's letter at the beginning of the tale is dated from Boulogne, 29 June 1839, and the date of Zamorna's abduction of Caroline is 7 December.

The imprint of Charlotte's recent experiences at Stonegappe is certainly visible in the opening scenes at Hawkscliffe, when Zamorna is shown superintending the hay-making in the fields below his house, accoutred in country clothes ("a broad-brimmed hat of straw and . . . a plaid jacket & trousers"), and all the talk is of crops and planting trees, subjects very pertinent to Mr Sidgwick's avocations, and new subjects to Charlotte Brontë's pen. Derived, too, from the Stonegappe household, is the "large Newfoundland dog laid under Zamorna's lodge-porch" who was actually mentioned in Charlotte's letter home of 8 June 1839.

Another new influence in Caroline Vernon *is the preoccupation with French matters—the defective morals of the ladies, the manners of Parisian society, and a markedly improved acquaintance with the language. This was due to Charlotte's reading at the time of French novels and newspapers loaned her by Mary Taylor's father, whose business took him frequently across the Channel to France and Belgium, Acknowledging the interest she had from such reading—sometimes receiving forty novels at a time—Charlotte commented that they were, like all the rest, "clever, wicked, sophistical and immoral, and gave one a thorough idea of France & Paris . . ."*

The subject of Caroline Vernon, *like* Mina Laury, *is love, but the author's advance in self-analysis makes it possible for her to detach herself from her heroine's situation, as she could* not *do in the earlier tale, and to see it whole.*

Caroline is a typical product of the Romantic Age (as was Charlotte Brontë). Her heroes are Byron, Bonaparte and Lord Edward Fitz-Gerald (because Moore wrote his "Life") and, like the young women in Byron's orbit, she is a ready victim to men's wiles.

Charlotte's concern with the destructive force of Love, inherent in all her best work, has made immense strides in this tale. How keenly she sought to abide by the truth inherent in her situation is seen by her rewriting of two passages—Caroline's farewell to Zamorna at Hawkscliffe at the end of Part I, and Zamorna's letter to Caroline in Chapter IV of Part II. The alternative text to the first of these is incomparably superior and shows not only a greater sense of realities, but a refinement in taste. Here, we are far from the clowneries of Charles Townshend. Had Zamorna and Caroline bared their feelings for each other in this scene, as in the first draft, there would have been no innocence left in their relationship, and Caroline could not have retained her illusions about her guardian which made her pursuit of him in Part II a guileless gesture and consequently a forgiveable one. The drama of Part II, which leads to Caroline's ruin, would not have existed if Zamorna had already shown himself in his true colours. In this edition, the main text uses the revised versions of these two passages, but the first drafts are printed separately in the Appendix.

Caroline Vernon—and her mother—had already figured in three previous narratives: in Passing Events, *where she is mentioned as Northangerland's acknowledged daughter; in* Julia, *where her appearance as a delightful child prefigures the perfection of Paulina Home in* Villette; *and in* Mina Laury, *where Louisa Vernon appears still under house-arrest to Zamorna for her part in the civil wars. The subject evidently held fascination for Charlotte Brontë, and received a fresh impetus, apparently, by the introduction, in* Captain Henry Hastings, *of Rosamund Wellesley, another of Zamorna's wards and victims, whose tale so resembles Caroline's.*

Charlotte Brontë's concern for the fate of Caroline Vernon did not end, however, with her ruin. How persistently it haunted her can be judged by her reintroduction of it in Jane Eyre, *where the child Adèle—the illegitimate fruit of Rochester's amours with Céline Varens, the Parisian dancer—was shown under other and better auspices than the guardianship of such a man as Zamorna. Adèle was given the chance that Caroline never had; she had, also, fewer of Caroline's natural good qualities; but, weak and vain as she is shown to be, she yet makes good, thanks to a moral upbringing and the steady,*

* Letter to Ellen Nussey, 20 August 1840

if somewhat repressive, affection of Jane Eyre. As a teacher in various schools, Charlotte was not without gaining some experience of child psychology, and of the effects of environment on character. Adèle's happier destiny compensates somewhat for poor Caroline's immolation to the Byronic fashion of Charlotte's youth. The evolution of the theme in the author's development shows better than any other her passage from apprenticeship to maturity.

The manuscript of Caroline Vernon *is currently in the possession of Harvard University Library, by whose kind permission it is printed here. It has previously been published in a modernised form and incomplete in F. E. Ratchford's* Legends of Angria *(Yale University Press, 1933).*

CAROLINE VERNON

When I concluded my last book I made a solemn resolve that I would write no more till I had somewhat to write about, & at the time I had a sort of notion that perhaps many years might elapse before aught should transpire novel & smart enough to induce me to resume my relinquished pen—but lo you—! Scarce three moons have waxed & waned ere

"the creature's at his dirty work again"

and yet it is no novelty—no fresh & startling position of affairs that has dipped my quill in ink & spread the blank sheet before me. I have but been looking forth as usual over the face of society—I have but been eating my Commons in Chapel Street—dressing & dining out daily—reading newspapers—attending the Theatres nightly—taking my place about once a week in the Fire-flaught Angrian Mail—rushing as far as Zamorna—sometimes continuing my career—till I saw the smoke of Adrianopolis. snatching a look at the staring shops & raw new palaces of that Great Baby [lon] Capital —then, like a Water-God, taking to the Calabar—not however robing myself in flags & crowning myself with sedge—but, with a ticket in my fist, getting on board a steamer & away, all Fizz & foam—down past Mouthton & coasting it along by Doverham back to Verdopolis again. When, subdued by a fit of pathose & sentimentalities—I've packed a hamper with sandwiches & gone to Alnwick or somewhere there 'awa'—but I try that no more—for last time I did it—chancing to sit down under a willow in the grounds to eat a cold fowl & drink a bottle of ginger-beer—I made use of the pedestal of a statue for my table—whereat a Keeper thought fit to express himself eminently scandalised, & in an insolent manner he gave me notice that such liberties were not permitted at the Castle, that strangers were excluded from this part of the grounds, that the statue was considered a valuable piece of sculpture being the likeness of some male or female of the house of Wharton who had died twenty years ago—with a lot of rhodomontade all tending to shew that I had committed sacrilege or something like it by merely placing a mustard-glass & pepper box— with a dinner-bun & knife & fork at the base of a stupid stone idol —representing somebody in their chemise—[illegible] gazing at their own naked toes.

Howsumdever, even in this course of life I've seen & heard a summat that, like the notes of a Tourist, may sell when committed to paper—Lord, a book-wright need never be at a loss. one can't expect earthquakes & insurrections every-day, there's not always

> An Angrian campaign going on in the rain,
> Nor a Gentleman Squire lighting his fire
> Up on the moors with his blackguards & boors,
> Nor a Duke & a lord drawing the sword,
> Hectoring & lying, the whole world defying,
>   Then sitting down crying.

There's not always

> A shopkeeper militant coming out iligant,
> With King Boy & King Jack both genteely in black,
> Forming Holy Alliance & breathing defiance,
> Nor a Prince finding brandy every day coming handy
> While he's conquering of lands with his bold nigger bands
>   Like a man of his hands.

There's not always

> A Death & a marriage—a Hearse & a Carriage,
> A Bigamy cause—A King versus laws,
> Nor a short Transportation for the good of the nation,
> Nor a speedy returning mid national mourning,
> While him & his father refuse to foregather
>   'Cause the earl hadn't rather.

reader, these things don't happen every day. it's well they don't, for a constant renewal of such stimulus would soon wear out the public stomach & bring on indigestion—But surely one can find something to talk about, though miracles are no longer wrought in the world—battle-fields, it is true, are now growing corn—according to a paragraph in a westland newspaper which I had a while since in my hand. "Barley & Oats are looking well in the neighbourhood of Leyden & all the hay is carried from the fields about Evesham, and they tell us the Navigation of the Cirhala is about to be improved by a canal which will greatly facilitate the conveyance of goods up the country, & that subscriptions are on foot for erecting a new & commodious Piece-Hall in the borough of Westwood." What then, is all interest to stagnate because blood has ceased to flow—? has Life no variety now? is all crime the child of war? Does Love fold his wings— when victory lowers her pennons?— Surely not—it is true a tone of respectability has settled over society

—a business-like calm—many that were wild in their youth have grown rational & sober. I really trust morals, even Court morals, have improved. we hear of no out-breaks now—some small irregularities indeed of a very elevated nobleman are occasionally rumoured in the public ear—but habit with him has become second nature—& the exquisite susceptibility of his feelings is too well known to need comment, & elsewhere there is certainly a change, a reformation, & let us now, who have so long gazed on glaring guilt, solace ourselves with a chastened view of mellowed morality.

CHAPTER I

On the morning of the 1st of July a remarkable event happened at Ellrington-House—the earl & Countess were both eating their breakfast, at least the Countess was, the earl was only looking at his—when all at once the earl, without previous warning or apparent cause—laughed!

Now the scene of this singular occurence was the Countess's own dressing-room—her ladyship had that morning coaxed his lordship to rise early—with the intention that, as it was a very fine summer day—they should take a drive out to Alnwick for the benefit of his lordship's health & spirits.—For about a fortnight or three weeks past his lordship had ceased certain eccentric deviations from his lawful path—the saloons, I should rather say the boudoirs, of certain noble mansions—had vainly waited to reverberate the gentle echo of his voice & step. Mesdames Greville, Lalande & St James—had been mourning like nightingales on their perches, or like forsaken turtle-doves cooing soft reproaches to their faithless mate—he came not, & bootless was the despatch of unnumbered & tender billets—charged at once with sighs & perfumes & bedewed with tears & rose-water—more than one such delicate messenger had been seen shrivelling "like a parched scroll" in the grate of his lordship's appartment, & answer there was none—Sick of music, surfeited with sentiment—the great ex-president had come home to his unmusical, plain-spoken Countess—the roll of languishing eyes gave him the [*illegible*] so he sought relief in the quick, piercing glances—that bespoke more hastiness than artifice of temper—Her ladyship was very cross-grained & intractable at first—she would not come to at all for about a week—but after the earl had exhibited a proper modicum of hopeless melancholy & lain on the sofa for two or three days in half real, half-feigned illness—she began first to look at him, then to pity him—then to speak to him, & last of all to make much of him & caress him. This reawakened interest was at its height about the time when my chapter opens—On the very morning in question—she had been quite disquieted to see how little appetite her noble helpmate evinced for his breakfast—& when, after an unbroken silence of about half an hour, he all at once, while looking down at his un-tasted cup—dissipated that silence by a laugh, an unexpected, brief, speechless but still indisputable laugh—Zenobia was half-alarmed. "What is it, Alexander?" said she—"What do you see?" "You, & that's enough in all conscience" answered the earl—turning upon her an eye that had more of sarcasm than mirth in it & more of languor than either. "Me! are you laughing at me then?" "Who, I? no" & he relapsed again into silence—a silence so pensive & dejected that the worthy Countess began to doubt her ears & to think she had only fancied the laugh which still rung in them—Breakfast being concluded—she rose from table &, advanc-ing to the window—drew up the blind which had hitherto screened the sunshine—she opened the sash top & a free admission of morn-ing light & air cheered the apartment—it was a fine day, too bright & summer-like for a city—every heart & every eye under the influence of such a day longs for the country.

"Let the carriage be got ready quickly" said the Countess, turn-ing to a servant who was clearing the breakfast-table, and as the servant closed the door, she sat down at her glass to complete the arrangement of her dress—for as yet she was only in deshabille —She had platted & folded her hair, & thought with some pride that its sable profusion became her handsome features as well now as it had done ten years ago. She had adjusted her satin apparel to a shape that, though it might not befit a sylph, did well enough for a fine tall woman—who had the weight of as much pride & cholor to support as would overwhelm any two ordinary mortals —She had put on her watch & was embellishing her white, round hands with sundry rings, when the profound hush which had till now attended her operations was interrupted by a repetition of that low involuntary laugh—"My lord!" exclaimed the Countess, turn-ing quickly round—She would have started if her nerves would have permitted such a proof of sensitiveness. "My lady!" was the dry answer—"Why do you laugh?" said she. "Don't know." "Well, but what are you laughing at?" "Can't tell." "Are you ill? is it hysterical?" "I'm never in rude health that I know of, Zenobia—but as to hysterical—ask Miss Delph—" With a gesture of scorn the Countess turned again to her Glass. Wrath is seldom prudent and as her ladyship's was vented upon her hair—on which she had so recently lavished such care & taste—combs & fillets flew—& the

becoming braids which had wreathed her temples & brow quickly
floated in a confused cloud of darkness over her shoulders—Again
the earl laughed, but now it was evidently at her—he approached
her toilette &, leaning on the back of the arm-chair she filled—
(emphatically I say filled, for indeed there was no room for anybody else), he began to talk—"Softly Zenobia. I thought you had
done your hair—it was well enough, rather a little sombre or so—
not quite enough in the floating, airy tendril style—but then, that
requires a lightish figure, & yours—ahem!" here the glass was
shifted with a hasty movement, & the brush thrown down & the
comb snatched up with emphatic promptitude—the earl continued
with gentleness. "The Furies, I believe, had hair of live snakes"
said he— "what a singular taste—how was it, eh Zenobia? eh?"
"How was it my lord! what do you mean? I have not the honour of
understanding your lordship—" "Don't know exactly what I mean
—it was some dim notion of analogy haunting my mind that made
me put the question. I've so many funny ideas nowadays, Zenobia,
that are crushed, blighted by the stormy climate I live in. a gentler
nurture, a little soft sunshine & quiet showers might encourage the
infant buds to expand—& in the tender shining after rain I might
now & then say a good thing—make a hit—but as it is I daren't
speak lest I should be snapped up & snarled at out of all reason—it
makes me quite low." the Countess, as she brushed her tresses,
whisked a thick dark mass over her face to conceal the smile she
could not repress—"You're hardly used" said she. "But Zenobia"
pursued the earl "I've something to tell, something to shew you"
—"indeed, my lord." "Aye—we all love them that love us,
Zenobia." "Do we?" was the succinct answer—"And" pursued his
lordship with pathos—"When we've neglected an attached friend
you know—turned a cold shoulder to him—kicked him perhaps by
mistake—how touching it is to find that after long years of separation & misunderstanding, he still remembers us & is still willing to
borrow that half-crown he has asked for seventy & seven times &
has seventy & seven times been refused—Zenobia, they brought
this letter last night." "Who, my lord?" "The people—James I
think—I don't often get a letter you know—Mr Steaton manages
these things." "And I suppose your letter is from Zamorna." "Oh
no—Mr Steaton generally relieves me of the trouble of correspondence in that quarter—besides, I think his documents are more
frequently addressed to you than me. I object, you know, to his
style—it is unpleasant—smells so very strong of oat-cake & grouse."
"Alexander!" expostulated Zenobia—"And then" continued the
earl—"you forget that he is in the country at present—& therefore

thoughtfully occupied in devising a new compost for Thornton's beans, farming Warner's turnips & curing the rot in Sir Markham Howard's sheep to think of writing letters—besides, his own hay about Hawkscliffe is not all carried—& depend on it he's making the most of this fine morning out in his shirt sleeves—with a straw hat on his head—swearing at the hay-tinkers, now & then giving a hand to help to load the waggons—& at noon or drinking-time sitting down on a cock—to eat his bread & cheese & drink his pot of ale like a King & like a clod-hopper. can't you fancy him, Zen—all in a muck of sweat, for it's hard work & hot weather, arrayed in his shirt & white tights & nothing else—& then you know, at the close of the day when the hamlet is still, going with his dear brother in arms, lord Arundel, to take a prudent dip & swim in the beck—& coming out with bad inflammation occasioned by a sudden check of the perspiration, & going home to be blistered & bled at libertum, & then with interesting wilfulness insisting on another tankard and a fresh go of bathing when he's in a raging fever, & being very properly yielded to—allowed to have his way, & so waxing delirious, cutting his throat & walking off stage with a flourish of trumpets worthy of the most mighty & magnanimous monarch that ever understood Dog-diseases or practised the noble science of farrier." "Who is that letter from, please my lord?" "Ah, the letter—you shall read it & the signature will tell you who it is from—" his Lordship took out his pocket-book & handed therefrom a singularly folded epistle—directed in a large black autograph—whose terrible down-strokes—cross-dashes & circular flourishes seemed to defy all hands—mercantile—genteel & juvenile—that ever existed. The Countess read as follows.

Boulogne June 29th 1839

Daddy Long-legs

Sober I am & sober I have been, and by the bleached bones of my father, sober I wish to be to the end of the chapter. Aye, by the bones of my fathers & by their souls, their burning souls—which in the likeness of Game-cocks cropped & spurred are even now sitting on my right hand and on my left & crowing aloud for vengeance!

The night was dark when I saw them, it lightened & there was thunder—who bowed from the cloud as it rolled?—who spake a word in mine ear?—Did'st not thou, dark but comely one, Sai Too-Too—thou the Brother of my mother's Grand-mother, Sambo, Mungo, Anamaboo.

I'll tell ye what, ye're a cozening old rascal, ye never made me a promise in your life but you broke it—Deny that, deny it I say, will ye? give me the lie—beard me—spit in my face—tweak my nose—come on—I'm your man—up with your daddles—who's afraid?—"What's the fun?"

The marrow of the affair—the root of the matter, is this—a more scoundrelly set of men than some that I could mention were never beheld—nor a more horrifying series of transactions than some that I have in my eye—why, the earth reels, the heavens stagger—the seas totter to their downfall—& old Ocean himself—trembles in his highest hills—& shudders horror-struck through all his woods.

To come to the point at once—may I forget myself & be counted as a child of perdition if the present Generation be not very little better than the last—why I remember when there was a bible in every house & as much Brandy sold for a cab of Dove's dung as you could buy now for half a sovereign—The fact is, & I am certain of it, religion's not popular—real genuine religion I mean—I've seen more christianity in the Desert than it would be worth any man's while to take account of.

Daddy, where are you, there seems to be a kind of a darkness, a sort of mist in the hoyle—a round-about, whirligig, circumferential cloudiness—prop the leg of this here table, will ye daddy, it's sinking with me through the floor—snuff out the candlestick—there, we've a better light now—we write steadier—hark ye then—the play's nearly played out.

Bloody old Robber—you walk in silks & velvets & live in a diamond House with golden windows—while I have foxes & holes, & birds of the air have neither—you toil & spin while I am Solomon in all his Glory arrayed like one of these—But I warn you, Scaramouch, you'd better provide for me—for my wife must share my poverty, & then what will you say? I've made up my mind to marry, I tell you it's a done thing—& the Queen of Heaven herself should not prevail on me to alter it.

Beautiful & benign Being! thou pinest in captivity! Loved lady of my heart, thou weepest in the prison house! but Heaven opens, & thy Bridegroom waits—she shall be mine!

Won't you give your consent, old scum? you promised me another—but she "like a lily drooping, bowed her head & died", at least as good as died, for was not that a living death that consigned her to the Arms of a Numb-Scull?

A better lot is thine fair maid,
  A happier lot is thine,
And who would weep in dungeon shade
  Whom fate had marked for Mine?

Come, do not pine,
But fly to arms that open to receive
  Thy youthful form divine.
Clasped to this heart of fire thoul't never grieve,
  No, thou shalt shine,
Happy as houris fair—that braid their hair,
  Glorious in Eden's bowers
  Where noxious flowers
With fragrant reptiles twine.
But thou, my blooming gem, wilt far out-flourish them,
  My radiant Caroline!

Now daddy, what d'ye say to that?—show her them lines & see if they won't plead my cause for me—she's young, you say, the more need she has of a father & won't I be both father & Husband to her in one? 'tother was not much older when you gave me the refusal of her fair snow-white hand—true I rejected her—but what then? I'd my eye on the younger, softer bud—Caroline's a more alluring name than Mary—more odoriferously & contumaciously musical —then she loves me—so did the other you'll say—desperately— divinely—I know it, old cock, I know it. I have it under her hand, sealed & signed in legal form—but this sweet blossom, this little fluttering—fickle, felicitous fairy—this dear, delicious, delirious mortal—comes into my arms & announces her intention of marrying me straight away off-hand whether I will or no.

I'll be moderate on the subject of settlements—a handsome house, ten thousand a year, the Custody of your Will & the making of it all over again according to my own directions—that's what I want & what I'll have—Answer by return of post & enclose a letter from my Lovely One—& a bank-note or two. in the shadows of approaching sunrise & the profound roar of the storm when it subsides to silence—in Love's Intoxication—Hope's Fury & Despair's wilderness—in Beauty's blaze—in Eden's bliss—in Hell's troubled & terrific turbulence—in Death's deep & dangerous delirium—

I am & was not A 'Squire of high degree
Q in the corner

"You know the fine Roman hand, I presume?" said the earl, when his Countess had finished reading this surprising lucubration. "Yes, Quashia of course*—but who does he mean, what is he driving at?"

* Quashia had previously, during the wars, invaded Zamorna's palace and occupied the apartments of his queen (*Roe Head Journal*, February 1836).

"he wants to marry a little girl of ten or eleven years old" returned Northangerland—"What, Miss Vernon?" said her ladyship, uttering the name between her teeth. "Aye." "And is Miss Vernon no more than ten or eleven?" "No—I think not—" A servant just then entered to announce the carriage—the Countess went on dressing herself very fast & looking very red & choleric. While she finished her toilette, Northangerland stood by the window thinking —his thoughts were wound up by a word that seemed to burst involuntarily from his lips. it was "D--n-t--n". He then asked his wife where she was going. she said to Alnwick. "no" he replied, "I'll go to Angria—bid them turn the horses heads east"—Mr Jas Shaver brought his hat & gloves & he went down into the Hall & so vanished.

CHAPTER II

Zamorna was literally standing in a hay-field—just below the House at Hawkscliffe—talking to a respectable man in black. It was a hot afternoon & he wore a broad-brimmed hat of straw, & though not exactly in his shirt-sleeves—yet a plaid jacket & trousers—testified but a remote approximation to full dress.

It was a large field and at the furthest end about a score of hay-makers, male & female, were busily engaged at their work. Zamorna, leaning against the trunk of a fine tree with a dog laid on the hay at his feet—was watching them—especially his eyes followed one or two smart active girls—who were amongst the number of the tenters. at the same time he talked to his companion, & thus their conversation ran—

"I reckon now" said the respectable man in black "if your Grace gets this hay well in—it'll be a varry fair crop."—"Yes, it's good land" returned the monarch. "Varry good grazing land—I sud thing grain would hardly answer so well—have ye tryed it wi' my mak o' corn seed?" "There's a croft on the other side of the beck— where the soil is just like this—I sowed it with red wheat last spring & it's bearing beautifully now"—"Humph—wha ye see, ye cannot err mich, for where trees grow as they do here, there's hardly any mak o' grain but what'll prosper—I find t'truth o' that at Girning-ton—now up i't North, about Mr Warner's place, it's clear different—" "Yes, Warner has a great deal of bother with tillage & manure—that bog-soil is so cold & moist—it rots the seed instead of cherishing it. well, my lass, are you tired?" going forward &

The style of this letter is very reminiscent of Branwell's letters to his friends at this period speaking to a tight girl with cheeks like a rose—who, with her rake, had approached nearer to the royal station—"Nay Sir" was the answer, while the young rustic's vanity, gratified by the notice of a fine Gentleman with whiskers & moustachios, sent a deeper colour than ever to her brown healthy complexion—"But it's hot, don't you think so?" continued his Grace. "Nay, not so varry—" "Have ye been working all day among the hay?" "Nay, nobbut sin' nooin"—"It's Hawkscliffe Fair to-morrow is not it, my lass?" "Yes Sir, they call't so." "And you'll go there no doubt?" "I happen sall" giggling & working with her rake very busily to conceal her embarassment. "Well, there's something to buy a fairing with." there was a show of reluctance to accept the present which was tendered—but his Grace said "Pshaw!" & pressed it more urgently —so the Damsel suffered her fingers to close upon it—&, as she put it in her pocket, dropped two or three short quick curtsies in acknowledgement. "You'd give me a kiss I daresay if that gentleman were not by—" said Zamorna, pointing to his friend—who regarded the scene with an expression that shewed he thought it excellent Fun—The lass looked up at both the Gentlemen— coloured again & laughing began to withdraw in silence. Zamorna let her go—

"There's a deal of vanity there" said he, as he returned to the oak-tree—"Aye, & coquetry too—look, the witch is actually turning back & surveying me with the corner of her eye." "I doubt she's a jilt" replied Thornton—His Grace pushed out his under lip —smiled & said something about "Palace & Cottage" & "very little difference". "But she's a bonny lass" pursued the laird of Girnington. "Tight & trim & fresh & healthy" was the reply. "There's many a lady would be glad to exchange shapes with her" remarked Sir Wilson again. "Varry like" said his Grace, leaning lazily against the trunk & looking down with a bantering smile at Thornton as he imitated his tone—"Does your Grace know the lass's name?" asked the General, not noticing his Master's aspect— —A pause, closed by a laugh, was the answer—Thornton turned to him in surprise—"What the D———l!" said he hastily—when he saw the sarcasm expressed by eye & lip. "Does your Grace mean to insinuate—?" "Nay, Thornton—be cool—I'm only thinking what a soft heart you have." "Nonsense—nonsense"—returned Sir Wilson, "But your Grace is like to have your own cracks, as if I had spokken to t'lass—when it was all your majesty 'at cannot let ought be under thirty—" "Cannot I? that's a lie—here I stand & I care as much for that foolish little jilt or any other you can mention— high or low—as Bell here at my feet does—Bell's worth them all—

my old girl—there's some truth in thy caress—there—there—
Down now, that's enough." "I know your Grace is steadier than
you used to be—& that's raight enough—but you *have* been wild"
—"Never" was the unblushing rejoinder. "But I know better—"
"Never by G–d, never" repeated his Grace—"O whah!" said
Thornton coolly "your majesty's a right to lie abaat ye se'n, it's
nought to me 'at I know on."

Could it possibly have been Quashia's mad letter which induced
Lord Northangerland to set off then & there to Hawkscliffe, at the
far end of Angria, a house & a country where he had not shewn his
nose for years? His Lordship's movements are often very inexplicable, but this, as Mr Jas Shaver expressed it (when he received
sudden orders to pack up the earl's dressing-case & wardrobe), was
the "beat 'em of all".

The Countess offered to go with her lord—but he made answer
that she "had better not"—so he was put into the carriage solus—
& solus he continued through the whole of the journey—neither
did he speak word to man or beast except to desire them "to get
on". Get on they did, for they stopped neither day nor night till
half the breadth of Angria was traversed & the Moray Hills began
to undulate on the Horizon.—He did not travel incognito & of
course he was known at every Inn & Ale-house where the horses
got a pail-ful of meal & water, & the postillions a bottle of Madeira.
Trivial preparations were commenced in Zamorna for a Riot & a
stoning—but before Mr Edward Percy could loose his mill &
furnish his people with brick-bats—the object of filial attention was
a mile out of Town & clearing the woods of Hartford in a whirlwind of summer dust. His progress was similarly hailed at the
other towns & villages that intercepted his route—at Islington
a dead cat, nimble as when alive, leapt up at the carriage window
& broke it—At Grantley the hissing & yelling rivalled the music
of a legion of cats, & at Rivaux the oblations of mud offered to
his divinity were so profuse as to spread over the chariot pannels
a complete additional coat of varnish. Whether the earl derived
pleasure or vexation from these little testimonials of national
regard it would be hard to say—inasmuch as the complexion
of his countenance varied no more than the hue of his coat—
his brow & features looked evermore to the full as placid as the
glass-face of a repeater which he held in his hand & continually
gazed at.

One thinks there is something pleasant in slowly approaching
Solitude towards the close of a bustling journey. Driving over the

burning pavements—through the smoke & filth of manufacturing towns in the height of summer, must form, one would fancy, no unimpressive preparation for the entrance on a fine green country of woods—where everything seems remote, fresh & lonely—Yet for all Jas Shaver Esqre. could see in Lord Northangerland & for all that Lord Northangerland could remark in Jas Shaver, neither of these illustrious persons found any remarkable difference—when a July afternoon saw their carriage entering the vast & silent domain of Hawkscliffe-Town, & tumult being left far behind & only a rustling of trees & a trickling of becks being audible.

Where the habitation of man is fixed, there are alway signs of its proximity—the perfect freshness of nature disappears, her luxuriousness is cleared away, & so, erelong, Hawkscliffe began to break into glades—the path grew rolled & smooth—& more frequent prospects of distant hills burst through the widening glimpses of foliage. Out at last, they rolled upon a broad & noble road as well beaten, as white & as spacious as the far-distant highway from Zamorna to Adrianopolis—that track, however, seems endless—but this, at the close of about a hundred yards, was crossed by the arch of an architectural-Gateway—the turret on each side served for a Lodge—& the heavy iron gates were speedily flung back by the Keeper. As the carriage paused for a moment ere it shot through, the yelping of a Kennel of hounds was heard somewhere near—& a large Newfoundlander laid under the lodge-porch rose up & gave a deep-mouthed bark of welcome.

Beyond these Gates there was no more forest, only detatched clumps of trees & vast solitary specimens varying the expanse of a large & wild Park which ascended & half-clothethed with light verdure—the long aclivity of one of the Sydenhams. the remoter hills of the same range rolled away clad in dusky woodland—till distance softened them & the summer sky embued them with intense violet. near the centre of the Park stood Hawkscliffe-House, a handsome pile—but by no means so large nor so grand as the extent of the grounds seemed to warrant—it could not aspire to the title neither of Palace nor Castle—it was merely a solitary Hall—stately from its loneliness—& pleasant from the sunny & serene effect of the green region which expanded round it—Deer—a herd of magnificent cattle & a troop of young unbroken Horses—shared the domain between them.

As the carriage stopped at the Front-door, Northangerland put up his repeater whose hand was pointing to six o'clock p-m &, the steps being let down & door opened, he alighted & quietly walked into the house—he had got half through the hall before he asked a question of any servant—but the butler, advancing with a bow, enquired to what appartment he should conduct him—North [angerland] stopped as if at fault—"Perhaps I am wrong", said he —"this is not Hawkscliffe" and he looked dubiously round on the plain unadorned walls & oak-painted doors about him—so unlike the regal splendours of Victoria Square—a noble branch of Stag's antlers seemed to strike him with peculiar horror—he recoiled instantly, & muttering something indistinct about "Angrian Squire's den a strange mistake", he was commencing a precipitate retreat to his carriage—when James Shaver interposed—"Your Lordship is in the right" said he, whispering low—"This is the royal residence"—(with a sneer) "but country plainness—no style kept. I fear I shan't be able to muster proper accomodations for your lordship—" "James" said the earl after a pause "will you ask those people where the Duke of Zamorna is—" James obeyed. "Gone out" was the reply. "his Grace is generally out all day—" And where was the Duchess? "Gone out too, but most likely would be back presently"—"Shew me into a room" said the earl, & his lordship was ushered into a library where, without looking round him, he sat down—his back to the window & his face to an enormous map half-unrolled & covering half the opposite wall—there was nothing else in the room except books, a few chairs, a desk & a table loaded with pamphlets & papers—no bust or pictures or any of the other elegant extras commonly seen in a nobleman's library —A large Quarto lay on the floor at Northangerland's feet—he kicked it open with a slight movement of his toe—it was full of gay feathers—coloured wools & brilliant flies for fishing—another & apparently still slighter movement sufficed to discharge the volume to the other end of the room—it fell by a row of thick volumes standing side by side in the lowest shelf—of books. the words Agricultural Magazine glittered in gilt letters on the back of each. When Northangerland was quite tired of sitting, he got up restlessly to pace through the appartment—pausing at a side-table where a small book was lying open—he began mechanically to finger the leaves—it was the planter's vade mecum—Northangerland withdrew his fingers as if they had been burnt. On the same table lay two packets neatly tied up & labelled—"Sample of red wheat from General Thornton"—"Sample of oats from Howard"—The earl was still gazing at these packets, riveted by them apparently as if they had been the two eyes of a basilisk—when a shade crossed the window outside—soon after, somebody was heard entering by the front-door—a word or two passed in the hall & then a step quietly approached the library—It was the Duchess who came. She went to her father & he had to stoop to give her a kiss—for which she looked up in silent eagerness—"I thought it was a farm-house" said he, when he had held her a moment & surveyed her face "but I suppose, Mary, you don't milk cows." "How long have you been here?" returned his daughter—evading his sarcasm with a smile— "They should have fetched me in before, I was only walking down the avenue." "Down the yard I thought you would say" continued the earl—"Surely, Mary—you term that a croft" (pointing to the Park) "And this bigging we are in no doubt is called the Grange— have you a room to yourself? or do you sit in the House & eat your porridge with the ploughman & dairy-maids?" The Duchess still smiled & she slipped the obnoxious packets into a drawer. "Is there a small Inn in the place?" went on her father "Because if there is—I'll put up there. you know I can't eat bacon & eggs &, though your kitchen may be very comfortable, it will smell perhaps of the stable which, you know, comes close up to the door for convenience sake—because when the Big Farmer comes home from his market a trifle sprung or so, it's more convenient to dismount him, rather nigh the house—as he's a good weight to carry in." "Don't father" said the Duchess, as half-vexed she held her head down—looking at her father's hand which she retained in hers, & pulling the ring from his little finger—"Which is he, a better Horse-Jockey or Cow-Jobber?" enquired the inexorable Northangerland —"Does he kill his own meat or he buys it—? does he feed Pigs, Mary?" The Duchess pouted—"I should like to see him riding home a horse-back—after driving a hard bargain down at Grantley there—about a calf which he is to bring home in a rope—the excellent fellow of course will be very drunk—extremely so—for the bargain has been on & off at least ten times & it took at least sixteen tumblers of whi[s]key & water to consolidate it in the end. then the calf will be amazingly contrary—as bad to get on as himself, & what with tumbling from his saddle—rolling in the mud— fighting with his bargain—&c. he will, I should imagine, cut much such a figure as I have seen that fool Arthur O'Connor do under similar circumstances." "Hush Father!" said the Duchess earnestly "Don't talk so—I hear him in the Passage—now pray—" she had not time to complete her entreaty—when the door was promptly opened & his Grace walked in—some Dogs walked in too—the whole party equally heedless of who might or might not be in the room—advanced to a cabinet with some drawers in it, & while the Duke sought in one of the drawers for a coil of gut that he wanted for his line—the Dogs pushed their noses in his face as he stooped down or smelt at his pannier which he had laid on the carpet.

"Be quiet, Juno" said Zamorna—putting a large pointer from him, whose caresses interrupted him in his sedulous search—then calling to somebody in the passage "William, tell Homes I can't find the tackle, it must be at his Lodge—but I shall not want it to night, so he may send it up first thing to-morrow-morning—" "Very well, my Lord" answered a gruff voice without—Zamorna shut up the drawers—"O stop!" said he, speaking suddenly to himself "I had almost forgotten." he walked quickly out of the room. "William!" standing on the front-door steps & calling down the Park—"Yes, please your Grace." "You may give my compliments to Homes & say that the river has been poached on—I was fishing there to day & I only got three trout—tell him he's a d———d idle dog & keeps no right look-out at all when I'm away, but things must be managed differently, I'll have Law & Order observed here, or else I'll try for it." He came back, crossing the Passage with firm even strides—He entered the library again rather more deliberately—He had now time to notice that it was occupied by other persons besides himself & his Dogs—his wife caught his eye first. "Well Mary, have you been walking?" "Yes" —"Rather late is not it, you should mind not to be out after sunset"—"It was very warm." "Yes, fine weather—" & he pulled off his gloves & began to take his long fishing rod to pieces—as he was busily intent on disengaging one hook from the line—Northangerland advanced a little step—from the sort of recess where he had been standing—Zamorna, attracted by the movement, turned. he looked keenly, pausing from his employment—he was evidently astonished for a moment at this unexpected apparition of his father-in-law—only for a moment—there was no salutation on either side—Zamorna stared—Northangerland gazed coolly— Zamorna turned his back, went on disjointing his rod—hung-up that & his pannier—took off a broad-brimmed straw hat which had hitherto diademed his head—& then at last, as he sat down in his arm-chair by the table—found time to ask "When the earl had arrived?" "Didn't look at the clock" was the answer & "Yet, faith, I remember I did—it was about six this evening—" "Hum— have you had any dinner?—we dine early, seldom later than three —" "James gave me a biscuit in the carriage—& 'tis as well he did so, for as I've been remarking to Mrs Wellesley—I can't take porridge or fried bacon—" "No—nor omlets & patès either for that matter" muttered the Duke in an undertone, "Nor hardly a mouthful of any christian edible under the sun." then he continued aloud—"Pray, have you been ordered to take a journey here for your health?"—"What? to a fish-mongers & farriers'? no, stale herring give me the nausea. I've come on business—but may that basket of stinking sprats be sent away?" pointing to the pannier & holding a perfumed cambric handkerchief to his nose. "It's fresh trout" answered his son calmly. "But you're a valetudinarian & must be excused for having sickly antipathies—come, I'll humour you for once—" he rung the bell & the nuisance was quickly removed.

"How did you get along through the country?" continued the Duke, taking up a newspaper & unfolding it—"were you much fêted & flattered when they forgot to ring the bells—& call out the bands in your honour—?" "I don't remember" responded Northangerland—"Don't you? Humph! but perhaps your postillions & horses will—I have some dim notion that the Kennel rubbish of Edwardston & Zamorna & Islington & some of those places has been made uncommon useful not so long since." The Duchess here approached his Grace's chair &, leaning over the back of it to look at the newspaper which he was still reading or feigning to read— she whispered "Don't try to vex him to-night, Adrian—I am sure he's tired with his journey"—The Duke merely seated her beside him—& resting his hand on her shoulder went on talking— "Where d'ye think you're most popular now, Sir?" said he— "With a small handful of coloured men under the command of Mr Kashua" returned Northangerland—"Long may your popularity be confined to that limited & devoted band" rejoined his dutiful son. "What for, Arthur?" enquired the earl in a gentle insinuating tone. "because you'll never more be fit for the confidence of decent Christians." "Was I once?" "Not that I can remember"—"No, only for such debauched Dogs as Douro—the Dandy" returned Northangerland—"Could you get up a meeting now any where in Angria—or form a Society for the Diffusion of Genuine Vitality?" "I could if my dear young friend Arthur Wellesley would stick the bills as he used to do—" "Arthur Wellesley, instead of sticking the bills now—would stick the whole concern—aye, to the D---l—" "As he does everything else he meddles with" said Northangerland, closing the verbal sparring-match with a gentle nicher. his Son's reply was prevented by the Duchess—who sat between the combatants trembling with anxiety lest this skirmish of words should overstep the brink of mere sarcasm & plunge into invective. "Well" said the Duke, in answer to her silent entreaty for forbearance—"he shall have it his own way this time in consideration that he's done up with riding a few miles in an easy carriage like a bed—but I'll balance the reckoning to-morrow." "Good-night, Mary—" said the earl, rising abruptly

—She followed her father from the room & the Duke, being left by himself, rang for candles & sat down to write a lot of letters.

CHAPTER III

Well, reader, you have not yet heard what business it was that brought Northangerland all that long way from Ellrington House to Hawkscliffe-Hall. but you shall if—you'll suppose it to be morning & step with the earl out of this little parlour where the Duchess is at work sitting by a window surrounded with roses—As soon as ever Zamorna had had his breakfast, he had set off, & the earl was now following him—fortunately he met him on the steps at the front door—leaning against the pillar & enjoying the morning sunshine & the prospect of his wild-park but half reclaimed from the forest—for one tranquil moment before—starting for a day-long campaign in the fields—"Where are you going, Arthur?" asked the earl—"To that wood beyond the river." "What to do there?" "To see some young trees transplanted"—"Will there be an earthquake if you defer that important matter until I have spoken a word with you on a trivial business of my own?"—"perhaps not, what have you to say—?" Northangerland did not immediately answer—he paused either from reluctance to commence or from a wish to ascertain that all was quiet & safe around, & that no intruder was nigh—The Hall behind was empty, the grounds in front were still dewy & solitary—He & his son-in-law stood by themselves—there was no listener—"Well, why don't you begin?" repeated Zamorna, who was whistling carelessly & evincing no inclination to attach special importance to the coming communication. When our own minds are intensely occupied with a subject, we are apt to imagine that those near us are able to pry into our thoughts. the side-glance with which Northangerland viewed his son was strange & dubious & distorted. At last he said in a remarkable tone "I wish to know how my daughter Caroline is?" "She was very well when I saw her last" replied the Duke of Zamorna—not moving a muscle but looking straight before him at the waving & peaked hills which marked the unclouded horizon. There was another pause, Zamorna began his whistle again—it was more studiedly careless than before—for whereas it had just flowed occasionally into a pensive strain—it now only mimicked rattling & reckless airs—broken into fragments.

"My daughter must be grown" continued Northangerland— "Yes, healthy children always grow." "Do you know anything about the progress of her studies, is she well educated—?" "I took care that she should be provided with good masters—& from their report I should imagine she has made very considerable proficiency for her age." "Does she evince any talent? musical talent she ought to inherit?" "I like her voice" answered Zamorna "& she plays well enough too for a child—" Northangerland took out a pocket book—he seemed to calculate in silence for a moment, & writing down the result with a silver pencil-case—he returned the book to his pocket, quietly remarking "Caroline is fifteen years old." "Aye, her birthday was the first or second of this month, was it not?" returned Zamorna. "She told me her age the other day—I was surprised, I thought she had hardly been more than twelve or thirteen." "She looks childish then, does she?" "Why no—she is well-grown & tall—but time in some cases cheats us—it seems only yesterday when she was quite a little girl." "Time has cheated me" said the earl—there was another pause—Zamorna descended the steps—"Well, good morning" said he—"I'll leave you for the present." he was moving off—but the earl followed him. "Where is my daughter?" asked he—"I wish to see her." "O, by all means —we can ride over this afternoon—the House is not above three miles off." "She must have a separate establishment instantly" pursued the earl. "She has—" said Zamorna. "That is, in conjunction with her mother"—"I shall either have Seldon-House—or Eden Hall fitted up for her—" continued his Lordship, without heeding this remark. He & his son-in-law were now pacing slowly through the grounds side by side—Zamorna fell a little into the rear—his straw hat was drawn over his eyes & it was not easy to tell with what kind of a glance he regarded his father-in-law.

"Who is to go with her & take care of her?" he asked after a few minutes silence—"Do you mean to retire into the North or South yourself & take up your abode at Eden-Hall or Seldon-House?" "Perhaps I may." "Indeed, & will Zenobia adopt her— & allow the girl to live under the same roof without the penalty of a daily chastisement—?" "Don't know—if they can't agree, Caroline must marry—but I think you once told me she was not pretty." "Did I? Well, tastes differ, but the girl is a mere child, she may improve—in the meantime—to talk of marrying her, is rather good—I admire the idea—if she were my Daughter, Sir— she should not marry these ten years—but the whole scheme sounds excessively raw, just like one of your fantastic expensive whims— about establishments—you know nothing of management nor of the value of money, you never did—" "She must be established— she must have her own servants & carriage & allowance" repeated the earl—"Fudge!" said the Duke impatiently—"I have spoken to Streaton & matters are in train" continued his father-in-law in a deliberate tone. "Unbusiness-like, senseless, ostentation!" was the reply—"Have you calculated the expense, Sir?" "No—I've only calculated the fitness of things." "Pshaw!"—Both Gentlemen pursued their path in silence—Northangerland's face looked serene but extremely obstinate—Zamorna could compose his features but not his eye—it was restless & glittering—"Well" he said, after the lapse of some minutes "Do as you like—Caroline is your Daughter not mine, but you go to work strangely, that is according to my notions as to how a young susceptible Girl ought to be managed—" "I thought you said she was a mere child—" "I said, or I meant to say, I considered her as such—She may think herself almost a woman—but take your own way—give her this separate establishment—give her money & servants & equipages—& see what will be the upshot—" Northangerland spoke not—his son-in-law continued.

"It would be only like you—like your unaccountable frantic folly to surround her with French Society or Italian if you could get it. If the circle in which you lavished your own early youth were now in existence, I verily believe you'd allow Caroline to move as a Queen in its centre."

"Could my little Daughter be the Queen of such a Circle?" asked Northangerland—"you said she had no beauty & you spoke as if her talents were only ordinary."

"There" replied his Son "that question confirms what I say—Sir" he continued, stopping & looking full at Northangerland—"aye" speaking with marked emphasis—"If your fear is that Caroline will not have beauty sufficient to attract licentiousness, & imagination warm enough to understand approaches—to meet them & kindle at them, & a mind & passions strong enough to carry her a long way in the career of dissipation if she once enters it—set yourself at rest, for she is or will be fit for all this & much more."

"You may as well drop that assumed tone" said Northangerland, squinting directly at his comrade—"You must be aware that I know your Royal Grace & cannot for a moment be deluded into the supposition that you are a Saint or even a repentant Sinner."

"I'm not affecting either Saintship or repentance" replied the Duke "& I'm well aware that you know me—but I happen to have taken some pains with the education of Miss Vernon—She has grown up an interesting clever Girl & I should be sorry to hear of her turning out no better than she should be—to find that I have been rearing & training a Mistress for some Blackguard Frenchman—& this or something worse would certainly be the result of your plans—I have studied her character—it is one that ought not to be exposed to dazzling temptation—She is at once careless & imaginative—her feelings are mixed with her passions—both are warm & she never reflects—Guidance like yours is not what such a girl ought to have—she could ask you for nothing which you would not grant—Indulgence would foster all her defects. when she found that winning smiles & gentle words passed current for reason & judgement—She would speedily purchase her whole will with that cheap coin, & that will would be as wild as the wildest bird—as fantastic as if the caprice & perversity of her whole sex were concentrated in her single little head & heart."

"Caroline has lived in a very retired way hitherto, has she not?" asked Northangerland—not at all heeding the Duke's sermonizing—"Not actually retired for her age" was the reply. "A Girl with lively spirits & good health needs no company—until it is time for her to be married." "But my daughter will be a little rustic" said the earl. "A milkmaid—she will want manners—when I want to introduce her to the world—" "Introduce her to the world!" repeated Zamorna impatiently. "What confounded folly! & I know in your own mind you are attaching as much importance to the idea of bringing out this half grown school-girl—providing her with an establishment & all that sort of humbug—as if it were an important political manoeuvre on the issue of which the existence of half the nation depended"—"Oh!" replied the earl with a kind of dry, brief laugh "I assure you, you quite underrate my ideas on the subject. as to your political manoeuvres, I care nothing at all about them—but if my Caroline should turn out a fine woman, handsome & clever—she will give me pleasure—I shall once more have a motive for assembling a circle about me to see her mistress & Directress of it"—an impatient "Pshaw!" was Zamorna's sole answer to this. "I expect she will have a taste for splendour" continued the Earl "& she must have the means to gratify it—" "Pray, what income do you intend to allow her?" asked his son. "Ten thousand per annum to begin with!" Zamorna whistled & put his hands in his pockets. After a pause he said "I shall not reason with you—for on this subject you're just a natural born fool incapable of understanding reason—I'll just let you go on your own way without raising a hand either to aid or oppose you— you shall take your little girl just as she is—strip her of her frock & sash & put on a gown & jewels—take away her child's playthings & give her a carriage & an establishment—place her in the midst of one of your unexceptionable Ellrington-House or Eden Hall

coteries—& see what will be the upshot—G–d d––n, I can hardly
be calm about it—well enough do I know what she is now—a
pretty intelligent innocent girl, & well enough can I guess what she
will be some few years hence—a beautiful, dissipated, dissolute
woman—one of your Syrens—your Donna Julias, your Signora
Cecillias—Faugh! Good-morning, Sir—we dine at three—after
dinner we'll take a ride over to see Miss Vernon"—His Grace
jumped over a field wall &, as he walked away very fast, he was
soon out of sight.

CHAPTER IV

Punctually at three o'clock, dinner was served in a large antique
dining-room at Hawkscliffe—whose walls, rich in carved oak &
old pictures, received a warm soft dim glow from the bow-window
screened with amber curtains. While one footman removed the
silver covers from two dishes, & another opened the folding-door
to admit a tall middleaged gentleman—with a very sweet young
lady resting on his arm & another Gentleman walking after—They
seated themselves, & when they were seated there was as much an
air of state about the table as if it had been surrounded by a large
party—instead of this select trio. the Gentlemen, as it happened,
were both very tall—they were both, too, dressed in black—for the
young man had put off the plaid jacket & checked trousers which
it was his pleasure to sport in the morning—& had substituted in
their stead the costume of a well-dressed clergyman—as for the
young lady—very fair neck & arms, well-displayed by a silk dress
made low & with short sleeves—were sufficient of themselves to
throw an air of style & elegance over the party—besides that, her
hair was beautiful & profusely curled & her mien & features were
exceedingly aristocratic & exclusive—very little talk passed during
dinner—the younger Gentleman eat uncommon well—the elder
one trifled a considerable time with a certain mess in a small silver
tureen which he did not eat—the young lady drank wine with her
husband when he asked her, & made no bones of some three or four
glasses of Champagne—The Duke of Zamorna looked as grave as a
judge—there was an air about him not of unhappiness but as if the
cares of a very large family rested on his shoulders—the Duchess
was quiet—she kept glancing at her help-mate from under her
eye-lids. when the cloth was taken away & the servants had left
the room—she asked him if he was well—a superfluous question
one would think to look at his delicate grace's—damask complexion
& athletic form & to listen to his sounding, steady voice—Had he

been in a good humour—he would have answered her question by some laughing banter about her over-anxiety—as it was he simply said he was well. She then enquired if he wished the children to come down. He said—"No—he should hardly have time to attend to them that afternoon—he was going out directly—" "Going out? What for?—there was nothing to call him out—" "Yes, he had a little business to transact—" The Duchess was nettled—but she swallowed her vexation & looked calm upon it—"Very well" said she "your Grace will be back to tea, I presume?"—"Can't promise, indeed, Mary." "Then I had better not expect you till I see you—" "Just so—I'll return as soon as I can"—"Very well" said she, assuming as complacent an air as she possibly could—for her tact told her this was not a time for the display of wife-like petulance & irritation—what would amuse his Grace in one mood, she knew would annoy him in another—So she sat a few minutes longer—made one or two cheerful remarks on the weather & the growth of some young trees his Grace had lately planted near the window—& then quietly left the table—She was rewarded for this attention to the Duke's humours by his rising to open the door for her—he picked up her handkerchief, too, which she had dropped, & as he returned it to her he favoured her with a peculiar look & smile—which as good as said he thought she was looking very handsome that afternoon. Mrs Wellesley considered that glance sufficient compensation for a momentary chagrin—therefore she went into her drawing-room &, sitting down to the piano, soothed away the remains of irritation with sundry soft songs—& solemn psalm tunes which, better than gayer music, suited her own fine melancholy voice.

She did not know where Northangerland & Zamorna were going, nor who it was that occupied their minds, or she would not have sung at all—most probably, could she have divined the keen interest which each took in little Caroline Vernon, she would have sat down & cryed—it is well for us that we cannot read the hearts of our nearest friends, & it is an old saying "where Ignorance is bliss 'tis folly to be wise", & if it makes us happy to believe that those we love unreservedly give us in return affections unshared by another—why should the veil be withdrawn & a triumphant rival be revealed to us? The Duchess of Zamorna knew that such a person as Miss Vernon existed—but she had never seen her—she imagined that Northangerland thought & cared little about her—& as to Zamorna, the two ideas of Caroline & the Duke never entered her head at the same time.

While Mrs Wellesley sung to herself "Has sorrow thy young days shaded?" & while the sound of her piano came through closed doors with faint sweet effect, Mr Wellesley junr & Mr Percy Senior sat staring opposite to each other like two bulls. They didn't seem to have a word to say, not a single word—but Mr Wellesley manifested a disposition to take a good deal of wine, much more than was customary with him, & Mr Percy seemed to be mixing & swallowing a number of little tumblers of brandy & water. at last Mr Wellesley asked Mr Percy whether he meant "to stir his stumps that afternoon or not?" Mr Percy said he felt very well where he was, but, however, as the thing must be done some day he thought they had better shog. Mr Wellesley intimated that it was not his intention to make any further objection, & that therefore Mr Percy should have his way, but he further insinuated that that way was the direct road to hell & that he wished with all his heart Mr Percy had already reached the end of his journey, only it was a pity a poor foolish little thing like Caroline Vernon should be forced to trot off along with him—"You, I suppose" said Mr Percy drily "would have taken her to heaven—now I've an odd sort of a crotchetty notion that the Girl will be safer in Hell with me than in Heaven with Thee—friend Arthur—" "You consider my plan of education defective, I suppose?" said his Grace with the air of a schoolmaster. "rather" was the reply—"You're drinking too much Brandy & water" pursued the royal Mentor. "& you have had quite enough champagne" responded his friend—"Then we'd better both be moving" suggested the Duke, & he rose, rung the bell & ordered Horses—neither of them were quite steady when they mounted their saddles &, unattended by servants, started from the front door at a mad gallop as if they were chasing wildfire.

People are not always in the same mood of mind, & thus, though Northangerland & Zamorna had been on the point of quarrelling in the morning—they were wondrous friends this afternoon—quite jovial—the little disagreement between them as to the mode of conducting Miss Caroline's future education was allowed to rest, & indeed Miss Caroline herself seemed quite forgotten—her name was never mentioned as they rode on through sombre Hawks-cliffe—talking fast & high & sometimes laughing loud—I don't mean to say that Northangerland laughed loud, but Zamorna did very frequently—for a little while it was Ellrington & Douro resuscitated—whether champagne & brandy had any hand in bringing about this change I can't pretend to decide—However, neither of them were [?ree], they were only gay—their wits were all about them, but they were sparkling.

We little know what fortune the next breath of wind may blow

us, what strange visitor the next moment may bring to our door—
So Lady Louisa Vernon may be thinking just now—as she sits by
her fireside in this very secluded house whose casements are darkened by the boughs of large trees—it is near seven o'clock & the
cloudy evening it [is] closing in somewhat comfortless & chill—
more like October than July—Her ladyship consequently has the
vapours, in fact she has had them all day—she imagines herself
very ill—though what her ailments are she can't distinctly say—
so she sits up-stairs in her dressing-room, with her head reclined on
a pillow & some drops & a smelling-bottle close at hand—did she
but know what step was now near her door—even at her threshold
—she would hasten to change her dress & comb her hair—for in
that untidy deshabille—with that pouting look & those dishevelled
tresses—her ladyship looks haggard.

"I must go to bed, Elise—I can't bear to sit up any longer"
says she to her French maid who is sewing in a window recess
near—"But your ladyship will have your gown tryed on first"
answered the girl. "It is nearly finished."

"Oh no! nonsense! what is the use of making gowns for me? who
will see me wear them?—my God! such barbarous usage as I
receive [from] that man who has no heart!"

"Ah Madame!" interposed Elise "He has a heart—don't doubt
it—attendre un peu—Monsieur loves you jusqu'à folie."

"Do you think so, Elise?" "I do, he looks at you so fondly—"
"He never looks at me at all—I look at him." "But when your back
is turned, Madame—then he measures you with his eyes—" "Aye,
scornfully."

"Non, avec tendresse—avec ivresse." "Then why doesn't he
speak?—I'm sure I've told him often enough that I'm very fond
of him—that I adore him, though he is so cold & proud & tyran-
nical & cruel." "C'est trop modeste" replied Elise very sagely—
apparently this remark struck her ladyship in a ludicrous point of
view—she burst into a laugh. "I can't quite swallow that either"
said she. "You are almost an idiot, Elise—I daresay you think he
loves you too—Ecoutez la fille—c'est un homme dur—quant'a
l'amour il ne sait guère qu'est ce que c'est—il regarde les femmes
comme des esclaves—il s'amuse de leur beautè pour un instant,
et alors il les abandonne—il faut haïr un tel homme et l'eviter, et
moi je le haïs—beaucoup—oui, je le deteste—Hèla! combien il est
different de mon Alexandre—Elise, souvenez-vous de mon Alexandre—du beau Northangerland!" "C'etait fort gentil" responded
Elise. "Gentil!" ejaculated her ladyship. "Elise, c'etait un ange!
il me semble que je le vois dans ce chambre mème—avec ses yeux

bleus, sa physiognomy qui exprimait tant de douceur—et son front de marbre environnè des cheveux chataignes—" "Mais le Duc a des cheveux chataignes aussi" interposed Elise—"Pas comme ceux de mon preux Percy" sighed her faithful ladyship, and she continued in her own tongue "Percy had so much soul, such a fine taste—il sut apprecier mes talens—he gave me trinkets—his first present was a brooch like a heart—set with diamonds. in return he asked for a lock of his lovely Allan's hair—my name was Allan then, Elise—I sent him such a long streaming tress—he knew how to receive the gift like a gentleman, he had it plaited into a watch-guard—& the next night I acted at the Fidena theatre—when I came onto the stage—there he was in a box just opposite—with the black braid across his breast. Ah Elise! talk of handsome men! he was irresistible in those days. Stronger & stouter than he is now—such a chest he shewed & he used to wear a green Newmarket coat & a white beaver—well, anything became him—But you can't think, Elise, how all the gentlemen admired me when I was a girl—what crowds used to come to the Theatre to see me act—& how they used to cheer me—but he never did, he only looked—Oh, just as if he worshipped me—& when I used to clasp my hands & raise my eyes just so—& shake back my hair in this way—which I often did in singing solemn things—he seemed as if he could hardly hold from coming on to the stage & falling at my feet, & I enjoyed that—the other Actresses did envy me so—there was a woman called Morton whom I always hated, so much—I could have run a spit through her—or stuck her full of needles any-day, & she & I once quarrelled about him—it was in the green-room—she was dressing for a character—she took one of her slippers & flung it at me—I got all my fingers into her hair & I twisted them round & round & pulled & dragged till she was almost in fits with pain—I never heard anybody scream so—the manager tryed to get me off —but he couldn't—nor could any-body else—at last he said "Call Mr Percy, he's in the Saloon". Alexander came—but he had had a good deal of wine—& Price, the manager, couldn't rightly make him comprehend what he wanted him for—He was in a swearing passionate humour & he threatened to shoot Price for attempting to humbug him as he said—he took out his pistols & cocked them —the green-room was crowded with actors & actresses & Dressers —every-body was so terrified—they appealed to me to go & pacify him—I was so proud—to shew my influence before them all—I knew that, drunk as he was, I could turn him round my little finger—so at last I left Morton with her head almost bald & her hair torn out by handfuls—& went to the Drover—I believe he would really have shot Price if I hadn't stopped him—but I soon changed his mood—you can't think, Elise, what power I had over him—I told him I was frightened at his pistols & began to cry—he laughed at me first, & when I cryed more he put them away—Lord George, poor man, was standing by watching—I did used to like to coquette between Vernon & Percy—Ah, what fun I had in those days—but it's all gone by now—nothing but this dismal house & that Garden with its high wall like a convent, & those great dark trees always groaning & rustling—whatever have I done to be punished so!" Her ladyship began to sob—"Monseigneur will change all this" suggested Elise.

"No—no—that's worst of all" returned her ladyship—"He does not know how to change—such an impenetrable iron-man—so austere & sarcastic—I can't tell how it is I always feel glad when he comes—I always wish for the day to come round when he will visit us again—& every time I hope he'll be kinder & less stately & laconic & abrupt, & yet, when he does come, I'm so tormented with mortification & disappointment—it's all nonsense looking into his handsome face—his eyes won't kindle any more than if they were of glass—it's quite in vain that I go & stand by him & speak low, he won't bend to listen to me—though I'm so much less than him—sometimes, when he bids me good bye, I press his hand tenderly—sometimes I'm very cold, distant, it makes no difference—he does not seem to notice the change—Sometimes I try to provoke him, for if he would only be exceedingly savage—I might fall into great terror & faint, & then perhaps he would pity me afterwards—but he won't be provoked—he smiles as if he were amused at my anger, & that smile of his is so, I don't know what—vexing, maddening—it makes him look so handsome—& yet it tears ones heart with passion—I could draw my nails down his face—till I had scraped it bare of flesh—I could give him some arsenic in a glass of wine—O, I wish something would happen—that I could get a better hold of him. I wish he would fall desperately sick in this house—or shoot himself by accident so that he would be obliged to stay here & let me nurse him. it would take down his pride if he were so weak that he could do nothing for himself—& then, if I did everything for him, he would be thankful —perhaps he would begin to take a pleasure in having me with him—& I could sing his kind of songs & seem to be very gentle—he'd love me, I'm sure he would—if he didn't & if he refused to let me wait on him—I'd come at night to his room & choke him while he was asleep—smother him with the pillow—as Mr Ambler used to smother me when he had the part of Othello & I had that

of Desdemona—I wonder if I daren't do such a thing—" Her
ladyship paused for a minute as if to meditate on the moral problem she had thus proposed for her own solution—ere long she proceeded—

"I should like to know now—how he behaves towards people
that he does love—if indeed he ever loved anybody—his wife now
—does he always keep her at a distance? & they say he has a
mistress or two—I've heard all sorts of queer stories about him—
it's very odd—perhaps he likes only blondes—but no, Miss Gordon
was as dark as me—& eight years ago what a talk there was in the
North about him & her—he was a mere school-boy then, to be sure
—I remember hearing Vernon & O'Connor bantering Mr Gordon
about it, & they joked him for being cut out by a beardless lad—
Gordon did not like the joke, he was an ill-tempered man that—
Elise, you're making my gown too long, you know I always like
rather short skirts—Morton used to wear long ones because, as I
often told her, she'd ugly thick ankles—my ankles now were a
straw-breadth less in circumference than Julia Corelli's, who was
the first figurante at the Verdopolitan Opera—How vexed Corelli
was that night that we measured & my ankles were found to be
slimmer than hers—then neither she nor any of the other Dancers
could put on my shoes—& its a fact, Elise—a Colonel in the Army
stole a little black satin slipper of mine & wore it a whole week in
his cap as a trophy—poor man, Percy challenged him—they had
such a dreadful duel across a table—he was shot dead—they called
him Markham, Sydenham Markham, he was an Angrian." "Madame, c'est finie" said Elise, holding up the gown which she had
just completed—"O well, put it away, I can't try it on, I don't feel
equal to the fatigue—my head's so bad & I've such a faintness—&
such a fidgetty restlessness—what's that noise?—" A distant sound
of music in a room below was heard—a piano very well touched—
"Dear—Dear—! there's Caroline strumming over that vile instrument again—I really *cannot* bear it & so it doesn't signify—that girl
quite distracts me with the racket she keeps up—" Here her ladyship rose very nimbly & going to the top of the stairs which was just
outside her room—called out with much power of lungs—"Caroline! Caroline!" no answer except a brilliant bravura run down the
keys of the Piano—"Caroline!" was reiterated—"give up playing
this instant! you know how ill I have been all day & yet you will act
in this way"—a remarkably merry jig responded to her ladyship's
objurgations—& a voice was heard far off saying "it will do you
good, mamma!" "You are very insolent" cried the fair Invalid,
leaning over the bannisters. "Your impertinence is beyond bearing.

You will suffer for it one day—you little forward piece, do as I
bid you—" "So I will, directly" replied the voice. "I have only to
play Jim Crow & then" & Jim Crow was played with due spirit
& sprightliness—Her ladyship cryed once again with a volume of
voice that filled the whole house "D'ye know I'm your mother,
Madam? you seem to think you are grown out of my control—
you have given yourself fine impertinent airs of late—it's high
time your behaviour was looked to, I think—Do you hear me?"
While Jim Crow was yet jigging his round, while lady Vernon, bent
above the bannisters, was still shaking the little passage with her
voice, the wire of the door-bell vibrated, there was a loud ring &
thereafter a pealing aristocratic knock—Jim Crow & Lady Louisa
were silenced simultaneously. her ladyship affected a precipitate
retreat to her dressing-room—it seemed also as if Miss Caroline were
making herself scarce—for there was a slight rustle & run heard
below—as of someone retiring to hidden regions.

I need not say who stood without, of course it was Messrs Percy
& Wellesley—in due time the door was opened to them by a
man-servant & they walked straight in to the drawing-room—
there was no one to receive them in that appartment—but it was
evident somebody had lately been there—An open piano—& a
sheet of music with a grinning capering nigger lithographed on the
title-page—a capital good-fire, an easy chair drawn close to it—all
gave direct evidence to that effect—His Grace the Duke of Zamorna looked warily round—nothing alive met his eye—he drew off
his gloves & as he folded them one in the other he walked to the
hearth—Mr Percy was already bent over a little work-table near
the easy chair—pushed out of sight under a drapery of half-
finished embroidery there was a book—Percy drew it out—it was
a novel & by no means a religious one either—While Northangerland was turning over the leaves, Zamorna rung the bell. "Where is
lady Vernon?" he asked of the servant who answered it. "Her ladyship will be down stairs directly. I have told her your Grace is
here." "And where is Miss Caroline—?" The servant hesitated—
"She's in the passage" he said, half-smiling & looking behind him
—"She's rather bashful I think because—there's company with
your Grace—" "Tell Miss Vernon I wish to see her, will you
Copper" replied the Duke—the footman withdrew—presently the
Door re-opened very slowly—Northangerland started & walked
quickly to the window where he stood gazing intently into the
Garden—meantime he heard Zamorna say "How do you do?" in
his deep low voice—most thrilling when it is most subdued—
Somebody answered "very well thank ye" in an accent indicating

girlish mauvaise honte mixed with pleasure. there was then a pause
—Northangerland turned round—it was getting dusk—but daylight enough remained to shew him distinctly what sort of a person
it was that had entered the room & was now standing by the fire-
place looking as if she did not exactly know whether to sit down or
to remain on her feet—he saw a girl of fifteen, exceedingly well
grown & well-made of her age—not thin or delicate—but on the
contrary very healthy & very plump—her face was smiling, she
had fine dark eyelashes & very handsome eyes—her hair was almost black—it curled as Nature let it, though it was now long &
thick enough to be trained according to the established rules of art
—this young lady's dress by no means accorded with her years &
stature, the short-sleeved frock, worked trousers & streaming sash
would better have suited the age of nine or ten than that of fifteen
—I have intimated that she was somewhat bashful, & so she was
—for she would neither look Zamorna nor Northangerland in the
face—the fire & the rug were the objects of her fixed contemplation—yet it was evident that it was only the bashfulness of a raw
school-girl unused to society—the dimpled cheek & arch animated
eye indicated a constitutional vivacity which a very little encouragement would soon foster into sprightly play enough—perhaps it was
a thing rather to be repressed than fostered.

"Won't you sit down?" said Zamorna, placing a seat near her—
she sat down—"Is your mamma very well?" he continued. "I
don't know—she's never been down to day —& so I haven't seen
her." "Indeed! you should have gone up-stairs & asked her how
she did." "I did ask Elise, & she said Madame had the migraine"
—Zamorna smiled & Northangerland smiled too—"What have
you been doing then all day?" continued the Duke. "Why, I've
been drawing & sewing. I couldn't practise because ma' said it
made her head ache—" "What is Jim Crow doing on the piano
then?" asked Zamorna. Miss Vernon giggled. "I only just jigged
him over once" she replied—"And ma' did fly—she never likes
Jim Crow—" Her Guardian shook his head. "and have you never
walked out this fine day?" he continued—"I was riding on my
pony most of the morning—" "Oh you were! then how did the
French & Italian lessons get on in that case?" "I forgot them" said
Miss Caroline—"Well" pursued the Duke "Look at this Gentleman now & tell me if you know him"—she raised her eyes from the
carpet & turned them furtively on Percy—frolic & shyness was the
mixed expression of her face as she did so—"No" was her first
answer. "Look again" said the Duke, & he stirred the fire—to elicit
a brighter glow over the now darkening appartment—"I do!"

exclaimed Caroline as the flame flashed over Northangerland's pallid features & marble brow—"it's papa!" she said, rising—& without agitation or violent excitement she stepped across the rug towards him—he kissed her, the first minute she only held his hand —& then she put her arms round his neck—& would not leave him for a little while though he seemed oppressed & would have softly put her away—"You remember something of me then?" said the earl at last—loosening her arms. "Yes papa, I do." she did not immediately sit down but walked two or three times across the room, her colour heightened & her respiration hurried.

"Would you like to see lady Vernon to-night?" asked Zamorna of his father-in-law—"no—not to-night—I'd prefer being excused —" but who was to prevent it—rustle & sweep—a silk gown traversed the passage—in she came—"Percy! Percy! Percy!" was her thrice-repeated exclamation—"My own Percy, take me again— Oh, you shall hear all—you shall—but I'm safe now, you'll take care of me—I've been true to you, however"—"God bless me, I shall be choked!" ejaculated the earl—as the little woman vehemently kissed & embraced him—"I never can stand this" he continued—"Louisa, just be quiet, will ye?" "But you don't knòw what I've suffered" cryed her ladyship "nor what I've had to contend against—he has used me so ill & all because I couldn't forget you"—"What, the Duke there?" asked Percy. "Yes—yes, save me from him—take me away with you—I cannot exist if I remain in his power any longer." "Ma', what a fool you are" interposed Caroline very angrily. "Does he make love to you?" said the earl. "He persecutes me—he acts in a shameful—unmanly brutal manner—" "You've lost your senses, Ma'" said Miss Vernon. "Percy, you love me, I'm sure you do" continued her ladyship. "O, protect me—I'll tell you more when we've got away from this dreadful place." "She'll tell you lies!" exclaimed Caroline in burning indignation—"She's just got up a scene, papa—to make you think she's treated cruelly—& nobody ever says a word against her." "My own child is prejudiced & made to scorn me" sobbed the little actress. "every source of happiness I have in the world is poisoned & all from his revenge, because—" "Have done, Mama" said Caroline promptly. "if you are not quiet, I shall take you up-stairs"—"You hear how she talks" cryed her ladyship—"my own daughter, my Darling Caroline—ruined, miserably ruined—" "Papa—Mama's not fit to be out of her room, is she?" again interrupted Miss Vernon. "let me take her in my arms & carry her up-stairs, I can do it easily"—"I'll tell you all—" almost screamed her ladyship—"I'll lay bare the whole vile scheme—your father shall know you, Miss—what you are & what *he* is—I never mentioned the subject before, but I've noticed, & I've laid it all up & nobody shall hinder me from proclaiming your baseness aloud—" "Good heavens, this won't do" said Caroline, flushing up red as fire. "Be silent, Mother—I hardly know what you mean, but you seem to be possessed—not another word now—Go to bed, do— come, I'll help you to your room." "Don't fawn—don't coax" cried the infuriated little woman—"it's too late—I've made up my mind —Percy, your Daughter is a bold impudent minx—young as she is —she's a—" she could not finish the sentence. Caroline fairly capsized her mother—took her in her arms & carried her out of the room—she was heard in the passage calling Elise & firmly ordering her to undress her lady & put her to bed—She locked the door of her bed-room & then she came down stairs with the key in her hand. She did not seem to be aware that she had done anything at all extraordinary—but she looked very much distressed & excited.

"Papa, don't believe Mamma" were her first words as she returned to the drawing-room—"she talks such mad stuff when she's in a passion—& sometimes she seems as if she hated me—I can't tell why—I'm never insolent to her, I only make fun sometimes." Miss Vernon lost command over herself & burst into tears—His Grace of Zamorna, who had been all this time a perfectly silent spectator of the whole strange scene—rose & left the room—Miss Vernon sobbed more bitterly when he was gone—"Come here, Caroline" said Northangerland—he placed his daughter on a seat close to his side & patted her curled hair soothingly—she gave up crying very soon & said, smiling, she didn't care a fig about it now, only mamma was so queer & vexatious—"Never mind her, Caroline" said the earl "always come to me when she's cross. I can't do with your spirit being broken by such termagant whims, you shall leave her & come & live with me"—"I wonder what in the world Mama would do quite by her self" said Caroline. "She would fret away to nothing, but to speak truth, papa, I really don't mind her scolding. I'm so used to it—it does not break my spirit at all— only she set off on a new tack just now—I did not expect it—she never talked in that way before—" "What did she mean, Caroline?" "I can't tell, I've almost forgot what she did say now, papa —but it put me into a regular passion." "It was something about the Duke of Zamorna" said Northangerland quietly. Caroline's excitement returned. "She's lost her senses" she said. "Such wild, mad trash." "What mad trash?" asked Percy. "I heard nothing but half sentences which amazed me, I confess, but certainly didn't inform me." "Nor me either" replied Miss Vernon "only I had an idea she was going to tell some tremendous lie." "Of what nature?" "I can't tell, papa—I know nothing about it—Ma' vexed me—" There was a little pause—then Northangerland said

"Your mother used to be fond of you, Caroline, when you were a little child—What is the reason of this change? do you provoke her unnecessarily?" "I never provoked her but when she provoked me worse—She's like as if she was angry with me for growing tall—& when I want to be dressed more like a woman & to have scarfs & veils & such things, it does vex her so—then, when she's raving & calling me vain & conceited—a hussey—I can't help sometimes letting her hear a bit of the real truth." "& what do you call the real truth?" "Why, I tell her that's she's jealous of me—because people will think she is old if she has such a woman as I am for her daughter—" "Who tells you you are a woman, Caroline?" "Elise Touquet—she says I'm quite old enough to have gowns & a watch & a desk & a maid to wait on me—I wish I might, I'm quite tired of wearing frocks & sashes, & indeed, papa—they're only fit for little girls—Lord Enara's children came here once—& the eldest, Senora Maria as they call her, was quite fashionable compared to me & she's only fourteen—more than a year younger than I am— when the Duke of Zamorna gave me a pony—Mamma would hardly let me have a riding habit—she said a skirt was quite sufficient for a child—but his Grace said I should have one & a beaver too—& I got them. Oh, how Ma' did go on—she said the Duke of Zamorna was sending me to ruin as fast as I could go—& whenever I put them on to ride out—she plays up beautifully. You shall see me wear them to-morrow—pa—if I may ride somewhere with you—do let me." Northangerland smiled. "Are you very fond of Hawkscliffe?" he asked after a brief interval of silence—"Yes, I like it well enough—only I want to travel somewhere—I should like, when winter comes, to go to Adrianopolis—& if I were a rich lady, I'd have parties & go to the theatre & opera every night—as Lady Castlereagh does—do you know Lady Castlereagh, papa?" "I've seen her." "And have you seen Lady Thornton too?" "Yes." "Well—they're both very fine fashionable ladies arn't they?" "Yes." "And very handsome too—do you think them handsome?" "Yes." "Which is the best looking, & what are they like? I often ask the Duke of Zamorna what they're like, but he'll tell me nothing except that Lady Castlereagh is very pale & that Lady Thornton is extremely stout—but Elise Touquet, who was Lady Castlereagh's dress-maker once, says they're beautiful—do you think them so?" "Lady Thornton is very well" replied Northangerland. "Well, but has she dark eyes & a Grecian Nose—?" "I forget" answered the earl. "I should like to be exceedingly beautiful" pursued Caroline. "And to be very tall—a great deal taller than I am—& slender. I think I'm a great deal too fat—& fair, my neck is so brown Ma' says I'm quite a negro—& I should like to be dashing & to be very much admired—who is the best-looking woman in Verdopolis, Papa?" Northangerland was considerably non-plussed. "There are so many, it's difficult to say" he answered. "Your head runs very much on these things, Caroline—" "Yes, when I walk out in the wood by myself—I build Castles in the air & I fancy all how beautiful & rich I should like to be & what sort of adventures I should like to happen to me—For you know, papa, I don't want a smooth commonplace life but something strange & unusual." "Do you talk in this way to the Duke of Zamorna?" asked Mr Percy. "In what way, papa?" "Do you tell him what kind of adventures you should like to encounter & what sort of nose & eyes you should choose to have?" "Not exactly—I sometimes say I'm sorry I'm not handsome & that I wish a fairy would bring me a ring or a magician would appear & give me a talisman like Alladdin's lamp that I could get everything I want." "And pray what does his Grace say?" "He says Time & Patience will do much—that plain Girls—with manners & sense, often make passable women, & that he thinks reading Lord Byron has half-turned my head." "You do read Lord Byron then?"—"Yes, indeed I do, & Lord Byron & Bonaparte & the Duke of Wellington & Lord Edward Fitzgerald are the four best men that ever lived." "Lord Edward Fitzgerald, who the D——l is he?" asked the earl in momentary astonishment. "A young nobleman that Moore wrote a life about" was the reply. "A regular Grand Republican—he would have rebelled against a thousand Tyrants if they'd dared to trample on him—he went to America because he wouldn't be hectored over in England, & he travelled in the American Forests, & at night he used to sleep on the ground like Miss Martineau." "Like Miss Martineau!" exclaimed the earl, again astounded out of his propriety. "Yes, papa—a lady who must have been the cleverest woman that ever lived—she travelled like a man—to find out the best way of Governing a country. She thought a republic far the best, & so do I—I wish I had been born an Athenian—I would have married Alcibiades—or else Alexander the Great—I do like Alexander the Great—" "But Alexander the Great was not an Athenian, neither was he a republican" interposed the earl in a resigned deliberate tone. "No, Papa, he was a Macedonian I know—& a King too—but he was a right kind of King—Martial & not luxurious & indolent—he had such power

over all his army—they never dared mutiny against him though he
made them suffer such hardships, & he was such an heroic man—
Haephaestion was nearly as nice as he was, though I always think
he was such a tall slender elegant man—Alexander was little—
what a pity!" "What other favourites have you?" asked Mr Percy
—the answer was not quite what he expected. Miss Caroline, who
probably had not often an opportunity of talking so unreservedly,
seemed to warm with her subject. in reply to her excellent father's
question, the pent-up enthusiasm of her heart came out in full tide
—the reader will pardon any little inconsistencies he may observe
in the young lady's declaration.

"O Papa, I like a great many people! but soldiers most of all, I
do adore soldiers! I like Lord Arundel, papa, & lord Castlereagh
& General Thornton, & General Henri Fernando di Enara, & I
like all Gallant Rebels—I like the Angrians because they rebelled
in a way against the Verdopolitans—Mr Warner is an Insurgent &
so I like him—as to Lord Arundel, he's the finest man that can be
—I saw a picture of him once on horseback, he was reining in his
charger & turning round with his hand stretched out—speaking to
his regiment—as he did before he charged at Leyden—he was so
handsome!" "He is silly" whispered Northangerland very faintly.
"What Pa!" "He is silly—my dear—a big man—but nearly idiotic
—calfish—quite heavy & poor-spirited—don't mention him"—
Caroline looked as blank as the wall, she was silent for a time.
"Bah!" said she at last "that's disagreeable—" & she curled her
lip as if nauseating the recollection of him. Arundel was clearly done
for in her opinion.

"You are a soldier, aren't you, Papa?" she said erelong—"No,
not at all"—"But you are a Rebel & a Republican" continued Miss
Vernon. "I know that, for I've read it over & over again." "Those
facts won't deny" said Northangerland—She clapped her hands &
her eyes sparkled with delight—"And you're a Pirate & a Demo-
crat too" said she—"You scorn worn-out Constitutions & old rotten Monarchies—& you're a terror to those ancient Doddered
Kings up at Verdopolis—that crazy ill-tempered old fellow
Alexander—dreads you I know—he swears broad Scotch whenever your name is mentioned—do get up an insurrection, Papa, &
send all those doting constitutionalists to Jericho." "Rather good
for a young lady that has been educated under royal auspices"
remarked Northangerland. "I suppose these ideas on politics have
been carefully instilled into you by his Grace of Zamorna, eh
Caroline?" "No, I've taken them all up myself, they're just my
unbiassed principles"—"Good!" again said the earl & he could

not help laughing quietly—while he added in an undertone "I suppose it's hereditary then—rebellion runs in the blood."

By this time the reader will have acquired a slight idea of the state of Miss Caroline Vernon's mental development, & will have perceived that it was as yet only in the chrysalis form, that in fact she was not altogether so sage, steady & consistent as her best friends might have wished—in plain terms, Mademoiselle was evidently raw, flighty & romantic, only there was a something about her, a flashing of her eye, an earnestness, almost an impetu-osity of manner which I cannot convey in words, & which yet if seen must have irresistibly impressed the spectator that she had something of an original & peculiar character under all her rubbish of sentiment & inconsequence—it conveyed the idea—that though she told a great deal, rattled on—let out—concealed neither feeling nor opinion—neither predeliction nor antipathy—it was still just possible that something might remain behind, which she did not choose to tell nor even to hint at—I don't mean to say that she'd any love secret, or hate-secret either—but she'd sensations some-where that were stronger than fancy or romance—she shewed it when she stepped across the rug to give her father a kiss & could not leave him for a minute—She shewed it when she blushed at what her mother said, &, in desperation lest she should let out more, whisked her out of the room in a whirlwind—all the rattle about Alexander & Alcibiades & Lord Arundel & Edward Fitzgeral was of course humbug, the rawest hash of ideas imagin-able—yet she could talk better sense if she liked, & often did do so when she was persuading her mother to reason. Miss Caroline had a fund of vanity about her but it was not yet excited—she really did not know that she was good-looking, but rather on the contrary considered herself unfortunately plain—sometimes indeed she ven-tured to think that she had a nice foot & ankle & a very little hand —but then, alas, her form was not half as slight & sylph-like enough for beauty according to her notions of beauty, which of course, like those of all school-girls, approached the farthest extreme of the thread-paper & May-pole style—in fact she was made like a model —She could not but be graceful in her movements, she was so perfect in her proportions—As to her splendid eyes—dark enough & large enough to set twenty poets raving about them—her spark-ling even teeth—& her profuse tresses, glossy, curling & waving— she never counted these as beauties, they were nothing. she had neither rosy cheeks nor a straight grecian nose, nor an Alabaster neck—& so she sorrowfully thought to herself she could never be considered as a pretty girl—besides, no one ever praised her, ever hinted that she possessed a charm. her mother was always throwing out strong insinuations to the contrary, & as to her royal Guardian, he either smiled in silence when she appealed to him, or uttered some brief & grave admonition to think less of physical & more of moral attraction—

It was after eleven when Caroline bade her papa good-night— His Grace the Duke did not make his appearance again that evening in the drawing-room. Miss Vernon wondered often what he was doing so long up-stairs—but he did not come—the fact is he was not up-stairs but comfortably enough seated in the dining-room quite alone with his hands in his pockets—a brace of candles on the table by him, unsnuffed & consequently burning rather dismally dim—It would seem he was listening with considerable attention to the various little movements in the house—for the moment the drawing-room door opened, he rose—& when Caroline's "good-night, Papa" had been softly spoken & her step had crossed the passage & tripped up the stair-case—Mr Wellesley emerged from his retreat—He went straight to the appartment Miss Vernon had just left—"Well?" said he, appearing suddenly before the eyes of his father-in-law. "Have ye told her?" "Not exactly", returned the earl "But I will do to-morrow." "You mean it still, then?" continued his Grace with a look indicating thunder—"Of course I do." "Your a d——d noodle" was the mild reply, & therewith the door banged to & the Majesty of Angria vanished.

CHAPTER V

To-morrow came—the young lover of rebels & regicides awoke as happy as could be—Her father, whom she had so long dreamed about, was at last come. One of her dearest wishes had been realized, & why might not others in due course of time?—while Elise Touquet dressed her hair, she sat pondering over a reverie of romance—something so delicious—yet so undefined—I will not say that it was all Love—yet neither will I affirm that Love was entirely excluded there-from—something there was of a Hero—yet a nameless, a formless, a mystic being—a dread shadow—that crowded upon Miss Vernon's soul—haunted her day & night when she had nothing useful to occupy her head or her hands—I almost think she gave him the name of Ferdinand Alonzo FitzAdolphus, but I don't know—the fact was he frequently changed his designation—being sometimes no more than simple Charles Seymour or Edward Clifford, & at other times soaring to the titles of Harold, Aurelius Rinaldo, Duke of Montmorency di Valdacella—a very fine man no doubt—though whether he was to have golden or raven hair or straight or aquiline proboscis she had not quite decided—however, he was to drive all before him in the way of fighting—to conquer the world & build himself a city like Babylon —only it was to be in the moorish style—& there was to be a palace called the Alhambra—where Mr Harold Aurelius was to live, taking upon himself the title of Caliph, & she, Miss C. Vernon, the professor of Republican principles, was to be his chief Lady & to be called the Sultana Zara-Esmerelda—with at least a hundred slaves to do her bidding—as for the gardens of roses & the Halls of Marble & the diamonds & fine pearls & the rubies—it would be vanity to attempt a description of such heavenly sights— the reader must task his imagination & try if he can conceive them.

In the course of that day Miss Vernon got something better to think of than the crudities of her over-stretched fancy—that Day was an era in her life—She was no longer to be a child—she was to be acknowledged a woman—farewell to captivity where she had been reared like a bird—her father was come to release her, & she was to go with him to be his Daughter & his Darling—The earl's splendid Houses, which she had never entered, were to be opened to her & she was to be almost mistress there—She was to have servants & wealth, & whatever delighted her eye she was to ask for & receive—She was to enter life, to see society—to Live all the Winter in a great City—Verdopolis—to be dressed as gaily as the gayest ladies—to have jewels of her own—to vie even with those demi-goddesses, the Ladies Castlereagh & Thornton—it was too much, she could hardly realize it—it may be supposed from her enthusiastic character that she received this intelligence with transport—that as Northangerland unfolded these coming glories to her view—she expressed her delight & astonishment & gratitude in terms of extacy, but the fact is she sat by the table with her head on her hand listening to it all with a very grave face—Pleased she was, of course—but she made no stir—it was rather too important a matter to clap her hands about—she took it soberly—When the earl told her she must get all in readiness to set off early to-morrow —she said "To-morrow Papa!" & looked up with an excited glance—"Yes, early in the morning—" "Does mamma know?" "I shall tell her." "I hope she'll not take it to heart" said Caroline. "Let her go with us for about a week or so, papa—it will be so dreary to leave her behind—" "She's not under my control" replied Percy. "Well" continued Miss Vernon "if she were not so excessively perverse & bad to manage as she is, I'm sure she might

get leave to go—but she makes the Duke of Zamorna think she's
out of her wits by her frantic ways of going on—& he says she's not
fit to be let loose on society—actually, papa, one day when the
Duke was dining with us, she started up without speaking a word
in the middle of dinner & flew at him with a knife—he could hardly
get the knife from her afterwards—he was obliged to tell Cooper to
hold her hands—& another time she brought him a glass of wine &
he just tasted it & threw the rest at the back of the fire—he looked
full at her & mamma began to cry & scream as if somebody was
killing her—She's always contriving to get laudanum & prussic
acid & such trash—she says she'll murder either him or herself—&
I'm afraid if she's left quite alone, she'll really do some harm."
"She'll not hurt herself" replied the earl "and as to Zamorna, I
think he's able to mind his own affairs—" "Well" said Miss Vernon
"I must go & tell Elise to pack up—" & she jumped up & danced
away as if care laid but lightly on her.

I believe the date of these present transactions is July—but I've
almost forgotten—if so, summer-days were not gone by—nor summer evenings either, & it is with summer evenings that I have now
to do—Miss Caroline Vernon alias Percy had finished her packing-
up & she had finished her Bed too—She was in the drawing-room
alone & she was sitting in the window-seat as quiet as a picture—I
don't exactly know where the other inmates of the house were, but
I believe Mr Percy was with Lady Louisa, & Lady Louisa was in
her own room—as sick as you please—whether, at this particular
moment of time, she was playing the Houri or the Fiend—kissing
or cuffing the earl, her lover, I really can't tell—neither, as far as
I know, does it much signify. However, be that as it may, Caroline
was by herself & also she was very still & pensive—What else could
she be, looking out on to the quiet walks of that Garden—& on to
that Lawn where the Moon is already beginning dimly to shine—a
summer moon is yellow, & a summer evening sky is often more
softly blue than pen can describe—especially when that same moon
is but newly risen, & when its orb hangs low & large over a back-
ground of fading hills & looks into your face from under the boughs
of Forest Beeches—Miss Caroline Vernon is to leave Hawkscliffe
to-morrow—so she is drinking in all its beauties to-night—so you
suppose reader, but you're mistaken—if you observe her eyes, she's
not gazing, she's watching—she's not contemplating the moon—
she's following the motions of that person who, for the last half
hour, has been leisurely pacing up & down that gravel-walk at the
bottom of the garden—It is her Guardian & she is considering
whether she shall go & join him & have a bit of talk with him for

the last time—that is, for the last time at Hawkscliffe, she's by no
means contemplating anything like the solemnity of an eternal
separation—This Guardian of hers has a blue frock-coat on, white
inexpugnables & a stiff black stock—consequently he considerably
resembles that angelic existence called a military man—You'll
suppose Miss Vernon considers him handsome—because other
people do—all the ladies in the world, you know, hold the Duke of
Zamorna to be matchless, irresistible—but Miss Vernon doesn't
think him handsome—in fact the question of his charms has never
yet been mooted in her mind—the idea as to whether he is a God
of perfection or a Demon of Defects has not crossed her intellect
once—Neither has she once compared him with other men—He is
himself—a kind of Abstract Isolated Being—quite distinct from
aught beside under the sun—he can't be handsome because he has
nothing at all in common with Messrs Ferdinand Alonzo Fitzadolphus, Harold Aurelius Rinaldo & Company—his complexion
is not like a lady's, nor has he cheeks tinged with transparent roses
—nor glossy golden hair, nor blue eyes—The Duke's whiskers &
moustaches are rather terrible than beautiful—& the Duke's high
mien & upright port & carriage are more awful than fascinating—
& yet Miss Caroline is only theoretically afraid of him—practically,
she is often familiar enough—to play with the Lion's mane is one
of her greatest pleasures—she would play with him now—but he
looks grave & is reading a book.

It seems, however, that Miss Vernon has at length conquered
her timidity—for lo! as the twilight deepens & the garden is all dim
& obscure, she, with her hat on, comes stealing quietly out of the
house—& through the shrubs, the closed blossoms & dewy leaves—
trips like a fairy to meet him—She thought she would surprise him,
so she took a circuit & came behind—She touched his hand before
he was aware—Cast-iron, however, can't be startled, & so no more
was he—"Where did you come from?" said the Guardian, gazing
down from supreme altitude upon his ward—who passed her arm
through his & hung upon him according to her custom when they
walked together—"I saw you walking by yourself & so I thought
I'd come & keep you company" she replied. "Perhaps I don't want
you" said the Duke. "Yes you do, you're smiling—& you've put
your book away as if you meant to talk to me instead of reading."
"Well, are you ready to set off to-morrow?" he asked. "Yes, all is
packed." "And the head & the heart are in as complete a state of
preparation as the trunk, I presume?" continued his Grace. "My
heart is wae"* said Caroline. "At last of all I'm sorry to go—

* An expression often found in the novels of Sir Walter Scott

especially this evening. I was not half so sorry in the middle of the day while I was busy—but now—" "You're tired & therefore low-spirited. well, you'll wake fresh in the morning—& see the matter in a different light—you must mind how you behave, Caroline, when you get out into the world—I shall ask after you sometimes." "Ask after me? you'll see me—I shall come to Victoria-Square almost constantly when you're in Verdopolis"—"You will not be in Verdopolis longer than a few days"—"Where shall I be, then—?" "You will go either to Paris or Fidena or Rossland—" Caroline was silent—"You will enter a new sphere" continued her Guardian "& a new circle of society which will mostly consist of French-People—don't copy the manners of the ladies you see at Paris or Fontainebleau. they are most of them not quite what they should be, they have very free obtrusive manners, & will often be talking to you about love & endeavouring to make you their confidante—you should not listen to their notions on the subject as they are all very vicious & immodest, & as to the men, those you will see will be almost universally gross & polluted—avoid them." Caroline spoke not. "In a year or two your Father will begin to talk of marrying you" continued her Guardian—"& I suppose you think it would be the finest thing in the world to be married—it is not at all impossible that your Father may propose a Frenchman for your Husband—if he does, decline the honour of such a connexion." still Miss Vernon was mute—"Remember always" continued his Grace "that there is one nation under heaven filthier even than the French—that is the Italians—the women of Italy should be excluded from your presence & the men of Italy should be spurned with disgust even from your thoughts." Silence still—Caroline wondered why his Grace talked in that way, he had never been so stern & didactic before.

She wanted to change the conversation* and so, by way of giving it another turn, she asked the Duke whether he would be so kind as to write to her somctimes when she was gone—He said "he did not know—he could not promise—his time was very much occupied." Caroline was again silent, she thought the answer scarcely kind. "Would he never write to her?" she said, after a pause. "Perhaps he might sometimes—there was no impossibility in the case—" again Miss Vernon was disappointed & saddened—his Grace was certainly displeased with her—he was not accustomed to speak so coldly—& instead of holding her hand as he generally

* From this point to the end of the chapter, the text used is the alternative version mentioned in the Introduction (see p. 274). The text of the first draft is printed in the Appendix

did—when she walked with him—he had allowed her arm to drop
—& barely suffered her to walk by his side—"And won't you even
think of me, my Lord?" she said at last. "I shall think of you when
I hear your name, I suppose" replied the Duke—Caroline slack-
ened her pace & dropped behind—this was too bad—she had
always thought herself a Favourite—she found she was mistaken,
her Guardian cared nothing about parting with her—the last
night, when she had thought he would be kinder & fonder than
ever, to treat her so coolly, so austerely! her heart swelled & a tear
or two was forced into her eye. "Now child, where are you?" said
the Duke, turning abruptly—she was only a pace or two behind
him & her handkerchief was at her eyes. "What ails you?" continued his Grace, taking her hand from her face. "A little touch of
sentimentalism about leaving Hawkscliffe, eh?—Come, come, all
will be right to-morrow—" "You don't know me"—said Miss
Vernon—"you think I'm pleased with all kinds of novelties—but
I'm not—" "Stuff! this little fit will go off soon—" His Grace stood
in the moonlight & looked at Miss Vernon & laughed—She turned
away, feeling about as bitter a pang at that moment as she had ever
known in her life—it was the anguish of discovering that her strongest & most genuine feelings were not appreciated—that a person
whom she was disposed to care for intensely—would not condescend
to let her tell him how much she regarded him—would not stoop
to understand her emotions—to enter into them or in the least
degree return them—Stifling her sobs & dashing away her tears as
well as she could, she would have hurried away to the house—but
his Grace said "Caroline!" the tone was not one to be disobeyed—
besides, she felt that if she parted from her Guardian so, without
a reconciliation, she would not sleep that night—so she returned to
him—they were near a little bower with a seat in it—he took her
there & having sat himself down he placed his ward beside him—
he divided her hair from her forehead &, as he smoothed away her
curls—said in a far different tone from what he had hitherto used
—a tone that changed the whole idea of his character "What is all
this little flutter about, Caroline?—tell me now"—Miss Vernon's
answer was plain truth at least. "I'm sorry" said she "that I'm
going to part with you, & still more sorry that you don't care for
parting with me—" "Who told you that I did not care?" asked his
Grace—"You're so cold" said she. "You call me child—& look as
if you despised me." It is probable that the Duke smiled at these
words though it was almost too Dusk to see, for the moon pene-
trated but faintly into the little bower. "Come Caroline" he said,
after a pause "You & I can't afford to quarrel—so we'll be friends

again—now, is all right—?" "I'm afraid you don't care for me" persisted Miss Vernon distrustfully—"Hush!—no more misunderstanding" said the Duke. "What is there to make you doubt whether I care for you now—can you be nearer to me?" All at once Miss Vernon's fears were removed, she was satisfied—it was not the Duke's words but his voice that produced this happy change—there was something in its tone that assured her he did not now at least regard her as a mere child. "Are you cold, Caroline?" he asked. "Does the air feel damp?" "No." "What are you looking at so earnestly, my little girl?" "Only the sky—it seems so full of stars—I shall always remember this night—Oh, I can't bear to go away to-morrow—but I won't think of to-morrow —" Just then a voice was heard in the Garden crying "Miss Caroline! Miss Caroline!" it was Mademoiselle Touquet who had been sent in search of the young lady.

[PART II]

CHAPTER I

We were talking of a young lady of the name of Miss Caroline Vernon who, by herself & her more partial friends, was considered to have pretty nigh finished her education—who consequently was leaving retirement & on the point of taking her station somewhere, in some circles of some order of highly fashionable society—It was in July when affairs reached their climax. it is now November, nearly December, & consequently a period of about four months has lapsed in the interim—We are not to suppose that matters have all this while remained in statu quo—that Miss Caroline has been standing for upwards of a quarter of a year with her foot on the carriage step—her hand on the lackey's arm—her eyes pathetically & sentimentally fixed on the windows & chimneys of the convent-like place she is about to leave for good—all in a cataleptic condition of romantic immutability. No, be assured the young person sighed over Hawkscliffe but once—wept two tears on parting with a Groom & a pony she had been on friendly terms with—wondered thrice what her dear mama would do without anybody to scold, & for four minutes had a childish feeling of pity that she should be left behind—sat a quarter of an hour after the start in a fit of speechless thought she did not account for, & all the rest of the way was as merry as a grig.

One or two instances did indeed occur on that route through

Angria which puzzled her a little—in the first place she wondered
to hear her noble father give orders—whenever they approached a
town, that the carriage should be taken through all sorts of odd,
narrow bye-ways so as to avoid the streets, & when she asked the
reason of this, he told her with a queer sort of smile—that the people
of Angria were so fond of him—he was afraid that a recognition of
the arms on his carriage might be attended with even a troublesome demonstration of their affection—When, towards evening,
they entered the City of Zamorna, which they were necessitated to
pass through because it lay directly in their way—Miss Caroline
was surprised to hear all sorts of groans & yells uttered by grimy
looking persons in paper-caps—who seemed to gather about the
lamp-posts & by the shop windows as they passed along. She was
almost confounded when, as the carriage stopped a moment at a
large hotel—an odd kind of howl broke from a crowd of persons
who had quickly collected by the door, & at the same instant the
window of plate-glass on her right-hand shivered with a crash, &
an ordinary-sized brick-bat leapt through it & settled on her lap—
spoiling a pretty silk frock which she had on & breaking a locket
which was a keep-sake & which she very much valued.

It will now be a natural question in the reader's mind, what has
Miss Vernon been about during the last four months—has she seen
the world? has she had any adventures? is she just the same as she
was? is there any change? where has she been? where is she now?
How does the globe stand in relation to her, & she in relation to the
globe? During the last four months, reader, Miss Vernon has been
at Paris—her father had a crotchety undefined notion that it was
necessary she should go there to acquire a perfect finish, & in fact
he was right in that notion—for Paris was the only place to give her
what he wished her to have—the ton, the air, the elegance of those
who were highest on the summit of fashion—she changed fast in
the Atmosphere of Paris—She saw quickly into many things that
were dark to her before. She learnt life & unlearnt much fiction—
the illusions of retirement were laid aside with a smile, & she wondered at her own rawness when she discovered the difference
between the world's reality & her childhood romance—She had a
way of thinking to herself & of comparing what she saw with what
she had imagined. by dint of shrewd observation she made dis-
coveries concerning men & things which sometimes astounded her,
& she got hold of books which helped her in the pursuit of knowledge—she lost her simplicity by this means & she grew knowing
& in a sense reflective—However, she had talent enough to draw
from her theories a safe practice, & there was something in her

mind or heart or imagination which, after all, filled her with wholesome contempt for the goings on of the bright refined world around her—People who have been brought up in retirement don't soon get hackneyed to society—they often retain a notion that they are better than those about—that they are not of their sort, & that it would be a letting down to them to give the slightest glimpse of their real nature & genuine feelings to the chance associates of a ball-room.

Of course Miss Vernon did not forget that there was such a thing in the world as Love. She heard a great deal of talk about that article amongst the gallant monsieurs & no less gallant madames around her—neither did she omit to notice whether she had the power of inspiring that superfine passion—Caroline soon learnt that she was a very attractive being & that she had that power in a very high degree. She was told that her eyes were beautiful—that her voice was sweet—that her complexion was clear & fine—that her brow was a model—she was told all this without mystery, without reserve—the assurance flattered her highly & made her face burn with pleasure, & when, by degrees, she ascertained that few even of the prettiest women in Paris were her equals—she began to feel a certain consciousness of power, a certain security of pleasing, more delicious & satisfactory than words can describe—The circumstance of her high parentage gave her eclat: Northangerland is a kind of King in Paris—& his youthful daughter received from her father's followers the homage of a princess—in the French fashion, & they hailed her as a rising & guiding star of their faction —the Dupin's, the Barra's & the Bernadottes—called her a new planet in the Republican Heaven—they knew what an ornament to their dark revolutionary Coteries a lady so young & so intelligent must be—& it will be no matter of wonder to the reader when I say that Miss Vernon received their homage & imbibed their sentiments & gave heart & soul to the politics of the Faction that called her Father its Leader—

Her career at Paris soon assumed the aspect of a Triumph. after she had made one or two eloquent & enthusiastic declarations of her adoration for republics & her scorn of monarchies—she began to be claimed by the Jeunes Gens of Paris as their queen & Goddess —she had not yet experience enough to know what sort of a Circle she had gathered round her, though she guessed that some of those Sons of Young France who thronged about her sofa in the saloon & crowded her box at the Theatre were little better than regular mauvais sujets—very different, indeed, were these from the polite, grimacing men-monkeys of the old regime—there was a touch of

Watercolour by Charlotte Brontë dated 6 October 1839, contemporary with the writing of *Caroline Vernon*

the unvarnished Blackguard about most of them—infinitely more
gross & unequivocal than is to be met with in any other capital of
civilized Europe—Miss Vernon, who was tolerably independent in
her movements because her Father restrained her very little &
seemed to trust with a kind of blind confidence to I know not what
conservative principle in his daughter's mind—Miss Vernon I say
—often at concerts & nightly soirèes—met & mingled with troops
of these men. She also met with a single individual—who was as
bad as the worst of the Jeunes Gens—He was not a Frenchman,
however, but a countryman of her Father's & a friend of his first
youth—I allude to Hector Montmorency Esqre.

She had seen Mr Montmorency first at an evening party at Sir
John Denard's Hotel in a Grand Reunion of the Northangerland
Faction—as usual her seat was surrounded by the youngest &
maddest men in the room, & as usual she was engaged in impassioned & declamatory conversation upon the desperate policies of
her party, & whenever she turned her head, she noticed a man of
middle age, of strong form—& peculiar, sinister, sardonic aspect—
standing with his arms folded, gazing hard at her. She heard him
ask Sir John Denard in the French language who the D——l cette
jolie petite fille à cheveux noirs could possibly be—she did not hear
Sir John's reply—it was whispered—but directly afterwards she
was aware of some one leaning over her chair-back—she looked
up, Mr Montmorency's face was bending over her—"My young
lady" said he "I have been looking at you for a good while, & I
wondered what on earth it could possibly be in your face that
reminded me so of old times—I see how it is now as I've learnt
your name—you're Northangerland's & Louisa's child I understand, hum—you're like to do them credit. I admire this—it's a bit
in Augusta's way—I dare say y'er father admires it too—you're in
a good line—nice young men you have about you. could you find
in your heart to leave them a minute & take my arm—for a little
promenade down the room?"—Mr Montmorency offered her his
arm with the manner & look of a Gentleman of the West*—it was
accepted, for strange to say Miss Vernon rather liked him—there
was an off-hand gallantry in his mien which took her fancy at
once—When the honourable Hector had got her to himself—he
began to talk to her in a half free, half confidential strain—he
bantered her on her numerous train of admirers, he said one or two
warm words about her beauty—he tryed to sound the depths of her
moral principles—& when his experienced eye & ear soon discovered that she was no Frenchwoman & no callous & hackneyed &

* By inference, of Irish temperament

well-skilled Flirt—that his hints did not take & his inuendos were not understood—he changed the conversation & began to inquire about her education—where she had been reared & how she had got along in the world. Miss Vernon was as communicative as possible—she chattered now with great glee about her mother & her masters—about Angria & Hawkscliffe—but she made no reference to her Guardian. Mr Montmorency inquired whether she was at all acquainted with the Duke of Zamorna. She said she was a little—Mr Montmorency then said he supposed the Duke wrote to her sometimes—she said no, never—Mr Montmorency said he wondered at that, & meantime he looked into Miss Vernon's face as narrowly as if her features had been the Lord's prayer written within the compass of a sixpence—there was nothing particular to be seen except a smooth brunette complexion & dark eyes looking at the carpet—Mr Montmorency remarked—in a random, careless way—"that the Duke was a sad hand in some things". Miss Vernon asked in what—"about women" replied Montmorency bluntly & coarsely. after a momentary pause, she said "indeed!" & that was all she did say—but she felt such a sensation of astonishment, such an electrical stunning surprise that she hardly knew for a minute where [she] was. it was the oddest—the most novel thing in the world for her to hear her Guardian's character freely canvassed—to hear such an opinion expressed concerning him, as that Mr Montmorency had so nonchalantly uttered, was strange to a degree. it gave a shock to her ordinary way of thinking—it revolutionized her ideas—she walked on through the room, but she forgot for a moment who was round her or what she was doing. "Did you never hear that before?" asked Mr Montmorency after a considerable interval which he had spent humming a tune—which a lady was singing to a harp.—"No"—"Did you never guess it? has not his Grace a rakish impudent air with him?" "No, quite different." "What, he sports the Simon Pure, does he?" "He's generally rather grave & strict." "Did you like him?" "No—yes—no—not much—" "That's queer, several young ladies have liked him a good deal too well—I daresay you've seen Miss Laury now, as you lived at Hawkscliffe—" "Yes"—"She's his Mistress"—"indeed!" repeated Miss Vernon—after the same interregnum of appalled surprise—"The Duchess has not particularly easy times of it" continued Montmorency, "she's your half-sister, you know—" "Yes." "But she knew what she had to expect before she married him, for when he was marquis of Douro he was the most consumed black-guard in Verdopolis—" Miss Caroline in silence heard &, in spite of the dismay she felt, wished to hear more

—there is a wild interest in thus suddenly seeing the light rush in on the character—of one well known to our eyes—but, as we discover, utterly unknown to our minds—& the young lady's feelings were not exactly painful, they were strange, new & startling—she was getting to the bottom of an unsounded sea, & lighting on rocks she had not guessed at—Mr Montmorency said no more in that conversation—& he left Miss Vernon to muse over what he had communicated—what his exact aim was in thus speaking of the Duke of Zamorna it would be difficult to say—he added no violent abuse of him, nor did he attempt to debase his character as he might easily have done—He left the subject there. Whether his words lingered in the mind of the listener I can hardly say, I believe they did—for though she never broached the matter to any one else, or again applied to him for further information—yet she looked into magazines & into newspapers—she read every passage & every scrap she could find that referred to Zamorna & Douro— she weighed & balanced & thought over every thing & in a little while, though removed five hundred miles from the individual whose character she studied—she had learnt all that other people know of him, & saw him in his real light—no longer as a Philosopher & Apostle—but as—I need not tell my readers what they know or at least can guess. Thus did Zamorna cease to be an abstract principle in her mind—thus did she discover that he was a man vicious like other men—perhaps I should say more than other men—with passions that sometimes controlled him—with propensities that were often stronger than his reason—with feelings that could be reached by beauty—with a corruption that could be roused by opposition—She thought of him no longer as "the Stoic of the woods, the man without a tear" but as—don't let us bother ourselves with considering as what.

When Miss Vernon had been about a quarter of a year in Paris, she seemed to grow tired of the society there—She begged her father to let her go home as she called it, meaning to Verdopolis— Strange to say, the earl appeared disquieted at this request—at first he would not listen to it—she refused to attend the soirèes, frequent the Opera—she said she had seen enough of the French people—she spent the evenings with her father & played & sung to him—Northangerland grew very fond of her—& as she continued her entreaties to be allowed to go home, often soliciting him with tears in her eyes—he slowly gave way, & at length yielded a hard-wrung & tardy assent—but though his reluctance was overruled, it was evidently not removed—he would not hear her talk of Verdopolis—he evidently hated the thoughts of her return thither— he seemed disturbed when she secluded herself from society & declined invitations. All this, to an ordinary observer, would seem to partake of a tincture of insanity—for well did his lordship know the character of those circles in which his daughter moved—the corrupt morality, the cold systematic dissoluteness universal there—yet he never hinted a word of advice or warning to her—he let her go seemingly unwatched & unguarded—He shewed no anxiety about her till the moment when she wished to withdraw from the vitiated atmosphere—& then he demurred & frowned as though she had asked to enter into some scene of temptation instead of to retire from it. in spite of this seeming paradox, however, the probability is that Northangerland knew what he was about—he was well acquainted with the materials he had to work upon—&, as he said himself, he deemed that Caroline was safer as the Prima-donna of a Parisian saloon—than as the recluse of a remote Lodge in Angria —But Northangerland is not proof to a soft imploring voice & a mournful look—Miss Vernon loathed Paris & pined after Verdopolis—& she got her way—one evening, as she kissed her Father good-night, he said she might give what orders she pleased on the subject of departure—a very few days after, a packet freighted with the earl & his household were steaming across the channel.

CHAPTER II

Northangerland was puzzled & uncomfortable when he got his daughter to Verdopolis—he evidently did not like her to remain there—He never looked settled or easy—there was no present impediment to her residing at Ellrington-House—because the Countess happened to be then staying in Angria—but when Zenobia came home, Caroline must quit—other considerations also disturbed the calm of the earl's soul—by him untold, by his daughter unsuspected.

Mr Percy has his own peculiar way of expressing his dissatisfaction, & rarely does a word drop from his lips—which bears the tone of expostulation, of reproof or even command—He does it all by looks & movements which the initiated only can understand. Miss Vernon discerned a difference in him, but could not dive to the origin thereof—when she came to him with her bonnet on, dressed to go out & looking, as her mirror had told her, very pretty & elegant—he did not express even his usual modicum of quiet pleasure—he would insinuate that the day was wet or cold—or windy, or in some way unfit for an excursion—when she came to his drawing-room after tea & said she had no where to go & was come to spend the evening with him—he gave her no welcome—hardly smiled, only sat passive—now his Daughter Mary would have keenly felt such coldness—& would have met it with silent pride & a bitter regret, but Caroline had no such acute sensitiveness, no such subtle perception—instead of taking the matter home to herself—& ascribing this change to something she had done or left undone, she attributed it to her father's being ill or in low spirits— or annoyed with business. She could not at all conceive that he was angry with her. & accordingly, in her caressing way, she would put her arms round his neck & kiss him—& though the earl received the kiss more like a peice of sculpture than anything living —Caroline, instead of retiring in silence, would begin some prattle to amuse him, & when that failed of its effect—she would try music —& when he asked her to give up playing—she would laugh & tell him he was as capricious as mamma, & when nothing at all would do, she would take a book—sit down at his feet & read to herself—She was so engaged one evening when Mr Percy said after a long—long lapse of silence—"Are you not tired of Verdopolis, Caroline?" "No" was the answer—"I think you had better leave it" continued the earl—"Leave it, papa! when winter is just coming on?" "Yes." "I have not been here three weeks" said Miss Vernon—"You will be as well in the country" replied her father—"Parliament is going to meet & the season is beginning" pursued she—"Are you such a monarchist?" asked the earl, "are you going to attend the debates—& take interest in the Divisions?" "No, but Town will be full." "I thought you had had enough of fashion & gaiety at Paris—" "Yes, but I want to see Verdopolitan gaiety—" "Eden-Cottage is ready" remarked Northangerland. "Eden-Cottage, papa?"—"Yes, a place near Fidena." "Do you wish to send me there, papa?" "Yes." "How soon?" "To-morrow, the day after if you like"—Miss Vernon's face assumed an expression—which it would be scarcely correct to describe by softer epithets than dour & [*illegible*]—she said with an emphatic slow enunciation "I should *not* like to go to Eden Cottage." Northangerland made no remark—"I hate the North especially" she pursued "& have no partiality to the Scotch." "Seldon-House is ready too" said Mr Percy. "Seldon-House is more disagreeable to me still" replied his daughter—"You had better reconcile yourself either to Fidena or Rossland" suggested Mr Percy quietly. "I feel an invincible repugnance to both" was her reply—uttered with a self sustained haughtiness of tone almost ludicrous from such lips. Northangerland is long-suffering. "You shall choose your own retreat" said he. "But as it is arranged that you cannot long remain in Verdopolis, it will be well to decide soon—" "I would rather remain at Ellrington-House" responded Mademoiselle Vernon. "I think I intimated that would not be convenient" answered her Father—"I would remain another month" said she. "Caroline!" said a warning voice. Percy's light eyes flickered— "Papa, you are not kind." no reply followed—"Will I be banished to Fidena?" muttered the rebellious girl to herself. Mr Percy's visual organs began to play at cross-purposes—he did not like to be withstood in this way—"You may as well kill me as send me to live by myself at the end of the world where I know no one except Denard—an old grey badger—" "It is optional whether you go to Fidena" returned Percy—"I said you might choose your station—" "Then I'll go to live at Paquena in Angria, you have a house there, papa." "Out of the question" said the earl. "I'll go back to Hawkscliffe then." "Oh no, you can't have the choice of that—you are not wanted there." "I'll live in Adrianopolis then, at Northangerland-House." "No"—"You said I might have my choice, papa, & you contradict me in everything—" "Eden-Cottage is the place" murmured Percy. "Do let me stay in Verdopolis" exclaimed Miss Vernon after a pause of swelling vexation—"Papa, do be kind & forgive me if I'm cross." Starting up, she fell to the argument of kisses & she also cryed abundantly. none but Louisa Vernon or Louisa Vernon's daughter would have thought of kissing Northangerland in his present mood—"Just tell me why you won't let me stay, papa" she continued. "What have I done to offend you? —I only ask for another month or another fortnight—just to see some of my friends when they come to Verdopolis—" "What friends, Caroline?" "Well, only two or three, & I saw in the newspaper this morning that they were expected to arrive in town very soon"—"Who, Caroline?" "Well, some of the Angrians, Mr Warner & General Enara & Lord Castlereagh. I've seen them many a time, you know papa, & it would be only civil to stop & call on them—" "Won't do, Caroline" returned the earl—"Why won't it do, papa? it's only natural—to wish to be civil, is it—?" "You don't wish to be civil—& we'd better say no more about it— I prefer your going to Fidena the day after to-morrow at the farthest." Caroline sat mute for a moment, then she said "So, I am *not* to stay in Verdopolis & I *am* to go to Eden-Cottage." "Thou hast said it" was the reply—"Very well" she rejoined quickly. She sat looking at the fire for another minute—then she got up, lit her candle, said good night & walked up-stairs to bed—as she was leaving the room, she accidentally hit her forehead a good knock against the side of the door—a considerable organ rose in an instant—she said nothing, but walked on—when she got to her own room the candle fell from its socket & was extinguished—she neither picked it up nor rang for another—She undressed in the dark & went to bed ditto. As she lay alone—with night round her —she began to weep—sobs were audible a long time from her pillow—sobs not of grief—but of baffled will & smothered passion —She could hardly abide to be thus thwarted, to be thus forced from Verdopolis when she would have given her ears to be allowed to stay—The reader will ask why she had set her heart so fixedly on this point. I'll tell him plainly & make no mystery of it.

The fact was she wanted to see her guardian. For weeks, almost months, she had felt an invincible inclination to behold him again by the new lights Mr Montmorency had given her as to his character. There had also been much secret enjoyment in her mind from the idea of shewing herself to him—improved as she knew she was after her long sojourn in Paris—She had been longing for the time of his arrival in Town to come—& that very morning she had seen it announced in the newspaper that orders had been given to prepare Wellesley-House for the immediate reception of his Grace the Duke of Zamorna & suite, & that the noble Duke was expected in Verdopolis before the end of the week—After reading this, Miss Caroline had spent the whole morning walking in the Garden behind Ellrington-House reflecting on the interesting future she imagined to be in store for her—picturing the particulars of her first interview with Mr Wellesley—fancying what he would say— whether he would look as if he thought her pretty—whether he would ask her to come & see him at Wellesley House—if she should be introduced to the Duchess—how the Duchess would treat her— what she would be like—how she would be dressed, etcetera—all this was now put a stop to—cut off—crushed in the bud—& Miss Caroline was thereupon in a horrid bad temper—choked almost with obstinacy & rage & mortification—it seemed to her impossible that she could endure the disappointment—to be torn away from a scene where there was so much of pleasure & exiled into comparative dark—blank solitude—was frightful—how could she live?—After long musing in midnight silence, she said half-aloud "I'll find some way to alter matters" & then she turned on her pillow & went to sleep.

Two or three days elapsed—Miss Vernon, it seemed, had not succeeded in finding a way to alter matters—for, on the second day, she was obliged to leave Ellrington-House, & she took her departure in tearless taciturnity—bidding no one good by except her father, & with him she just shook hands & offered him no kiss—the earl did not half like her look & manner—not that he was afraid of anything tragic—but she seemed neither fretful nor desponding —she had the air of one who had laid a plan & hoped to compass her [*illegible*]. She scrupled not to evince continued & haughty displeasure towards his lordship—& her anger was expressed with all her mother's temerity & acrimony—with something too of her mother's whimsicality—but with none of her fickleness—She seemed quite unconscious of any absurdity in her indignation— though it produced much the same effect as if a squirrel had thought proper to treat a Newfoundland dog with Lofty hauteur— Northangerland smiled when her back was turned—still he perceived that there was character in all this & he felt far from comfortable—However, he had written to Sir John Denard desiring him to watch her during her stay at Eden-Cottage, & he knew that Sir John dared not be a careless Sentinel—The very morning after Miss Vernon's departure—Zenobia—Countess of Northangerland, arrived at Ellrington-House &, in the course of the same day, a Cortège of six carriages conveyed the Duke & Duchess of Zamorna, their children & Household to the Residence in Victoria Square—Mr Percy had made the coast clear only just in time.

CHAPTER III

One day, when the Duke of Zamorna was dressing to go and dine in state at Waterloo-Palace—with some much more respectable company than he was accustomed to associate with, His young man, Mr Rosier, said, as he helped him on with his Sunday coat— "Has your Grace ever noticed that letter on the mantle-piece?" "What letter? no—where did it come from—?" "it's one that I found on your Grace's library-table the day we arrived in town— that's nearly a week ago—& as it seemed to be from a lady I brought it up here intending to mention it to your Grace, & somehow it slipped down between the toilet & the wall, & I forgot it till this morning when I found it again." "You're a blockhead— give me the letter—" It was handed to him. He turned it over & examined the superscription & seal—it was a prettily-folded, satin-paper production—nicely addressed & sealed with the impression of a Cameo—His Grace cracked the pretty classic head—unfolded the document & read.

My Lord Duke
    I am obliged to write to you because I have no other way of

letting you know how uncomfortable everything is—I don't know whether you will expect to find me in Verdopolis—or whether you've ever thought about it—but I'm not there, at least I shall not be there to-morrow—for Papa has settled that I am to go to Eden Cottage near Fidena & live there all my life I suppose— I call this very unreasonable—because I have no fondness for the place & no wish ever to see it—& I know none of the People there except an old plain person called Denard whom I exceedingly dislike—I have tryed all ways to change papa's mind, but he has refused me so often that I think it would seem a want of proper spirit to beg any longer. I intend, therefore, not to submit—but to do what I can't help doing—but I shall let Papa see that I consider him very unkind & that I should be very sorry to treat him in such a way—He was quite different at Paris & seemed as if he had too much sense to contradict people & force them to do things they have a particular objection to—Will your Grace be so kind as to call on Papa—& recommend him to think better of it & let me come back to Verdopolis—it would perhaps be as well to say that very likely I shall do something desperate if I am kept long at Eden-Cottage—I know I cannot bear it—for my whole heart is in Verdopolis—I had formed so many plans which are now all broken up—I wanted to see your Grace—I left France because I was tired of being in a country where I was sure you would not come, & I disliked the thought of the sea being between your Grace & myself—I did not tell papa that this was the reason I wished to remain in Verdopolis—because I was afraid he would think me silly —as he does not know the regard I have for your Grace. I am in a hurry to finish this letter as I wish to send it to Wellesley-House without papa knowing, & then you will find it there when you come—your Grace will excuse faults because I have never been much accustomed to writing letters—though I am nearly sixteen years old—I know I have written in much too childish a way— however, I cannot help it &, if your Grace will believe me, I talk & behave much more like a woman that I did before I went to Paris—& I can say what I mean to say much better in speaking than I can in a letter—This letter, for instance, is all contrary to what I had intended—I had not meant to tell your Grace that I cared at all about you—I had intended to write in a reserved dignified way that you might think I was changed—which I am, I assure you—for I have by no means the same opinion of you that I once had—Now that I recollect myself—it was not from pure friendship that I wished to see you—but chiefly from the desire I had to prove that I had ceased to respect your Grace so much as formerly

—you must have a great deal of cover in your character, which is not a good sign.

I am, my Lord Duke
Your obedient Servant
Caroline Vernon

P.S. I hope you will be so kind as to write to me—I shall count the hours & minutes till I get an answer—if you will write directly, it will reach me the day after tomorrow—do write—my heart aches —I am so sorry & so grieved —I had thought so much about meeting you—but perhaps you don't care much about me & have forgotten how I cryed the evening before I left Hawkscliffe—not that this signified, or is of the least consequence—I hope I can be comfortable whoever forgets me—& of course you have a great many calls on your thought being a sort of King—which is a great pity— I hate Kings—it would conduce to your Glory—if you would make Angria into a commonwealth & make yourself Protector— Republican Principles are very popular in France—*you* are not popular there—I heard you very much spoken against—I never defended you—I don't know why—it seemed as if I disliked to let people know that I was acquainted with you—believe me—Yours respectfully, C.V.

Zamorna having completed the perusal of this profound & original document—smiled & thought a minute—smiled again—popped the epistle into the little drawer of a cabinet which he locked— pulled down his brief black silk waistcoat—adjusted his stock— settled himself in his dress-coat—ran his fingers three times through his hair & took his hat & new light lavender kid gloves—turned a moment to a mirror—backed, erected his head, took a survey of his whole longitude from top to toe—walked down stairs—entered a carriage that was waiting for him—sat back with folded arms & was whirled away to Waterloo Palace—He dined very heartily with a select Gentlemen Party—consisting of his Grace the Duke of Wellington—his Grace the Duke of Fidena—the right honourable the earl of Richton—the right honourable Lord St Clair—General Granville & Sir R. Weaver Pelham—During the repast he was too fully occupied in eating to have time to commit himself much by any marked indecorum of behaviour—& even when the cloth was withdrawn & the wine placed on the table—he comported himself pretty well for some-time, seeming thoughtful & quiet. after a while he began to sip his glass of champagne & crack his walnuts with an air of easy impudence much more consistent with his usual habits

—erelong he was heard to laugh to himself at some steady constitutional conversation going on between General Granville &
Lord St Clair—he likewise leaned back in his chair, stretched his
limbs far under the table & yawned—His Noble Father remarked
to him aside that if he were sleepy he knew the way upstairs to bed
& that most of the guests there present would consider his room
fully an equivalent for his company—he sat still, however, &
before the party were summoned to coffee in the drawing-room,
he had proceeded to the indecent length of winking at Lord
Richton across the table. When the move was made from the
dining-room—instead of following the rest upstairs, he walked
down into the Hall—took his hat—opened the door whistling, to
see if it was a fine night—having ascertained that it was—turned
out into the street without carriage or servant—& walked home
with his hands in his breeches pockets grasping fast hold of a bob
& two [?jayes].

He got home in good time—about eleven o'clock—as sober as a
water-cask—let himself in by the Garden-door at the back of
Wellesley-House—& was ascending the private stair-case in a most
sneaking manner—as if he was afraid of some body hearing him &
wanted to slink to his own den unobserved—when, hark, a door
opened in the little Hall behind him—it was her Grace the Duchess
of Zamorna's drawing-room door—Mr Wellesley had in vain
entered from the Garden like a Thief & trodden across the Hall
like a large Tom-Cat & stepped on his toes like a magnified danc-
ing-master as he ascended the softly carpeted stairs—some person's ears are not to be deceived, & in a quiet hour of the night—
when people are sitting alone—they can hear the dropping of a
pin within doors or the stirring of a leaf without—"Adrian!" said
one below—& Mr Wellesley was obliged to stop midway up the
stairs. "Well, Mary" he replied without turning round or commencing to descend—"Where are you going?" "Up stairs I rather
think, don't I seem to be on that tack?" "Why did you make so
little noise in coming in?" "Do you wish me to thunder at the door
like a battering-ram, or come in like a troop of horse?" "Now that's
nonsense, Adrian—I suppose the fact is you're not well—now just
come down & let me look at you." "Heaven preserve us—there's
no use in resisting—here I am—!" He descended & followed the
Duchess from the Hall to the room to which she retreated—

"Am I all here? do you think?" he continued, presenting himself
before her—"Quite as large as life?" "Yes, Adrian, but—" "but
what?—I presume there's a leg or an arm wanting—or my nose is
gone, or my teeth have taken out a furlough—or the hair of my

head has changed coulour—eh? examine well & see that your wor-ser half is no worse than it was." "There's quite enough of you such as you are" said she "but what's the matter with you? are you sure you've been to Waterloo-Palace?" "where do you think I have been? just let us hear?—keeping some assignation I suppose —if I had, I would not have come home so soon, you may be pretty certain of that—"

"Then you have been only to Waterloo-Palace?"

"I rather think so, I don't remember calling anywhere else—" "And who was there? & why did you come home by yourself without the carriage—did the rest leave when you did?"

"I've got a head-ache, Mary." this was a lie—told to awaken sympathy & elude further cross-examination.

"Have you, Adrian, where?"

"I think I said a *head*-ache, of course it would not be in my great toe."

"And was that the reason you came away so soon?"

"Not exactly: I remembered I had a love-letter to write—" This was pretty near the truth—The Duchess, however, believed the lie & disregarded the truth. the matter was so artfully managed that jest was given for earnest & earnest for jest—"Does your head ache very much?" continued the Duchess—"Deucedly"—"rest it on this cushion—" "Hadn't I better go to bed, Mary?" "Yes, & perhaps if I was to send for Sir Richard Warner—you may have taken cold." "Oh no—not to-night—we'll see to-morrow morning —" "Your eyes—don't look heavy, Adrian"—"but they feel so, just like bullets"—"What kind of a pain is it?" "A shocking bad one." "Adrian, you are laughing—I saw you turn away your head & smile"—His Grace smiled without turning away his head—that smile confessed that his head-ache was a sham. the Duchess caught its meaning quickly—she caught also an expression in his face which indicated that he had changed his mood since he came in & that he was not so anxious to get away from her as he had been—She had been standing before him—she now took his hand—Mary looked prettier than any of her rivals ever did. She had finer fea-tures, a fairer skin—more eloquent eyes—no hand more soft & delicate had ever closed on the Duke's than that which was de-taining him now—He forgot her superiority often & preferred charms which were dim to hers—still she retained the power of wakening him at intervals to a new consciousness of her price—& his Grace would every now & then discover with surprise that he had a treasure always in his arms that he loved better a great deal than the far-sought gems he dived amongst rocks so often to bring up.

"Come, all's right" said his Grace sitting down, & he mentally added "I shall have no time to write a letter to-night. it's perhaps as well let alone." dismissing Caroline Vernon with this thought— he allowed himself to be pleased by her elder & fairer sister, Mary —The Duchess appeared to make no great bustle or exertion in affecting this, nor did she use the least art or agacerie as the French call it—which, indeed, she full well knew, with the subject she had to manage, would have instantly defeated its own end. She simply took a seat near the arm-chair into which his Grace had thrown himself—inclined herself a little towards him—& in a low agree-able voice began to talk on miscellaneous subjects of a household & family nature. She had something to say about her children & some advice to ask. She had also quietly to inquire into his Grace's opinion on one or two political points—& to communicate her own notions respecting divers matters under discussion—notions she never thought of imparting to any living ear except that of her honourable spouse, for in everything like gossip or chit-chat the Duchess of Zamorna is ordinarily the most reserved person im-aginable—to all this the Duke hearkened almost in silence— resting his elbow on the chair & his head on his hand—looking sometimes at the fire & sometimes at his wife—he seemed to take her talk as though it were a kind of pleasant air on a flute—& when she expressed herself with a certain grave naïve simplicity—which is a peculiar characteristic of her familiar conversation—which she seldom uses but can command at will—he did not smile, but gave her a glance which somehow said that those little original touches were his delight. The fact was she could, if she liked, have spoken with much more depth & sense—she could have rounded her periods like a blue if she had had a mind, & discussed topics worthy of a member of parliament, but this suited better—Art was at the bottom of the thing after all—it answered, his Grace set some store on her as she sat telling him everything that came into her mind— in a way which proved that He was the only person in whom she reposed this confidence—now & then—but very seldom raising her eyes to his, & then her warm heart mastered her prudence, & a glow of extreme ardour confessed that he was so dear to her— that she could not long feign indifference or even tranquillity while thus alone with him, close at his side.

Mr Wellesley could not help loving his Mary at such a moment, & telling her so too—& I daresay swearing with deep oaths that he had never loved any other half so well—nor ever seen a face that pleased his eye so much or heard a voice that filled his ear with such sweetness—That night she certainly recalled a Wanderer—

How long it will be before the wish to stray returns again is another thing—Probably circumstances will decide this question—we shall see, if we wait patiently.

CHAPTER IV

Louisa Vernon, sixteen years ago, gave the name of Eden to her romantic cottage at Fidena, not, one would suppose, from any resemblance the place bears to the palmy shades of an Asiatic Paradise—but rather because she there spent her happiest days in the society of her Lover: Mr Percy the Drover—& because that was the scene where she moved as a Queen in the midst of a certain set—& enjoyed that homage & adulation whose recollection she to this day dwells on with fondness, & whose absence she pines over with regret.

It was not with her mother's feelings that Caroline Vernon viewed the place when she arrived there late on a wet & windy November night—too dark to shew her the amphitheatre of Highlands towards which her cottage looked—for the mountains had that evening muffled their brows in clouds—instead of crowning them "with the wandering star".

Caroline, as may be supposed, cherished other feelings towards the place than her mother would have done—other than she herself might very probably have entertained had the circumstances attending her arrival there been somewhat different—had the young lady, for instance, made it her resting-place in the course of a bridal tour—had she come to spend her honeymoon amid that amphitheatre of Highlands towards which the cottage looked— she might have deigned to associate some high or soft sensations with the sight of the dim mountains—only the portals, as it were, to a far wilder region beyond—especially when in an evening "they crowned their blue brows with the wandering star"—But Miss Caroline had arrived on no bridal tour—She had brought no inexpressibly heroic-looking personage as her camarade de voyage, & also her camarade de vie—she came a lonely exile, a persecuted & banished being according to her own notions—& this was her Siberia & not her Eden. Prejudiced thus, she would not for a moment relax in her detestation of the villa & the neighbourhood —Her heaven for that Season she had decided was to be Verdopolis—there were her hopes of pleasure—there were all the human beings on earth in whom she felt any interest—there were those she wished to live for—to dress for—to smile for—when she put on a becoming frock here, what was the good of it—were those great staring mountains any judges of dress?—when she looked pretty, who praised her?—when she came down of an evening to her sitting-room, who was there to laugh with her—to be merry with her?—nothing but arm-chairs & ottomans & a cottage piano—no hope here of happy arrivals, of pleasant rencontres—then she thought if she were but at that moment passing through the folding-door of a saloon at Ellrington-House—perhaps just opposite to her —by the marble fire-place—there would be somebody standing that she should like to see—perhaps nobody else in the room—she had imagined such an interview—she had fancied a certain delight-ful excitement & surprise connected with the event—the Gentle-man would not know her at first—she would be so changed from what she was five months ago—she was not dressed like a child now, nor had she the air & tournure of a child—she would ad-vance with much state—he would perhaps move to her slightly—she would give him a glance—just to be quite certain who it was—it would, of course, be him, & no mistake—& he would have on a blue frock coat & white irreproachables, & would be very much bewhiskered & becurled as he used to be—also his nose would be in no wise diminished or impaired, it would exhibit the same aspect of a tower looking towards ? Lebanon that it had always done—After a silent inspection of two or three minutes, he would begin to see daylight—& then came the recognition—there was a curious un-certainty about this scene in Miss Caroline's imagination—She did not know exactly what his Grace would do or how he would look—perhaps he would only say "what, Miss Vernon, is it you?" & then shake hands—that, the young lady thought, would be sufficient if there was anybody else there—but if not—if she found his Grace in the Saloon alone—such a cool acknowledgement of acquaintanceship would never do—he must call her his little Caroline & must bestow at least one kiss. Of course there was no harm in such a thing, wasn't she his ward, & then there came the outline of an idea of standing on the rug talking to him—looking up sometimes to answer his questions about Paris, & being sensible how little she was near him—She hoped nobody would come into the room, for she remembered very well how much more freely her Guardian used to talk to her when she took a walk with him alone —than when there were other persons by—So far Caroline would get in her reverie, & then something would occur to rouse her, perhaps the tinkling fall of a cinder from the grate—to speak emphatically—it was then dickey with all these dreams—she awoke & found herself at Fidena & knew that Verdopolis & Ellring-ton-House were just three hundred miles off—& that she might wear her heart with wishes—she could neither return to them nor attain the hope of pleasure they held forth. At this crisis, Miss Vernon would sit down & cry, & when a cambric handkerchief had been thoroughly wet, she would cheer up again at the remembrance of the letter she had left at Wellesley House—& commenced another reverie on the effects that profound lucubration was likely to produce—though day after day elapsed & no answer was returned—no messenger came riding in breathless haste—bearing a recall from banishment. She still refused to relinquish this last consolation—She could not believe that the Duke of Zamorna would forget her so utterly as to neglect all notice of her request. But three weeks elapsed & it was scarcely possible to hope any longer—her father had not written—for he was displeased with her—her Guardian had not written—for her sister's charms had succeeded in administering a soft opiate to his memory— which for the time lulled to sleep all recollection of any other female & deadened every faithless wish to roam.

Then did Miss Caroline begin to perceive that she was despised & cast off—even as she herself hid away a dress that she was tired of or a scarf that had become frayed & faded—in deep meditation in the watches of the night, she discerned at first by glimpses & at last clearly—that she was not of that importance to the earl of Northangerland & the Duke of Zamorna which she had vainly supposed herself to be—"I really think" she said to herself doubtfully "that because I am not papa's proper daughter, but only his natural daughter—& mamma was never married to him, he does not care much about me—I suppose he is proud of Mary Henrietta —because she married so highly & is considered so beautiful & elegant—& the Duke of Zamorna—just considers me as a child— Whom he once took a little trouble with in providing her with masters & getting her taught to play a tune on the piano—& to draw in French chalk & to speak with a correct Parisian accent—& to read some hard, dry, stupid, intricate Italian poetry—& now that I'm off his hands—he makes no more account of me than of one of those ricketty little Flowers whom he sometimes used to take on his knee for a few minutes to please Lord Richton. Now this will never do, I can't bear to be considered in this light. But how do I wish him to regard me? what terms should I like to be on with him?—really, I hardly know—let me see. I suppose there's no harm in thinking about it at night to oneself when one can't sleep but is bored to lie awake in bed looking into the dark—& listening to the clock strike hour after hour—" & having thus satisfied herself with the reflection that Silence could have no

Drawing by Charlotte Brontë bearing close resemblance to her authenticated portrait of the Duchess of Zamorna at Alnwick

listener & solitude no watcher—she turned her cheek to her pillow & shrouding her eyes even from the dim outline of a large window which alone relieved the midnight gloom of her chamber— she would proceed thus with her thoughts:

"I do believe I like the Duke of Zamorna very much—I can't exactly tell why—he is not a good man it seems from what Mr Montmorency said—he is not a particularly kind or cheerful man. when I think of it, there were scores of Gentlemen at Paris who were a hundred times more merry & witty & complimentary than ever he was—young Vaudeville & Troupeau said more civil things to me in half an hour than ever he did in all his life.—But still I like him so much—even when he is behaving in this shameful way—I think of him constantly—I thought of him all the time I was in France—I can't help it—I wonder whether—" she paused in her mental soliloquy—raised her head & look[ed] forth into her chamber. all was dark & quiet—She turned again to her pillow —the question which she had thought away returned, urging itself on her mind—"I wonder whether I love him?" "O, I do!" cryed Caroline, starting up in fitful excitement—"I do, & my heart will break—I'm very wicked" she thought, shrinking again under the clothes—"Not so very" suggested a consolatory reflection—"I only love him in this way. I should like always to be with him & to be doing something that would please him—I wish he had no wife—not because I want to be married to him, for that is absurd— but because, if he were a bachelor, he would have fewer to think about & thus there would be more room for me—Mr Montmorency seemed to talk as if my sister Mary was to be pitied—stuff! I can't imagine that—he must have loved her exceedingly when they were first married at any rate, & even now she lives with him & sees him & talks to him—I should like a taste of her unhappiness. if she would be Caroline Vernon for a month & let me be Duchess of Zamorna—if there was such a thing as magic & if his Grace could tell how much I care for him & could know how I am lying awake just now & wishing to see him—I wonder what he would think? perhaps he would laugh at me & say I was a fool. O, why didn't he answer my letter? what makes Papa so cruel? How dark it is— I wish it was morning—the clock is striking only one—I can't go to sleep, I'm so hot & so restless—I could bear now to see a spirit come to my bed-side and ask me what I wanted—wicked or not wicked, I would tell all—& beg it to give me the power to make the Duke of Zamorna like me better than ever he liked any body in the world before—& I would ask it to unmarry him & change the Duchess into Miss Percy again & he should forget her, & she should not be so pretty as she is—& I believe—yes—in spite of fate —he should Love me & be married to me—now then—I'm going mad, but there's the end of it."

Such was Miss Vernon's midnight soliloquy & such was the promising frame of mind into which she had worked herself by the time she had been a month at Fidena. Neglect did not subdue her spirit, it did not weaken her passions—it stung the first into such desperate action that she began to scorn prudence & would have dared anything, reproach, disgrace, disaster, to gain what she longed for—& it worked the latter into such a ferment that she could rest neither day nor night—She could not eat, she could not sleep—she grew thin—she began to contemplate all sorts of strange, wild schemes—She would assume a disguise, she would make her way back to Verdopolis, she would go to Wellesley-House & stand at the door & watch for the Duke of Zamorna to come out—She would go to him hungry, cold & weary—& ask for something—perhaps he would discover who she was, & then surely he would at least pity her. it would not be like him to turn coldly away from his little Caroline—whom he had kissed so kindly when they had last parted on that melancholy night at Hawkscliffe— Having once got a notion like this into her head—Miss Vernon was sufficiently romantic, wilful & infatuated—to have attempted to put it into execution—in fact she had resolved to do so, she had gone so far as to bribe her maid by a present of her watch, a splendid trinket set with diamonds, to procure her a suit of boy's clothes from a tailor's at Fidena—that watch might have been worth two hundred guineas—the value of the clothes was at the utmost six pounds. this was just a slight hereditary touch of lavish folly—with the attire thus dearly purchased—she had determined to array herself on a certain day—slip out of the house unobserved —walk to Fidena—four miles, take the coach there & so make an easy transit to Verdopolis—Such was the stage of mellow maturity at which her wise projects had arrived—when, about ten o'clock one morning, a servant came into her breakfast-room—& laid down on the table beside her coffee-cup a letter—the first, the only one she had received since her arrival at Eden-Cottage. She took it up— she looked at the seal—the direction, the post-mark—the seal was only a wafer-stamp—the direction, a scarcely legible scrawl—the post-mark Free-Town—here was mystery. Miss Caroline was at fault—She could not divine who the letter came from—she looked at it long—she could not bear to break the seal, while there was doubt there was hope—Certainty might crush that hope so rudely—At last she summoned courage, broke it, opened the missive & read.

Wood-House-Cliff—Freetown Novbr 29th

My dear little Caroline.

Miss Vernon read so far—& she let the letter fall on her knee & her head drop forward on to the table—& fairly burst into a flood of tears. this was odd—but romantic young ladies are said to be often unaccountable—Hastily wiping away the tears from her eyes, she snatched the letter up again—looked at it, cryed once more—smiled in the midst of her weeping—rose, walked fast about the room—stopped by the window—& while the letter trembled in the hand that held it, read with dim eyes that still flowed over—the singular epistle that follows:

My dear little Caroline*

Business has called me for a few days to Woodhouse-Cliffe, a place of Mr Warner's in the neighbourhood of Freetown—Freetown is a hundred miles nearer to Fidena than Verdopolis, & the circumstance of closer proximity has reminded me of a certain letter left some weeks ago on the library-table at Wellesley-House —I have not that letter now at hand for, as I recollect, I locked it up in the drawer of a cabinet in my dressing-room, intending to answer it speedily—but the tide changed & all remembrance of the letter was swept away as it receded—now, however, that same fickle tide is flowing back again & bringing the lost scroll with it —No great injury has been done by this neglect on my part—because I could not fulfil the end for which your letter was written —you wished me to act as intercessor with your Father & persuade him, if possible, to change his mind as to your place of residence, for it seems Eden-Cottage is not to your taste. On this point I have no influence with him—Your father & I never converse about you, Caroline—it would not do at all—It was very well to consult him now & then about your lessons & your masters when you were a little girl—we did not disagree much on those subjects, but since you have begun to think yourself a woman—your guardians have started on a different tack in our notions concerning you—You know your Father's plan—you must have had sufficient experience of it lately at Paris & now at Fidena—You don't know much about mine, & in fact it is as yet in a very unfinished state, scarcely fully comprehended even by its originator—I rather think,

* The text of Zamorna's letter is that of the revised version (which shows a change of pen and possibly a lapse of time) mentioned in the Introduction (see p. 274). The text of the first draft is printed in the Appendix

however, your own mind has anticipated something of its outline—
there were moments now & then at Hawkscliffe when I could
perceive that my ward would have been a constituent of her
Guardian's in case the two schemes had been put to the decision
of a vote, & her late letter bears evidence that the preference has
not quite faded away—I must not omit to notice a saucy line or
two concerning my character—indicating that you have either
been hearing or reading some foolish nonsense on that head—
Caroline, find no fault with it until experience gives you reason so
to do—Foolish little girl! What have you to complain of? not much,
I think—and you wish to see your Guardian again, do you? you
would like another walk with him in the Garden at Hawkscliffe?—
you wish to know if I have forgotten you? Partly—I remember
something of a rather round face with a dimpled childish little chin
& something of a head—very much embarassed by its unreasonable quantity of black curls, seldom arranged in anything like
christian order—but that is all—the picture grows very dim—I
suppose, when I see you again, there will be a change—you tell
me you are grown more of a woman—very likely—I wish you
good-bye. If you are still unhappy at Eden cottage, write and tell
me so—Your's &c.   Zamorna

People in a state of great excitement sometimes take sudden resolves & execute them successfully on the spur of the moment—
which, in their calmer & more sane moments, they would neither
have the phrenzy to conceive nor the courage & promptitude to
put in practice—as somnambulists are said in sleep to cross broken
bridges unhurt, & walk on the leads of houses in safety—where
awake, the consciousness of all the horrors round them would
occasion instant & inevitable destruction. Miss Vernon, having read
the letter & folded it up & committed it to the bosom of her frock—
she then, without standing more than half a minute to deliberate—
left the room, walked quickly & quietly up-stairs—took out a plain
straw bonnet and a large shawl, put them on—changed her thin
satin slippers for a pair of walking shoes—unlocked a small drawer
in her bureau—took therefrom a few sovereigns—slipped them into
a little velvet bag—drew on her gloves—walked down stairs very
lightly & very nimbly—crossed the hall, opened the front door—
shut it quickly after her—passed up a plantation, out at a wicket
gate—entered the high road—set her face towards Fidena with an
intrepid, cheerful, unagitated air, kept the crown of the causeway,
and in about an hour was at the door of the General Coach Office
asking at what time a coach would start for Free-town—the answer

was that there were conveyances in that direction almost every hour of the day—& that the Verdopolitan Mail was just going out. She took her place & paid her fare—entered the vehicle & before any one at Eden Cottage was aware of her absence—was already a good stage on the road to Wood-house-Cliff. Here was something more than the Devil to pay—a voluntary elopement without a companion—alone entirely of her own free-will—on the deliberation of a single moment that letter had so crowded her brain with thoughts, with hopes, with recollections & anticipations—had so fired her heart with an unconquerable desire to reach & see the absent writer—that she could not have lived through another day of passive captivity—there was nothing for it but flight—the bird saw its cage open—beheld a free sky—remembered its own remote Isle & grove & nest—heard in spirit a voice call it to come—felt its pinion nerved with impatient energy, launched into air & was gone—Miss Vernon did not reflect, did not repent, did not fear—Through the whole day & night her journey lasted, she had no moment of misgiving—some would have trembled from the novelty of their situation, some would have quailed under the reproaches of prudence—some would have sickened at the dread of a cold or displeased reception at their journey's end—none of these feelings daunted Caroline a whit—she had only one thought, one wish, one aim, one object—to leave Fidena, to reach Freetown—that done, Hell was escaped & Heaven attained—She could not see the blind folly of her undertaking—She had no sense of the erroneous nature of the step—her Will urged it—her Will was her predominant quality & must be obeyed.

CHAPTER V

Mrs Warner, a quiet, nice little woman as every-body knows—had just retired from the dinner-table to her own drawing-room, about six o'clock one winter's evening. it was nearly dark—very still—the first snow had begun to fall that afternoon—& the quiet walks about Woodhouse-Cliffe were seen from the long low windows all white & wildered. Mrs Warner was without a companion— She had left her husband & her husband's prodigious Guest in the dining-room—seated each with a glass before him & decanters & fruit on the table—she walked to the window, looked out a minute, saw that all was cold and cheerless—then came to the fireside, her silk dress rustling as she moved over the soft carpet, sank into a bergère (as the French call it) & sat down alone & calm—her earings only glittering & trembling—her even brow relieved with smooth, braided hair—the very seat of serene good temper.

Mrs Warner did not ring for candles—she expected her footman would bring them soon, & it was her custom to let him choose his own time for doing his work—an easier mistress never existed than she is—A tap was heard at her door—"come in" said the lady, turning round—she thought the candles were come—She was mistaken. Hartley, her footman, indeed appeared—with his silk stockings & his shoulder knots—but he bore no shining emblems of the seven churches which are in Asia. The least thing out of the ordinary routine is a subject of gentle wonderment to Mrs Warner, so she said—"What is the matter, Hartley?" "Nothing, Madam, only a post-chaise has just driven up to the door." "Well, what for?" "Some one has arrived, Madam." "Who is it, Hartley?" "Indeed, madam, I don't know." "Have you shewn them into the dining-room?" "No." "Where then?" "The young person is in the Hall, madam." "Is it some one wanting Mr Warner, do you think?" "No, ma'am, it is a young lady who asked if the Duke of Zamorna were here." Mrs Warner opened her blue eyes a trifle wider—"Indeed, Hartley! What must we do?" "Why, I thought you had better see her first, madam, you might recognise her—I should think from her air she is a person of rank." "Well, but Hartley I have no business with it—His Grace might be displeased, it may be the Duchess or some of those other ladies." What Mrs Warner meant by the term other ladies I leave it to herself to explain—however, she looked vastly puzzled & put about —"What had we best do?" she inquired again, appealing to Hartley for advice. "I really think, Madam, I had better shew her up here—you can then speak to her yourself & inform his Grace of her arrival afterwards." "Well, Hartley, do as you please—I hope it's not the Duchess, that's all—if she's angry about anything it will be very awkward—but she would never come in a post-chaise, that's one comfort." Hartley retired—Mrs Warner remained fidgetting from her arm-chair to her work-table—putting on her gold thimble, taking it off—drawing her foot-stool to her feet—pushing it away—In spite of the post-chaise, she still entertained a lurking dread that the new-comer might be her Mistress, the Duchess—& the Duchess was in Mrs Warner's idea a very awful, haughty, formidable little personage—there was something in the high melancholy look of the royal lady's eyes—which, when Mrs Warner met it, always made her feel uncomfortable & inspired a wish to be anywhere rather than in her presence—Not that they had ever quarelled, nothing of the kind, & her Grace was usually rather con-

spicuously civil to the lady of one of the most powerful men in
Angria—Still, the feeling of restraint did exist & nothing could
remove it—Steps were heard upon the stair-case—Hartley threw
open the pannelled folding-door of the drawing-room—ushered in
the visitor & closed it—first, however, depositing four thick & tall
tapers of wax upon the table—Mrs Warner rose from her arm-
chair, her heart fluttering a little & her nice face—a modest
countenance—exhibiting a trivial discomposure—The first glance
at the stranger almost confirmed her worst fears. She saw a figure
bearing a singular resemblance to the Duchess of Zamorna in air,
size & general outline—a bonnet shaded the face & a large shawl
partially concealed the shape.

"I suppose you are Mrs Warner" said a subdued voice, and the
stranger came slowly forward—"I am" said that lady, quite re-
assured by the rather bashful tone in which those few words were
spoken, & then, as a hesitating silence followed, she continued in
her kind way—"Can I do anything for you? will you sit down?"
The young person took the seat which was offered her. it was
opposite Mrs Warner & the brilliant wax lights shone full in her
face—all remains of apprehension were instantly dissipated—here
was nothing of the delicate, fair & pensive aspect characteristic of
Mary Henrietta—instead of the light shading of pale-brown hair,
there was a profusion of dark tresses crowded under the bonnet—
instead of the thoughtful poetic hazel eye gazing rather than glancing, there was a full black orb, charged with fire, fitful, quick &
restless—for the rest, the face had little bloom but was youthful &
interesting—

"You will be surprised to see me here" said the stranger after a
pause, "but I am come to see the Duke of Zamorna—" this was
said quite frankly—Mrs Warner was again relieved—she hoped
there was nothing wrong, as the young lady seemed so little embarassed in her announcement. "You are acquainted with his
Grace, are you?" she inquired. "O yes" was the reply—"I have
known him for a great many years—but you will wonder who I am,
Mrs Warner—my name is Caroline Vernon, I came by the coach
to Free-Town this afternoon. I was travelling all night." "Miss
Vernon!" exclaimed Mrs Warner. "What! the earl of Northangerland's daughter—O, I am sorry I did not know you—you are
quite welcome here—you should have sent up your name, I am
afraid Hartley was cold & distant to you." "No, not at all—
besides that does not much signify—I have got here at last—I
hope the Duke of Zamorna is not gone away—" "No, he is in
the dining-room." "May I go to him directly? do let me, Mrs

Warner?" Mrs Warner, however, perceiving that she had nothing
to fear from the hauteur of the stranger & experiencing likewise an
inclination to exercise a sort of motherly or elder-sisterly kindness
& protection to so young & artless a person, thought proper to
check this extreme impatience. "No" said she "you shall go up-
stairs first & arrange your dress—you look harassed with travelling
all night"—Caroline glanced at a mirror over the mantlepiece—
she saw that her hair was dishevelled & her face pale & her dress
disarranged—"You are right, Mrs Warner, I will do as you wish
me—may I have the help of your maid for five minutes?" a ready
assent was given to this request. Mrs Warner herself shewed Miss
Vernon to an appartment up stairs, & placed at her command
every requisite for ennabling her to appear in somewhat more credit-
able style. She then returned to her drawing-room, sat down again
in her arm-chair, put her little round foot upon the foot-stool—&
with her finger on her lip began to reflect more at leisure upon this
new occurrence. not very quick in apprehension—she now began
to perceive for the first time—that there was something very odd in
such a young girl as Miss Vernon coming alone—unattended, in a
hired conveyance to a strange house, to ask after the Duke of
Zamorna—what could be the reason of it? had she run away—
unknown to her present protectors?—it looked very like it—But
what would the Duke say when he knew? she wished Howard
would come in, she would speak to him about it—But she didn't
like to go into the dining-room & call him out—besides, she did not
think there was the least harm in the matter—Miss Vernon was
quite open & free, she made no mystery about the business—The
Duke had been her Guardian, it was natural she should come to see
him—only the oddity was that she should be without carriage or
servants—she said she had come by the coach. Northangerland's
daughter by the coach!—Mrs Warner's thinking faculties were
suspended in amazement—The necessity of pursuing this puzzling
train of reflections was precluded by Miss Vernon coming down—
she entered the room as cheerfully & easily as if Mrs Warner had
been her old friend and she an invited guest at a house perfectly
familiar—

"Am I neat now?" were the first words as she walked up to her
hostess. Mrs Warner could only answer in the affirmative, for
indeed there was nothing of the traveller's negligence now remaining in the grey silk dress, the smoothed curled hair—the delicate
silk stockings & slippers—besides, now that the shawl & bonnet
were removed, a certain fine turn of form was visible which gave a
peculiarly distinguished air to the young stranger—a neck &

shoulders elegantly designed, & arms round, white & taper—fine ankles & small feet, imparted something classic, picturesque & highly patrician to her whole mien & aspect—in fact, Caroline looked extremely lady-like—& it was well she had that quality for her stature & other proportions of her size were on too limited a scale to admit of more superb & imposing charms.

She sat down—"Now I do want to see the Duke" said she smiling at Mrs Warner. "He will be here presently" was the answer "he never sits very long at table after dinner." "Don't tell him who I am when he comes in" continued Caroline. "Let us see if he will know me, I don't think he will." "Then he does not at all expect you?" asked the Hostess—"O no! it was quite a thought of my own coming here—I told nobody. You must know, Mrs Warner, Papa objected to my staying in Verdopolis this season—because I suppose he thought I had had enough gaiety in Paris—where he & I spent the autumn & part of the summer—well, as soon as ever town began to fill, he sent me up beyond Fidena to Eden-Cottage, you've heard of the place I daresay—a dismal solitary house at the very foot of the Highlands—I have lived there about a month, & you know how stormy & wet it has been all the time. well, I got utterly tired at last for I was determined not to care anything about the misty hills—though they looked strange enough sometimes— yesterday-morning I thought I'd make a bold push for a change— directly after breakfast—I set off for Fidena with only my bonnet & shawl on as if I were going to walk in the grounds—when I got there I took the Coach & here I am." Caroline laughed. Mrs Warner laughed too, the nonchalant off-hand way in which this story had been told her, completely removed any little traces of suspicion that might still have been lurking in her usually credulous mind—The reader will by this have discerned that Miss Vernon was not quite so simple & communicative as she seemed—She knew how to give her own colouring to a statement without telling any absolute lies—The very warm sentiments which she indulged towards her guardian, were, she flattered herself, known to no living thing but the heart that conceived & contained them. As she sat on a sofa near the fire, leaning her head against the wall so that the shade of a projecting mantle-piece almost concealed her face— she did not tell Mrs Warner that while she talked so lightly to her —her ear was on the stretch to catch an approaching foot-step— her heart fluttering at every sound—her whole mind in a state of fluttering & throbbing excitement—longing, dreading for the door to open—eagerly anticipating the expected advent—yet fearfully shrinking from it—with a contradictory mixture of feelings.

The time approached—a faint sound of folding doors unclosing was heard below—the grand stair-case ascending to the drawing-room was again trodden—& the sound of voices echoed through the lobby & hall—"They are here" said Mrs Warner—"now don't tell who I am" returned Miss Vernon, shrinking closer into her dim corner—"I will introduce you as my niece, as Lucy Grenville" was the reply, & the young matron seemed beginning to enter into the spirit of the young maid's espieglerie—

"Your Grace is perfectly mistaken" said a gentleman opening the drawing-room door & permitting a taller man to pass. "It is singular that reason does not convince your Grace of the erroneous nature of your opinion; those houses, my lord Duke, will last for fifty years to come, with the expenditure of a mere trifle on repairs. With the expenditure of two hundred pounds on the erection [of] new walls & roofs, plaster, painting & wood-work—they will last a few years longer." "I make no doubt" was the reply—"Your Grace speaks ignorantly" rejoined Warner Howard Warner Esqre. "I tell you those houses have stood in their present state for the last twenty years—I recollect them perfectly when I was only twelve years old & they looked neither better nor worse than they do now." "They could not well look worse" returned the taller man— walking up to the hearth & pushing away an ottoman with his foot to make room for himself to stand on the rug. "Are you talking about the Cliff-Cottages still?" asked Mrs Warner looking up— "Yes, Mistress, they have been the sole subject of conversation since you left the room—your master has increased his estimate of their value every five minutes, & now at last he describes the rotten, roofless hovels as capital well-built mansion-houses, with convenient out-houses—to wit a pig-stye each, & large gardens, id est—a patch of dunghill two yards square—suitable for the residence of a genteel family—& he tells me, if I would only buy them, I should be sure to make a rental of twenty pounds per annum—from each —that won't wash, will it, Mistress?" "What won't wash, please your Grace—? the rug?" "No, Mr Ferguson's pocket-handker-chief." "I don't know who Mr Ferguson is, & what kind of hand-kerchiefs does he wear?" "Very showy ones—manufactured at Blarney-Mills. your Master always buys of him"—'Now, your Grace is jesting—Howard does nothing of the kind, his pocket-handkerchiefs are all of cambric."

A half-smothered laugh, excited no doubt by Mrs Warner's simplicity, was heard from the obscure sofa-corner—The Duke of Zamorna, whose back had been to the mantle-piece & whose elbow had been supported by the projecting slab therefo—quickly turned—so did Mr Warner—both Gentlemen saw a figure seated & reclining back—the face half hid by the shade & half by a slim & snowy hand—raised as if to screen the eyes from the flickering & dazzling firelight. The first notion that struck his majesty of Angria was the striking similarity of that grey silk dress—that pretty form & tiny slender foot, to something that ought to be a hundred miles off at Wellesley House—in fact, a vivid though vague recollection of his own Duchess was suggested to his mind by what he saw—In the surprise & conviction of the moment, he thought himself privileged to advance a good step nearer—& was about to stoop down to remove the screening hand & make himself certain of the unknown's identity—when the sudden & confused recoil— the half-uttered interjection of alarm with which his advances were received, compelled him to pause. at the same time Mrs Warner said hurriedly "my niece, Lucy Grenville." Mr Warner looked at his wife with astonishment—he knew she was not speaking the truth—she looked at him imploringly—the Duke of Zamorna laughed—"I had almost made an awkward mistake" said he. "Upon my word I took Miss Lucy Grenville for some one I had a right to come within a yard of without being reproved for impertinence—if the young lady had sat still half a minute longer I believe I should have inflicted a kiss—now I look better though, I don't know, there's a considerable difference—as much as between a dark dahlia & a lily—" his Grace paused—stood with his head turned fixedly towards Miss Grenville, scrutinized her features with royal bluntness—threw a transfixing glance at Mrs Warner—abruptly faced round, turning his back on both in a movement of much more singularity than politeness—erelong dropped into a chair—& crossing one leg over the other—turned to Mr Warner & asked him if he saw day-light—Mr Warner did not answer for he was busily engaged in perusing a newspaper— The Duke then inclined his head towards Mrs Warner & leaning half across her work-table—inquired in a tone of anxious interest whether she thought "*This* would wash?" Mrs Warner was too much puzzled to make a reply—But the young lady laughed again fitfully & almost hysterically—as if there was some inward struggle between tears & laughter. again she was honoured with a sharp-hasty survey from the King of Angria. To which succeeded a considerable interval of silence—broken at length by his majesty remarking that he should like some coffee—Hartley was summoned & his majesty was gratified—He took about six cups—observing, when he had finished—that he had much better have taken as many eight pennorths of brandy & water & that, if he had thought of it before, he would have asked for it—Mrs Warner offered to ring the bell & order a case-bottle & a tumbler then—but the Duke answered that he thought on the whole he had better go to bed as it was about half-past eight o'clock, a healthy primitive hour—which he should like to stick to—He took his candle—nodded to Mr Warner, shook hands with Mrs Warner—& without looking at the neice, said in a measured, slow, manner as he walked out of the room "Good-night, Miss Lucy Grenville".

CHAPTER VI

How Miss Vernon passed the night which succeeded this interview, the reader may amuse himself by conjecturing—I cannot tell him, I can only say that when she went up-stairs she placed her candle on the dressing-table—sat down at the foot of the bed where she was to sleep—& there remained, perfectly mute & perfectly motionless till her light was burnt out. She did not soliloquize, so what her thoughts were it would be difficult to say—Sometimes she sighed—sometimes tears gathered in her eyes, hung a little while on her long eye-lashes & then dropped to her lap, but there was no sobbing, no strong emotion of any kind—I should say, judging from her aspect, that her thoughts ran all on doubt—disappointment & suspense—but not on desperation or despair—After the candle had flickered a long time, it at last sank into darkness—Miss Vernon lifted up her head which had been bent all the while—saw the vital spark dying on the table before her, rose & slowly undressed—She might have had a peculiar penchant for going to bed in the dark when anything happened to disturb her—if you recollect, reader, she did so on the night her father announced his resolution to send her to Eden-Cottage.

The next morning she woke late, for she had not fallen asleep before the dawn began to break—when she came down, she found that the Duke & Mr Warner were gone out to take a survey of the disputed Cliffe-Cottages—two superannuated old hovels, by the bye, fit habitations for neither man nor beast—they had taken with them a Stone-mason & an Architect—also a brace of guns, two brace of pointers & a game-keeper. the probability therefore was that they would not be back before night fall—When Miss Vernon heard that—her heart was so bitter that she could have laid her head on her hand & fairly cryed like a child—if the Duke had recognised her, & she believed he had, what contemptuous negligence, or cold displeasure his conduct evinced—However, on second thoughts, she scorned to cry—she'd bear it all—at worst she could take the coach again & return to that Dungeon at Fidena—& what could Zamorna have to be displeased at?—he did not know that she had wished her sister dead & herself his wife—he did not know the restless, devouring feeling she had when she thought of him— who could guess that she loved that Powerful & austere Zamorna, when, as she flattered herself, neither look, nor word, nor gesture had ever betrayed that frantic dream. could he be aware of it when she had not fully learnt it herself till she was parted from him by mountain, valley & wave? Impossible, & since he was so cold, so regardless—she would crush the feeling & never tell that it had existed—She did not want him to love her in return—no—no— that would be wicked—she only wanted him to be kind—to think well of her, to like to have her with him—nothing more—unless indeed the Duchess of Zamorna was to happen to die, & then —but she would drop this foolery—master it entirely—pretend to being in excellent spirits—& if the Duke should really find her out, affect to treat the whole transaction as a joke, a sort of eccentric adventure undertaken for the fun of the thing. Miss Vernon kept her resolution, she drest her face in smiles & spent the whole day merrily & sociably with Mrs Warner—its hours passed slowly to her, & she, still in spite of herself, kept looking at the window & listening to every movement in the hall—as evening and darkness drew on, she waxed restless & impatient—When it was time to dress, she arranged her hair & selected her ornaments with a care she could hardly account for herself.

Let us now suppose it to be eight o'clock. the absentees returned an hour since & are now in the drawing-room—But Caroline is not with them; she has not yet seen them, for some cause or other she has preferred retiring to this large library in another wing of the house—She is sitting moping by the hearth like Cinderella—she has rung for no candles. the huge fire alone gives a red lustre & quivering shadows upon the books, the ceiling, the carpet— Caroline is so still that a little mouse, mistaking her no doubt for an image, is gliding unstartled over the rug & around her feet—On a sudden the creature takes alarm, makes a dart & vanishes under the brass fender—has it heard a noise? there is nothing stirring— Yes, something moves somewhere in the wing which was before so perfectly still—while Miss Vernon listened—yet doubtful whether she had really heard or only fancied the remote sound of a step— the door of her retreat was actually opened & a second person entered its precincts—The Duke of Zamorna came straying listlessly in as if he had found his way there by chance—Miss Vernon looked up, recognised the tall figure & overbearing build & felt that now at last the crisis was come. her feelings were instantly wound to their highest pitch, but the first word brought them down to a more ordinary tone.

"Well, Miss Grenville, good evening." Caroline, quivering in every nerve, rose from her seat & answered "Good evening, my lord Duke." "Sit down" said he "& allow me to take a chair near you—" She sat down—she felt very queer when Zamorna drew a seat close to her & coolly installed himself beside her—Mr Wellesley was attired in evening dress with something more of brilliancy & show than has been usual with him of late—he wore a star on his left breast & diamonds on his fingers—his complexion was coloured with exercise, & his hair curled round his forehead—with a gloss & profusion highly characteristic of the most consummate cox-comb going—

"You & I" continued his Sublimity "seemed disposed to form a separate party of ourselves to-night, I think, Miss Lucy—we have levanted from the Drawing-room & taken up our quarters else-where—I hope, by the bye, my presence is no restraint? you don't feel shy & strange with me, do you?" "I don't feel strange" answered Miss Vernon—"But rather shy just at the first—I pre-sume—well—a better acquaintance will wear that off—in the meantime, if you have no objection, I will stir the fire & then we shall see each other better"—His Grace stooped, took the poker—woke up the red glowing mass—& elicited a broad blaze which flashed full on his companion's face & figure—He looked first with a smile, but gradually with a more earnest expression—he turned away & was silent—Caroline waited, anxious, trembling—with difficulty holding in the feelings which swelled her heart—Again the Duke looked at her & drew a little nearer—"He is not angry" thought Miss Vernon "when will he speak & call me Caroline?" She looked up at him—he smiled—she approached—still seeking in his eye for a welcome—her hand was near his—he took it, pres-sed it a little, "Are you angry?" asked Miss Vernon in a low, sweet voice—she looked beautiful, her eye bright & glowing, her cheek flushed—& her dark wavy hair resting lightly upon it like a cloud.

Expectant, impatient, she still approached the silent Duke till her face almost touched his—

This passive stoicism on his part could not last long—it must bring a reaction—it did. Before she could catch the lightning change in face & eye, the rush of blood to the cheek—she found herself in his arms—He strained her to his heart a moment, kissed her forehead & instantly released her—"I thought I would not do that" said Zamorna, rising & walking through the room—"but

what's the use of resolution?—a man is not exactly a Statue."
Three turns through the appartment restored him to his self-
command—he came back to the hearth.

"Caroline! Caroline!" said he, shaking his head as he bent over
her—"How is this? what am I to say about it?" "You really know
me, do you?" answered Miss Vernon—evading her Guardian's
words—"I think I do" said he. "But what brought you from
Fidena? have you run away?"—"Yes" was the reply—"And where
are you running to?" "Nowhere" said Caroline. "I have got as far
as I wished to go—didn't you tell me in your letter—that if I was
still unhappy at Eden Cottage I was to write & tell you so—I
thought I had better come." "But I am not going to stay at
Woodhouse-Cliffe, Caroline, I must leave to-morrow—" "And will
you leave me behind you?" "God bless me!" ejaculated Mr Wellesley, hastily raising himself from his stooping attitude & starting
back as if a wasp had stung his lip—he stood a yard off, looking at
Miss Vernon, with his whole face fixed by the same expression that
had flashed over it before—"Where must I take you, Caroline?"
he asked—"Anywhere." "But I am to return to Verdopolis—to
Wellesley-House—it would not do to take you there—you would
hardly meet with a welcome." "The Duchess would not be glad to
see me, I suppose" said Miss Vernon. "No, she would not"
answered the Duke—with a kind of brief laugh. "And why should
she not" enquired the young lady—"I am her sister—Papa is as
much my Father as he is her's—but I believe she would be jealous
of any-body liking your Grace besides herself." "Aye, & of my
Grace liking anybody too, Caroline." This was a hint which Miss
Vernon could not understand. these words & the pointed emphasis
with which they were uttered broke down the guard of her simplicity & discomforted her self-possession—they told her that Zamorna
had ceased to regard her as a child—they intimated that he looked
upon her with different eyes to what he had done, & considered
her attachment to him as liable to another interpretation than the
mere fondness of a Ward for her Guardian—her secret seemed to
be discovered—She was struck with an agony of shame—her face
burned—her eyes fell—she dared look on Zamorna no more.

And now the genuine character of Arthur Augustus Adrian
Wellesley began to work—in this crisis, Lord Douro stood true to
his old name & nature—Zamorna did not deny by one noble &
moral act the character he had earned by a hundred infamous
ones. Hitherto we have seen him rather as restraining his passions
than yielding to them—he has stood before us rather as a Mentor
than a Misleader—but he is going to lay down the last garment of

light & be himself entirely—In Miss Vernon's present mood, burning & trembling with confusion, remorse & apprehension, he might by a single word have persuaded her to go back to Eden-Cottage— She did not yet know that he reciprocated her wild frantic attachment—he might have buried that secret—have treated her with an austere gentleness—he well knew how to assume—& crushed in time the poison flowers of a passion whose fruit, if it reached maturity, would be crime & anguish—Such a line of conduct might be trodden by the noble & Faithful Fidena —it lies in his ordinary path of life—he seldom sacrifices another human being's life & home on the altar of his own vices—but the selfish Zamorna cannot emulate such a deed—He has too little of the moral Great-Heart in his nature, it is his creed that all things bright & fair live for him— by him they are to be gathered & worn as the flowers of his Laurel Crown—The green leaves are victory in battle—they never fade, the roses are conquests in Love—they decay & drop off— Fresh ones blow round him, are plucked & woven with the withered stem of their predecessors—such a wreath he deems a glory about his temples, he may in the end find it rather like the snaky fillet which compressed Calchas's brows, steeped in blue venom.

The Duke reseated himself at Miss Vernon's side—"Caroline" said he, desiring by that word to recall her attention which was wandering wide in the distressful paroxysm of shame that overwhelmed her—he knew how to give a tone, an accent to that single sound—which should produce ample affect—it expressed a kind of pity—there was something protecting & sheltering about it as though he were calling her home—She turned, the acute pang which tortured her heart & tightened her breath dissolved into sorrow—a gush of tears relieved her.

"Now then" said Zamorna, when he had allowed her to weep awhile in silence. "The shower is over—smile at me again, my little dove—what was the reason of that distress?—do you think I don't care for you, Caroline?" "You despise me—you know I am a fool" —"Do I?" said he quietly—then, after a pause, he went on "I like to look at your dark eyes & pretty face—" Miss Vernon started & deeply coloured—never before had Zamorna called her face pretty—"Yes" said he "it is exquisitely pretty—& those soft features & dusky curls are beyond the imitation of a pencil—You blush because I praise you—did you never guess before that I took a pleasure in watching you—in holding your little hand, & in playing with your simplicity—which has sported many a time, Caroline, on the brink of an abyss you never thought of?" Miss Vernon sat speechless—She darkly saw or rather felt the end to which all this tended, but all was fever & delirium round her—The Duke spoke again—in a single blunt & almost coarse sentence compressing what yet remained to be said. "If I were a bearded Turk, Caroline, I would take you to my Harem"—His deep voice, as he uttered this—his high-featured face, & dark large eye, beaming bright with a spark from the depths of Gehenna, struck Caroline Vernon with a thrill of nameless dread—Here he was—the man that Montmorency had described to her—all at once she knew him—Her Guardian was gone—Something terrible sat in his place—The fire in the grate was sunk down without a blaze—this silent lonely library, so far away from the inhabited part of the house—was gathering a deeper shade in all its Gothic recesses. She grew faint with dread—she dared not stir—from a vague fear of being arrested by the powerful arm—flung over the back of her chair—At last—through the long & profound silence, a low whisper stole from her lips. "May I go away?" No answer—She attempted to rise—this movement produced the effect she had feared, the arm closed round her—Miss Vernon could not resist its strength, a piteous upward look was her only appeal—He, Satan's eldest Son, smiled at the mute prayer—"She trembles with terror" said he, speaking to himself. "Her face has turned pale as marble within the last minute or two—how did I alarm her? Caroline, do you know me?—you look as if your mind wandered—" "You are Zamorna" replied Caroline. "But let me go." "Not for a Diadem, Not for a Kroomad's head— not every inch [? of land] the Joliba waters"—"Oh, what must I do?" exclaimed Miss Vernon. "Crede Zamorna!"* was the answer. "Trust me, Caroline, you shall never want a refuge—I said I would not take you to Wellesley-House, but I can take you elsewhere—I have a little retreat, my fairy, somewhere near the heart of my own Kingdom, Angria—sheltered by Ingleside & hidden in a wood—it is a plain old house outside—but it has rooms within as splendid as any saloon in Victoria-Square—you shall live there, nobody will ever reach it to disturb you—it lies on the verge of moors—there are only a few scattered cottages & a little church for many miles round. it is not known to be my property—I call it my treasure-house, & what I deposit there has always hitherto been safe—at least" he added in a lower voice "from human violence— & living force—there are some things that even I cannot defy—I thought so that summer afternoon when I came to Scar House & found a King & Conqueror had been before me—to whom I was no Rival; but a trampled slave."

The gloom of Zamorna's look as he uttered these words told a

* A paraphrase of Byron's motto

tale of what was passing in his heart—What vision had risen before him which suggested such a sentence at such a moment it matters little to know—However dark it might have been, it did not hush his vehemence nor quell his eager tone—He smiled as Caroline looked at him with mixed wonder & fear—his face changed to an expression of tenderness more dangerous than the fiery excitement which had startled her before—he caressed her fondly & lifted with his fingers the heavy curls which were lying on her neck. Caroline began to feel a new impression—She no longer wished to leave him, she clung to his side—infatuation was stealing over her—The thought of separation or a return to Eden was dreadful—The Man beside her was her Guardian again but he was also Mr Montmorency's Duke of Zamorna—She feared, she loved—Passion tempted, conscience warned her—But, in a mind like Miss Vernon's, Conscience was feeble opposed to passion, its whispers grew faint & were at last silenced—& when Zamorna kissed her & said in that voice of fatal sweetness which has instilled venom into many a heart "Will you go with me to-morrow, Caroline?" she looked up in his face with a kind of wild devoted enthusiasm & answered "Yes".

The Duke of Zamorna left Woodhouse-Cliffe on Friday the 7th of Decbr next morning & was precisely seven days in performing the distance between that place & Verdopolis—at least seven days had elapsed between his departure from Mr Warner's & his arrival at Wellesley-House—It was a cold day when he came & that might possibly be the reason that he looked pale & stern as he got out of his carriage, mounted the Kingly steps of his mansion & entered under its roof—He was necessitated to meet his wife after so long a separation—& it was a sight to see their interview—He took little pains to look at her kindly & his manner was sour & impatient—& the Duchess, after the first look, solicited no fond embrace—She receded even from the frozen kiss he offered her, dropped his hand —& after searching his face & reading the meaning of that pallid, harassed aspect—told him, not by words but by a bitter smile, that he did not deceive her—turned away with a quivering lip, with all the indignation, the burning pride, the heart-struck anguish stamped on her face that those beautiful features could express— She left him & went to her room which she did not leave for many a day afterwards.

The Duke of Zamorna seemed to have returned in a business mood—he had a smile for no one—When Lord Richton called to pay his respects—the Duke glared at the card which he sent up, threw it on the table & growled like a Tiger "not at home"—He received only his ministers—he discussed only matters of state. When their business was done, he dismissed them, no hour of relaxation followed the hour of labour—he was as scowling at the end of the council as he was at the beginning.

Enara was with him one night & in his blunt way had just been telling him a piece of his mind—& intimating that he was sure all that blackening & sulking was not for nothing & that he had as certainly been in some hideous mess as he now wore a head—The answer to this was a recommendation to Enara to go to Hell—Henri was tasting a glass of spirits & water preparatory to making a reply. When a third person walked in to the appartment, & advancing up to him, said "I'll thank you to leave the room, Sir." The Colonel of Bloodhounds looked up fierce at this address—but having discerned from whom it proceeded, he merely replied "Very well, my lord—but with your leave I'll empty this tumbler of brandy & water first—here's to the King's health & better temper —" He drained his glass—set it down & marched away.

The new-comer, judging from his look, seemed likely to give the Duke of Zamorna his match in the matter of temper. One remarkable thing about his appearance was that, though in the presence of a crowned King—he wore a hat upon his head which he never lifted a hand to remove—the face under that hat was like a sheet it was so white, & like a hanged malefactor's it was so livid—he could not be said to frown—as his features were quiet, but his eye was petrifying—it had that in its light iris which passes shew.

This Gentleman took his station facing the Duke of Zamorna, & when Lord Enara had left the room—he said in a voice such as people use when they are coming instantly to the point & will not soften their demand a jot—

"Tell me what you have done with her?"

The Duke of Zamorna's conscience—a vessel of a thousand tons burthen—brought up a cargo of blood to his face, his nostrils opened—his head was as high, his chest as full & his attitude, standing by the table, as bold as if, from the ramparts of Gazemba, he was watching Arundel's Horsemen scouring the Wilderness.

"What do you mean?" he asked.

"Where is Caroline Vernon?" said the same voice of fury.

"I have not got her."

"And you have never had her—I suppose? and you will dare to tell me that lie."

"I have never had her—"

"She is not in your hands now?"

"She is not."

"By G–d, I know differently, Sir—I know you lie."

"You know nothing about it."

"Give her up, Zamorna."

"I cannot give up what I have not got."

"Say that again."

"I do."

"Repeat the lie."

"I will."

"Take that, miscreant."

Lord Northangerland snatched something from his breast, it was a pistol—he did not draw the trigger—but he dashed the but end viciously at his son-in-law's mouth—in an instant his lips were crimson with gore—if his teeth had not been fastened into their sockets like soldered iron—he would have been forced to spit them out with the blood with which his mouth filled & ran over. He said nothing at all to this compliment, but only leaned his head over the fire & spat into the ashes—& then wiped his mouth with a white handkerchief which in five minutes was one red stain—I suppose this moderation resulted from the deep conviction that the punishment he got was only a millionth part of what he deserved.

"Where is she?" resumed the excited Percy.

"I'll *never* tell you."

"Will you keep her from me?"

"I'll do my best."

"Will you dare to visit her?"

"As often as I can snatch a moment from the world to give to her."

"You say that to my face?"

"I'd say it to the D——l's face."

A little pause intervened in which Northangerland surveyed the Duke & the Duke went on wiping his bloody mouth.

"I came here to know where you have taken that Girl" resumed Percy—"I mean to be satisfied—I mean to have her back—you shall not keep her—the last thing I had in the world is not to be yielded to you—you brutal, insatiable Villain."

"Am I worse than you, Percy?"

"Do you taunt me? you are worse—I never was a callous brute."

"And who says I am a brute, does Caroline? Does Mary?"

"How dare you join those names together—how dare you utter them in the same breath?—as if both my daughters were your purchased slaves—you coarse Voluptuary, filthier than that filthy Jordan."

"I am glad it is you who give me this character & not Miss Vernon—or her sister."

"Arthur Wellesley, you had better not unite those two names again, if you do, neither of them shall ever see you more except dead—"

"Will you shoot me?"

"I will."

Another pause followed, which Percy again broke.

"In what part of Angria have you put Caroline Vernon—for I know you took her to Angria—?"

"I placed her where she is safe & happy—I should say no more if my hand were thrust into that fire, & you had better leave the matter where it is—for you cannot undo what is done."

Northangerland's wild blue eye dilated into wilder hatred & fury. He said, raising his hand & striking it on the table—

"I wish there was a Hell for your sake—! I wish—"

The sentence broke of & was resumed as if his agitation shortened his breath too much to allow him to proceed far without drawing it afresh.

"I wish you might be withered hand & foot & struck into a paralytic heap—" again it broke.

"What are you? you have pressed this hand & said you cared for me—You have listened to all I had to tell you. What I am, How I have lived & what I have suffered—You have assumed enthusiasm—blushed almost like a woman & even wearied me out with your boyish ardour—I let you have Mary—& you know what a curse you have been to her—disquieting her life with your constant treacheries & your alternations of frost & fire—I have let you go on with little interference—though I have wished you dead many a time when I have seen her pale harassed look—knowing how different she was before she knew you & was subjected to all your monstrous tyrannies & tantalizations—your desertions—that broke her spirit—& your returns that kept her lingering on with just the shadow of a hope to look to—"

"Gross exaggeration!" exclaimed Zamorna with vehemence. "When did I ever tyrannize over Mary? ask her at this moment—when she is so much exasperated against me as ever she was in her life—Tell her to leave me—She will not speak to me or look at me—but see what her answer would be to that—"

"Will you be silent & hear me out?" returned Percy—"I have not finished the detail of your friendship—That Hebrew imposter Nathan tells David, the man after God's own heart—a certain parable of an ewe lamb & applys it to his own righteous deeds—you have learnt the Chapter by heart I think & fructified by it—I gave you everything but Caroline, you knew my feelings to her—

you know how I reckoned on her as my last & only comfort—& What have you done? She is destroyed, she can never hold her head up again, she is nothing to me—but she shall not be left in your hands—"

"You cannot take her from me, & if you could—how would you prevent her return?—She would either die or come back to me now—& remember, Sir, if I had been a Percy instead of a Wellesley, I should not have carried her away & given her a home to hide her from scorn & shelter her from insult—I should have left her forsaken at Fidena to die there delirious in an Inn as Harriet O'Connor did."

"I have my last word to give you now" said Percy. "You shall be brought into the Courts of Law for this very deed—I care nothing for exposure—I will hire Hector Montmorency to be my Counsel— I will furnish him with ample evidence of all the atrocities of your character—which, handled as he will delight to handle it, will make the flesh quiver on your bones with agony—I will hire half the press & fill the newspapers with libels on you & your court, which shall transform all your tools of followers into jealous enemies—I will not stick at a lie—Montmorency shall indite the paragraphs in order that they may be pungent enough—he will not scruple at involving a few dozen of court ladies in the ruin that is to be hurled on you—He shall be directed to spare none, your cabinet shall be a herd of horned cattle—the public mind shall be poisoned against you—a glorious triumph shall be given to your political enemies— before you die you shall curse the day that you robbed me of my daughter."

So spoke Northangerland—his Son answered with a smile "The Ship is worthless that will not live through a storm."

"Storm!" rejoined the earl. "This is no storm—but fire in the hold, a lighted candle hurled into your magazine! see if it will fall like a rain-drop."

The Duke was still unquelled—He answered, as he turned & walked slowly through the room "In nature there is no such thing as annihilation—blow me up & I shall live again."

"You need not talk this bombast to me" said Percy. "Keep it to meet Montmorency with when he makes you the target of his shafts—Keep it to answer Warner & Thornton & Castlereagh when their challenges come pouring on you like chain-shot."

His Grace pursued his walk & said in an undertone—

"Moored in the rifted rock,
Proof to the tempest shock,
Firmer he roots him the ruder it blow."

APPENDIX

CAROLINE VERNON

Charlotte Brontë's first draft for the passage describing Caroline Vernon's parting with the Duke of Zamorna (see p. 316) reads as follows :

His allusions to matrimony, too, confounded her—it was not that the idea was altogether foreign to the young lady's mind—she had most probably studied the subject now & then in those glowing day-dreams before hinted at—nay, I would not undertake to say how far her speculations concerning it had extended, for she was a daring character—but as yet those thoughts had all been secret & untold—her Guardian was the last person to whom she would have revealed their existence—& now it was with a sense of shame that she heard his grave counsel on the subject. What he said, too, about the French Ladies & the Italian men & women made her feel very queer—She could not for the world have answered him & yet she wished to hear more—she was soon gratified.

''It is not at all improbable'' pursued his Grace after a brief pause—during which he & Caroline had slowly paced the long terrace walk at the bottom of the Garden which skirted a stately aisle of trees ''It is not at all improbable that you may meet occa-sionally in society a Lady of the name of Lalande & another of the name of St James—& it is most likely that these ladies will shew you much attention—flatter you—ask you to sing or play—invite you to their houses & introduce you to their particular circle & offer to accompany you to public places—you must decline it all.'' ''Why?'' asked Miss Vernon. ''Because'' replied the Duke ''Madame Lalande & Lady St James are easy about their char-acters, their ideas on the subject of morality are very free—they would get you into their boudoirs, as the ladies of Paris call the little rooms where they sit in a morning & read gross novels—& talk over their own secrets with their intimate friends—you would learn of many love-intrigues—& of a great deal of amorous manoeuvering—you would get accustomed to impudent conversa-tion & perhaps become involved in foolish adventures which would disgrace you.'' Zamorna still had all the talk to himself—for Miss Vernon seemed too busily engaged in contemplating the white pebbles on which the moon was shining—that lay here & there on the path at her feet—to take much share in the conversation—at last she said in rather a low voice ''I never intended to make friends with any Frenchwoman & I always thought that when I was a woman I would visit chiefly with such people as Lady Thornton & Mrs Warner & that lady who lives about two miles from here—Miss Laury—they are all very well-behaved are they not?" Before the Duke answered this question, he took out a red-silk handker-chief & blew his nose—he then said "Mrs Warner is a remarkably decent woman—Lady Thornton is somewhat too gay & flashy—in other respects I know no harm in her—"" "And what is Miss Laury like?" asked Caroline. ""What is she like? she is rather tall & pale but—"" ""I mean, what is her character—ought I to visit with her?" "You will be saved the trouble of deciding on that point as she will never come in your way—she always resides in the Country—"" "I thought she was very fashionable" continued Miss Vernon ""for I remember, when I was in Adrianopolis, I often saw pictures in the shops of her & I thought her very nice-looking." The Duke was silent in his turn. ""I wonder why she lives alone" pursued Caroline ""and I wonder she has no relations—is she rich?" "Not very." ""Do you know her?" ""Yes." ""Does Papa?" ""No." ""Do you like her?" ""Sometimes." ""Why don't you like her always?" "I don't always think about her." ""Do you ever go to see her?" ""now & then." ""Does she ever give parties?" ""No." ""I believe she's rather mys-terious & romantic" continued Miss Vernon. ""She's a romantic look in her eyes—I should not wonder if she has had adventures." ""I daresay she has" remarked her Guardian. ""I should like to have some adventures" added the young lady—""I don't want a dull droning life." ""You may be gratified" replied the Duke. ""Be in no hurry—you are young enough yet, life is only just opening." ""But I should like something very strange & uncommon—something that I don't at all expect—"" Zamorna whistled—""I should like to be tryed to see what I had in me" continued his ward—""O, if I were only rather better looking—adventures never happen to plain fat people—"" ""No—not often—"" ""I'm so sorry I'm not as pretty as your wife the Duchess—if she had been like me she would never have been married to you—"" ""Indeed—how do you know that?" ""Because I'm sure you would not have asked her—but she's so nice & fair—& I'm all dark, like a mulatto mamma says—"" "Dark yet comely" muttered the Duke involuntarily, for he looked down at his ward & she looked up at him & the moonlight disclosed a clear forehead—pencilled with soft dusk curls—dark & touching eyes & a round youthful cheek, smooth in texture & fine in tint—as that of some portrait hung in an Italian Palace, where you see the raven eyelash & southern eye relieving a complexion of pure colourless olive—& the rosy lips smiling brighter & warmer too for the absence of bloom elsewhere.

Zamorna did not tell Miss Vernon what he thought—at least not in words, but when she would have ceased to look up at him & returned to the contemplation of the scattered pebbles—he retained her face in that raised attitude by the touch of his finger under her little oval chin—his Grace of Angria is an Artist—it is probable that that sweet face touched with soft lunar light struck him as a fine Artistical Study—No doubt it is terrible to be looked fixedly at by a tall powerful man who knits his brows—& whose dark hair & whiskers & moustaches—combine to shadow the eyes of a Hawk & the features of a Roman Statue. when such a man puts on an ex-pression that you can't understand—stops suddenly as you are walking alone with him in a dim garden—removes your hand from his arm & places his hand on your shoulder—you are justified in feeling nervous & uneasy. "I suppose I've been talking nonsense" said Miss Vernon, colouring & half-frightened—"In what way?" "I've said something about my sister Mary that I shouldn't have said." "How?" "I can't tell—but you don't like her to be spoken of perhaps—I remember now you once said that she & I ought to have nothing to do with each other & you would never take me to see her." "Little Simpleton!" remarked Zamorna—"No" said Caroline—deprecating the scornful name—with a look & smile, & shewed her transient alarm was evaporating—"No, don't call me so—" "Pretty little simpleton, will that do?" said her Guardian. "No—I'm not pretty." Zamorna made no reply—"whereat, to con-fess the truth, Miss Vernon was slightly disappointed—for of late she had begun to entertain some latent embryo idea that his Grace did think her not quite ugly—what grounds she had for supposing so it would not be easy to say—it was an instinctive feeling & one that gave her little vain female heart too much pleasure—not to be encouraged & fostered as a secret prize—Will the reader be ex-ceedingly shocked if I venture to conjecture that all the foregoing lamentations about her plainness, were uttered with some half-defined intent of drawing forth a little word or two of cheering praise?—Oh, human nature! human nature! & Oh, Inexperience! in what an obscure, dim unconscious dream Miss Vernon was enveloped—How little she knew of herself—However, time is advancing & the hours, those "wild-eyed Charioteers" as Shelley calls them*—are driving on—She will gather knowledge by degrees—She is one of the Gleaners of Grapes in that Vineyard—where all man & woman-kind—have been plucking fruit since the world began, the Vineyard of Experience—At present, though, she rather seems to be a kind of Ruth in a Corn-field—nor does there want a

* *Prometheus Unbound* II, 130–3

Boaz to complete the picture—who also is well-disposed to scatter handfuls for the damsel's special benefit—In other words she has a Mentor who, not satisfied with instilling into her mind the precepts of wisdom—by words—will, if not prevented by others—do his best to enforce his verbal admonitions by practical illustrations—that will dissipate the mists on her vision at once & shew her in light both broad & burning—the mysteries of humanity now hidden, its passions & sins & sufferings—all its passages of strange error & all its after-scenes of agonised atonement. A skilful Preceptor is that same; one accustomed to tuition. Caroline has grown up under his care a fine & accomplished Girl—unspoilt by Flattery—unused to compliment—unhackneyed in trite fashionable conventionalities—Fresh, naïve & romantic, really romantic—throwing her heart & soul into her dreams, Longing only for an opportunity to do what she feels she could do—to die for somebody she Loves—that is, not actually to become a subject for the undertaker—but to give up heart, soul, sensations to one adored Hero—to lose Independent Existence in the perfect adoption of her Lover's Being. This is all very fine isn't it, reader—almost as good as the notion of Mr Rinaldo Aurelius. Caroline has yet to discover that she is as clay in the hands of the Potter—that the process of moulding is even now advancing & that ere long she will be turned off the wheel a perfect polished vessel of Grace—

Mr Percy Senr had been a good while up-stairs—Lady Louisa had talked him almost deaf—so at last he thought he would go down into the drawing-room by way of change & ask his Daughter to give him a tune on the piano—That same Drawing-room was a nice little place—with a clean bright fire, no candles—& the furniture shining in a quiet glow—but, however, as there was no-body there, Mr Percy regarded the vacant sofa—the empty easy-chair & the mute instrument with an air of gentle discontent. He would never have thought of ringing & asking after the missing individuals, but, however, as a footman happened to come in with four wax candles—He did just enquire ''Where Miss Vernon was''. The footman said ''He really didn't know—but he thought she was most likely gone to bed as he had heard her saying to Mademoiselle Touquet that she was tired of Packing''.—''Mr Percy stood a little while in the room—erelong he strayed into the passage—laid his hand on a hat & wandered placidly into the garden—Mr Percy was very poetical in his youth—consequently he must have been very much smitten with the stillness of the summer night—the fine, dark, unclouded blue of the sky—& the glitter of the pin-point stars—that swarmed over it like mites & all this must have softened his spirit, not to mention anything of a full moon which was up a good way in the element just opposite & gazed down on him as he stood on the front door-steps—just as if she mistook him for Endymion.

Mr Percy, however, would have nothing to say to her—he pulled the brim of his hat a trifle lower down on his forehead—& held the noiseless tenor of his way amongst the shades & flowers of the garden. he was just entering the terrace walk when he heard somebody speak—the voice came from a dim nook where the trees were woven into a bower & a seat was placed at their roots—

"Come, it is time for you to go in," were the words, "I must bid you good-bye." "But won't you go in too?" said another voice, pitched in rather a different key to that of the first speaker—"No, I must Go Home." "But you'll come again in the morning before we set off—" "No." "Won't you?" "I cannot." there was silence—a little suppressed sound was heard like a sob—"What is the matter, Caroline? are you crying?" "O, I am so sorry to leave you. I knew, when Papa told me I was to go—I should be grieved to bid you good-bye—I've been thinking about it all day—I can't help crying," the sound of weeping filled up another pause. "I love you so much" said the mourner. "You don't know what I think about you or how much I've always wanted to please you—or how I've cryed by myself whenever you've seemed angry with me—or what I'd give to be your little Caroline & to go with you through the world—I almost wish I'd never grown a woman, for when I was a little girl you cared for me far more than you do now—you're always grave now—" "Hush & come here to me" was the reply—breathed in a deep tender tone. "There, sit down as you did when you were a little girl—why do you draw back?" "I don't know—I didn't mean to draw back." "But you always do, Caroline, now—when I come near you—& you turn away your face from me if I kiss you, which I seldom do—because you are too old to be kissed & fondled like a child—" Another pause succeeded—during which it seemed that Miss Vernon had had to struggle with some impulse of shame, for her Guardian said, when he resumed the conversation—"Nay now, there is no need to distress yourself & blush so deeply—& I shall not let you leave me at present, so sit still—" "You are so stern" murmured Caroline, her stifled sobs were heard again—"Stern am I? I could be less so, Caroline—if circumstances were somewhat different—I would leave you little to complain of on that score." "What would you do?" asked Miss Vernon. "God knows." Caroline cried again, for unintelligible language is very alarming. "You must go in, child" said Zamorna

—"there will be a stir if you stay here much longer—Come, a last kiss—" "Oh my lord!" exclaimed Miss Vernon, & she stopped short as if she had uttered that cry to detain him & could say no more—her Grief was convulsive. "What, Caroline?" said Zam- orna, stooping his ear to her lips. "Don't leave me so—my heart feels as if it would break." "Why?" "Oh, I don't know." long was the paroxysm of Caroline's sore distress—she could not speak, she could only tremble & sob wildly—Her mother's excitable tem- perament was roused within her—Zamorna held her fast in his arms, & sometimes he pressed her more closely—but for a while he was as silent as she was. "My little darling" he said, softening his austere tone at last—"Take comfort you will see or hear from me again soon—I rather think neither mountains nor woods nor seas will form an impassable barrier between you & me—no, nor human vigilance either. the step of separation was delayed too late —they should have parted us a year or two ago, Caroline, if they had meant the parting to be a lasting one—now leave me—Go in" —with one final kiss he dismissed her from his arms—She went— the shrubs soon hid her—the opening & closing of the front door announced that she had gained the house—

Mr Wellesley was left by himself on the terrace-walk—he took a cigar out of his pocket, lighted it by the aid of a Lucifer-match, popped it into his mouth, & having reared himself up against the trunk of a large beech—looked as comfortable & settled as possible —At this juncture he was surprised by hearing a voice at his elbow gently enquiring whether his mother knew he was out? He had barely to turn his head to get a view of the speaker—who stood close to his side, a tall man—with a pale aspect & a particular ex- pression in his eyes which shewed a good deal of their whites & were turned laterally on to Mr Wellesley—

Charlotte Brontë's first draft for the opening of Zamorna's letter to Caroline Vernon (see p. 339) reads as follows:

My dear little Caroline
You trusted to an unsafe plan—when you left your letter at Wellesley-House to wait for me till my coming there—the chances were ten to one that I might never have received it—& indeed it was not put into my hands till many days after my arrival—even then I had no leisure to answer, as the first week or two of my stay in town brought continual & pressing calls on my attention—I am at present a little more disengaged, having contrived to get away from Verdopolis in order to complete a small business-transaction— relative to an affair of some old houses, which has for many years

been pending between myself & Mr Warner—the matter is not one likely ever to be settled because it only relates to a rental of some ten pounds per annum—arising from a brace of tenements —whose roofs are nearly off—however, it gives Mr Warner pretext in demanding my presence at his place, Wood-house-Cliff, about twice a year—in order to survey the buildings & direct afresh the disputed point of their value—Mr Warner, my little Caroline, wishes me to take them off his hands without requiring any re-pairs, and I am considerably too much a man of business to consent to any such arrangement. My young Ward will wonder what all this has to do with her

Map of the Great Glasstown Confederacy by Branwell Brontë